D0238034

THE PEOPLE NEXT DOOR

Also by Tony Parsons

Man and Boy
One For My Baby
Man and Wife
The Family Way
Stories We Could Tell
My Favourite Wife
Starting Over
Men from the Boys
Catching the Sun
The Murder Bag (Max Wolfe #1)
The Slaughter Man (Max Wolfe #2)
The Hanging Club (Max Wolfe #3)
Die Last (Max Wolfe #4)
Girl on Fire (Max Wolfe #5)
#taken (Max Wolfe #6)
Your Neighbour's Wife

Max Wolfe Digital Shorts
Dead Time
Fresh Blood
Tell Him He's Dead

THE
PEOPLE
NEXT
DOOR
TONY PARSONS

C
CENTURY

1 3 5 7 9 10 8 6 4 2

Century
20 Vauxhall Bridge Road
London SW1V 2SA

Century is part of the Penguin Random House group of companies
whose addresses can be found at global.penguinrandomhouse.com

Copyright © Tony Parsons 2022

Tony Parsons has asserted his right to be identified as the author of this
Work in accordance with the Copyright, Designs and Patents Act 1988

First published by Century in 2022

www.penguin.co.uk

ISBN 9781529124750 (hardback)
ISBN 9781529124767 (trade paperback)

Typeset in 14/17.75 pts Fournier MT
by Integra Software Services Pvt. Ltd, Pondicherry

Printed and bound in Great Britain by Clays Ltd, Elcograf S.p.A.

The authorised representative in the EEA is Penguin Random House Ireland,
Morrison Chambers, 32 Nassau Street, Dublin D02 YH68

Penguin Random House is committed to a sustainable future for
our business, our readers and our planet. This book is made from
Forest Stewardship Council® certified paper

For my mother's six brothers –
Rich, Jim, Bert, John, Tub and Alfie Wood.
The best uncles that any boy ever had.

THE NIGHT I LEFT YOU

I did not want to leave you.

You know that, don't you? You know it in your blood and bones, you know it in your heart and soul.

Leaving you felt like the end of the world. It was *the end of the world – at least that other world, that lost world where we didn't know how lucky we were, the world where we were too young and dumb to count our blessings.*

But I woke up near the end of the night and you were gone.

I knew – it's true – that you were not gone far, and you were not gone long, for your side of the bed was still warm from your body, and the soft dent of you was still there.

But you were no longer where you should have been.

You were no longer sleeping by my side.

And still caught somewhere between dreams and waking, I whispered your name into the darkness. And as if in response, from somewhere deep inside our home, there were sounds that should not be there.

Muffled, scuffling sounds, angry but muted.

These were unmistakably the sounds of violence but it was not a violence that felt the need to raise its voice. These were choked, suffocated noises, brutal and coarse and smothered, as if all of this nasty business could be done and over and finished without ever waking the neighbours.

I slid from our bed, heart pounding, and my palm brushed against the place where you had slept by my side, and your body heat touched my hand even as my bare toes felt the night-time cold, making me shiver.

There was only the deep night silence as I reached our bedroom door and eased it open. The choked, scuffling sounds were gone and I wondered if I had heard them in a bad dream, only a dream, but one of those dreams that seem so real.

Then the sounds began again, and I said your name – louder now, calling for you to come back to me, suddenly terrified that this was the night that I had always dreaded.

The night I would lose you.

I said your name again – louder, insistent – as if it was the only word I had ever known. Then I said your name a third time as if it was, in the end, the only word in the world that really mattered a damn to me.

But still you did not come back to me.

And so I went looking for you.

I walked along the dark hall – did I hear urgent murmuring voices or were they just inside my head? – and then I went down the stairs until finally I stood outside the closed door of the living room.

Such a strange name, isn't it? The living room. It makes you wonder what all the other rooms are for. I turned the doorknob to the living room and took two paces into pitch-black darkness heavy with silence, a silence that seemed to be holding its breath.

And all the lights came on at once.

And those lights were blinding and there it was waiting for us just as it had always been waiting, the thing that explodes in a life and changes it forever.

And I thought – this is how our world ends.

I felt total, all-consuming panic in the blaze of light so bright that I had to squeeze my eyes shut for a moment, a glare so dazzling it tattooed a black star on my retina.

They were in our home.

They were in this living room, these strangers with blood in their eyes.

They were here in our home that all at once was no longer a home.

Their hands all over everything we loved. And then they were on me as they were already on you, and I saw your face as they forced you to your knees, then to the floor. Two of them were forcing you to the ground, your head twisted sideways, your mouth and nose contorted against the hardwood floor and even then I thought it might all go away, even as late as that I believed they might just take what they wanted and flee, and I would go after them half-heartedly, not wanting to catch them, not really, and then the night would be split by the sound of a police siren coming to the rescue and I could stop running and it would be over and I would return to you and you would be unbroken and we would be as we were before.

But none of that happened.

What happened was this.

They had you down on the ground, one of them facing you with his hands on the back of your head, gripping it like a basketball, pushing your face into the floor, while the other was kneeling on your back, placing a knee at the base of your spine, pressing his full weight down, pinning you to the ground.

And as I watched with my arms pinned behind my back I thought that the knee against the base of the spine was not something that came naturally, it was a move that needed to be learned, to be taught and practised and mastered.

There was a terrifying efficiency about their cruelty.

They were professionals.

And I struggled and I fought but the one who had me put his hands on my neck from behind, expertly choking the life out of me, swinging me from side to side like a large animal with something smaller and weaker and dying in its mouth.

And as my breathing stopped it was the sudden jolt of terror that made my head spasm backwards, connecting hard with something both soft and hard – a combination of eyeball, bridge of the nose and the fragile bone of eye socket – that made him let me go.

And as he reeled away, clawing at his ruined eye, I saw that our front door was still slightly ajar.

A halo of street light gleamed around its ragged edges where they had forced it open and then pushed it not quite shut.

And I know I should have stayed and fought for you.

Do you think I don't know that?

On the day I die I will tell myself that I should have stayed.

I should have got a knife from the kitchen and shoved it in their rotten faces.

I should have fought them for you.

I should have killed them all.

I should have stayed.

I should never have left you.

But I screamed your name.

And then I ran.

PART ONE
LANA

1

Saturday, 29 August

We were moving into our new home when an old hippy lady came out of the cottage opposite carrying a large glass jar of home-made honey. Her home was beautiful, the front almost completely covered with a pink tangle of oleander, so that her cottage seemed to be spun from the flower, like a magical home in a deep dark wood in a fairy tale.

'Welcome!' she called. 'I do hope you like honey.'

As a city girl – born, bred and by nature – I was not very comfortable with the whole knocking-on-your-neighbours'-door thing. I was more of the avoid-eye-contact-with-your-neighbour-at-all-costs type.

In my city, my long-lost city, if you lived next door to someone for ten years or so then you might possibly nod coldly to them at Christmas. But out here it was clearly different. Out here among the green rolling hills of Oxfordshire – only an hour's commute to the city although it felt like another planet – your new neighbour brought you home-made honey before the removal men had started unloading the lorry. She told me her name – Sally Berry. She was an elderly flower child, part of the hippy diaspora that had headed for the country half a lifetime ago, seventy-five if she was a day, with fine, snow-white hair still streaked with natural blonde highlights like souvenirs of all those lost Sixties summers. Her silver-and-gold locks fell to the shoulders of a faded denim jacket embroidered with little flowers and peace signs.

Her lovely blue eyes sparkled behind wire-rimmed specs.

I told her my name – Lana Wade – and mumbled my thanks, tongue-tied and shy in the presence of this kind stranger, our new neighbour, as I stared at her golden gift, the late summer sun warming the glass jar of honey in my hands.

'Store it as long as you like,' Sally Berry said. 'You can keep honey forever. Honey was found in the tombs of the pharaohs.'

I must have looked doubtful.

'Honey never goes bad!' she assured me. 'Eat it after a thousand years and it's the same as eating it after a day!' She turned to look at the removal lorry. 'Is that your husband? The one in the white T-shirt? He's very good-looking, isn't he?'

Roman, my husband, had one of those faces that looks made to be seen in profile – a strong chin and a high forehead and an attractively broken nose, like the face you might see on a coin in the British Museum or on a bottle of Paul Newman salad dressing.

His tight blond curls were darkened and matted with sweat and his white T-shirt, so pristine when we had set out today, was now smeared with the grime of moving. My boy looked good. He stood at the back of the lorry, grinning at us, one hand raised in salute.

'Is he an actor?' Sally asked.

'A doctor,' I said, feeling that familiar pang of pride that I knew would never fade. 'Roman's a doctor.'

Roman was helping the removal men to unload our only sofa. My husband was not the type who liked to stand around and watch the help.

Roman and the youngest, fittest, most elaborately tattooed of the removal men came staggering up the short gravel driveway with the sofa between them.

Sally Berry watched him approvingly.

'Welcome,' she smiled. 'Dr Wade.'

People like being around doctors, I find. They trust doctors. They respect doctors. They find doctors a reassuring presence. But I guessed that Sally would have brought home-made honey for any new neighbour.

'I *love* honey,' Roman said, slightly breathless at the far end of the sofa, but maintaining his impeccable bedside manner. 'Thank you so much.'

His smile was dazzling.

'I do hope you'll be happy here,' Sally said, beaming at the pair of us. 'Nobody ever leaves the Gardens.'

'Why would they?' Roman gasped. 'Clean air. No crime. Good schools. All this living space. What could you get in the city for this money? Why would anyone ever move out?'

He sounds like an estate agent, I thought – a mean thought – as they lugged the sofa into the house. But I knew that Roman was not simply being polite to our new neighbour. He was still selling our new home to me, as if I still needed convincing.

And I did.

I desperately wanted this to be a happy day. A new start for us. To leave the past behind and all of that.

But today was not the same for Roman as it was for me. For my husband, we were moving home. And for me, it felt more like exile.

Roman came out of the house and stood panting by my side, staring at the street with something like wonder. Drenched in the sunshine of a late summer afternoon, Castle Gardens – although I never heard anyone call it anything but the Gardens – looked like a city dweller's dream of the countryside. Sally's small thatched cottage, swathed in all those pink oleander shrubs, must have originally been the home of some kind of gatekeeper or estate worker or minor retainer. Roman smiled at it with wonder, as if it might be made out of gingerbread.

Apart from Sally's pink cottage, there were four honey-coloured houses, all postcard-perfect Cotswold architecture, two on each side of the Gardens, none of them exactly the same size. We were in the smallest.

At the far end of the Gardens stood the manor house – much older and larger than its neighbours, its stone a shade darker from the passing of a few extra centuries, more flaxen than honey, the ancient walls lush with the deep dark green of Boston ivy, looking like the distilled essence of some lost England of a hundred years ago.

The manor house stood apart from the rest of the Gardens behind iron gates designed for horse and carriage, not car, with gently rising lawns that looked as though they had been cut with nail scissors, at the end of a grey ribbon of a driveway, behind tall trees that I could not name. It looked like the grand old house in a Gothic novel, waiting to be woken from some bewitched sleep.

Roman sighed by my side, and I leaned against him.

The Gardens might lose some of its romance in the middle of a cold grey winter but on a big blue day in late August with the smell of cut grass in the air and the sun gently toasting all that soft yellow stone, it was beautiful.

Our new home, I thought.

Then there was a sensation so light on the back of my hand that I took it for a summer breeze. But a bee had landed, attracted no doubt by my jar of home-made honey, and I held my breath, waiting for it to sting me. The bee seemed to stare around, getting its bearings, its wings making a blurry rotation movement like a tiny helicopter, its inky legs kicking in strange jerking movements.

'Human beings can learn a lot from bees,' Sally told me, watching the one on my hand, making it clear that I shouldn't even think about swatting it. 'Their work ethic. Their sense of duty. Their compassion and their sacrifice. Bees live their brief lives in the service of a greater good. Bees are the essence of resilience!'

The bee abruptly lifted from my hand and meandered off into the unbroken blue sky. As we watched it go Roman slipped his arm around my waist and I could smell the sweat mixing with his cologne and feel his hopes for this place coming off him in waves.

I smiled at him, touched by his happiness, and he grinned, scooping me up in his arms, and Sally Berry clapped and the removal guys cheered as my husband carried me across the threshold of this house of dreams, our second shot at building a happy home, the place where we would try to begin again.

2

Our back garden was a jungle.

Someone must have loved it once because it was edged with the tiny graveyards of dead flowers, but nature and neglect had long since reclaimed it for the wild. The grass was waist high and a collapsed trellis of blackened roses sagged and dipped into the deep end of a swimming pool that looked more like a stagnant pond. A pair of scrawny foxes dozed by the pool's rusting metal ladder, almost invisible in the late afternoon shadows of a droopy willow. The level of the pool's filthy water was a good metre lower than it should have been.

Taking a break from unpacking, I settled in a nook I had discovered at the top and the back of the house, a secret little alcove with a window seat that was just about big enough for tea for two although there wouldn't have been room to swing a chocolate digestive – cosy was definitely the word. I contemplated how much work it was going to be to tame our jungle.

In contrast, the garden next door had a lawn as smooth as a snooker table, the grass cut in sharply alternative shades of pale green and dark green, the neat flower beds a riot of colour – pale lemon Japanese primroses and fresh white roses, the garden's tall fences covered with banks of purple wisteria. Immaculately green-uniformed gardeners silently watered and pruned, manicured and fussed as a young woman did lazy laps of a swimming pool that was as blue as a David Hockney Californian canvas with nothing on its surface but dappled late summer sunshine. The woman emerged at the far end and, even from this distance, she was stunning. Tall and tanned – no, mixed race – she looked like one of those genetically blessed girls I had once photographed for fashion magazines, but ten years older now and married into serious money.

The beauty next door wrapped a white towel around her bony shoulders and, checking her phone, walked slowly around the pool and into her honey-coloured house, ignoring the gardeners who, it seemed to me, were all trying their best not to stare at her.

It was several hours after the removal men had left us. Roman was in the master bedroom at the front of the house, tearing open boxes, trying to get it all done at once, as if we could really move home in just one day. But I looked at the contrast between the two back gardens and I needed a drink of something cold, alcoholic and rosé-coloured.

I went downstairs to the kitchen where the big black American fridge was empty apart from a bottle of Léoube, my favourite wine. It took me a while to find the box containing a corkscrew, and a little longer to find the box with wine glasses. But I was getting on a pleasant rosé buzz when Roman came down.

'It's organic,' I said. 'Good for you.'

He raised his eyebrows, smiled and said nothing. I was not the only one making an effort today. Roman didn't like me drinking before sundown. He filled a wine glass with tap water and gulped it down. Then he filled another and joined me at the long marble-topped island that dominated the kitchen. A kitchen island. I ran my palms over the mottled granite. We had never had a kitchen island before. Our new house was countryside quaint on the outside, the oleander and wisteria a riot of colour over the old gold of the distinctive Cotswolds stone, but inside it was all state-of-the-art tech and expensive surfaces of marble, granite and glass. We raised our drinks of wine and water, and I felt the familiar ache that I always got when I looked at my husband's face.

Sally Berry's welcome gift stood between us.

'Does honey really last a thousand years?' I said.

Roman flipped into nerd mode.

'As long as you keep the lid on,' he said. 'No best-by date on that stuff. It's the science – low moisture, high acidity, hydrogen peroxide. The bees flap their wings, dry out the juices so nothing can ever spoil it. Shelf life is the end of the universe. And honey is Mother Nature's bandage. You can put it on a burn or a cut because nothing can grow on it. But you have to watch out for the side effects.'

'What's that?'

'You might get a bit sticky.'

I punched his arm.

'We've got a pool in our back garden,' I said. 'Did you see? And also an Amazon rain forest.'

'Yes, we're going to have to get a fence built around that pool,' he said.

That's Roman for you. Always anticipating disaster, and always trying to head it off at the pass.

I persuaded him to have a half-glass of wine with me to celebrate our arrival and he persuaded me to do a bit more unpacking before we knocked off for the day. There was a floor-to-ceiling triple-door wardrobe in the master bedroom. I hung up my end-of-summer clothes in the first part, and Roman's Paul Smith suits and Prada shirts in the second – he was a very dapper doctor, my husband – but the third door on the right-hand side would not open.

'Push,' Roman said, with a secret smile.

And so I pushed and the third door swung open towards me. Beyond, there was not a wardrobe but a small room. More of a large cell, in fact. Roman was watching me with that faint smile. He had hardly touched his wine. I looked inside the secret space. There was nothing inside but a sofa bed and an old school desk with a monitor, keyboard and some kind of video recorder.

I shook my head. 'What's all this?'

Roman grinned at me. 'Narnia!'

'I don't remember the estate agent mentioning Narnia.'

'Because she didn't know it was there,' Roman said.

I remembered that estate agent. A glossy young thing who talked – with a little smirk full of unearned intimacy – as much about children as she did about property. Did we have any? Were we planning to 'start a family' soon – as if we weren't a family already! As if you couldn't be a proper family without children. Excellent schools around here, she had said, until she saw the look on my face and swiftly changed the subject. I had not cared for her much.

'I saw this space when I came alone, the second time, with her boss,' Roman was saying. 'Didn't I tell you? I thought I might have.'

'You definitely didn't tell me, Roman.'

I stepped inside, hit a random button on the keyboard and the monitor came alive, revealing nine little screens, three rows of three, showing black-and-white images of the rear of the house, the front of the house, the street, the stairs, the kitchen, everything, in fact, from the entrance to the Gardens to the big manor house at the end of the road. I tapped the walls of the room and they felt like solid steel.

'I know what this is,' I said. 'This is a panic room.'

'Don't call it that,' Roman said, frowning, as though I was spoiling a lovely moment. 'It's a *safe* room.'

'Why do we need a *safe* room?'

'We don't! This can be your studio. You can keep your photography kit in here. You can hang up your Dorothea Lange. And all your photographs.'

I thought about it.

'You really know what to say to a girl, don't you?' I said.

My Dorothea Lange was in a big cardboard box that we had carried on the back seat of our car because it was far too precious to trust with any removal men. Most people might not know Lange's name but they certainly know her work, because Dorothea Lange took some of the most famous photographs of the Depression. The most famous Dorothea Lange photograph of all was the one that we now carefully unpacked – *Migrant Mother* from 1936.

A young woman, her face etched deep with worry, stares off into the distance, two of her children hanging on her threadbare dress. Their clothes are rags and, after almost a century, their desperation is still raw. The woman holds her right hand to the side of her sunburned face and in that gesture, you can feel the misery of millions. It is a terrible and beautiful image, one of the most famous photographs of the 1930s, taken by Lange in a migrant workers' camp in California.

Roman helped me put it up on the back wall.

The photograph was 24 by 30 inches, which meant that unforgettable face was life size. I had a silver gelatin, hand-processed fibre print, and the irony was not lost on me, owning a portrait of human suffering in an expensive, exhibition quality limited edition. But this was exactly the kind of photograph I had dreamed of taking, once upon a time, before life got in the way.

We unpacked two more framed photographs of a slightly smaller size. *The Crack Shack* by Sandy McKay, my old mentor, teacher and friend. Sandy's photograph was taken inside a derelict building on the outskirts of the city, the frame packed with drug-ravaged faces staring out of the twilight.

And finally my own photograph, *Chicken Soup,* a shot of a homeless man waiting in line for his dinner. I took it the night that I met Roman. I was trying hard to be the new Dorothea Lange or Sandy McKay, taking photos in a homeless hostel, and Roman was an idealistic medical student working for a charity that taught first aid to people living on the street. Later I had to take whatever work I could get – mostly fashion, but with a bit of corporate and even a few weddings – because I had to keep earning to support my boyfriend when he was in med school, and then I had to keep earning when Roman was my husband and a junior doctor working in an inner-city A&E ward, dealing with assault-with-a-sharp-object victims every night of the year – and I mean, *every* night – while I took pictures of young women like the bathing beauty next door.

We held hands, admiring *Chicken Soup*. Other couples had a favourite song that brought the memories flooding back of the night they met. Roman and I had a photograph of a bloke with no teeth waiting for a free bowl of chicken soup.

'We'll be all right here,' Roman said. 'I promise. New start and all that.' A pause. 'You heard our new neighbour. Sally? Nobody ever leaves this place.'

I smiled my agreement. But that night, when Roman was sleeping the sleep of the physically exhausted, I could not switch off my head.

There were no blinds or curtains in our bedroom – that was one of the ten thousand things on tomorrow's to-do list – and the pulsing orange light of a security guard's van slowly crept across the ceiling as he did his rounds.

And it couldn't be true, could it?

Roman was talking like an estate agent again.

It couldn't be true that nobody ever left the Gardens. It could not be true that you moved into this place and then just lived here happily ever after. Because if nobody ever left, then whatever happened to the people who had lived here before us?

*

We spent the rest of the weekend with the never-ending job of moving in. Calling utility companies whose recorded messages told us how important we were to them, but they were experiencing unprecedented waiting times, and unpacking the Himalayas of cardboard boxes that were still stacked high in every room, Roman and I trying to be gentle with each other until the light was growing dark and we needed to wash off the day and we wanted dinner delivered to our door and we badly needed a big glass of rosé.

Or was that just me?

Roman was taking a shower when I knocked over the second glass of wine and I saw what was carved into the doorway of the master bedroom.

How had I not noticed before?

There were what looked like claw marks on the polished hardwood floor, scratched deep into the wood, as if made by a dog demanding to be let out of the house.

Or someone fighting for their life.

3

Sunday, 30 August

A father was running with his son.

I watched from the window of our bedroom as the pair of them jogged into the Gardens. A youngish dad trailed by a skinny boy in his awkward, loose-limbed middle teens who had a black dog of indeterminate breed panting happily by his side. The man and boy both wore camouflage tracksuit bottoms and bright yellow T-shirts, the kind cyclists wear for the Tour de France or to avoid getting hit by a bus, but their matching kit was where the resemblance ended. The dad was muscular, crop-haired, his face flushed with all that pumping blood and fresh air. There was something slightly amiss about his handsome face but from this distance I could not name it. The man looked ferociously fit, as if he could run forever. But the boy – a weedy fifteen or maybe sixteen, small for his age – was clearly in some distress. When they stopped on the driveway of the house next to Sally's pink cottage, the boy looked as if he was in a great deal of pain. Hands on his hips, bending double, his long dark hair fell over his face. It was striking – they were so different and yet they were unmistakably father and son. The man patted the boy encouragingly on his back, slipped an arm around his shoulders and they went inside their home.

I should have had my camera with me, I thought.

Dorothea Lange would have captured that moment.

A thickset, bustling woman with a wild mess of frizzy hair came out of the house on the other side of Sally's cottage, followed by a good-looking blonde girl of seventeen or so, her hair carelessly tied up in a loose bun, dressed for Sunday-morning football but sullenly lugging a cello in a cherry-red case as if it was a drunk she was throwing out of a pub.

The woman glanced at her watch and spoke sharply to the girl – her daughter, the reluctant musician and sportswoman. They got into a brand-new Range Rover and tore off.

Sunday morning in the Gardens, I thought. Jogging, music lessons and competitive sport. Self-improvement all round.

Roman was at work. Or rather he was in his surgery, preparing for tomorrow. He started at the doctor's practice in what they called 'the village' on Monday morning and was checking out his office so that he could hit the ground running. He had left me with a kiss on the cheek and a vague promise to call me about lunch.

Daunted by all the boxes that were still waiting to be unpacked, I made myself a coffee and came back upstairs to my new studio, sipping it under the watchful gaze of *Migrant Mother* as I flicked on the monitors.

Nine small screens came to life.

Nothing much was happening in the Gardens. I thought I might see the beautiful woman in the swimming pool next door but her garden was empty. Nothing was stirring at Sally's cottage or the big house at the end of the road. No sign of the running man and boy. I looked at the image of our overgrown jungle in our back garden, wondering how we would even begin to clear it.

And then, among the shadows of the collapsed rose trellis and drooping willow tree, I saw the face of a man.

The face was motionless.

There was a stone Buddha hiding somewhere in the long grass, one of those figures that are placed in gardens to attract positive energy and repel negative forces, a feng shui-conscious garden gnome for the spiritually enlightened, and for a moment I thought that was what I was looking at, some half-buried garden furniture.

But then a phone was raised to the face.

And he took a picture of the back of our house.

Suddenly terrified, I rushed out of the safe room and into the nook at the back of the house. I stared down at the back garden. Whoever was out there was on the move now, wading through the high grass that skirted the swimming pool, the phone still raised to his face, clicking away.

Getting closer.

I banged hard on the glass.

The man looked up at me and stood paralysed, as if he had seen a ghost. Then he turned and fled through the trees at the back of the garden and into the fields beyond just as the doorbell rang. I went downstairs to answer it, my heart pounding.

It was the beauty from the swimming pool next door and the woman with the multi-talented daughter.

They were smiling at me.

'We're just checking you got your honey,' said the woman from next door.

They were unlikely friends.

Willow – the stunner from the swimming pool – was not quite thirty and she had retired from modelling in Paris when she met her husband, Guy, who had apparently made an early fortune with some tech bros from school. Krissy was ten years older, American, a pretty woman who would always fret about her weight, a former equity research analyst – whatever that was – at Lehman Brothers.

'Until the world went to shit in the GFC,' she said as we all settled at my kitchen island.

I must have looked blank.

'KFC?'

'GFC,' she smiled, rolling her eyes but not in a nasty way. 'Not KFC. There were no chicken wings involved. 2008? The Great Financial Crash? Ring a distant bell?'

In the city they would never have been friends, I thought. Krissy had a law degree from Harvard and Willow had a Home Economics GCSE for looking after her hamster and had headed for Paris as soon as the school gates were left slightly ajar.

No, they could never have been friends in the city because there would have been too many people of the same age, background and life experience, too many friendship opportunities. But out here in our privileged corner of the countryside, Willow and Krissy were practically a double act.

They finished each other's sentences, laughing in perfect harmony, exchanged knowing little looks, shared private jokes. Sally's honey was clearly a source of endless amusement. They considered my pot with delight.

'The bee is the essence of resilience!' Krissy laughed.

'We can learn a lot from bees!' Willow chuckled.

They took me for brunch in the village. It was not really a village at all, just two picture-perfect streets of cafés and restaurants and antique shops, a river with white swans and a languid rowing crew running through it, a village green covered with fallen chestnuts and gently rising above it all a jumbled hill of small, milk-and-honey-coloured houses.

The village was a fifteen-minute walk from the Gardens or a three-minute drive – even less, the way Krissy drove her Range Rover. We headed for a café by the river – Teahouse on the Tracks – where the young staff all knew them.

I felt shy – the new kid in school – but they quickly put me at my ease.

Willow was not the deep-frozen beauty I had taken her to be when I first saw her, and there was a very un-English warmth about Krissy, a native New Yorker who had moved to the UK some twenty years ago for her masters at the London School of Economics. We drank our coffee and they gave me a beginner's guide to the Gardens.

The big house at the end of the road was owned by an elderly academic and his brilliant wife, Professor Hall and Doctor Hall – or was it the other way round? Sally Berry had had sex with Jimi Hendrix at Woodstock. The father I had seen running with his son was a single parent, Ben, and the boy was Oscar. His black dog was Buster.

'Ben's raising Oscar alone?'

Willow and Krissy exchanged a look.

'Juno – Ben's wife – ex-wife, I guess – did a runner,' Willow said. 'A year ago.'

They exchanged a look, and apparently decided to let me in on the secret.

'Juno fell in love with her yoga trainer,' Krissy said. 'A Brazilian hunk of spunk called Paulo.'

'*Manolo*,' Willow said. 'Not *Paulo*. Why do you always get it wrong?'

Krissy shook her head.

'It's the memory of Manolo's yoga pants – it does something to my brain. The reinforced seams, the elasticated waistband, the signature crotch panelling ...'

They leaned their heads together, chuckling.

'We shouldn't laugh,' Willow said, suddenly serious. 'It was awful for Ben and Oscar.'

'Juno ran off to London with *Manolo* to work on her Downward Facing Dog,' Krissy said. She stared at Willow, her face impassive. 'I imagine it must be quite good by now.'

'A mixed marriage, Sally called it,' Willow said. 'Local boy – Ben – marries a townie – Juno. Never works, according to our Sally.'

'But Juno had a troubled life,' Krissy pointed out. 'Her mother was some kind of addict. Drink? Drugs?'

Willow shrugged.

'Anything that was going, Juno told me.'

'Juno had a dad who was long gone, or never there in the first place. And she had a younger brother, but they were separated when they both went into care. She had a lot of unwanted attention from men all her life. Then she met Ben.'

'Juno told me he was the first man who ever told her she was pretty.'

'But their love was not to be,' Krissy said.

'Shame,' Willow said. 'Because Juno was a great mum. Doted on Oscar. Never marry the first man who tells you that you're pretty.'

'It's all right for you, Willow,' Krissy said. 'I'm still waiting!'

They laughed in perfect harmony.

I stared out the window at the river. 'A mother leaving her child,' I said. 'That's unusual.'

'It happens,' Krissy shrugged.

'And you didn't see Manolo,' Willow said.

'Poor Ben,' Krissy sighed. 'He does such a brilliant job with that boy. And he's not the easiest of kids, young Oscar.'

And then we talked about ourselves, telling those the-wonder-of-me stories that are shared among people meeting for the very first time.

Willow's husband – I got the impression they were seriously rich – had struck gold in the digital world.

'Guy had a small inheritance from his parents in South Africa and his friends at school had the brains and dreams. You know this Instagram influencer – Mata-chan?'

I shook my head.

'Well, Guy's friends invented Mata-chan and Guy provided the seed money. Mata-chan gives advice to troubled teens. She's half-Korean and half-Cuban. Supports fashionable causes. Got some big brands behind her now.'

I was struggling to keep up. 'Wait? So she's not real?'

'Google virtual Instagram influencer,' Krissy said. 'You can't miss her.'

'Guy cashed out early – *too* early,' Willow said, her eyes wide in her stunning face.

'Don't feel too sorry for her,' Krissy smiled. 'Guy's loaded. She's talking about the difference between the Haves and Have Yachts.'

'Krissy, those boys Guy knew from school are on *rich lists*!' Willow said. 'It's the difference between flying first class and having your own private jet.'

'That's what they call it, don't they?' Krissy said. 'School. *Were you at school?* Meaning – Eton. I love it. As though it's the only school in the country! The only school in the world!'

I told them how I met Roman – the young photographer trying to capture the desperation of the homeless and the idealistic medical student working pro bono among the poor. And our eyes met across a crowded soup kitchen.

It was a cute story and, back in our old life in the city, I would have felt the need to explain that Roman was only going into private practice now after years tending to stab victims at inner-city A&Es and then more years as a criminally overworked NHS GP in a very deprived neighbourhood.

But Willow and Krissy didn't care.

They liked it that handsome young Dr Wade was going to be their doctor at their local private surgery, replacing the retiring and unloved Dr Cox.

'Dr Cox and his ice-cold stethoscope,' shivered Willow.

Krissy told me the story of the Gardens and the great house that dominated it.

'This place is listed in the Domesday book,' she said, with what felt like an American reverence for a thousand years of history. 'There was a manor house, farm buildings, a few shacks for the carrot-munching peasants. Sally's place was originally an estate cottage housing some trusty retainer back in the day. Although what you see of it now – and what we live in – is largely twentieth century. Our houses – the new builds, they call them – have been there over a hundred years. Built by some financier who lost everything in the Great Crash of 1929.'

'Stepped off the roof of a tall building in Cheapside,' Willow said, spooning three sugars into her flat white. 'Poor man.' Then she brightened. 'Shall we have a drink? I do hope you drink, Lana.'

'Bit early,' Krissy laughed. 'Even for you, Willow.'

And again I felt it, as I had with Sally and her gift of honey – the unforced warmth of my new neighbours. There was no way I would be having brunch with people I had only just met in the city, discussing if it was too early for a bottle of wine.

'There was a man in our back garden,' I said.

They exchanged a look.

'Text Goran,' Krissy said. 'He's the security guard for the Gardens. That's what Goran's *for* – strangers in your back garden. I'll send you his details. What's your number?'

I told her. Her fingers flew across her phone.

'Goran's been in two wars,' Willow said. 'He's from – where is it? The Balkans or the Baltic?'

'I thought Goran was from Swindon,' Krissy said.

'We all pay for him,' Willow said. 'You'll get an invoice every six months.'

My phone went ping with Goran's number. I felt better already. Seeing the man in the garden had frightened me. I had thought we would be safe out here. That was the whole point of our move.

To feel safe again.

'Your house has been empty for ages,' Krissy said. 'Sometimes people come through a hole in the fence at the back. It's all open farmland back there. And they look at the house. *Your* house. They don't go inside, do they, Willow?'

'It used to be worse,' Willow said. 'A lot worse. When – you know – it happened.'

I didn't understand what they were talking about.

'When *what* happened?' I said. 'Who looks at the house? And why would anyone look at *my* house?'

They stared at me. And then at each other.

'You don't know, do you?' Krissy said. And to Willow. 'Wow. She doesn't know.'

Krissy nodded, staring at me.

'But it was *everywhere*,' Willow said. She seemed suddenly upset. She looked at her friend. 'How can she *not* know?'

'Because there are things – lots of things – estate agents don't tell you about,' Krissy said. 'It was big news around here – the biggest news ever – but perhaps not so big everywhere else. That's why there was someone in your back garden.'

'You should have seen it after it happened,' Willow said. 'The bloody ghouls were everywhere. Gawping. Taking their pictures with their little phones. Getting their thrills out of somebody else's misery. Guy threatened a few of them with a horse whip.'

'Fucking sightseers,' Krissy said, her accent suddenly pure Brooklyn. 'Cranks. The dregs of the Internet.'

The house price, I thought. It was too cheap. It did not make sense at the time. But it did now. I should have known. Something terrible had taken place in our beautiful new home.

'Tell me,' I said.

They hesitated, as if unsure where to begin.

'There was a tragedy,' Krissy said.

'A tragedy with the family who were there before you,' Willow said. 'The Clutters.'

'The Clutters were a lovely family,' Krissy said. 'Bill – the husband – was a pilot. Long-haul 777s.'

'Very dashing in his uniform,' Willow said. 'April was a flight attendant on Singapore Airlines. Gorgeous girl. Some kind of beauty queen in her youth – what was it?'

'Miss Kuala Lumpur 2000.'

'And Bill and April's son, Josh, he was one of those beautiful Anglo-Asian mixed-race kids.'

'Josh was a few years older than Sailor – my daughter,' Krissy said. 'They were very close. Grew up together. Bill used to tell them these great stories about flying when they were small. Flying at 35,000 feet in the high latitudes and suddenly his plane was in the middle of the Northern lights. And flying east to west, Sydney to London, he saw the sun rise twice on the same day over the Indian Ocean.'

'The Clutters were talking about moving away. Cornwall. The Highlands. The Lake District. Getting right away from the Gardens.'

'Please,' I said. '*What happened in my house?*'

Krissy and Willow looked at each other.

'They all died,' Willow said.

'Bill Clutter lost his job at the same time as me,' Krissy said. 'When it all went to shit in 2008. The GFC. But then Bill lost his again in 2020 when it all went to shit once more for an encore. And that second time it happened, he broke. The poor man. He just . . . broke.'

'Bill had a nervous breakdown,' Willow said. 'Fell out with everyone in the Gardens. All of us. All the people who were his friends. All the people who loved him, and

April, and Josh. He was on antidepressants.' She looked meaningfully at Krissy. 'Old Dr Cox always handed out the happy pills a bit too freely.'

I was waiting with a feeling of mounting dread.

'Bill Clutter had a double-barrelled 12-bore shotgun,' Krissy said. 'That's not unusual around here. There are more shooting clubs in Oxfordshire than any county in the country. So having a shotgun in your house is not unusual in this neck of the woods. We've all got them.'

I wanted to run. I didn't want to know what was coming.

But they were about to tell me.

'A year ago Bill Clutter took his shotgun and he shot April while she was sleeping,' Krissy said.

'We all heard the shot,' Willow said.

'It was the middle of the night but a 12-bore shotgun wakes up the neighbourhood,' Krissy said. 'By the time we all got some clothes on, Goran was trying to smash down their front door. Then we heard the second shot, when Bill killed their son, when he killed Josh. And then Bill shot himself just as Goran kicked down the door.'

Willow signalled for the waitress and asked her for the wine list.

We were going to have that bottle after all.

I sat in stunned silence.

A family had died in our new home. And it was the father who had killed them, and then himself.

My hand was shaking as I reached for my wine.

No wonder they gave us a discount.

'That's what happened to the previous family,' Willow said. 'That's what happened in your house. And that's why you get creeps taking pictures in your back garden.'

4

Clutter Family Annihilation
From Wikipedia, the free encyclopaedia

In the early hours of 1 November 2020, **William Clutter** murdered his wife **April Clutter** and their seventeen-year-old son **Josh Clutter** with his legally owned Browning B525 Sporter shotgun before committing suicide with the same firearm. William Clutter was a forty-year-old long-haul airline pilot who had recently been made redundant following the 2020 contraction of the airline industry. The Clutter **familicide** received widespread publicity due to the idyllic setting of the crime – an affluent community in rural Oxfordshire – and because Clutter's recent unemployment was directly attributed to the economic downturn of the Covid-19 pandemic, also known as the coronavirus pandemic. The Clutter family killings also sparked debate within the medical community around the routine prescription of **antidepressant medication** at a time of **mass unemployment** and **mental disorder.**

See also: Familicide, Family Annihilation, Family Murders, Murder-Suicide, Antidepressant-induced mania.

There was much more. About the Clutter family killings, and about men like William Clutter who decide that the only way out of the black pit they are in is wiping out their entire family and then themselves.

Willow was right. The Clutters were everywhere online. Tap their name into any search engine and their terrible end came rolling out in all its horror.

Google suggestions.
Clutter family killings
Clutter family house
Clutter family crime scene

So how had I missed them?

How could Roman and I have been so oblivious to this horror?

Because William Clutter murdering his family and then himself had been news but not for very long and, quite frankly, it had never been front-page news, and it had never been any media outlet's lead story. Because their story happened too often.

Clutter was a newly unemployed man – one of many – who cracked up and then took it all out on his family. There was a horrible lack of surprise about the horrific act.

Men did it all the time. Husbands and fathers, pushed somewhere beyond their breaking point, then reaching for the fist and the boot, or even the knife and the gun. Always, always the man.

If murderously depressed women did it – if unemployed mothers did it, if despairing wives did it, if some doped-to-the-eyeballs missus reached for the family shotgun – then I could find no evidence.

I sat in the safe room – my studio, my safe studio – with a big glass of Léoube, watched over by *Migrant Mother* and the others, wandering the digital labyrinth, going where it took me, sipping my wine, trying to drink slowly, already too buzzed from the bottle I had shared with Willow and Krissy at the Teahouse on the Tracks, clicking on the links like a fisherman casting his line until I found a blog called *Truer Crime*, illustrated with a picture of our new home.

Familicide Narrative

There are four categories of familicide murder – nihilistic, disappointed, self-righteous, paranoid.

The nihilistic killer sees his family purely as a status symbol; when his economic status collapses, the nihilistic killer sees them as surplus to his requirements.

The disappointed killer seeks to punish the family for not living up to his ideals of family life.

The self-righteous killer destroys the family to exact revenge upon the mother, in an act that he blames on her.

Finally, the paranoid killer kills their family in what they imagine to be an attempt to protect them from a fate far worse.

And I thought – worse than being shot in the head with a 12-bore shotgun?

And I also thought – nihilistic, disappointed, self-righteous, paranoid – oh, which one were you, Captain Bill?

Or were you all of the above?

All over the developed world, a child and a spouse are statistically far more likely to be killed by a parent than by a stranger. In cases of family annihilation, the killer takes his life after the act and so there is no court case, no way of knowing if this was a premeditated, carefully planned murder or a spontaneous act of slaughter.

And so the central mystery of every familicide – *why?* – is never solved.

Three images came up again and again and again. William Clutter in his pilot's uniform, dashingly handsome and delighted with life, some kind of official airline shot. And the youthful April Clutter wearing a bathing suit and a winner's tiara and sash in her Kuala Lumpur hometown the year before she became a flight attendant. And a family photograph with baby Josh and his beautiful parents laughing under a sparkling Christmas tree.

But to really meet the Clutter family, you needed to find them on Instagram. And I was shocked to see that they were still there.

The Clutter presence on social media had abruptly stopped, it seemed, around a month before their deaths – a last wistful shot of the family dog running ahead on barren autumn fields, the sun low in the sky, April and Josh wrapped up in anoraks, their faces unseen by the photographer.

They were dead and gone but their social media timeline lived on. The family holidays, the lazy weekends, all of them getting younger as I scrolled backwards through the posts. Would these images stay online forever, like space junk floating through the universe?

It was on Instagram that I felt I truly got a sense of the Clutters for the first time. But the impression was misleading – wasn't it? – because the Clutters looked *normal*. They looked *happy*.

They looked as if they had mastered the great trick of living, the one we must all master, and learned how to count their blessings, and to understand how lucky they were to have their life, and how to stay close to the things that they loved. They were a family who looked as though they had many golden years ahead of them. I looked at the father, Captain William Clutter, and I had no sense that this man had a raging madness inside him that would claim all their lives. The Clutters looked like a loving, lucky family who enjoyed life's simple pleasures.

I traced their faces with my fingertip on the screen of my laptop and I could have wept for them.

Bill the proud husband and father and handsome pilot.

April the former beauty queen and retired flight attendant and hot young mum. And Josh, the sporty kid, the beloved only child.

How does a world like that fall apart?

And how the hell, I asked myself again as Roman's car pulled into our drive, had we not known about what had happened in this house? How had we missed it? How could we be so oblivious? So ignorant?

As Roman got out of the car and stood staring at the street, the soft evening sunlight on his perfect face, I felt my stomach fall away.

Because perhaps only one of us had been ignorant.

Roman found me upstairs at the back of the house, sitting in my alcove with an empty wine glass, staring out over the overgrown garden. Next door there was a man lounging by the pool in a dress shirt and shorts, reading the *Financial Times*. He was balding, overweight, already forty – not quite what I had in mind for Willow's husband, Guy, genius co-inventor of an Instagram virtual influencer.

Roman placed a hand against my face and I flinched.

'There was someone out there this morning,' I said. 'In our back garden. He ran off when I banged on the window.'

There was a muscle just under Roman's left eye and it began to pulse. That rogue muscle by Roman's left eye always did that when he was frightened or anxious. It actually happened quite a lot.

'Who?'

'I don't know! Some freak. Some ghoul. How should I know?'

He stared at the garden. 'What was he doing out there?'

'He was taking photographs. And just staring, staring, staring. Nosing around – *because of what happened in this house*. Because our house is famous, Roman.'

We stared at each other.

'And you knew, didn't you?' I said. 'You knew exactly why this house is famous, didn't you? Did that estate agent tell you about it – full disclosure and all that – when you came alone for that second viewing without me?'

He shook his head, the muscle by his left eye throbbing harder, then blinked once, trying to control it. But nothing could stop that muscle once it got going.

'Do you seriously think estate agents tell you these things?' he said. 'I only learned about it this morning because the Clutters were all patients of Dr Cox, my predecessor, and I've been reading their medical records.' He took a breath. 'William Clutter was suffering from clinical depression, Lana. He was on levels of antidepressant medication that, between you and me, should never have been prescribed. Bill Clutter was a man having a complete nervous breakdown on industrial-strength medication who happened to be a shooting enthusiast with a loaded gun in the house. That's never going to be a good combination. But it has nothing to do with *us,* Lana.'

He made to take me in his arms, but I pulled away.

I felt we had been tricked. I felt as if I had been tricked. We both found out only today? I wasn't sure that I believed him.

'It would have been nice to have known,' I said. 'It's not as if it's just noisy neighbours or a touch of rising damp, is it? *A family died here, Roman.* That's why it was empty for so long! That's why it was so cheap! Some poor mad bastard took his shotgun and killed his wife and son and then himself. Who would want to live in a place like that?'

He shrugged. He sighed. He had the nerve to sigh.

'Why can't you just be happy, Lana?' he said.

'I'm fucking trying! But I thought we were going to be *safe* here!'

'Of course we're safe here!'

'Really?

'William Clutter was a deeply troubled man.'

'No kidding! *You* wanted this move, Roman. You were so desperate to get away from our old flat.'

I saw him flinch and I felt bad that I had hurt him. But it was true. He was the one most desperate to escape from our past. He was the one who had wanted to run from our old home.

'What happened here was textbook,' he said quietly. 'The man of the house was clinically depressed, economically desperate, probably intoxicated and certainly drugged up to the gills. And *armed*. It's a tragedy – of course it's a tragedy! – but there's nothing complicated about it, and there's no mystery, and there's nothing difficult to understand.' He took my hands and I let him, our fingers wrapped around the stem of the empty wine glass. 'And it has got nothing to do with us or the life that we are going to build here.'

My eyes filled with tears. I pulled my hand away and put my glass on the windowsill of my little alcove.

'What happened to their dog?'

'What dog?'

'They had a dog. The Clutters had a dog. It's all over their Instagram posts. What happened to the dog?'

'I have no idea, Lana.'

But I could guess what had happened to the dog. Exactly the same thing that happened to all of them. Everybody had died.

'You want to move?' Roman said. 'Fine. We can move. We don't have to stay here. But we would still be the same people, and we would take our own scars with us. You know that wouldn't change, don't you?'

I stared at the overgrown back garden.

Then I nodded.

He sank to his knees beside me, and he put his hands on me, and I felt his love for me, and his need to make me understand.

'Whatever sadness or tragedy has happened, it has nothing to do with *our* life,' he said. 'What house doesn't have its stories of misery? What house is all sweetness and light? Bad things – horrific, life-rending things – can and do happen everywhere. Oh Lana! *Don't we know that better than anyone?* Our old home – what happened there – it nearly ruined us, didn't it?'

Now we were both crying.

And I was sorry, I was sorry for everything, and I didn't need to tell him.

We clung to each other for a long time and then he lifted me from my cosy little alcove and my anger with him suddenly drained away.

Roman took me in his arms and I let him and I wanted to stay there forever.

Bad things can – and do – happen everywhere.

5

Monday, 31 August

Willow and Krissy were grinning on my doorstep, both of them in Sweaty Betty leggings and vests, fresh from a Monday morning yoga class with their spongy blue mats still rolled up under their arms.

'We brought you something,' Krissy said, and the two of them stepped apart to reveal an unsmiling guy of around thirty, lean as the Marlboro Man, so deeply tanned that he looked as if he had never spent a day of his life out of harsh sunlight. He could have been carved out of teak. He stared at me without expression. He had a six o'clock shadow, and it was only just after breakfast.

'Lana, this is Vince,' Krissy said, and the sunburned man gave me the briefest of nods. 'And Vince is our – what are you, Vince?'

Vince said nothing.

'Our handy man,' Willow said.

'Our handy man. And Vince is kindly going to sort out your garden. Aren't you, Vince?'

They regarded him brightly.

Vince continued to stare at me.

'Need to have a butcher's first,' he muttered, the accent vaguely West Country but using the rhyming slang of a long-lost London. Butcher's hook – look.

There was a high wooden gate at the side of the house that led to the back garden. I found the key that unlocked it and opened it up. Vince brushed past me and my nose twitched, for there was a smell about him that I could not quite place – a burnt, musky, skunky odour that somehow reminded me of the city.

Insistent and sickly sweet. I knew it from somewhere.

'Can I get you …'

'I'm all right,' he grunted, and disappeared into the overgrown garden.

Willow and Krissy were in the kitchen. I must have looked doubtful.

'Vince is a sweetheart,' Krissy said. 'A man of few words, it's true – but a sweetheart.'

I thought of the immaculately attired gardeners in their green uniforms who had tended the garden next door while Willow did her languid laps. They could hardly be more different to Vince with his gruff manner and strange smell.

'We use Albion's Avant Gardeners, and you will too,' Willow said, reading my mind. 'You can bring them in later for the subtle stuff. But you need Vince for the heavy lifting. Please don't be put off by his pong.'

From the big glass doors at the back of the house we could see Vince wading through the undergrowth. Willow smiled her fabulous smile and mimed puffing on a joint.

I nodded. Of course, I thought. That distinctive eau de Vince was weed. You smelled it all the time in our old neighbourhood, especially in the early evening when the building sites were clocking off. It was our new century's equivalent of a pint after work, the smell of a working man winding down.

'He does like his puff, our Vince,' Krissy said. 'He lives in a tent just outside the village and that's what he does in the evening. He inhales.'

'It's not a *tent*,' Willow smiled. 'It's a *yurt*.'

'A tent-like residence,' Krissy said. 'A middle-class tent. A tent of the bourgeoisie. Willow's been round there.'

'I was only getting a quote!'

'But for what, dear?'

They cackled in perfect accord.

Vince banged on the back window and we all looked.

'Going to need a skip,' he called. 'And I'm going to have to fill it a few times.' He glanced back at the garden. 'And it looks like your pool's got a leak.'

'Yes, yes, off you go then, Vince!' Krissy said, waving him away.

Vince had a battered white van parked on the street and he went off to hire a skip. Money was not mentioned. Willow and Krissy, I realised, assumed that money would never be a problem. They were used to being served. People came into the Gardens every day to attend to their needs, and the needs of their homes and families. It was a different way of living. They had help, they had staff, and they took being served as the natural order of the universe.

I watched the street as the man I had seen running – Ben? – came out of the house opposite with his son – Oscar? – and the black mongrel – Buster – trailing behind. Sally Berry emerged from her cottage and waved to them as they drove off. Willow and Krissy were talking about the place that cannabis had occupied in their previous lives.

'Smoking was never very popular among the girls,' Willow was saying, meaning girls like her, the professionally beautiful, the slinky drop-dead-gorgeous catwalk models of Paris. 'We always had to keep the weight off – even the naturally thin girls, like me – so the drugs of choice tended to be all the fast white powders. Smoking – when it wasn't cigarettes – just made you hungry.'

'Christ, I needed a bit of the wacky baccy to get through the day at Lehman Brothers,' Krissy said. 'The fucking Titanic of financial services.'

When I had first seen the pair of them – the impossibly beautiful ex-model and the prematurely retired financial analyst – I had thought that they would not be friends with each other in the city. And now as we drank our coffee I realised that, in my old life, I would not be friends with either of them.

I would have thought that Willow was spoilt, vain, full of herself – when actually she was nothing but sweet and kind and open, the girl next door hiding behind the face of an angel.

And Krissy would have been too much the hard-nosed, money-orientated city slicker for my arty tastes – but I loved her self-confidence, and her toughness, and her energy. And Krissy was kind, too – they both were – and I could see they wanted me to be happy in this place.

Willow and Krissy were nothing like the friends I had left behind in the city. So much of my old life, and the lives of my friends, had revolved around our work. It was not like that for Willow and Krissy. In their own way, they were both post-work – one of them happily retired, the other one traumatically redundant. Yet they were totally confident about their place in the world. And they seemed to genuinely care about me. Bringing Vince to tame our back garden was like Sally's home-made honey. I felt it again – the generosity of my new neighbours.

Then I saw them.

The man in black who had been lurking in our back garden was now standing bold as brass at the end of our driveway. He had his phone attached to some kind of small tripod which he was holding by one of its legs, pointing it at himself with our house in the background. I saw him more clearly now. He looked like a grown man who was dressed like a teenager – black hoodie, black jeans, like some overgrown Goth.

'That's *him*,' I said, and Willow and Krissy joined me at the window. 'The same bastard who was taking pictures in my back garden!'

There was a little gang of them now. A girl, somewhere in her early twenties, with cheaply dyed pink hair and a boy, around the same age, who reminded me of Piggy in *Lord of the Flies*. Portly, bespectacled, abnormally fair.

I felt something surge in me and I could not tell if it was rage or fear.

There was a wooden block with half a dozen Wusthof chef knives and I grabbed one of the larger knives.

'Oh baby!' Krissy cried.

'No-no-no!' Willow said, holding up her hands in horror.

The look in their eyes made my face burn with shame.

I put down the knife. 'But they're taking bloody selfies outside my home!'

'No,' Krissy said, pulling her phone out of her bag. 'I think they're probably making another documentary.'

'Internet sleuths,' Willow said, patting my arm as we stared at the shabby figures shuffling around at the end of my driveway.

'Internet – what?' I said.

'Internet sleuths,' Willow said.

'It's a euphemism for pathetic fucking losers,' Krissy said, sending a text message.

'They're interested in this house,' Willow said. 'Obsessed with it. Because of what happened with the Clutters.'

Then a voice from the street, not friendly.

'Oy!'

Our security guard, Goran, was shouting out the window of his white van as he pulled up outside. The Internet sleuths quickly folded their tripod and jogged nervously from the Gardens.

Willow and Krissy were staring at me. And I was staring at the Wusthof chef knife on the kitchen island.

'They're creeps,' Krissy said. 'And they're a pain in the butt. But you don't have to be scared, Lana.' She raised her hand to the security guard, out of his van now and standing watch like a postcard of a German Shepherd. 'Thank you, Goran!' she called pleasantly.

I was shaking and close to tears.

'Hey,' Willow said, stroking my back. She delicately took the knife and tossed it into the sink so I didn't have to look at it any more. 'Hey, Lana, it's nothing, just some little creeps. Come on now.'

'Sorry, sorry,' I said, wiping at my eyes, embarrassed by my emotion, humiliated about waving a knife around as though I would actually use it.

'Nothing to be sorry about,' Willow said, still soothing me but glancing at Krissy.

There was silence in the kitchen.

'It's just that we need this place to work,' I said. 'Roman and me.' I lifted my head to take it all in. 'This home. This move. It *really* has to work for us. We have to be safe here. Because in our old place – we weren't safe there.'

They looked at each other and then at me.

'Did something happen?' Krissy said.

They were nothing like the people I had known in my old life. But somehow, I felt that I could talk to them.

I nodded. Took a few deep breaths.

'We had what the law calls an aggravated burglary,' I said. I took another long breath and slowly let it out. It's meant to calm you down. 'It was devastating for both of us.'

'Did they catch them?' Willow said.

I shook my head. 'The police never catch anyone, do they? That's only on TV. We're all on our own, aren't we?'

'No,' Krissy said, her face creased with concern, watching me with an almost maternal gaze. 'That's just not true, Lana! You're *not* alone.'

She placed her hands on my hands.

Willow placed her hands on top of Krissy's hands.

We sat there staring at our pile of hands on the kitchen island and I laughed – embarrassed, relieved, grateful, all of it.

'You're not alone, Lana,' Willow repeated. 'Not here. Not now.'

She grinned at me, as if normal service had been resumed, but Krissy – older, shrewder – knew there was more that I was not saying.

Uncomfortable under her gaze, I tried to pull my hands away so I could put on the kettle, make us coffee, and we could talk about something else.

But Krissy held our hands in place, effortlessly strong.

There was silence in the kitchen. In the street we could hear the happy chatter of Filipina housekeepers on their way to work, talking to each other in Tagalog.

'What happened?' Krissy asked quietly. 'You and Roman. What did they do to you?'

I pulled my hands away, reeling away from the kitchen island, avoiding their eyes.

I will never tell anyone what happened that night.

I don't talk about it with old friends. I don't talk about it with Roman.

We didn't even tell the police.

So I wasn't about to tell my new neighbours, was I?

6

Tuesday, 1 September

Of all the things I missed about the city, my friend Sandy was the thing I missed the most.

That makes Sandy sound like a woman my own age, one of those girlfriends from Bridget Jones's diaries, always up for a night sharing a bottle of Sauvignon Blanc and talk of man trouble in Café Rouge. *50 cals, VG.* But my friend Sandy was a seventy-seven-year-old Glaswegian man who had made his name as a photographer of conflict during the golden age of the Sunday supplements with a CV – Vietnam, Bangladesh, Belfast, Biafra, London's ripped backside – that Dorothea Lange herself would not have sniffed at. It was Sandy's photograph of those massed druggies – *The Crack Shack* – that hung in my new studio. Sandy McKay was a real photographer in a way that I suspected that I was not really, not in the way that Dorothea Lange or Sandy McKay were real photographers, the indisputable genuine article.

In the morning I waved Roman off to work, and then I called Sandy.

'Lana,' he said, gruff and warm, and I could feel how pleased he was to hear from me. 'How's paradise?'

I stared down from the upstairs alcove. In our back garden, Vince had started hacking back the undergrowth. That eau de Vince weed pong had been particularly potent when he arrived in his van today, suggesting that he had just had a spliff the size of a Cornetto to set him up for the day. But Krissy and Willow were right – despite the high times back in his yurt, Vince was a grafter.

Next door, Willow was doing her languid, lazy lengths of their pool with her slow-motion American crawl as her husband Guy read the *FT*. He lifted his head as Willow emerged from the deep end, wrapping a white towel around her long limbs.

'It looks like heaven,' I said. 'It's beautiful, Sandy. The countryside is full of these green, gently rolling hills and the houses – all these beautiful, wheat-coloured houses – they change colour with the light. The colour of the stone is not static. It can be honey, gold, butterscotch. It all sits up and begs to be photographed.'

When I was still learning my trade, when Roman was at medical school and I had to keep earning, I had worked as Sandy's assistant in his quiet studio in Primrose Hill. Sandy was already knocking on a bit and no longer jumping on planes to war zones. By the time I first met him, he was taking black-and-white portraits for the glossy magazines of the posh Sundays – a long way from Saigon and the Falls Road – but there was still a gritty realism about those mug shots, even when he was taking a photo of some bright young thing fresh out of RADA and starring in their breakout role in some Jane Austen bonnet-drama.

'Even the people are beautiful,' I said, as Willow brushed past her husband and he reached for her wrist. He grabbed, held her for a moment, but then she pulled away, laughing, and disappeared into their house. Guy stood up, his belly poking out of his unbuttoned dress shirt and over his shorts. He stared after Willow, bemused, as if she was some perfect stranger who he couldn't quite account for rather than his wife.

'And the ones who are not beautiful are rich,' I said.

'So you're working?' Sandy said. 'Tell me you're working. You're capturing all this beauty for the ages, are you? Tell me you're pleading the fleeting moment to remain? Tell me that you remember you are a photographer, Lana.'

Slightly mocking, in that gruff Glasgow hard-man manner, just in case anyone might suspect that he had a heart of solid gold.

But he was dead serious about photography, and that was why he was my hero. And Sandy was a kind man, and that was why I loved him.

'The house is very demanding right now,' I said, watching Vince dragging away the collapsed rose trellis. 'We're still unpacking ...'

Sandy sighed. 'Don't stop working, Lana. Just because you've moved out of the city. Just because you and Roman have your Grand Plan. Just because you're suddenly surrounded by all that pastoral glory. I know – beauty's hard. The other stuff is easier to photograph. Misery. Desperation. The dark stuff. But you're far too good to stop working.'

I wasn't sure that was true. I had been good enough at my craft to support Roman and myself during his five years at medical school. And unlike a lot of photographers on the glossy magazines, I had never been too proud to do corporate work after the great print plunge – and technically I knew I was good enough for that, too. But as I wandered the house, pausing by the room we now called my studio to look at *Migrant Mother*, I could not kid myself.

No matter how much I wanted it, I was no Dorothea Lange, and I was no Sandy McKay.

'Lana?' Sandy said. 'Will you promise me you are going to keep taking pictures?'

'Only if you promise to visit me.'

That gruff Sandy laugh.

'Deal,' he said.

The receptionist at the surgery was confused.

She was a glossy blonde cresting forty, good-looking but tempered with the arrogant politesse of the doctor's gatekeeper. I knew the type and I always enjoyed messing with their pompous highlighted heads.

'I'm Dr Wade's one o'clock,' I said, deadpan.

She consulted her screen.

'Dr Wade doesn't have a one o'clock,' she said.

Roman came out of his office preceded by an old man in sports gear.

They both beamed at me, the old chap blinking owlishly behind massive specs.

'And this is my wife,' Roman said. 'Lana, this is Professor Alan Hall – our neighbour.'

'My dear,' he said, clasping my hands. 'How wonderful to have you and Dr Wade living in our neck of the woods.'

The owner of the big house, I thought.

Professor Hall looked fit in the manner of the elderly affluent – frail but hearty, a heartiness that had been worked at for decades. He was decked out in Adidas and Asics and there was not a gram of spare fat on him. His eyes were sharp blue little tacks behind his big black-framed George Smiley glasses. The only real sign of Professor Hall's advanced age – knocking on for eighty, I guessed – was his skin, which was as devoid of moisture as the Dead Sea scrolls.

He reluctantly let go of my hands and we small-talked about the magic of the Gardens as I tried to remember what Krissy and Willow had told me about the old couple who lived in the big house. The Halls were both hotshot academics, now retired, and this old chap, Professor Hall, had been something of a media celebrity back in the day, one of those academics who make it to the small screen, ruminating on late-night BBC2 and writing popular history bestsellers at the end of the last century. His German wife – Magda, Dr Magda Hall – had apparently been unwell.

'Touch of the old timer's disease,' Willow had said, tapping her head, and rolling her huge brown eyes.

Professor Hall was all charm – people like doctors, and by default they tend to like doctor's wives. We let him go, moving quite slowly on his Asics, and when he had finally disappeared, Roman nodded to the receptionist.

'I'll be back for my two o'clock, Rachel,' he said, and Rachel nodded, giving me a stiff little smile of her painted mouth.

Roman and I walked out into the chestnut tree-lined high street.

The village had been a seventeenth-century wool town, a minor stopping post on the road from London to Wales, and although it was largely unchanged it was mercifully far enough off the beaten track to avoid the tourism that blighted so many parts of the area. The broad main drag by the river was full of local restaurants rather than tourist tearooms, and the former coaching inns were now pubs catering to regulars grabbing a quick lunch, rather than touting for buses of tourists from China. Our village was achingly beautiful, but it was a place where people earned a living and lived their lives.

'Professor Hall was Regius Professor of History Emeritus at Oxford,' Roman said.

'Wow,' I said. 'I mean, I have absolutely no idea what that means – but definitely – wow.'

'I told him we would come for dinner.'

I groaned.

'Let's not get stuck with elderly neighbours, Roman. Once they take a shine to you, you can never get shot of them.'

He laughed.

'Don't you want to see the big house? And Professor Hall is an interesting man. He wrote bestselling books on the world wars. He did a lot of great stuff on the BBC. Always wore a bow tie. You must have seen it? It's all over YouTube.'

I shook my head.

'His wife – Magda – she's Dr Hall – was born in Berlin in 1940. Imagine the life she must have lived. Imagine the things she's seen.'

I could tell we were not going to get out of dinner with the old folks.

'What's Professor Hall's presenting problem?' I said.

After all those years supporting someone at medical school, you pick up the lingo. A patient's presenting problem is what he comes moaning about to the doctor. The presenting problem is the patient's own diagnosis of what is ailing him or her.

'Professor Hall's presenting problem is that he wants to live forever,' Roman said. 'And maybe he will. His biggest problem is that he is on one of the Z-drugs for his insomnia, thanks to old Dr Cox, my predecessor. And the Z-drugs went out with banana rationing.' Roman patted his flat stomach. 'I need some carbs – that all right with you?'

I slipped my arm around my husband's waist. 'I don't care what we eat,' I said.

We found an old-school Italian restaurant, all white linen tablecloths and ancient male waiters wearing glistening hair products, right on the village green. There were a few tables outside and we took one of them because summer was hanging on, reluctant to leave us. Then the streets began filling up with schoolchildren on their lunch break, packs of them in green blazers with purple piping, their volume turned up to ten, so we went inside the restaurant, relocated to a window table, and ordered the pasta of the day. Roman took my hand, leaned back and sighed.

'What a relief to be out of the city,' he said. 'What a stone-cold joy to escape all that obesity, diabetes, asthma, teenage pregnancy, domestic violence ...'

I laughed. 'That's not the city you've escaped, Doctor – it's poverty.'

He pulled his hand away, looking hurt.

'It's all right for you,' he said, studying the menu. 'You grew up with all of this.'

'All of what?'

'You know – all this middle-class abundance. Real coffee and someone to clean the bathroom. Piano lessons and ski trips. Having just enough money that you never have to think about money.'

That was unfair, I thought, as we ordered. And untrue.

Actually, Roman came from a more economically secure home than me. His parents had both been GPs in the Home Counties while my folks were both head teachers at inner-city state schools. But when Roman was sixteen his mother and father were in a head-on collision with a lorry with a driver who was compiling a playlist at somewhere above the speed limit. Apparently statistically it happens all the time – parents dying in the same car crash together – and obviously it is a desperately tragic thing to happen to anyone. But Roman was almost grown, just at the start of sixth form – and surely it was far worse if it happened when you were a child? After his folks died, he had been shunted around between a couple of half-hearted relatives – an emotionally distant maternal grandmother and an uncle, his father's brother, who was a functioning alcoholic in a cold, collapsing marriage. It wasn't *The Little House on the Prairie*. But after two years of this, he escaped to medical school, always claiming he grew up one step ahead of a care home. That was not strictly true. Losing his parents as he started his A-levels was difficult and desperately sad. But it didn't make him Oliver Twist.

And when he was at medical school, he had me to pay his way.

'Let's not argue,' I said, touching his withdrawn hand. I hated it when we argued.

'We're not arguing,' he said, making no attempt to take my hand.

The pasta arrived. Two steaming plates of penne arrabbiata. We ate in deafening silence, one of those silences that can suddenly settle upon any married couple, watching the village green being annexed by green-blazered brats. A pack of older boys, some of them with wispy beards, buzzed around two laughing, slightly younger girls. For a moment I did not recognise Krissy's daughter, Sailor.

The first time I had seen her she was dressed for soccer and carrying a cello, every inch the dutiful student. Today she was in her school uniform, her grey skirt rolled up to the outer limits of decency, the muscles in her legs well-toned from all that competitive sport. Her friend was pretty enough but it was Sailor who had the older boys barking at the moon. The girls clung together while the older boys preened, and bellowed, and capered for their amusement and attention.

The hormonally excited pack drifted past a lone boy sitting on a bench reading a postcard.

That's odd, I thought.

Who sends postcards any more?

And who reads them?

When the lone boy lifted his head, as if lost in thought at what the postcard contained, I recognised him as

Oscar – the boy I had seen running with his father, Ben, the single dad in the house opposite us.

'Hey, Bones!'

Through the open windows of the Italian restaurant, I could hear one of the older boys taunting Oscar.

'Hey, Bones? How's your mum these days, Bones?'

Oscar did not respond. He slowly stood up and walked away, heading for the village, carefully tucking his postcard into his old-fashioned school satchel. Then one of the older boys picked up something from the ground and threw it at him.

'Catch, Bones!'

A conker. The village green was covered in ripe horse chestnuts, bursting out of their spiky lime green shells, the dark brown nuts so shiny they looked as if they had been freshly polished.

The conker struck Oscar on the back of the head to much hilarity.

Then the older boys were all throwing conkers at him. Pelting him. Oscar flinched with pain. It was the kind of high jinks that can crack skulls.

Sailor and her friend clung to each other, whispering together, as if this had nothing to do with them, as if it wasn't being done to impress them.

'We should do something,' I said to Roman. 'That boy they're bullying is our neighbour's son. That's Ben's son. That's Oscar.'

'Kids are cruel.' Roman shrugged.

The largest of the older boys sprinted to catch up with Oscar and hurled a conker at the back of his head at point-blank range.

It caught him just above the ear, nearly knocking him off his feet and leaving him bent with pain. The other kids roared with laughter.

I looked at Sailor's face. She was not laughing now.

Because Oscar had straightened up, reached into his school bag and pulled out a knife.

It looked like the kind of knife you would use for camping. A long shiny blade with a black rubber grip. The kind of blade that Robert Baden-Powell might mug you with.

Oscar held the blade up to the face of the bearded bully, and lifted his chin, as if inviting him to keep coming.

They scattered.

The pack of older boys, plus Sailor and her friend.

They all saw that stainless-steel blade pointed at the beardy boy's face and they all fled as fast as they could. Oscar slipped the knife back into his satchel and carried on across the village green. His expression had not changed. Roman was staring at him, and I knew he was thinking of all those graveyard shifts as a junior doctor at the A&E in Homerton, patching up what the medical profession call *assault with a sharp object*. Every night Roman had treated stab wounds in that hospital, every night for a year. It had been a long year.

'We should do something,' I said.

'What exactly can we do, Lana?'

'I don't know! Tell his father. Tell the school. Talk to the boy himself. We should get that knife taken away from him before he kills someone.'

Roman shook his head, dismissing it all, as Oscar disappeared into a milling herd of green blazers making their way back to school.

Once upon a time my husband would have got involved, I thought.

Once upon a time, he would have cared.

But this was our new life, and instead he ordered a double espresso and the tiramisu.

7

After our lunch Roman went back to the surgery for his two o'clock and I wandered the village alone, climbing to the top of the hill above the green where it was all modest residential property, mostly former weaver's cottages with thatched roofs and wonky windows, half-timbered façades and spiky chimneys, untouched by the modern world apart from the odd satellite dish. It was pleasant enough, but once you've seen one former weaver's cottage, quite frankly, you've seen them all.

I made my way back down towards the village, through winding lanes full of one-off shops selling what in the city they would market as the *previously loved* – heaps of bric-a-brac, decorated teacups and cutlery and vases and china and antiques that were one or two steps away from being junk, and shops selling vintage designer bags and clothes, and even a small music shop selling second-hand guitars and keyboards. All the discarded booty of bored, affluent people with too much stuff in their lives. The village green was directly below me now and I began to make my way down the steep, winding road.

And that was when I saw them.

The little bastards who had been taking pictures outside our house. The Goth I had first seen lurking in the back garden and the other two – the girl with badly dyed pink hair and the big fair-haired lump with glasses, the Piggy-lookalike, the three of them staring into the dusty window of a second-hand bookshop as if they had no particular place to go this afternoon.

'Hey,' I said. 'Remember me?'

They turned as one to look at me.

I saw panic flare in the eyes of Goth Boy and Piggy, but the girl, a few years younger than her friends, considered me with cool, unflinching eyes.

'You should be ashamed of yourselves,' I said.

'Sorry,' said Piggy quickly.

'You were in my back garden,' I said to Goth Boy. 'That's trespassing. And you scared the daylights out of me.'

He was not old, somewhere in his twenties, but his thinning brown hair made him look prematurely aged, a moon-faced man-boy dressed in his all-black teenage drag. He plastered a hideously ingratiating smile onto his milky face.

'We thought the house was still empty,' he said in a strong accent, far closer to poor urban Wiltshire than well-heeled rural Oxfordshire. 'I didn't mean to freak you out. I'm really sorry.'

Oy'm not. Oy didn't. Oy yum really sorry.

'How dare you,' I said. 'How fucking *dare* you.'

'Sorry,' he said again. 'I didn't know there was anyone in the house or I wouldn't have been in your garden. Honest! Then I just wanted a couple of shots for my files. I know I should have cleared it with you.'

Oy should have cleared it. Moy files.

'We're awfully sorry,' said Piggy, all metropolitan middle class, as if he must be down here in Mummy and Daddy's second home.

And I saw that my friends were right. These overgrown kids were not a threat. They were pathetic losers who got their kicks from somebody else's misery. *Internet sleuths!* What a joke. I felt the rage draining out of me. Piggy and Goth Boy were genuinely contrite. Only the girl with pink hair looked defiant, the hint of a smile playing around her lolling, half-open mouth.

'Your goon threatened us,' she said. 'That bald bloke from the Balkans. He said he would fill us in if he caught us there again.'

She meant Goran, shaven-headed gatekeeper of the Gardens.

'He's not my goon,' I said. 'I don't have a goon.'

Pink Hair turned to her friends for support.

'It's true,' Goth Boy agreed. 'He told me the next time he catches me hanging around the Gardens, he'll take out one of my eyes.'

I laughed at them.

'Am I meant to feel sorry for you? Dial down the self-pity a notch. I don't believe Goran would do that to you. And, anyway, you shouldn't be poking around someone's home.'

'Just doing my job,' Goth Boy said, slightly sheepish. 'Our job.'

I shook my head. 'And what's that?'

'I do a blog. A like podcast.'

'Is it *like* a podcast or is it *actually* a podcast?'

'It's a podcast,' he said, and I thought he was going to call me *miss*. 'Truer Crime.'

It rang a distant bell. And then I remembered. Truer Crime was one of the sites I had seen when I was reading about the Clutter family. I vaguely recalled ghoulish, overwritten purple prose. *The central mystery of every familicide* – why? – *is never solved*. There was something repellent about him, about them, about all of it. This lip-smacking interest in a family's tragedy.

I felt the anger rising again.

'You're all weirdos,' I told him. I jabbed a finger at Piggy and Pink Hair. 'Sad little creeps who are playing games with a real family.' I wasn't sure if I meant the poor dead Clutters, or me and Roman, but it didn't matter.

'Stay away from my home,' I told them. 'Or it's not Goran you'll have to worry about. It's me.'

Goth Boy and Piggy stared at their trainers.

Only Pink Hair maintained eye contact, an infuriating little smile playing around her mouth as I turned away.

'Bill Clutter didn't kill his family,' she said.

I reeled around, furious with her.

'Look – I never knew the man, but he was clearly very sick. He was having a nervous breakdown. He was stuffed full of antidepressants. He kept a loaded shotgun in the house.'

'That's nothing special around here!' Pink Hair laughed. 'None of it. The pills, the gun. That's all *normal*. That's what people *do*.'

'He had been made redundant,' I said, hating myself for debating with the bolshy little bitch. '*Twice*. So you can throw money problems into the mix.'

'Bill Clutter had another job lined up,' she said.

It was really annoying me – it was infuriating me – the way she called him *Bill Clutter*, the appalling assumed intimacy of it.

'Bill was a long-haul pilot in the prime of his career,' Goth Boy said, emboldened by Pink Hair, wanting me to understand. 'A captain. He would always be able to find work in the end, no matter what was happening in the aviation industry and the wider economy. Planes are going to keep flying, aren't they? And he wasn't the kind of man who would hurt his family.' He had found his courage, his pale spotty Goth face growing rosy with indignation. 'Everyone who knew him said he loved his family. April and Josh. Bill Clutter loved them. He worshipped them.'

'And you know this – how? By hanging out in my back garden? By pressing your nose up against my kitchen window?'

'I didn't *know* it was your back garden. I thought the house was still *unoccupied*. I said I was *sorry*, didn't I?'

He was like some sulky teenager now, feeling sorry for himself.

'Watch the documentary about them on Netflix,' Piggy said sheepishly. 'Read the autopsy report. It just doesn't—'

'Stop talking or I'm calling the police about your trespassing,' I told him, and he immediately looked as though he might cry. 'Just. Shut. The. Fuck. Up.' I glared at Pink Hair, the smirking ringleader of this cabal of web sleuths. 'All of you.'

And they shut up.

'And leave me and our house alone. Sticking your nose in, taking your pictures, offering your views online. It's all so *wrong*. Can't you see how wrong it is? Please.'

But I remembered something that Krissy had said, something about Bill Clutter telling stories to the children when they were small, Sailor and Josh, tales of flying east to west, Sydney to London, watching the sun rise twice on the same day over the Indian Ocean, and there was something reassuring about thinking of William Clutter not as a broken wreck who wanted to end everything around him, but as a man who loved life and his family.

It was reassuring.

But it was an illusion.

'William Clutter cracked,' I said. 'He cracked up for a lot of reasons that we will never know and then he reached for that shotgun.'

They looked at each other.

'That's not what happened,' Pink Hair said.

I stared at her.

'Bill Clutter didn't kill himself and he didn't kill his family,' she said. 'You *live* in that house.' She met my stare. 'Don't you want to know who did?'

8

I went home and found the Netflix documentary on the Clutters.

Daddy's Home began with a shot of our house. This house. But it was seen in a different season, early spring, maybe, the world just turning green.

And then it all went to black and white with a clap of thunder and there was what sounded like a voiceover by God himself, if God was an elderly American who you thought you remembered from a couple of Star Wars movies.

'Everyone thought they knew the story of the Clutter family killings,' boomed God. 'The police. The coroner. And the neighbours.'

A shot of a woman – Krissy? – placing her hand over a camera, not wanting to be filmed, as she bundled a teenager – Sailor? – into the back of an expensive car, her snarled Brooklyn-flavoured expletive beeped out. I smiled to myself. Yes, Krissy.

'But the true story of what happened to the Clutters that night has never been told,' said God.

Another clap of thunder.

'*Until now.*'

I watched this hokum for twenty minutes and learned nothing new. The voiceover talked of Bill Clutter's battle with depression following his unemployment, then there were TV news reports of the night of the murders of April and Josh Clutter and Bill Clutter's own suicide, and then a lurid montage of newspaper headlines to squeeze every last drop of sensation out of a family's tragedy. Web sleuths were wheeled out. I half expected to see Goth Boy, Pink Hair and Piggy make an appearance but the web sleuths in *Daddy's Home* were from a bigger league and on a bigger budget. They were older, with American accents, high-end digital Sherlocks who made a living out of this stuff, the booming True Crime industry. But their clothes were the same – a lot of black – and so were their theories. Bill Clutter would never kill his family, they boldly asserted, no matter how depressed he became, no matter how far adrift from his inner self and blah blah blah.

I yawned, went to the fridge and cracked open a bottle of Léoube. When I came back to my laptop sitting on the kitchen island, one of the web sleuths – not a kid, a grown man who was losing his hair but still dressed like a roadie for The Cure – was talking about the autopsy.

'In the UK all coroner inquest records are closed to the public for seventy-five years, although next of kin can apply to have them released,' he said. 'In the case of the Clutters, there was no next of kin. But during the inquest, the pathologist who did the three autopsies revealed there was a cadaveric spasm in their legs – all of their legs – and only in their legs.'

Dramatic music. Pay attention, Lana.

I sipped my rosé and shook my head, wondering about the life of a web sleuth, picturing this bald man-child lost in his laptop in some dreary little room, poring over the gory details of the tragedy of someone he never met, poleaxed by a truth that only he could see.

I was suddenly angry. Angry with myself for watching this trash, angry with this digital dick for not letting the Clutters rest in peace, angry with a world that made light entertainment out of a family's catastrophe.

I reached for the quit button.

'They were all keen to call it a murder-suicide and move on,' said the web sleuth. 'It's *incredible* that nobody thought those deaths were suspicious. It's *obscene*. They looked at the blood on the walls and the shotgun blasts and that was the story they told. It is *still* the story they tell. But the cadaveric spasms in their legs tell a different story.'

I found I had not pressed quit.

And now there was a youngish woman in a white coat on the screen. A moderately hot forensic pathologist with great teeth.

'A cadaveric spasm is a stiffening of the muscles after death – a much stronger stiffening than regular rigor mortis,' she said. 'Rigor mortis takes two to four hours to happen, but a cadaveric spasm happens *instantly*. They call it instant rigor or instant stiffness and it tells you what someone was doing at the moment of death. Specifically – a violent death.'

A slow tracking shot of anonymous naked bodies waiting on the stainless-steel slabs of a mortuary. A solo piano picking out a mournful melody. The tools of the autopsy trade were carefully placed by a cadaver's skull.

And I still hadn't pressed quit.

'You only see cadaveric spasm in a part of the body that has been pushed to the physical limits,' she said. 'So a drowning man's hands might be found in tightly clenched fists as if he was holding on to something that he hoped would save his life at the moment he died.' She clenched her fists, held them up, her eyes bright with excitement, her pearly whites gleaming. 'A cadaveric spasm causes a chemical reaction – a loss of adenosine triphosphate, ATP – that makes the muscles stiffen and contract. So the stiffening in their legs means just one thing – that there was severe muscular activity in the legs prior to death.'

Shots of the family. An airline mug shot of Captain William Clutter, grinning in his uniform, ready to fly you to the moon on gossamer wings.

And April Clutter, winning Miss Kuala Lumpur in 2000, resplendent in high heels and a bathing costume and her fresh-faced youth, twenty years old, grinning self-consciously as she adjusted her slightly wonky tiara.

And young Josh Clutter, a team shot of what looked like a school rugby team, his face muddy and euphoric, proudly holding up a small golden cup.

'All of them had it,' said the web sleuth. 'The wife and son, April and Josh Clutter, who were meant to have died *in their sleep*, and Bill Clutter, who is meant to have got out of bed, loaded his shotgun, killed his family and then put that shotgun in his mouth and taken off the top of his head. In other words, these *were not people who died in bed*.'

And then there was just the same sad piano sonata and those three recurring images.

The pilot. The bathing beauty. The player of the match.

The people who lived in this house before us, I thought. The family who died here.

'April and Josh Clutter were meant to have been shot in their sleep but there was extreme muscular activity in the legs prior to death,' the woman in the white coat repeated, smiling grimly, stunned that the world was too stupid to see the obvious. 'Twenty years of experience in forensic pathology makes me believe that at the moment of death, they were not sleeping but *running*. And perhaps not simply running – *but being chased*.'

God had the final word.

'A tragedy? Yes. But also a mystery.'

Roll credits. Spooky music. Fade to black.

I sat there sipping my rosé.

And then I poured myself another glass, and as the house grew dark around me, I watched *Daddy's Home* again.

Roman kissed me on the top of the head when he came home, and I saw him recoil slightly as he always did when he got a whiff of a bottle of rosé during daylight hours. He picked up the empty bottle of Léoube and took it to the sink. Then he pulled up a chair and sat opposite me at the kitchen island.

'What's wrong?' he said.

'The Clutters,' I said.

He waited.

'At the inquest it was reported that the autopsy found they all had cadaveric spasm in their legs,' I said. Then I hesitated. 'Severe rigor from extreme muscular activity.'

My husband the doctor tried not to look patronising. 'Yes, I know what cadaveric spasm is, Lana.'

He seemed very tired.

'And there's a theory that the whole truth didn't come out at the inquest,' I said. 'That more – much more – should have been made of the cadaveric spasm at the autopsy.'

Roman nodded. 'And there's a theory that the moon landing was shot in a studio in LA. And another theory that the royal family bumped off Princess Diana. And another theory that the CIA blew up the World Trade Center on 9/11.'

'This is not some batshit-crazy conspiracy theory,' I said. 'This is according to the evidence that nobody wanted to hear. The stuff about the cadaveric spasm is all there in the autopsy! The pathologist who did the post-mortem recorded cadaveric spasm but all anyone saw – all anyone was *interested* in – was the 12-bore shotgun and the blood on the beds. They all acted as if that told the whole story. They ignored their own evidence because it didn't fit their narrative. But the extreme rigor in their legs means only one thing, doesn't it?'

'You've been watching that documentary on Netflix, haven't you? *Daddy's Home*. Why do you fill your head with this rubbish, Lana?'

'Have you seen it?'

'No,' he said, and I thought – *liar.*

'Roman—'

'Come with me,' he said.

I followed him down to the basement, a large white room with a low ceiling, accessed by a door at the rear of the house, facing French doors that opened onto the back garden. I had only been in here on the day we moved in, carting down boxes of stuff we did not have the need or the will to open immediately. We still had unopened boxes of clothes, books and God knows what down here.

'Do you know what this room was before we moved in? Have a guess, Lana.'

'Some kind of storage room?'

He shook his head. 'Try again.'

'Roman—'

'Look.'

He was pointing out some marks on the thin grey carpet that covered the floor. Two long, deep parallel lines. And then indicating another part of the room that had tiny ruts in the carpet, but more of them.

'Those long lines look as though they were from a treadmill or an elliptical trainer – some kind of machine for cardio,' he said. 'Those shorter, deeper lines are probably from free weights.' He nodded at an ancient rubber carpet rolled up and covered in cobwebs. 'What do you reckon that's for, Lana? Yoga or Pilates?' There was a metal plate drilled to the wall. 'That held some kind of bag for boxing, wouldn't you say?'

I could feel my face burning.

'This room was a gym,' I said.

He nodded. 'It was *a gym*. And do you know why there was muscular activity in the Clutters' legs that night? *Because they had all been working out*. That's why there was cadaveric spasm. April was still an incredibly striking woman. Josh was an athletic teenage boy who played rugby for his school. And Bill Clutter was a keep-fit fanatic, probably vain about his looks. The Clutters were a very sporty family, Lana. They all stayed in shape. It's not a mystery. There was muscular activity in their legs on the night they died because they had been down here in their gym. They had been *exercising*.'

I said nothing. I felt foolish.

'Do you know what I think happened that night?' Roman said. 'Exactly what all those experts said had happened. The experts – that's who I believe, Lana. Not a bunch of self-promoting narcissists looking for a book deal or a slot on breakfast TV. I believe the paramedics and the doctor and the coroner and the police and the pathologist.'

'Sorry.'

'I'm sorry too. Look, I don't want you to get upset. Come here.'

He gave me a hug and I hugged him back and we both laughed, a strange mix of embarrassment and relief, but as we came apart Roman glanced at me in a way that he had never looked at me before.

As if I might be crazy.

9

Wednesday, 2 September

Willow and I had nearly polished off a bottle of Léoube when I noticed her tattoo. She had her elbows on the kitchen island, her long brown arms bare as she cradled a glass of the pale rosé, and I saw what looked like the letter *L* branded in the crook of her right arm.

'So who was *L*?' I said. 'A boy you knew in school? Some fashion photographer in Paris?'

She smiled and pressed a chewed fingernail against her skin.

'Girl, you're looking at it upside down,' she said, swivelling on her seat to face me. 'It's the number *7*, see?' Her perfect face became serious. 'Seven is a significant number in every major religion. God rested on the seventh day, didn't He? The Koran speaks of seven heavens. It's a number with mythic powers – the seventh son of the seventh son.' She turned her back towards me and lifted the gorgeously tangled mass of black curls. 'I've got lots of numbers tattooed. I have a *911* on the back of my neck. See?'

'I see it. And what does *911* stand for?'

'Call the cops!' She turned, hiking up her right leg. She was wearing a long, floaty summer skirt with snow-white trainers, and just under the bone of her left ankle there was a *0*. 'The number zero is the mother of existence. Everything comes from this void. And on my back, just above my butt ...'

She pulled down the waistband of her floaty skirt and just above the crack in her ridiculously perfect ass, there was the number *8*.

'I had a friend – sweet girl from Shanghai – what was her name? I'll remember it in a minute – who told me that the number *8* was the luckiest number of all in Chinese culture because *8* in Mandarin – *bā* – sounds the same as "to prosper".' She pulled up her skirt and lifted her drink in salute. 'I would show you the rest, but I don't want Vince to slip with his buzzsaw,' she said with her lopsided grin.

I raised my glass to her. Willow was the most beautiful girl I had ever seen, and possibly the craziest.

'I had them done in Paris, all of my tattoos.'

'And they're all numbers?'

She nodded. 'But they all mean something. Even if it's just "be lucky" or "call the cops".'

I may have raised a wry eyebrow.

'I just liked the feeling of being tattooed,' she laughed. 'It's great! That kind of vibrating scratch, like an animal gently cutting into your skin? Can you cut flesh gently? Have you got any?'

I shook my head. I had once contemplated getting one in the name of modest self-expression, but Roman, still at medical school, had given me his doom-laden speech about contaminated tattoo needles and bloodborne diseases and so I went to the hairdresser instead.

'But although I really liked being tattooed, I could never really settle on anything that I wanted to be there forever,' Willow said. 'Dolphins? Butterflies? Who gives a shit, right? I mean, I *like* dolphins but I wouldn't want to look at the same dolphin for a lifetime. I knew a girl who had a Ferrari stallion on her butt and everyone said – why have you got a tattoo of a donkey on your arse?'

She drained her glass and held it out to me.

Willow was a woman who was used to being served.

I topped her up and then myself and that was the bottle done. That had gone fast.

'You have to remember – I was pretty messed up in Paris,' she said. 'Modelling is *not* a healthy environment for a growing girl. Even when you are at your maximum beauty – when, say, you're nineteen years old – there is always some cruel little stylist or bitchy photographer who tells you that you are too fat – *'Babes, tone up! You need to tone up!'* – tone up means lose weight – or that nobody wants a mixed-race girl this season, or that the girls have got to be a lot darker than you are or a little bit lighter than you are because that's what bloody *Vogue* wants right now.'

We sipped our drinks. Vince noisily slashed through the undergrowth out in the back garden. Willow rubbed at the number *7* in the crook of her elbow, as if she might erase it.

'Guy hates my tats,' she said. 'When we met, I thought the old body art might even be a deal-breaker. I remember how shocked he was when he first saw that number *8* on my butt. For a second there, I thought he was going to lose his erection.'

'But how could tattoos stop him loving you?'

'Well, Guy was quite fussy when we met,' she said. 'Very high standards in his women. He was a hardcore modeliser.'

'Guy only went out with models?'

She nodded. 'The money had just come in from selling out his share of Mata-chan, the virtual influencer, to his clever friends. So Guy was working his way through the catwalks of Europe – Milan, London, Paris, repeat. Then he met me at *semaine de la mode de Paris* – Paris fashion week – and we just fit.' She flashed me her wicked smile. 'Youth and beauty meets wealth and cocaine – that old chestnut. And here we all are – happy ever after in England's Eden.'

'I'm sure it was more romantic than that,' I said. 'I bet he was mad about you.'

'A dick pic was Guy's idea of a romantic gesture,' she said.

To me, Willow was like a mixed-race Holly Golightly, and for all her wild talk about drugs and rich men and being a messed-up teenage model far from home, there was a grace about her, and a vulnerability, and a kindness, and a certain softness, and a self-deprecating humour. She was the only person in the world who was not remotely impressed by the way she looked.

The buzzsaw had stopped.

Vince staggered into the kitchen carrying the stone garden Buddha that had sat out there for so long, contemplating the transient nature of all things and the back of the house, its hands clasped together in prayer, its eyes closed in meditation.

'Want me to chuck this on the skip?' he said.

There was a big yellow skip parked on our drive, already overflowing with garden waste.

'April Clutter loved her Japanese Zen Buddhist artefacts,' Willow said.

I told Vince to leave it in the hall.

For some reason, the idea of throwing it on the skip filled me with a dread that I could not name.

It was late afternoon now and across the street Ben and Oscar came out of their house, father and son apparently ready for their evening run. They stood on their driveway, stretching and staring at the skip outside my house, and I remembered the bullied boy on the village green with the knife in his hand.

They crossed the road, hailing Goran, and came up my drive. I went to the door and Ben Cave introduced himself.

'We saw you were having some work done,' he said, his accent local but softened by a few years at university and a working life around the middle class. 'And wondered if you needed some extra help?' His boy stood silently behind him. 'This is Oscar. He doesn't want paying. He's happy to help a neighbour.'

I saw now what was strange about Ben Cave's face. There was a scar that ran all the way from his hairline down one side of his face to just under his chin. His face looked as though someone had tried to unzip it. And yet he seemed like a gentle man, even shy – when we made eye contact, his gaze seemed to flinch. I wondered what he would think if he knew his son was waving a knife around in public. But once again I felt it – the generosity of our new neighbours.

'That's really kind of you,' I said. 'I imagine Vince could use some help in the garden.' I stared at the boy lurking behind his father. 'If it's no trouble for Oscar.'

The boy shrugged. A reluctant affirmative.

Ben's damaged face lit up with parental pride. He told his son he would be back to cook dinner and took off on his run. Oscar came inside, avoiding all eye contact. He was perhaps older than I first thought, edging seventeen, but small for his age and agonisingly shy.

'Hello, handsome,' Willow hailed him. 'When are we running off together?'

Oscar blushed hotly in reply. 'I'll go and see Vince,' he said.

I indicated the stone Buddha sitting at the foot of the stairs. 'This needs taking upstairs. Could you give me a hand first?'

Oscar and I lugged the statue up to my studio and set it down under the Dorothea Lange photograph of the migrant woman. He stared at it with interest.

'Do you like that photograph?' I asked him.

'I don't know.' He thought about it. 'Is it your mum?'

I laughed. 'No, it's not my mum! She's a woman in a migrant camp in California in 1936.'

'What – like a refugee?'

I nodded. 'Exactly. But a refugee in her own country.'

Oscar and I considered the photograph together.

'Nobody knows her name, but she was looking for a better home.'

'She looks really worried.'

'Doesn't she? There were millions of refugees like her. But we can't really imagine millions of people, can we? We can't get our heads around millions. But that one woman's face – we can understand what *she* was going through. And I guess that makes it easier to understand the millions like her.'

Oscar shrugged and looked away towards the back garden.

Who was this crazy old lady his dad had parked him with?

'Everything OK?' I said.

'With the human race?' he said.

'With you.'

He looked haughty. 'Why wouldn't it be?'

'I saw you on the village green, Oscar.'

He scrutinised the carpet.

'There's an Italian restaurant facing it and I was having lunch in there with my husband and I saw those boys throwing conkers at you.'

'It didn't even hurt, if that's what they think.'

'And I saw you pull that knife.'

'I should go help Vince.'

'Does your father know you carry a knife?'

He said nothing.

'What happens if the other boy pulls out a knife? What then? Look, just because someone's bullying you, you can't threaten them with a knife.'

He was suddenly upset.

'They weren't bullying me because I didn't let them, OK?' He hesitated. 'They were talking about *my mum*. They always talk about *my mum*. Because she's the only mum who is never around. Even the kids whose parents are divorced have their mums around. So I showed them my knife. As a warning, OK? And they soon shut their cakeholes.'

'I get all that. But what would have happened if he had kept coming?'

'I don't know. He didn't, did he?'

'And what if he had pulled out his own knife?'

'I don't know! I don't know! Are you going to rat me out?'

'I'm not going to rat you out. But you see that skip outside? You should throw your knife on that skip, Oscar. Or drop it down a drain. Because it's not going to get you out of trouble. It's only going to get you into more trouble than you can ever imagine.'

'I thought you wanted me to help Vince.'

'My husband is a doctor.'

'I know. Everybody knows. Taking over from old Dr Cox.'

'And Roman – my husband – he treated a lot of stab wounds at his old job. And those young people he saw with stab wounds, they were just boys like you.'

I did not say the other thing, the thing that Roman often said after the end of another long shift in A&E. I did not say that every boy he ever saw didn't carry the knife because he was tough, but because he was weak.

'What would your mum think about you carrying a knife?'

'I don't live with my mum any more.'

'I know you don't. But I bet she wouldn't like it, would she?'

'Probably not.'

'Is your mum nearby?'

'She's in the city.' He seemed to be remembering his lines. 'It didn't work out between her and my dad. But these things happen. So it's better all round.'

They were the reassuring clichés that an adult parrots about a divorce, empty slogans to be memorised by bewildered children, and they broke my heart.

'Do you see her often?'

'Not at the minute because she's so busy.' His face brightened. 'But she sends me postcards.'

'I love postcards!' I said. 'Nobody sends postcards any more, do they?'

'My mum does,' he said proudly. The thought of his mother's postcards had calmed him down. 'I should go help Vince.'

'Yes, you go and help Vince now.'

He happily turned away.

'And Oscar?'

He paused at the top of the stairs.

'Throw your knife away.'

I joined Willow at the kitchen island.

Out in the back garden I could hear Vince welcoming Oscar – they sounded like old friends – and giving him instructions.

'Oscar's a sweetheart,' Willow said. 'He blushes when he looks at me.'

'I saw him pull a knife.'

Willow laughed with disbelief. 'What?'

'Some bigger kids were picking on him in the village, showing off for a couple of girls, including Krissy's daughter. Apparently, they were teasing him about his mother. And he pulled out a blade.'

'Oh, well,' Willow said brightly. 'Boys will be boys!'

'What really happened with his mum?'

She sighed. 'Juno just did a runner. Guy said he could always tell that one was a bolter. Ben is a great father, but I think it's like being in the army for that boy over there. Ben is a bit of an old-school disciplinarian. Ex-cop, ex-military. Runs his own security company. Goran works for him.'

'Our security guard is employed by Ben?'

She nodded.

'All the paramilitary discipline caused a clash with the wife. I think Juno just wanted a bit more of a liberal regime. A few less press-ups and a bit more getting in touch with your feelings. All of that malarkey. And then the inevitable happened. She met someone else, and she bailed.'

'This is the Brazilian Yoga teacher?'

'It could have been anyone, between you and me. Juno was looking for a way out of that marriage. She had a troubled life. A difficult life. Apparently, she adored her younger brother, but they got separated when they both went into care. Their mother sounds like a nightmare. Some kind of addict. Heroin. Drink. Anything that was going, Juno told me. And doing whatever it took to pay for it. The way Juno told it, she got unwanted attention all her life. From foster fathers. From the children of her foster homes. When she was in care. Horrible stuff. And then she met Ben. And Ben told her she was pretty. And she had never heard that before, so she married the guy. Can you imagine?'

Willow laughed, the laugh of someone who had been told she was drop-dead gorgeous for as long as she could remember.

'Juno was a great mum,' she said. 'She doted on young Oscar. She loved the boy. But she had that wild side in her. From her mother, I guess. Or maybe from the way she grew up. And that always comes out in the end. You can't stop it, that wildness. It has to come out, no matter the damage that it does.'

An Aston Martin roared up the driveway next door.

Willow rose from the kitchen island, loose-limbed and feeling good from our shared bottle of rosé, ready to greet her husband.

10

Thursday, 3 September

I met Sandy at the station.

He came out of the first-class carriage with a few of the early commuters already heading home in the afternoon, the big shots who could leave the office without explanation when they wanted. Sandy looked nothing like them – he was older, better dressed and more at ease with himself and the world as he ambled slowly down the platform, immaculate in his blazer and chinos and white shirt with a dark blue tie, a representative of that last generation who all believed in *looking smart*, suddenly older than I remembered – he was in his late seventies now – a big man who was relaxed in his body, his sun-baked, serious, lived-in face breaking into a smile when he saw me waving, calling his name and jumping up and down with pure joy to see him again.

'Lana!'

I took his arm and led him out of the station and for a moment he stood there, taking it all in.

I don't know what I was expecting or hoping for – possibly that he would take one look at my new country home and tell me that it was not for me, that I should be back in the city, taking photographs, hanging out in his studio in Primrose Hill and living the life I was meant to be living. But he just patted my arm and told me in his understated, unsentimental way that it was good to see me again. We stood outside the station, halfway up the hill above the village proper, and under a cloudless blue sky it was all spread out before us.

The river dappled with burnished gold in the dying summer sunlight, a scattering of dog walkers and joggers on the village green, and the first nip of autumn in the air. The fading light turned the stone of the picturesque jumble of buildings to a pale lemon colour. Beyond the village the green fields gently rose and rolled on forever.

'Beautiful,' Sandy said.

My plan was to show him around the village and then walk back to the Gardens. But he moved more slowly than I remembered, and he walked with greater care now, as if all the years that had piled up needed to be shown due respect, and so we went to the Teahouse on the Tracks and watched the river.

'Really beautiful,' he said.

'But Sandy – there's nothing to photograph!' I said, laughing, although I wasn't joking. 'The alms houses and the thatched cottages and the quaint villages. The sheep safely grazing in the meadows. It's all been done to death.'

'There's *always* something to photograph,' he said, and I remembered how much I loved that voice, so calm and steady and wise, still full of the working-class Scotland he had left a lifetime ago.

We drank our tea and talked shop. The decline of the print industry, the budget cuts in the surviving newspapers and magazines, and the happy fact that he was still on a retainer at his Sunday paper after all these years.

It was so good to see him. Sandy was more than my friend. I learned my trade by his side, in that studio in Primrose Hill. He was my first boss, and my mentor, and my inspiration. When I was doing all the depressing hack work I took on to pay the rent as Roman slogged his way through medical school, when I was doing catalogue shoots of girls not quite thin enough or pretty enough or young enough for the catwalks, I thought of Sandy in Vietnam, Bangladesh and Belfast – or rather, I thought of the images he had captured in those places.

Sandy McKay was usually described – even now – as a 'war correspondent' but in truth he had migrated to studio-based portrait work for his posh Sunday paper decades ago. The photographs that he was best known for were all taken more than half a lifetime ago. How long ago was his shot of the sleeping bar girl in Saigon? The crying child in Bangladesh? The terrified housewife in Belfast? The drug addicts staring blankly at his camera in *The Crack Shack* – the one I had on the wall of my studio – was more recent, but even that was over ten years ago.

But they were all images that would be remembered forever, and for me they would always show where the bar was set. Sandy and I had a genuine friendship but there's no denying it was the kind of friendship that was built on unstated hero worship.

We finished our tea and took a taxi back to the Gardens, arriving just as Willow was returning from her tennis lesson.

She looked radiant, as always, impossibly leggy in her short white tennis skirt and sleeveless Lacoste top. I introduced them and they were perfect together – Willow the instinctive flirt and Sandy acting with the restrained courtesy of the lifelong ladies' man. He did not kiss her hand, but it was touch and go there for a moment.

'You want something to photograph?' Sandy said, when we were inside the house. 'I'd start with her.'

I gave him the grand tour.

The garden was still a jungle out there despite Vince filling a few skips with chopped-down undergrowth and looking even more desolate because he had drained the pool and it was now home to a couple of scrawny foxes, who groomed themselves totally oblivious to Sandy and me as we watched them from the French doors.

I took him upstairs and showed him my little alcove at the back of the house where I went to think and drink, and I showed him my studio and he smiled at my framed *Migrant Mother*, and winced with embarrassed pride when he saw one of his own works framed on the wall.

'My most recent hit,' he said, staring at *The Crack Shack*.

'There's more,' I said. 'I wish I had room for them all.'

I had a leather-bound portfolio with prints of some of his best-known work. I handed it to him and he was silent, slowly leafing through them.

I hesitated.

'Something happened here, Sandy,' I said. 'In this house, I mean.'

I realised this was why I wanted to see him, and that I was desperate to tell him everything.

As he stood there with the portfolio of his old photographs in his hands, looking at an image of the bar girl in Saigon, perhaps not seeing her, he listened while I told him about the Clutters.

All of it. What had happened. The ghouls that were obsessed with it. The web sleuths who hung around my back garden and filmed the house. The *Daddy's Home* documentary on Netflix. And the lunatic idea that there had been some kind of cover-up.

When I had finished, he turned the page, saying nothing. What could he say? What did I expect him to say?

Then the foxes started howling at the bottom of the empty swimming pool, and his face broke into a wry smile.

'The peace of the countryside,' Sandy said.

I wanted him to relax while I was preparing dinner but, even moving at a slower pace these days, Sandy was still unable to just do nothing. He announced he was going for a walk, and I had an irrational stab of fear for him, and then the immediate awareness of the absurdity of fretting about a man who had caught malaria in Vietnam and been shot at on the Falls Road in Belfast and hung out with morgue-eyed junkies in London. He was only going for a pre-dinner stroll in the Oxfordshire countryside.

I watched him through the kitchen window as he stepped out onto the street, then paused, taking it all in. The four honey-coloured houses, Sally's gingerbread cottage wreathed in its riot of pink oleander, the imposing manor house at the far end of the Gardens. He stood there for a long moment, looking around, and I saw this place through Sandy's eyes, and I felt the timeless peace of this place, and I suddenly knew that it was much like this one hundred years ago and it would be much like this one hundred years from today.

My friend Sandy was right.

It was beautiful.

An hour later I heard voices on the street, and I looked out to see Sandy talking to Professor Hall, who was making his way back to the big house with Ben Cave, who I now realised acted as the old man's personal trainer.

A lot of hours in the Gardens were devoted to health and fitness. Willow's tennis, Sailor's school sports, Professor Hall's dedication to staying hale and hearty and living forever.

I opened the door as Sandy came up the drive, and Professor Hall and Ben gave me a friendly wave as they began slowly jogging towards the big house.

'You met our neighbours,' I said.

'I *know* your neighbour. The older gentleman. At least, I met him once before. He reminded me that I took his photograph for the *Sunday Times* magazine. Long time ago, back in the Harry Evans days. Professor Alan Hall. He was some kind of celebrity historian, wasn't he?'

'Roman says he was semi-famous back in the day. He did some TV lecture series. Wore bow ties on BBC2.'

'I shot him when he had a book out.'

'How was he?'

'Interesting face. A good subject. Co-operative, patient, did what I asked. Low maintenance. All you want, really. There was some kind of controversy after he appeared in the magazine though – I can't remember what it was about. Something to do with his book. It caused a bit of a stink, as I recall. He gave me a copy but I never read it. Have to dig it out, if I didn't give it to Oxfam. People seemed to think he was a deeply unpleasant man.'

I was shocked. 'Really? Professor Hall?'

'He seemed perfectly fine to me. Still does.'

'He's taken quite a shine to Roman.'

'Well,' Sandy said drily. 'Everyone loves Roman.'

Sandy and Roman had never been friends.

Roman had always seen Sandy – ludicrously – as some kind of rival. Sandy had – far more reasonably – seen Roman as a distraction from my life's work. When Roman came home just after six, the pair of them attempted to greet each other like old friends but couldn't quite manage it. They were two men who had known each other for a long time but had never been close. The only connection they had ever had was me.

'I've been meeting your neighbours,' Sandy said.

'Sandy fancies Willow,' I said, fishing a bottle of champagne out of the fridge and three flutes from the freezer. 'It's a good job he's not eighteen months younger.'

'And the other neighbours,' Sandy smiled. 'The chap with the impressive scar – Ben?'

'Ben's a great father,' Roman said, a little offended, as if Ben's scar was the least interesting thing about him. 'He's a single dad.'

'And Professor Hall.'

'Professor Hall is a great man,' Roman said.

Sandy laughed with surprise, and a cloud passed across my husband's face as he bolted down his drink.

And the evening went downhill from there.

I attempted to remain wreathed in smiles, even as I smelled something beginning to burn in the kitchen, and the mood was becoming strained between my friend and my husband.

I watched Roman choosing a second bottle.

I always find drinking difficult with three people. Two can share a bottle. But three can't share one bottle and three should never share two bottles. When three share one bottle a third isn't enough to get a buzz on. But two thirds of two bottles is always too much. Someone always gets rat-faced.

Tonight it was going to be Roman.

Sandy had once had a wife called Angie.

Angie McKay was a former Lead Principal at English National Ballet, and then later a dance teacher, and even when I first met her in her late middle years, she looked like one of those Swinging London beauties, effortlessly adorable with shoulder-length hair and an uneven gap between her front teeth, one of them chipped and never repaired. You could imagine Angie in an open-top sports car cruising down the King's Road with some pretty boy cockney from RADA.

They had met after Sandy came off the road but their time together was painfully brief.

Angie was already sick when I first went to work in Sandy's studio and, after she died, I always felt that I was filling some kind of gap, not for the wife Sandy lost to breast cancer, but for the children they never had.

But Roman always acted as if I was filling the gap left by Angie.

By the time I joined them in the living room, Roman was unburdening himself. There was a stillness about Sandy, and a patience, and it was a demeanour that allowed him to work at his trade but it also made people think they could open up to him.

'It's different for Lana out here,' Roman was saying. 'Because her family never fell apart when she was a child. And that makes all the difference, Sandy, it really does.'

Sandy murmured non-committedly.

In the back garden the foxes began to scream. Roman flinched, shook his head, gathered his thoughts, already drunker than he should be.

'As you know, I was one step from care and when you are one step from care, home means more because you always expect someone to come along and take it away.'

This was all a bit rich. Roman loved playing his Little Orphan Annie routine but the truth was that money had never really been a problem for him. It was the insurance payment from his parents that got us a toehold on the property ladder, and it was my work as a jobbing photographer that got him through med school.

'I was telling Sandy you're still settling in,' he said to me.

'It's a bit of a culture shock,' I smiled. Awkward silence. 'I'm allowed to find it a bit of a culture shock, aren't I?'

Roman placed a possessive hand on my hip. 'Of course. But it's glorious, right, Sandy?' Roman smiled at me, dialling up his best bedside manner. 'I know that we're going to be happy here.' A beat. 'If we just give it a chance.'

Roman and I looked at each other and shared one of those unspoken exchanges that are unique to married couples.

Why can't you just embrace this place?

Because people died here. Because it makes my skin crawl.

I tried to laugh it off. 'But – please – allow that there is something just a *little* weird about this street, Roman. And not just because of the Clutters.'

His fabulous face scowled. 'Oh, come on, Lana!'

I began laying the table. The bloody chicken I had in the oven was overdone on the outside but still uncooked on the inside. I was never exactly Nigella Lawson but I didn't want to rely on Deliveroo for dinner with Sandy as our special guest.

'Can I help?' Sandy said, standing up, anxious to be doing something, anything.

I shook my head, gave him a tense smile.

'Can't you see how odd it is?' I went on, turning to Roman. 'It might be the twenty-first century in the rest of the world but it's 1955 around here. The men are all these big-earning breadwinners and the women have all given something up that they were rather good at.' I placed water glasses and our best cutlery on the table. 'And the children are kept in line with all these constant activities. Exercise, music, and school bags they can hardly carry.'

'I think they call it getting an education,' Roman said.

'But the women have grown passive out here. Even Krissy – this is our American neighbour, Sandy – she was the big rising star at Lehman Brothers, apparently, and now she's this stay-at-home helicopter mother, whipping her daughter all the way to Oxbridge!'

'But what's wrong with wanting your child to go to a great university?' Roman said. 'I'd love it.'

We both looked at Sandy, as if he was some king of the court of appeal.

He just sat there like a great big Glaswegian Buddha, nursing his drink. He had hardly touched it.

Roman laughed, nearly said something, and thought better of it. Then finally couldn't stop himself.

'Can't you be happy, Lana?' he smiled.

'I'm trying,' I said, smiling back at him.

Roman laughed, drained his drink. 'My wife wants suffering, Sandy!' He looked at me, his smile slipping. 'Misery. The human condition in all its bleak despair. So she can take a picture of it and show the world how much she cares.'

'That's really fucking unfair,' I said, slamming down the cutlery as tears sprang to my eyes.

'Lana wants to show the world what a rotten place it is,' Roman said. 'As if the world doesn't know already!' He wagged a mocking finger at our guest. 'I blame you, Sandy.'

I could smell roast chicken immolating in the kitchen. I had tried so hard tonight and it was all a waste of time.

'You were far more respectful to my work in the past, Roman,' I said, heading off to the charred chicken. 'When it was paying your way through med school.'

The foxes began to shriek louder from the swimming pool and the three of us turned towards the back garden to listen.

'They're mating,' I said.

'Or murdering each other,' Roman said, draining his glass.

Sandy did not stay long after dinner.

I had anticipated that he would spend the night in our guest room and that after Roman had gone to work in the morning we would have a chance to really talk over a long lazy brunch at the Teahouse on the Tracks before he went back to town.

But as Roman and I simmered in strained silence over my burned Ocado-bought roast chicken followed by tiramisu, Sandy announced – as casually as he could manage, and that was really convincingly casual – that he would be heading back on the last train to London.

I drove him to the station.

'I'm sorry,' I said. 'That was horrible.'

'Nothing to be sorry about. It was lovely to see you. And Roman, too.'

Sandy hated conflict. That was the irony of his life. He had recorded conflict so meticulously, so brilliantly, and yet he couldn't stand to be around harsh words between a half-cut husband and a homesick wife.

The lights of his train were in the distance and I suddenly wanted to weep, feeling as if all I had loved had gone forever, feeling trapped between my old life and my new life, belonging to neither.

'What am I going to do, Sandy?'

He lightly patted my back. 'Enjoy it,' he said. 'I don't even know what that means. But be kind to each other. Both of you. Don't give up work. Have a baby. Enjoy this place, Lana. The city will still be there when you and Roman have had enough.' He laughed shortly. 'Although the magazines and the newspapers we worked for might not be.'

'You're a wise old coot, aren't you?'

'One more thing,' Sandy said as his train pulled into the station.

I thought he was going to give me a few words of wisdom about marriage, about how every relationship is a series of compromises, about how he and Angie made it work, how Roman and I were still the golden couple, envied by the world.

But no.

'I grew up in the sticks,' he said.

'Glasgow,' I said.

He shook his head. 'That's what the bio says but it was more like Paisley. And it wasn't even really Paisley. It was the countryside.'

The train stopped, sighed, waited for its one passenger to board.

'Foxes mate once a year,' Sandy said. 'They mate in January and their cubs are born in March. So those foxes in your swimming pool – I don't think they're fighting and I know they're not mating.'

'Then what are they doing?'

'They're digging, Lana.'

11

Friday, 4 September

I had never seen Sailor laugh.

I had seen her looking like a blank-faced, dutiful student as Krissy ferried her through her busy schedule, from school to music lesson to soccer practice and back again, and I had seen her looking like a smirking little minx, dangerously mature beyond her years, long legs flashing as older boys trailed her and her friend across the village green. But I had never seen Sailor looking truly happy, laughing out loud, until I watched her talking with the charming young man at the entrance to the Gardens. He was wearing an old-fashioned Newsboy cap, one of those baggy, eight-panel flat caps that was the colour of the Old Holborn tobacco my grandfather had favoured for his cherished hand-rolled cigarettes, and it gave this lad a cocky military air, like a larky corporal who was heading for the glasshouse.

Sailor's face was lit up with joy. She liked him a lot, and she was of the tender age when liking someone a lot is so hard to hide. It was good to see her looking so happy. She had the longest day of anyone in the Gardens, often setting off with Krissy before breakfast for sport or music, and in the evening, long after I had cracked open a bottle of Léoube, the sound of her practising would drift across on the night air. Sailor playing cello, Sailor singing, Sailor dropping the ball in the basketball hoop bolted to the side of their garage, over and over again. Sticking at it all for hours.

Krissy usually provided a taxi service for her daughter's crowded schedule but today Sailor must have walked home from school, because she was still in her green blazer and toting her paramilitary load – a backpack stuffed with a small library, a violin case – how many instruments did she play? – and a sports bag.

She licked an ice cream cone as the young man watched her with open admiration. He liked her too.

He must have been in his late teens – not tall, nowhere near it, but handsome in a curiously old-time, matinee-idol kind of way, with jet-black wavy hair and a wide, winning smile. Someone must have once told him that he looked a bit like Tom Cruise, and he had never forgotten it. I looked up at the Cave house and I saw Oscar watching them with a bereft expression. Goran was glowering from his van. The men and the boys all liked Sailor.

Krissy came out of their house and stood on the doorstep with her arms folded across her chest, watching her daughter.

Nothing happened. The young man kept up his smooth, smiley chat, and Sailor was his willing audience, lazily licking her Magnum, her eyes never leaving him. Then Krissy barked her daughter's name once and Sailor turned reluctantly away, her fingertips briefly touching the arm of the black-haired boy, before dragging her heavy burden home.

Krissy stood guard until Sailor had disappeared inside, glaring at the young man. When Sailor was gone, he approached her tentatively, still beaming the same high-wattage smile that had bewitched her daughter. It wasn't a social call. He was offering some kind of service, or trying to sell something, and Krissy didn't even bother to say no as she turned away with a contemptuous shake of her head, and closed her front door. And then there were other men, older than Sailor's friend, appearing at the entrance of the Gardens, exchanging terse words with Goran, as if explaining that they had every right to be here.

Roman was at my side, slipping an arm around my waist and pressing his mouth against the side of my face. I leaned my head against him, pushed my body closer.

We had made up. We always made up. That was one of the best things about us as a couple – our genius for making up.

One of us would reach out – Roman had said, 'I'm sorry,' as soon as I got back from taking Sandy to the station – and the other one would respond. And I did. That was our deal and it was where a lot of married couples go wrong. When someone tries to make up, you have to meet them halfway, you can't decide they need to be punished a while longer.

Roman and I had made up last night. And then in the half-light of dawn, lazy and slow and sweet, we had made up again. We were getting good at making up.

'Who are those men?' I said.

'I've seen them in the village,' Roman said. 'The Carter family. There are two houses on the council estate for socially disruptive families. Families that have been kicked out of everywhere else. The Carters have got both of them.'

Somewhere out there beyond the high-achieving families and the beautiful honey-stone houses, on the outskirts of our picture-book village, there was a council estate that could have been anywhere in the country. And on the council estate, there were the Carters.

'Goran will see them off,' Roman said. 'You should come and see the garden.'

We went out to the back. The last of the skips had been taken away that morning.

Where there had once been untamed overgrown jungle there was now a wide-open space, a surprisingly large expanse of scrubby grass. A hose was pouring water into the swimming pool and it was almost full.

'Good job, Vince,' Roman said.

Vince seemed immune to flattery. He scooped stray leaves from the surface of the swimming pool and did not react. But I saw now why he was valued in the Gardens. All Vince needed was a cup of builder's tea every few hours and to be left alone to get on with the job. He never even requested to use the bathroom, so either he had a bladder of cast iron or he was too proud to ask.

Vince was hardly the most socially outgoing of handymen, but it was true – with the help of Oscar, he had reclaimed our garden from the wild. Roman and I walked to the edge of the pool. At the deep end, the water level was lower than where it should have been. At the shallow end, the bottom was clearly showing, the tiles cracked and scarred, the grouting blackened with neglect.

'It's not filling up as fast as it should,' Vince said. 'There's probably a leak somewhere. If it keeps leaking then you're going to have to drain it, have a look at the bottom.' He slipped into an absent-minded reverie, his narrow, sunburned face lost in thought. 'Should have been done years ago,' he said, talking to himself as much as us. 'Takes a lot of maintenance, a pool does.'

He dropped the leaves on what had once been a flower bed and was now a mound of churned soil. And I imagined the Clutters in this pool, before their world fell apart.

We walked Vince to his van as he waved off Roman's offer of payment with a brusque, 'Settle up later.'

By now there were five men roaming around the Gardens, clearly touting for work. One of them, an enormously fat man in a tracksuit, was talking to Sally Berry on her doorstep, the man gesturing excitedly at her driveway while Sally regarded him with her benign hippy courtesy. They were knocking on other doors. Ben Cave appeared across the street, frowning with irritation. Goran trailed the men, remonstrating, but they ignored him with a kind of casual derision.

One man, the oldest, in his sixties, suddenly turned on Goran. 'You're not a real copper,' he barked. 'So back up.'

Vince regarded them without interest as he got into his van. The young matinee idol who had been chatting up Sailor smiled at me from the end of our driveway.

'Special offer this week,' he called. 'Tarmac your driveway. Fifteen per cent off. One week only.'

Roman smiled politely. In my mind I saw them working on our driveways, a gang of Carters, sweaty and shirtless over the boiling black tarmac. Was it all a con? Would they take the money and run? Would they have done a good job? I had no idea. But I could see they were not going to get any work on this street.

My neighbours, I sensed, did not like strangers appearing in the Gardens.

Across the street I could see Ben Cave raising his voice at the Carters' hard sell, cutting one of them off, while Goran watched anxiously, getting out of his van again.

Roman and I had been invited for drinks at the manor house. We started down the Gardens with Sailor's friend tagging along just behind us, smiling hopefully as he kept up his sales pitch. But we were no longer listening to him, because the big house held your attention, and you could not look away.

There was an otherworldliness about the manor house, like somewhere seen in a dream, and as we walked closer I saw it was not simply older and grander than its pretty, honey-coloured neighbours. The big house had a beauty that had been mellowed by centuries, marinated in time, here long before anyone had even thought about building the other homes. We passed through its iron gates and under the tall trees that lined the driveway, breathing in the sweet scent of the deep green Boston ivy that covered its walls.

Sailor's young man was still jabbering mindlessly by our side, almost forgotten, and he only hung back as we climbed the stone steps that led up to the front door.

Professor Hall appeared, smiling at Roman and me, and then at the young man hovering at the foot of the steps, and for a moment it was as if the three of us were all expected and welcome guests at the big house.

'Very special offer this week, sir,' the young man blurted, remembering his lines, taking his cap off in an act of deference that was almost comical. 'Tarmac your driveway. Fifteen per cent off. One week only.'

Professor Hall nodded, smiling, as if he was seriously considering the proposition.

'From your accent, I detect that you are a local man.'

The boy seemed derailed by the elderly academic. 'We're on the Rosa Parks estate, sir.' He gestured back at the other men. 'My uncles and my dad and my cousins and all of us.' He paused. 'Council moved us in two years back.'

'Real local men,' said Professor Hall approvingly. 'Worthy of the name. Excellent!'

The young man's smile faltered. 'Special offer,' he said, his confidence slipping. 'One week only.'

'Tempting,' Professor Hall said, smiling. 'Very tempting indeed. But I think our drive is in serviceable condition for now.' He nodded at the immaculate grey ribbon of a driveway. 'But thank you so much!'

He stood back and we went inside. We walked down a stone-flagged, oak-panelled passageway, and I glimpsed a drawing room, lined with books, and built around a giant stone hearth piled with logs, the fireplace so large that it seemed to occupy almost half of one wall. At the far, gabled end of the ground floor was a two-storey-high space and what was more of a wall made of glass than a window.

'We call it the Sunshine Room,' Professor Hall murmured.

The glass wall looked out over a deeply loved garden and beyond the trees there lay the neat squares of the Oxfordshire countryside, those perfectly symmetrical fields that feel more like a dream of England than working countryside, all of it rising softly to a distant treeline blurry with the last of the daylight.

Roman and I gawped at the view, for it was impossible to do anything else. There was a gentle pop as our host opened a bottle of pink champagne. There were four glasses in an ice bucket but no sign of his wife.

'Welcome,' he said. He handed us glasses of pink fizz. I took a big gulp.

'You have such a beautiful home,' I said.

'Thank you. It has an interesting history. I think it was originally a hunting lodge. The man who built the latest incarnation made his fortune in wool after the first war. Lost everything in 1929. Stepped off a rooftop on Threadneedle Street. Cheers.'

We carried our glasses to the glass wall of the Sunshine Room. It was an open, bright, uncluttered home, not what you would expect from a pair of elderly academics. In the silence we could faintly hear the Carter family exchanging words with Goran as they finally left the Gardens.

'They seem harmless enough,' Professor Hall said. 'I shouldn't think they'll give our Goran any problems. Did you get a chance to talk to him? Interesting man. He was in two wars before he turned twenty.'

'But I wonder,' I said. 'What is he for?'

Professor Hall blinked. 'Goran?'

I nodded, smiling. 'This area is not exactly a hotbed of crime, is it?'

Roman laughed nervously beside me.

'Thankfully not,' said Professor Hall. He took a slug of champagne. 'Although we get a substantial discount on Goran, thanks to Ben   Ben Cave, who owns the security company – but you're right. There's no crime here.'

'No crime – but we have our own security guard,' I said. 'No crime – but there's a panic room in our house.'

'A *safe* room,' Roman said quickly. 'Now your studio.'

Professor Hall smiled at us. 'I understand a safe room is quite handy in a hurricane.'

I nodded. 'And when exactly is the hurricane season in Oxfordshire? It seems quite mild out.'

He chuckled appreciatively, a man who clearly relished debate. 'We're lucky with the weather!' Then he was serious. 'But the central thesis behind the safe room is that your life can change *in an instant* and, as a historian, I would have to concur. Belgrade in 1914. Poland in 1939. Hiroshima and Nagasaki in 1945. Rwanda in 1994. The Holocaust, of course. And natural disasters – earthquakes and tsunami in Fukushima, the Indian Ocean and Haiti. On and on and on. Ask those people if life can change in an instant. Ask Magda – my wife – who was living with her mother and her older sisters in Germany in the spring of 1945.'

He sipped his champagne and smiled at me. He still had all his own teeth, but they were weathered and stained with time's wear and tear.

'I can't imagine a safe room would have been much good when the Red Army arrived,' I said.

'True enough,' he said. 'But my central point remains the same. *Bad things happen*. Not merely bad – catastrophic, life-rending things that nobody sees coming and nobody can control.'

'Black swan events,' Roman said. 'Extinction level events.'

'Exactly.' He turned to Roman. 'Do you believe your life can change in an instant?'

I felt Roman stiffen by my side.

'Yes,' he said softly. 'Yes, I do.'

And then back to me. 'In answer to your question, Goran is for – the unexpected,' Professor Hall said.

'The unexpected?'

'Many people feel – anxious,' Professor said. 'You must have noticed. Increasingly, in our modern world, they feel an anxiety they can't even explain or put a name to. There's a fear abroad – very widespread, very common, very real.' He was smiling again, a friendly old duffer with a glass of pink champagne in his hand, just chewing the fat with the new neighbours. 'I imagine that's why so many want to come to live somewhere like this, Mrs Wade.'

'Lana.'

'Lana.'

He gestured towards the window. 'These local men who would like to tarmac our driveways – as I say, they seem harmless enough. But Goran is there in case the *next* uninvited visitors are not quite so charming. Or the ones who come after them.' He smiled, warming to his theme. 'Everyone expects to be taken care of these days, don't they? By the Government, by the police, by some-one – anyone! But what if they *can't* take care of you? What if we're all on our own?' He placed the hand that was not holding his glass on his heart. 'Forgive me. I'm rambling. But history is full of people who thought that someone was going to take care of them. And then nobody did.'

'Professor Hall taught history at Oxford,' Roman said.

I looked suitably impressed, as if this was breaking news, as if Roman had not told me this already.

'What period of history?' I said, trying to be polite to our host.

'The twentieth century.' He focused on me, as if I was the one he needed to convince. 'A century of the unexpected. Economic collapse. Natural disasters. Gen-ocide. Nuclear bombs. The Somme and Auschwitz and Hiroshima. Nobody anticipated *any* of these things at the start of the century – they were all quite literally unimaginable.'

He raised an index finger, placed it against his chin, an almost theatrical gesture of reflection, and I could see how he had bewitched generations of students at Oxford or the audience of late-night BBC2, his bow tie gleaming under the studio lights.

'One example, if I may. When the US was compiling a list of Japanese cities to obliterate with their new atomic bomb in 1945, Nagasaki was *not* one of them. Hiroshima, Yokohama, Kyoto, Niigata, Kokura. That was the list of five Japanese cities. But US Secretary of War Henry Stimson had spent his honeymoon in Kyoto thirty years earlier. So Kyoto dropped off the list and was replaced by Nagasaki. And so eighty thousand men, women and children died in Hiroshima, and then forty thousand in Nagasaki – and tens of thousands more from radiation over the coming decades – just because one sentimental old American had his honeymoon in Kyoto!' He raised his glass in salute. 'The unexpected, Lana.'

'But we don't live in Nagasaki or Germany and it's not 1945, is it?' I said.

'But even in the midst of all this civilisation, all this privilege, all our multiple blessings, we are adjacent to chaos. Even in this beautiful part of the world, even in this essence of England.' He was quite jolly now. 'We are only ever five meals away from anarchy, Lana. Miss five meals and your children will be screaming with hunger. And do you know what you will do to feed them?'

I waited, my mouth tightening. I did not much like being treated as the mouthy student who needed to be shown the error of her sloppy thinking.

'Anything,' Professor Hall said quietly. 'That's what you would do after missing five meals. That's what *any* of us would do.' He beamed at us. 'You're settling in, I trust?'

Roman murmured his assent but our host must have sensed a moment's hesitancy on my part.

'Ah, you're thinking about the Clutter family,' he said. 'Of course you are. It was a tragedy for them, and for all of us who loved them.'

'But what happened?' I said. 'They looked so *happy*.'

I felt Roman's sigh of exasperation. 'We *know* what happened, don't we?'

'It's a reasonable question,' Professor Hall said. 'How does a loving father and husband come to kill the two people he loves most in the world? I ask myself the same question every single day. And I think I have finally arrived at something resembling a conclusion.'

I stared beyond him at the spectacular countryside stretching off to the horizon, sipping my champagne, waiting for him.

'In April 1945, Magda – my wife – Dr Hall – was five years old,' he said.

'Living in Germany. You said.'

'Berlin,' he said. 'Magda lived with her mother and two older sisters in an area called Grunewald on the western outskirts of Berlin. A very nice area, full of large villas, even at the end of the war, although bombed to smithereens, of course. Her father had been quite a successful architect before they stuffed him in a Wehrmacht uniform, but he had vanished into the Eastern Front years ago and Magda has absolutely no memory of him. The war had lasted all her life. It had been a terrible winter, but that spring of 1945 was warm and sunny. There was damage everywhere in Grunewald – Magda's little world. Everywhere there was the war, but everywhere too, there was something like normal life. There was heavy artillery in the park, but the trees were in bloom. There was the constant noise of the shells, always getting closer, but she still played with her dolls and her sisters still made a fuss of their hair. And then the Russians came.'

'I don't understand,' I said.

He showed me his tea-stained old teeth.

'Berlin in the spring of 1945 was a time and a place when cyanide was easier to get than chicken,' he said.

'But what's that got to do with the Clutters?'

'Dying is not the worst thing that can happen to you,' he said.

12

Then there was a sound on the stairs and Professor Hall turned towards it.

'Magda!' he called. 'Come and meet our new neighbours.'

Dr Magda Hall was helped into the room by a bespectacled Filipina.

Like her husband, Dr Hall was knocking on for eighty years old, but she had aged at a different pace. Professor Hall was a spry old man, careful in his movements but still robust, and very proud of his fitness, while Dr Hall was settled into a chair by her tiny helper as if she might break. But she settled herself with a sigh and smiled warmly up at Roman and me. Now she was still, I saw her face had a fine, chiselled quality and I could easily imagine her as a young beauty.

'What an attractive young couple,' Dr Hall said, with only a trace of the Germany she had left a lifetime ago.

She had the carefully clipped English of a foreigner who had learned to speak the language around the educated and the wealthy. 'Aren't they an attractive young couple, Al?'

'They shine,' Professor Hall smiled.

'Dr Hall,' Roman said. 'How lovely to see you again.'

'Magda,' she said.

Her husband offered her a glass of champagne and she pulled a disdainful face and waved it away. Her helper dutifully placed it untouched on a small side table.

'I don't *want* it, Rosa,' Magda muttered.

'You might want it later,' Rosa told her.

Krissy and Willow had explained to me that there were three generations of Mendoza women who worked in the Gardens – Angel the daughter, Virginia her mother and this one, Rosa, Granny Mendoza. Cooking, cleaning and caring in loose rotation, although apparently this oldest Mendoza only worked in the big house, watching over Dr Magda Hall.

Magda smiled up at me. 'Remind me what you do again, dear?'

'I'm a photographer,' I said, feeling a bit of a fraud, for it had been a while since I had held a camera.

Her eyes lit up. 'Ah, *plead the fleeting moment to remain*,' she said. 'Isn't that how Henri Cartier-Bresson put it?'

I smiled. 'The quote is always attributed to Cartier-Bresson but I think it may have been someone else who actually put it exactly like that.'

'Plead the fleeting moment to remain,' she repeated. 'Wouldn't that be lovely? If the fleeting moments would remain?'

'Ken Burns called photography *an arrested moment of reality*,' I said.

She shook her head. 'I don't know that one, dear.'

I turned to Roman for support. Rather remarkably, he was examining Professor Hall's elbow, which our host was complaining felt painful and tender. Sounded like bursitis to me, the inflammation of a bursa sac, the small bag of tissue formed round joints to allow ligaments and tendons to pass over bones. The old boy was probably going to have to have it drained.

I fought back wild laughter. What was meant to be casual drinks was turning into a house call.

Magda was still staring at me, nodding and smiling.

'And how's the Captain?' she asked.

Mrs Mendoza shot me a look and gave a quick, panicked shake of her head. I didn't get it.

'The Captain?' I said.

'I always call him that when I see him in his pilot's uniform. So very smart! And your boy? Your beautiful boy – Josh. Is he well? Has he been enjoying the cricket this summer?' She smiled broadly. 'Josh was always surprised to hear that I liked cricket too. But my husband, you see. He's a member of the MCC – Marylebone Cricket Club – and we always went when we were in town and it was the season. I quite enjoyed a day at Lord's! Very English.

So of course, I developed an interest in cricket. Josh couldn't believe it – an old German lady who liked cricket!'

Mrs Mendoza was no longer looking at me. In fact, she seemed to be avoiding eye contact. Roman was still examining Professor Hall's sore elbow. I stared at Magda's smiling face and had no words.

Because of course by now I understood.

She thought I was April Clutter.

Something in my face must have spooked her because Magda turned to Mrs Mendoza for help, looking suddenly distressed.

Mrs Mendoza was staring at Professor Hall. 'Sir?'

But the old man was watching Roman as he gently manipulated the problem elbow.

'Ma'am?' Mrs Mendoza said to her charge. 'Shall we go upstairs and have a nice lie-down now, ma'am?'

There were sudden confused tears in Magda's eyes and I knelt before her and took her hand.

'Please,' I said. 'Don't be sad about anything. I am so happy to meet you, Magda, truly I am.'

She pulled her hand away, suddenly affronted, and then Professor Hall was crouching beside her, placing his hands upon her hands with the tender familiarity of the lifelong husband and for the first time, I felt a surge of warmth towards him.

'Dr Wade and Mrs Wade – Roman and Lana – are *the new people*, Magda,' he said gently. 'You're thinking of the people who lived here before.'

'I know that!' she said angrily. But there was something close to terror in her eyes. 'I do *know*, don't I?' she said to her husband. 'I do *know*, don't I? I haven't forgotten everything, have I?'

Then she began to weep. Soft, sad, confused tears as Mrs Mendoza and her husband leaned close and soothed her and told her that everything was all right.

Roman shot me a look. We drank more quickly.

Time to go home.

We walked back down the long, winding driveway of the big house and when we reached the iron gates, Roman stopped and took my hand.

'I'm sorry,' he said. 'That was a nightmare.'

'No, it's fine,' I said. 'She's a confused old lady. She liked the Clutters and she doesn't understand what happened. And I like her. What is it – vascular dementia?'

Roman shook his head. 'Vascular dementia is usually caused by a specific event, like a stroke. It's like falling off a cliff. This is the start of Alzheimer's. They're both types of dementia but Alzheimer's is like a road with a slow downward slope. The first thing to go is memory. That's where Magda is now. But sometimes the road rises a little bit. So she has good days and bad days.'

'It's sad.'

'Yes. But I'm sure she'll be better the next time we see them.'

I had a sinking feeling. I knew that Roman and Professor Hall were a bit of a mutual admiration society and I had a vision of us getting stuck with the wrinklies down the road and never being able to shake them off. But I said nothing because the memory of our last fight was too recent.

Instead I leaned into him, loving the way his warmth felt in the evening chill, sensing the turning of the seasons.

'Shall we make up again when we get home?'

He laughed. 'Making up three times in twenty-four hours?'

'Is that too much making up for you?'

'It's just about right.'

'Better keep eating your greens, Doctor.'

He kept hold of my hand as we walked home, the Gardens empty now, and I was enjoying the light buzz of champagne and the bitter-sweet feeling that catches you right at the end of summer, and although we didn't talk about it, I know we both felt how blessed we were to have moved to this beautiful place.

I had always thought there was nothing between the Gardens and the village but unbroken Oxfordshire countryside, the sort of working farmland that always looks as though it is primarily there to make you marvel at the glory of nature. But there was something else out there among the fields, visible in the gathering darkness.

Scattered across a stumpy little hill a mile or two away, a cluster of low yellow lights were shining.

'What is that place?' I said.

'That's the council estate,' Roman said.

I stared at the lights with surprise.

The poor were always closer than you thought.

13

Sunday, 6 September

The invitation to the summer party at the big house said cocktails at noon and it was already just after the hour. I was all good to go, in a light floaty cotton dress with heels so high they would slow the walk up that long driveway, but from my upstairs alcove I could see Willow was still out there in her pool, doing laps with her languid American crawl, as if she had all the time in the world, as if Willow always did only what Willow wanted to do when Willow wanted to do it. She made me smile.

I watched as she hoisted herself out of the deep end and sat on the edge, kicking her long legs in water a blue so perfect that I always felt David Hockney should be out there painting it.

She was towelling her exploding tangle of brown curls as Guy came waddling into the garden, an overweight toff in blue blazer and chinos, looking almost comically old-fashioned. He walked around the pool, his black leather loafers slipping on the immaculate lawn with its contrasting green stripes, tapping his watch and saying something that I couldn't hear. Willow just squinted up at him, smiled adorably, and shrugged. Guy watched in disbelief as she slowly got up and stood poised by the edge of the pool.

His mouth moved, saying her name, or perhaps giving a command, but she did not react, she just kept staring straight ahead, deadly serious now, her lithe brown arms by her side.

Then Guy shouted her name, slapped his watch as she raised her arms above her head, bounced twice on the balls of her feet and dived in, hardly disturbing the surface of the pool.

Her long body shimmered and glowed under the water and she did not surface until she was halfway down the length of the pool. Guy was waiting for her at the shallow end. She rose out of the water, rested her arms on the edge of the pool, smiling sweetly up at him.

Then he reached down and grabbed her by the hair.

She cried out with pain and tried to pull away, but he did not let her go, shaking her by the fistful of her tumbling curls. She swung a leg onto the side, desperately attempting to clamber out now but he still did not let go and I wanted to scream because he was only making it harder for her to get out and could he really not see that?

He shouted something that sounded like a curse and finally released her. Willow quickly hauled herself out of the pool and knelt at his feet, chastised at last, her body shuddering with sobs as Guy stared down on her and spoke quietly, as if explaining that she had brought all this on herself.

Then he took her by the elbow and gently helped her to her feet and together they walked back towards their house, Guy walking one step behind her like a chaperone, or bodyguard, or prison warden.

Then Roman was by my side, absurdly handsome in his lightweight Paul Smith suit with a white Sunspel polo shirt.

'You look pretty,' he smiled, taking my hand.

And then we went to the party.

On the terrace above the garden of the big house we sipped Bellinis and looked out across what was said to be the best view in the county.

Beyond the clipped lawn and riot of flowers in the Halls' immaculate garden there was a field with grazing horses, softly falling to a spinney where game birds called and cooed to each other. Beyond this dense knot of trees, the open farmland rose and unfurled, the neat symmetrical fields stretching away for miles before rising to an impossibly distant treeline, purple in the late summer haze.

'Let me ask you a medical question, Doc,' Tucker, Krissy's husband, said to Roman.

Krissy groaned. 'Tucker, that's the man's *job*. You don't want to spend your weekends talking about quantitative easing, do you? And stop calling him "*Doc*".'

Roman smiled patiently.

Tucker was a big, bluff Texan who had played football and basketball at college level some fifteen years ago. He had put on a few kilos since then but still had the swagger of the school jock. The two younger Mendoza women glided among us, Angel – a Manga-eyed twenty-year-old, and Virginia, her buxom, smiling mother – carrying trays, refreshing drinks, exchanging brief snatches of Tagalog to each other. Tucker reached out and snatched a fistful of sashimi from the tray held by the middle Mrs Mendoza. She smiled at him. He didn't notice.

'The antibiotics industry is worth fifty billion US a year,' Tucker said through a mouthful of fatty tuna. 'But the stuff we put in fish tanks to keep the water clean is made of *exactly* the same stuff, right? Amoxicillin, penicillin, all that good shit. So dirt-cheap fish antibiotics – which you can buy without a prescription – are *identical* to FDA-approved antibiotics sold expensively to humans, right?'

Roman was still smiling patiently. 'But no doctor would recommend self-medication with something you bought at a pet shop,' he said.

Tucker cackled. 'Of course not! You'd put yourself out of a job, right, Doc? And big pharma would be kicked right in the bottom line. But millions of Americans use fish antibiotics to treat themselves, don't they? Because they're broad-spectrum antibiotics, correct?'

Roman nodded. 'True, although personally fish antibiotics are not something I would recommend. Unless you're a goldfish.'

'Are you a goldfish, Tucker?' Krissy said, drawing a line under the conversation. Then she looked around the terrace. 'Where's Willow?' she said, and I wondered if Krissy knew about the abuse in that house.

I shook my head, looking around the party, fearing for my friend.

Dr Hall – Magda – waved enthusiastically to me, the tears and confusion of our last meeting completely forgotten. Today must be one of the good days, I thought. Sailor stood by her side, demure in a billowing white summer dress, like a lady in waiting at court, while the oldest Mrs Mendoza was offering Magda a plate she had fetched from the impressive buffet. Professor Hall stood close by, neat and spry in a polo shirt and pressed jeans, deep in conversation with Ben Cave. Sally Berry laughed with Oscar, who was telling some long, complicated anecdote, the boy dressed in some little man lounge suit and a clip-on bow tie. His black dog, Buster, waited patiently at the boy's side, gimlet-eyed and salivating at the sight of all that food piled high on paper plates.

There was no sign of Willow and Guy.

The air seemed to stir, a breeze picking up. Rain clouds massed over the hazy treeline of the horizon. The landscape turned a darker shade of green. I shuddered. It was like watching the end of summer.

And Tucker would not let it go.

'But if you needed – say – penicillin, and you took a fish antibiotic *containing* penicillin, then what would be the side effect?'

'The side effect is that it would make you well,' Roman said, the first note of irritation in his voice. 'But the argument against self-treatment is that it invariably means self-diagnosis. And that can be – in fact, it is extremely likely to be – faulty. And it can also be fatal. And that's what makes self-treatment with fish antibiotics what we call in the trade clinically unsound.'

Tucker nodded, apparently satisfied.

Ben Cave came over to us, sweating inside what looked like golfing clothes, a mineral water in his hand. He smiled a greeting and I tried not to stare at the long livid scar that ran down one side of his friendly face.

'I told you, man,' Tucker said to him, as if they had had a bet. 'Fish antibiotics *work*.'

Ben nodded, processing this information. There was a distant rumble of thunder and we all looked at the sky. The perfect blue was now broken up by dark, billowing clouds, getting closer as we watched.

I felt the first drop of rain splatter on my arm.

'Here's Willow,' Krissy said.

Willow was dressed for a Rodeo.

While everyone else on the terrace wore some approximation of clothes that were appropriate for cocktails in an English garden, she was in a Stetson, denim mini skirt, short cowboy boots and tasselled jacket, looking ready to rope cattle.

She looked sensational.

She hung back at the long buffet table as Guy crossed the garden to greet our hosts. I glared at him, but he was smiling warmly at the Halls, oblivious or perhaps simply indifferent to what I thought of him.

Krissy and I approached Willow.

She was staring dreamily at the lavish spread. She picked up a langoustine and nibbled it tentatively.

'Are you eating?' Krissy asked her, reaching for a pair of plates.

'With buffets,' Willow slurred, 'I prefer to just look.'

Krissy sighed with exasperation, as if she had seen all of this before, and started down the buffet, piling two plates high.

I stepped close to Willow's side as she gazed thoughtfully at the food. 'Are you all right?'

'Me? Why wouldn't I be?'

I hesitated. There was a red mark on her hairline, as if the skin had been scuffed by a ring or a watch.

'I saw what Guy did to you, Willow. Sorry, I really didn't mean to snoop. But I couldn't miss it. And it's not right. You know it's not right.'

She narrowed her big brown eyes. And then she understood.

'Ah,' she said. 'We're not used to having neighbours, you see. Your house has been empty for so long. Sorry you had to see all of that. Or at least the part that happened in the garden. You missed the best bit.'

Then there was a furtive light in her eyes of something that I recognised but at first could not name. And then I placed it.

Shame. The unearned, unwarranted shame of the victim.

She leaned in conspiratorially, trying to laugh it off, or at least get me to back off and treat it more lightly than it deserved. She self consciously touched the mark on her face.

'Walked into something. Can you believe it? Clumsy me.'

'Yes,' I said. 'You walked into an asshole. Does it happen often?'

'What? No!' she said. 'No, no, no.'

'Willow – I know it's got nothing to do with me – but you really don't have to let him put his hands on you.'

'But I *provoke* him.'

'It doesn't *matter*.'

'But it kind of *does*. I knew it was time to get ready. I knew it was time to go.'

'Don't make excuses for him.'

'And I give as good as I get, Lana.'

I shrugged and looked away. 'I find that hard to believe.'

The middle Mrs Mendoza – Virginia – approached us with a tray of drinks and Willow took a Bellini in each hand. She knocked one back like it was fruit juice and took an appreciative sip of the other one. Then she bolted that one down too. She stepped unsteadily away from the buffet, the high heels of her cowboy boots suddenly off balance, and she banged hard into the youngest Mendoza – Angel – who dropped her tray of chicken satay all over the flagstones of the terrace.

'Whoops,' Willow said. 'So sorry, Angel.'

'Hey,' Krissy called from the far end of the buffet, both her plates heaped far too high. She nodded at the glasses Willow held in both hands. 'Maybe slow down, cowgirl.'

'Just trying to get through my social obligations.'

Krissy shook her head. 'Time to grow up, Willow.'

'So soon?' Willow said.

I had seen them as a double act, inseparable and the same, but that was wrong. Willow was more like me. Krissy was at home in the Gardens while Willow was in exile from the life she should have been living. At least, that's what it felt like as Krissy carried her overloaded plates over to Tucker while Willow and I started to help Angel pick up the ruined satay. Then Angel's mum, the middle Mrs Mendoza, was there, waving us away and telling us it was her job.

Guy approached his wife, his pudgy face twisted into some strange cocktail of emotion – half-amused, half-deeply pissed.

I glared at him again. But if he noticed, or if he gave a damn, then he gave no sign.

'Try not to smash the place up, darling,' he drawled. 'Would you like some black coffee?'

'I need a drink,' Willow said, looking around for more Bellini.

'But you always need a drink,' her husband said with a tight smile.

Willow laughed. 'Oh, fuck off, Guy!'

He slipped an arm around her waist, more restraint than embrace.

'Amorous? I like it!' she said, pulling away from him. 'Did you take one of your pills, darling? Shall we give it thirty minutes so it can kick in?'

His doughy face red with fury, Guy reached for her wrist.

'Hey!' I said.

He looked at me, and it was as if he suddenly realised what I had seen.

'God,' he said. 'Spare me from nosy neighbours.' He turned to Willow. 'Please stop embarrassing me, darling. And yourself. You're having black coffee if I have to pour it down your throat.'

He clicked his fingers twice for attention, and two Mendozas came rushing to answer the call as the thunder rumbled, the summer lightning cracked, the skies opened and the rain beat down on the terrace of the big house.

We all went inside and huddled in what the Halls called the Sunshine Room, watching the rain lash down from the floor-to-ceiling window that filled the back of the house. Professor Hall stood facing us and smiling, dark spots of rain on his neat polo shirt and pressed jeans, as if the vagaries of the English summer were all part of the fun.

And then we heard the front door slam.

Our host's face froze.

'I believe we may have an uninvited guest,' Professor Hall said.

The men moved quickly – Ben Cave first, quickly followed by Tucker and Guy – and the rest of us trailed after them, not yet understanding.

In the book-lined room at the front of the house we saw the window that had been smashed and then jemmied open.

Broken glass sparkled on the flagstones of the great hearth. I recalled two silver candlesticks above the massive fireplace, which had stuck in my mind because they were ornate enough for a cathedral.

They were gone.

Ben Cave threw open the front door and as the rest of the party came trailing down the long hall from the Sunshine Room, I saw the young man, Sailor's friend, the Carter who had once been told he looked like Tom Cruise, sprinting down the long driveway of the big house with a silver candlestick in each hand. His tobacco-coloured Newsboy hat went flying but he did not pause to pick it up.

'Candlesticks.' Guy chuckled. 'It's Jean Valjean, doing a runner. Bloody pitiful, isn't it?'

'Call Goran,' Professor Hall said.

Ben pulled out his phone, punched a number and jumped down the stone steps in a single bound, speaking urgently into the phone as he took off down the driveway.

Tucker and Guy were not far behind him. But Guy was swiftly out of puff and bent double wheezing for breath while Oscar was chasing his dad with Buster yapping excitedly by his side and Krissy was going after them, not a natural runner, and I saw Roman jog past her and I was out of the house too, kicking my shoes off and running after him, Professor Hall shouting something behind me that I didn't catch, and then there was a pack of us running down the drive.

Shouts, cries.

And the sound of a distant engine.

And then, coming from the far end of the Gardens, there was Goran in his white security van, racing towards the big house. The van was briefly hidden behind the ancient trees that lined the driveway but as I turned the final bend the trees were suddenly gone.

And so I had a perfect view of what happened next.

The Carter boy had almost reached the iron gates of the big house. The chasing pack had spread out behind him, Ben followed by Oscar and his deliriously happy dog and then Roman. But Carter was fast, and afraid, and he was getting away, while the rest of us – me and

Krissy and Sailor and finally Guy – were only jogging now, wanting him to be gone, knowing it was best all round if he just got away.

Goran's white van arrived at the iron gates of the big house at the same time as the boy, who skidded to a sudden halt. He stood there with his hands raised, caught bang to rights, the chasing pack paused behind him, uncertain what to do next, Ben shouting at Oscar to stay back.

But Goran's van did not slow down. If anything, it seemed to accelerate as it approached the great iron gates of the manor house.

Carter raised his hands higher, rooted to the spot. He was still holding the candlesticks. The van kept speeding towards him.

At the very last moment, the Carter boy shouted with disbelief, and Goran drove straight through him, and the shout died.

Carter's body seemed to snap double, the top half slapping hard against the hood of the van, the sickening sound of flesh and bone being struck by two tons of metal and then flinging him to one side.

The van screeched to a halt just inside the gates.

The body did not move.

Somebody else was screaming now.

Sailor.

Krissy went to her daughter and turned her face away from the sight of the broken body, twisted and bleeding and terribly still by the iron gates.

But Sailor did not stop screaming.

Then it was Roman who was giving orders as he bent over the boy.

'Back!' he shouted.

He meant all of us. And everyone got back. Apart from me. I came forward so I could stand by Roman's side.

Kneeling in the driving rain, Roman tenderly placed his hand on the boy's forehead and gently tilted it back, lifting the scuffed and bloody chin, and then put his cheek by the boy's mouth, listening for a long moment.

'I'm going to stay with you as long as you need me, OK?' he said calmly.

Then he carefully eased the body on its side, still talking, so calm it seemed almost conversational, the rain lashing down as he supported the Carter boy's head and neck, keeping the airways open.

Roman looked around, saw me, nodded once, and I found my phone and I was calling the emergency services, my eyes never leaving Roman and the boy.

Ben Cave slowly approached with a blanket that he had found somewhere and hesitated, as if waiting for permission from Roman, and Roman nodded curtly and Ben draped it over the boy's legs.

Roman pulled it up to his neck, like tucking in a baby, and eased him onto his back.

He was holding the boy's hand and we were all standing there just watching and there was a moment of total stillness until something changed, and Roman was suddenly frantic, placing the heels of his hands in the centre of the boy's chest, one hand on top of the other as he pushed the full weight of his body down again and again and again, one hundred times in a minute, that's how you do it, with only the briefest of pauses to let the chest recoil.

Then Roman pinched Carter's nostrils shut, and his mouth was on the boy's mouth, the rain pounding down as Roman breathed into his lungs, forcing life into him, and then he stopped to check the chest for movement, and then once again placed his mouth against the boy's mouth.

Roman kept breathing into the boy's lungs, and he kept up that desperate kiss even after we heard the sirens and the Carter boy's eyes were staring wide with fear at the summer rain.

And Sailor did not stop screaming.

14

There was a uniformed policeman at our front door.

'Dr Wade?' he said. 'The detective is ready for you now.'

It was early evening as we came out of our house, and there were police all over the Gardens.

Half a dozen squad cars lined the road, blue lights pulsing as uniformed officers went from door to door with their questions for our neighbours. The entrance to the big house was taped off with black-and-yellow emergency tape and lit up like a film set, bright arc lights shining on the white-suited search team who scraped in the dust for clues.

On the far side of the street, a female detective in a beige raincoat stood with her back to the pink oleander bushes of Sally's cottage. She was an Amazon of a woman, broad-shouldered and over six feet tall, her white-blonde hair cut severely short, slowly looking one way and then the other, as if working it all out in her head. She looked up as Roman and I approached her and started towards us, and then we all paused to let a squad car pass, heading out of the Gardens, its tyres hissing on the wet tarmac. She nodded to the driver and then crossed the street.

'Dr Wade?' she said. 'Mrs Wade? I'm Detective Inspector Hunter.'

She shook hands with both of us, unsmiling, but it wasn't me she was interested in.

'Sorry to make you wait,' she said to Roman. 'I know you talked to one of the attending officers about what happened to John Carter.'

She said his name as if she knew him.

'I've spoken to the two neighbours who were with you,' she said, fishing a crumpled notebook out of her raincoat. 'Mr ... Ben Cave and Mr ... Tucker Jordan – and the security guard who accidentally hit Carter. Mr ... Goran Petrovic.'

I stared at Roman.

Accidentally?

He did not look at me.

DI Hunter was still talking. 'We'll get formal taped statements later, but I just wanted to get an IBA – initial brief account – from you.'

Roman nodded. 'As I told the attending officer,' he said. 'It was a complete accident.'

I could not believe what I was hearing.

In the immediate aftermath, I had been with Willow and Krissy in the Sunshine Room of the big house, trying to understand what had just happened, trying to calm

Sailor down, trying to stop her screaming, and I had missed Roman's interview with the first police to arrive on the scene.

But I had never doubted that Goran had deliberately run the boy down.

'The man – the boy – Mr ... John Carter,' Roman said, adopting the detective's language, 'had apparently broken into Professor and Dr Hall's house when we were out on the terrace. We came inside when it began to rain, and he – Mr Carter – made a run for it. Ben – Mr Cave – called our security guard, who clearly came as fast as he could.' Roman licked his lips. 'And I guess he just didn't have the chance to stop.'

DI Hunter nodded. 'He's pretty shaken up, the security guy.' Looking at her notes. 'Goran Petrovic.' She looked back at Roman, two professionals together, doing what needed to be done. 'And you administered CPR to Mr Carter?'

'Is he dead?' I blurted.

DI Hunter and Roman both looked at me, as if surprised I was still there.

'The last I heard,' the detective said, 'he was in a medically induced coma.'

'Mr Carter was semi-conscious when I reached him and I administered CPR,' Roman said.

We stood there saying nothing for a long moment. The wheels of another squad car hissed on the wet road, heading from the big house. The rain had stopped hours ago but the atmosphere was still heavy with the storm.

DI Hunter tapped her notebook. 'So – just to be clear – it was the three of you who were closest to the gate – Mr Cave, Mr Jordan and yourself. And you saw – just to be clear – what *exactly* did you see, Dr Wade? One more time. If you don't mind.'

'He ran – the boy – John Carter – he ran and – I don't know.' He ran a hand through his hair. 'He was looking back at us, I guess – yes, I'm pretty sure he was looking back at us – and Goran – Mr Petrovic – he kept coming – he had answered the emergency call from Ben, and he had no chance to stop.'

DI Hunter consulted her notes, nodding. 'Yes, that's what Mr Cave and Mr Tucker told us in their IBAs.' She glanced up at me and then away. 'And the other people from the party – they were behind you, Dr Wade?'

'A few of them. Krissy – Mrs Jordan. Ben's son, the boy, Oscar. But they were some distance down the drive.'

A beat. I waited for Roman to mention me.

But he didn't.

DI Hunter finally looked at me.

'Were you there, Mrs Wade?'

I nodded dumbly. 'Yes, I was there.' I glanced at Roman. 'It's true, I was a bit further back when it happened.'

Tell her you saw the boy deliberately run down.

But what did I remember? Get it right, Lana.

I remembered overtaking Guy as he bent double in the driveway and then suddenly stopping when the rest of them stopped.

Because the car was coming, and Goran was driving very fast, responding to an emergency call, and we stopped because it was suddenly very dangerous on that driveway.

I remembered standing with Krissy and Sailor, afraid to go forward, all of us stopped dead – all of us, including the boy, including John Carter with his pathetic booty. I tried to conflate what I had seen with what Roman was saying, I tried to make it work, I tried to make it somehow true, or a grotesque mistake, or a misunderstanding.

But I couldn't do it.

It just didn't fit. None of it fit.

Roman was lying to the police.

DI Hunter was nodding her head at me. 'So you didn't really witness the accident, Mrs Wade?'

I shook my head and it was a lost, meaningless gesture, neither confirming nor denying what she was asking.

To tell her what I saw would make my husband a liar.

'No,' Roman said, not looking at me. 'They didn't see what happened. You had to be standing right where we were standing.'

We went back inside our home and Roman poured two large brandies.

'I don't want brandy,' I said.

He threw the drink down his throat and then picked up the one that was meant for me. The muscle by his eye was twitching. He was shaking.

The blue lights were pulsing on the kitchen walls.

'What just happened?' I said.

He could not look at me. He set down the second glass of brandy. Too much. Already too much.

'What are you talking about?'

'What you told the police,' I said. 'It didn't look like an accident from where I was standing. It didn't look anything like that to me. He ran that boy down, didn't he? Goran tried to kill him.'

Roman touched the knees of his trousers, as if suddenly realising that they were soaked from where he had been kneeling in the road, trying to save John Carter's life. He touched his elbows, the sleeves of his Paul Smith suit. All filthy, all soaked through. He shuddered with the sudden chill.

'*Look at me, will you?*'

I grabbed his arm and the brandy swilled over the kitchen island.

'Jesus Christ, Lana!'

'*What you told that detective – that's not what happened!*'

He turned on me with a sudden fury.

'You didn't *see*. You couldn't see where you were. Not really.'

'Is that the story? Did you and Ben and Tucker and Guy get it straight when we were waiting for the police to show up?'

'I was a lot closer than you! You know that's true. We were all a lot closer than you.'

'I was close enough to *see*. I was closer than Guy. I know what it looked like.'

'And what did you see?'

I shook my head. 'Goran ran him down.'

'Lana—'

'This is all wrong, Roman. You must know that. This place is wrong. It's beautiful but it's wrong. What you told them, Roman – you know it's wrong, don't you?'

But there was a hardness in his eyes, something that I had never seen before.

'He shouldn't have been here, OK?' Roman said quietly. 'He shouldn't have broken into that house. He shouldn't have invaded someone's home.'

'But you tried to save him! You tried to save his life! I *saw* you. I saw how hard you tried! And you did, Roman, you saved him. He would have died today without you there.'

'Of course I tried! I took an oath to always try. But nobody asked him to come here, did they?'

'His name was John Carter.'

'I don't care what his name was, Lana. It was all his decision – to break into someone's house, to rummage around in someone's life to see what he felt like taking.

That was his choice and – you know what, Lana? – he got what he deserved.' His eyes were shining with angry tears. 'Have you forgotten what happened to us?'

I shook my head. 'How could I ever forget?'

'He shouldn't have been here today! I'm sorry he's probably going to lose his life for petty theft. But he smashed his way into someone's home. And he got what he deserved.'

'No,' I said. 'He didn't get what he deserved. And it's wrong.'

Roman came to me, and he held me, and we were both crying now. With my face pressed against the sweet familiar feeling of him, I whispered what I was struggling to understand.

'Why are you lying?' I said.

And then he pulled away from me, drying his eyes with the back of his hand, and he shook his head, sick of talking about it, and he went outside where Guy stood in the street talking to Ben, Guy back in a T-shirt and jeans but Ben still in his golfing party clothes. Then Krissy and Tucker joined them, and eventually Sally Berry came out of her cottage, and the neighbours stood talking among themselves in the middle of the Gardens as the police went about their business.

Then Ben slapped Roman on the back, just once, comforting him, or encouraging him, or something, and Guy laughed, and it was as if something had been settled forever between them.

Then the neighbours all turned, and as one they began walking slowly towards the big house.

I caught a glimpse of Sailor watching them from an upstairs bedroom window, her eyes raw with wild grief, her long blonde hair still plastered to her face by the summer rain, but then the blinds were suddenly shut tight, and she was gone.

PART TWO
ROMAN

15

Monday, 7 September

At the end of the night, something pulled me awake.

The security light was blazing in the back garden and for a foggy moment I thought it was the light that had disturbed me.

But then I saw Lana standing by the window in her T-shirt and pants, staring out at the garden. She stood stock-still, her fabulous face lit by moonlight, and for a confusing moment, there was only the silence of the night.

And then I heard the screaming.

It came from somewhere outside, unearthly animal noises that chilled my blood.

I sat up in bed, more asleep than awake, glancing at the clock by the bedside – just after 4 a.m. – and then, rubbing my eyes, at Lana.

She was a slim figure in her boyish sleepwear of T-shirt and pants, her body slightly built but with some natural-born strength, like a marathon runner, small but lean and hard and leggy, and I felt the old familiar ache. Those arms, those legs, that face. All I wanted was to feel her beside me.

'Lana? It's just the countryside. Come back to bed.'

She turned her head towards me, her hair moving in a way that always tugged at some secret chamber in my heart. For Lana's hair swung – it was black, thick and lush, like Japanese hair, and it was cut in a bob, like a flapper from a hundred years ago.

Her face, as wide-eyed as some sad beauty on a Fornasetti vase, was set in serious lines.

She kept staring at me but gave no indication that she had heard me.

Was it possible I had not spoken?

My mind was groggy. I had taken one of my pills. Sleep was a problem for me these days. Not falling asleep, but staying asleep, and the pills I prescribed for myself brought a kind of self-imposed unconsciousness, a poor imitation of restorative sleep, and they sometimes left me blurry and exhausted the next morning. I tried hard to limit my intake of the pills, but I had taken one last night after the detective had gone, just to stop my thoughts from churning.

I shook my head and slipped out of bed, joining Lana at the window. I saw what she was looking at. Down in the drained swimming pool there were two foxes, scrawny with youth or starvation or both, facing off against each other in the empty well of the deep end.

Their bodies were perfectly still with terror or excitement, and they were howling in each other's faces.

'I know the standard country line about foxes being murderous vermin who nick all your chickens, but I can't help it,' Lana said. 'There will always be something magical about them to me.'

The foxes stood stock still as they screamed at each other, a sound that was full of pain or longing, and then – as one – they hurled themselves together, biting and snapping and circling, their cries now punctuated with grunts of exertion.

'Try to sleep,' I said.

'I can't sleep,' she said. 'Because I can't stop thinking about that boy.' She looked at me. 'And I'm so thirsty, Roman.'

I brought her the bottle of mineral water that we kept by our bedside, and she glugged it down, her black hair swinging.

'You know what you need tomorrow morning?' I said. 'Sunshine. Toast. And Coca Cola – Regular not Diet.'

She wiped her mouth with the back of her hand. 'I don't need a cure for a hangover,' she said. 'And I'm not dehydrated. Because I wasn't drunk at the party, OK?'

I held up my hands. I didn't want to fight. She didn't want to hear my lectures about her drinking. And I had learned that in every marriage there were things that you did not talk about. Or was that just us?

'OK.'

'You think I was drunk?'

I shrugged. 'You had a couple. I'm not criticising you.'

She took an exasperated breath. 'Are you really telling me that I don't know what I saw? That's what you're implying, isn't it? I *know* what I saw, Roman.'

I gently touched her bare arm.

'You know what you *think* you saw.'

She angrily pulled away.

'It was an accident, Lana. The boy was so keen to get away he wasn't looking where he was going and Goran didn't have the chance to stop.'

She laughed. 'Is that the story? Did you all work out what to tell the police? And is that what you all decided?'

'There's no story to work out,' I said, trying to stay calm. 'Goran has a wife and two kids back in – I don't know. Belgrade or Zagreb or Swindon or wherever. Do you *really* want to see him locked up for manslaughter? What possible good would that do anyone?'

She smiled at me. 'Oh, Roman! You make lying to the police sound so bloody reasonable.'

'*It was an accident*. A horrible accident. Do you think our neighbours would lie about such a thing? These are good people, Lana.'

'They are the rich,' she said. 'And the rich always think they can do what they like. Even the nice ones.'

We were silent, staring at our back garden rather than each other.

'And will he die?' Lana said. 'John Carter? Will he die?'

'I don't know,' I said. 'He has severe internal injuries. He has head trauma. He's in a medically induced coma.'

'That sounds like a yes, Doctor.'

'It's a probably. He's probably going to die.'

She took a deep breath and when she released it, it came out ragged and strained. 'At last you're being honest with me.'

'I'm always honest with you. I've always told you everything, haven't I?'

She leaned closer to the window, watching the foxes, ignoring me.

I was numb with exhaustion.

'Come back to bed, Lana.'

'I'm going to be up for a while,' she said, turning away from the window.

She went downstairs and soon I heard her in the kitchen, the slam of the fridge door, the clink of glass, the sound of a bottle being opened.

And I thought – *In the middle of the night, Lana? Even in the middle of the night?*

I got back in bed and lay awake for a long time, listening to the cries in our back garden, the two foxes howling as if they were still trying to decide between mating or murder. I could never sleep without Lana by my side. The bed was always too big without her, the sheets too cold, the night too long.

I remembered other nights when I woke and she was not there – not gone far and not gone long, because her side of the bed was still warm, the soft dent of her body still in the mattress.

I reached out now, touching her side of the bed.

But the cotton sheets were already cold.

I listened for sounds from the kitchen but she was drinking silently, trying not to disturb me. I lay awake until finally the exhaustion pulled me under, that moment that always comes just before your alarm goes off.

And in the morning I was bolting black coffee when the police came back to talk to us.

16

It was a married kind of silence.

At breakfast Lana spoke to me when she needed to but kept exchanges to a minimum. *More coffee? Thank you. Breakfast? I'll grab something later.* Eye contact kept to a minimum, and as I readied myself for the working day, there was a lack of warmth between us that gnawed at my heart.

I hated it when we argued.

Lana was more than my wife. She was my best friend; she was the only family I had left. But she was better at arguing than me, adept at letting her hair fall forward to half cover her face, more capable of sustaining resentment over an extended period, and I knew I wasn't going to escape this married silence until the far end of the day, at least.

Then the unmarked police car pulled into the Gardens, the huge, distinctive figure of DI Hunter hunched over the wheel, and Lana and I looked at each other.

We were in this together.

'What does she want now?' Lana said, a note of panic in her voice.

I shook my head. 'I'm sure it's just routine.'

But what they wanted was us.

They parked outside our house. DI Hunter eased her large frame out of the driver's seat and ran a hand through her cropped hair, so white that I wondered if she had albino blood. An older man emerged from the passenger side, almost totally bald but with a neatly trimmed goatee, slim and diffident and neat, with leather patches on the elbows of his sports jacket that made him look like an old-fashioned teacher. They took their time, talking over the roof of the car, DI Hunter indicating the big house, the pair of them working it out.

How it had happened.

Then they started up our driveway and I went to the door to meet them.

The older man was smiling as if this was a social visit. He paused and smiled dreamily, taking in the postcard perfection of the Gardens.

'What a beautiful road,' he said, glancing towards the big house, and then back to me, all apologies. 'Detective Chief Inspector Jim Baxter,' he said, and we shook hands. 'Sorry to disturb you, Dr Wade. And Mrs Wade,' he said, smiling at Lana hovering just behind me. He gestured towards the inside of our house, still smiling. 'We need your CCTV footage. Funnily enough, you have the only CCTV on the Gardens. Can you believe it?'

From the doorway I stared up at the cameras that adorned the honey-stone house, as if seeing them for the first time.

'We haven't really started using the CCTV,' I said.

'We can show you how,' DI Hunter said.

'A panic room?'

The two detectives seemed fascinated, examining the hidden door with what I took to be professional curiosity. DCI Baxter tapped the reinforced walls as DI Hunter ran a hand over the door jamb, making a little red light come on in the motion sensor.

'A safe room,' I said, embarrassed. 'The previous owners had it installed.'

'It's my studio now,' Lana said, brushing her hair from her face. 'I'm a photographer.'

'A photographer?' DCI Baxter nodded, professionally polite.

They stepped inside. Lana and I followed them.

The room was a bit of a squeeze with four adults inside and we tried to give each other space. DCI Baxter was taking it all in with a smile of appreciation, first Lana's little gallery – Dorothea Lange's *Migrant Mother*, the shot of the homeless man that Lana had taken the night we met, and Sandy McKay's *Crack Shack* – a photograph that I have always despised, because it seems to give a *Vogue* magazine gloss to a group of hopeless addicts. I looked at that photograph for the ten-thousandth time and I saw HIV and hepatitis, broken homes and children taken into care, rotting bodies and homelessness. What did the great Sandy McKay see? Glorious squalor, I imagine.

DCI Baxter's eyes roamed over the stone Buddha that still had flecks of grass on his impassive face, and everywhere there were the stacks of photography books, on the floor and piled high on the desk with the CCTV monitor.

DCI Baxter politely nodded his bald head. 'A photographer,' he said, seeming genuinely impressed now.

He picked up the nearest book. A library-binding of *Slightly Out of Focus* by Robert Capa, a birthday gift to Lana from Sandy, the cover Capa's classic blurry shot of a terrified GI wading onto a Normandy beach on D-Day.

DI Hunter was stooped over the desk, hitting buttons, turning on the monitor then standing back.

'Sir?' she said.

The screen revealed nine live shots of the Gardens in three lines of three.

'You've got a lot of cameras,' DCI Baxter said, with a degree of admiration. 'And are they all working?'

He looked at me, then at Lana, then back to me. As if the man of the house would know about these things. I felt rather than saw Lana stiffen with irritation.

I stared at the monitor. 'I imagine so,' I said, feeling slightly stupid that I was not yet proficient with our CCTV. 'I don't know.'

'They all look as though they are working just fine, sir,' DI Hunter said. Then she turned to me with her stern, unforgiving cop's face. 'May I?'

I nodded and she plonked herself into a chair that was almost comically small for her great frame, leaning into the CCTV monitor, tapping on the keyboard.

Within seconds the main menu had appeared on the screen.

'Just the street,' DCI Baxter murmured, still looking at the Robert Capa shot of the GI wading ashore on Omaha Beach, and nine screens instantly became one, a widescreen shot of the Gardens.

'Sir, do you want to search by time or event?' DI Hunter said, not turning around.

'Is your CCTV operated by a motion sensor?' DCI Baxter asked us, and Lana and I must have looked blank. 'Does it record when it senses movement or is it always on?' he said, still very patient with us.

'I'm sorry, we really don't know,' I said.

Lana said nothing.

'Search by time,' DCI Baxter said.

DI Hunter hit some keys and a calendar appeared in a corner of the screen.

'How is he?' Lana said.

DCI Baxter stared at her for a moment before he realised she was asking about John Carter. 'The Carter boy has head trauma,' he said, wincing with what felt like more than a professional token show of regret. He looked at me. 'I think you worked a small miracle keeping him alive, Dr Wade.'

I didn't speak.

'You knew him, didn't you, Beth?' he said to DI Hunter. '*Know* him, I mean. Present tense. The Carter boy.'

'Every copper round here gets acquainted with the Carter family,' she said, her eyes on the screen. 'You don't even have to be with the force. Everyone from these parts has heard about the Carters. I've known young John since I was in uniform, and he was knee high to his probation officer.' She allowed herself a small chuckle. 'He didn't leave school until he was thirteen. That's practically a PhD in his family.'

DCI Baxter was smiling too, as if they were reminiscing about an old friend.

'John Carter was the oldest thirteen-year-old I ever met in my life,' DI Hunter said, still scrolling through the menu on screen. 'Quite a nice chap for a professional thief. And there was a charm about him. The girls loved him.'

'Love him,' DCI Baxter said, a prissy but indulgent English teacher.

'Yes, sir. They love him still. And so does everyone else. John is a popular lad.' DI Hunter leaned into the computer screen. 'That's why they're getting so hysterical,' she said. 'His family, I mean. And of course, because of who his mother is – Mary Carter.'

DCI Baxter chuckled. 'Typhoon Mary! Criminal aristocracy is our Mary. At least, in our little pond.'

'More like minor royalty.'

'What will his family do to us?' Lana said. 'Will they come back here?'

DCI Baxter was suddenly serious, all professional reassurance. I had seen it before, the police being reassuring that everything will turn out fine.

I felt something clench in my gut.

'There's nothing for you or the other residents to be concerned about,' DCI Baxter told Lana. 'Carter's family and his friends and associates are not going to do anything as some misguided act of revenge because we are not going to let them. It will only escalate now if the worst comes to the worst.'

'And what does that mean?' Lana said.

DCI Baxter looked surprised.

'If the boy dies,' he said.

He smiled at me with a sort of fraternal courtesy, as if we were two old pros who understood the way the world worked, and then he turned his attentions back to DI Hunter, who was now staring at a blank screen.

'What's wrong?' he asked.

'This should be it,' DI Hunter said. 'This is the time and place.' She shook her head with disbelief.

'Try it again,' DCI Baxter said.

She called up the calendar again and tapped in a time and date, and I realised it must be the time and date when Goran's van struck John Carter.

The screen remained defiantly blank.

DI Hunter picked up the black box next to the monitor, shook her head and laughed shortly as she felt the weight of the thing, and then looked in the back to confirm her suspicions.

'No hard drive,' she said, putting it back down.

'No hard drive?' DCI Baxter said.

'Someone's removed it, sir. So, all those cameras on the front of the property – they see, and they watch the street, but they don't remember a thing.'

The two detectives stared at us.

'You've got a CCTV DVR system,' DI Hunter said coldly. 'The DVR stands for a Digital Video Recorder. That's where the CCTV stores images.'

I could feel my face burning. 'Yes,' I said. 'I get it. I understand how it works.'

'Was the hard drive in there yesterday?' DCI Baxter said quietly, looking at Lana.

'I thought so,' she said, turning to me for help. 'I mean – I don't know.'

'Was it there when you moved in?' DI Hunter said, a hardness in her voice now.

She looked at Lana, then at me. The room felt very small. I felt a trickle of sweat at the base of my spine.

I shook my head, more in confusion than denial. 'We really don't know.'

The two of them stared at the blank screen and then back at us. DI Hunter sighed, shifting her bulk in the tiny chair.

And for the first time Lana's studio felt far too small to comfortably contain all four of us, or even to uncomfortably contain us.

I found it difficult to breathe. I tried to calm my heart, slow my breathing, because I knew where this terror led, I knew it ended in the blind panic that made you feel that your heart was going to burst, and this was going to be the day you died.

And I knew this feeling so well because I had felt it so often since the night our world came apart.

'Here's the thing,' DCI Baxter said, and I tried to place the city that I heard buried deep in his accent. Manchester? Leeds? He was from meaner streets than these, and he was suddenly not nearly as affable.

'The story we've got, the security chap – Mr Petrovic – didn't see the boy – John Carter – and that's why he drove into him without bothering to use his brakes. But from one end of the Gardens to the manor house is a straight run.' He stared at me levelly. 'And we don't quite understand how he could have failed to see him.'

I glanced at Lana, who looked torn, paralysed.

I spoke quickly. 'Goran – the driver – is employed by Mr Cave – our neighbour, Ben – and I know that Goran was responding to Ben's call. Maybe – I don't know – he didn't see the boy because he was looking at his phone.'

DI Hunter swivelled her bulk in the little chair and stared at her boss. Something seemed to pass between them.

DCI Baxter put down the Robert Capa book and turned to us.

'Is there anything that either of you would like to tell us?' he said. A silence. 'Dr Wade? Mrs Wade? Anything you remember about yesterday that has only just come back to you?' He was plainly giving us both every chance. 'Anything that might help us in our inquiries about this incident?' A pause. 'The accident?'

I felt Lana shift beside me.

She opened her mouth to speak.

'No,' I said.

17

Thursday, 10 September

'You can get dressed.'

As Ben Cave put his clothes on in a corner of the surgery that was reserved for examinations, I sat at my desk and scrolled through his medical record.

My neighbour was a fit man for his age – in fact he was a fit man for any age – but his blood pressure was off the chart. It was lucky for him he was built like a middleweight boxer. If he had been overweight, Ben Cave would be a heart attack waiting to happen.

There were notes on his working life. Ben had spent ten years running his own security company, I learned from the notes of my predecessor, Dr Cox. Before that he served five years with the police, and before that five more in the army, including two tours of Afghanistan.

No record of PTSD but that didn't mean it wasn't there. He didn't strike me as the type of man who would embrace therapy, or even admit to a problem.

He slid into the seat opposite me, a boyish-looking man of forty, despite the livid scar that ran down one side of his face. I wondered if that was a souvenir from his years in the army or the police.

'You're looking at my scar,' he smiled.

I smiled back. 'I didn't mean to stare.'

He laughed. 'I came off my BMX bike when I was twelve,' he said. 'Trying to jump some barbed wire. Everyone usually thinks it must be from hand-to-hand combat with the Taliban. Nothing so dramatic, I'm afraid.'

I looked at his notes.

'I'm not surprised you can't sleep, Ben,' I said. 'Your blood pressure is 150 systolic over 100 diastolic.'

'That's a tad high, right?' he said, still smiling, a man who liked to look on the bright side, and I could hear rural Oxfordshire deep in his accent. A local lad who had done well. 'Maybe it's white-coat syndrome.'

'Do you still have the sleeping pills that Dr Cox prescribed for you?'

He slid a battered white packet across the desk.

I looked at the prescription and, as I suspected, saw it was one of the Z-drugs.

I tossed them in the bin.

'That stuff will knock you out but it's not going to do anything to help your insomnia,' I said. 'Believe me, I understand how elusive sleep can be.'

He raised his eyebrows. 'You too?'

I nodded. 'Me too. But the Z-drugs should only be prescribed on a short-term basis. Personally, I would never prescribe them.' I scribbled a prescription. 'This is just a sedating antihistamine you can get from the pharmacist,' I said. 'It should ease you into a good night's sleep.'

'Never have too much trouble nodding off. It's staying there that's the difficult bit.'

'I know the feeling. These will help with that too. But we'll keep an eye on your BP and if it stays elevated, you will need to take some calcium channel blockers to widen your arteries.'

'How long for?'

I paused. 'The rest of your life.'

He thought about it, those boyish features frowning. Nobody likes the idea of having to take pills for life.

'Side effects?' he said.

'The side effects are they make you well,' I said. It was the line they had taught us in medical school that was most likely to result in patient compliance.

He nodded, satisfied. In the distance, coming from faraway fields, we heard the *pof-pof-pof* of shotguns.

'What are they shooting?' I said. 'Pheasant?'

'It's too soon for pheasant. It's partridge now, from September to February, and pheasant from October to February.' He smiled shyly. 'You should join us sometime. The guns. We all shoot. Guy. Tucker and Krissy. And even Professor Hall.'

'I'm not sure my wife would approve.'

'A real city girl!' he grinned.

'Exactly.'

We listened to the distant guns. Lana would more than disapprove but I could see the attraction of walking through beautiful countryside carrying a weapon that you knew how to use.

'I saw the law came back to your place Monday morning,' Ben said.

I nodded. 'Looking for CCTV that's unfortunately not there. Because of the accident.'

'It was sad. Poor Goran didn't have a chance to stop. He's really cut up about it.'

I nodded.

'Burglary is almost non-existent in the Gardens,' Ben continued. 'I hope Lana isn't too upset.'

'It's shaken her.'

'Yes. I've seen a few dead bodies. In the police. In the army. I can't say it ever got any easier. And of course you've seen your share.'

'But John Carter isn't dead.'

'Not yet,' he said, and there was both sympathy and resignation in his soft country burr. For all his affable manner, Ben Cave was a former policeman and there was a limit to his empathy for the criminal class.

'He was lucky, that boy,' he said. 'Lucky you were there to save his life.'

'Frankly I think his luck was out,' I said.

Then I steered the conversation back to his presenting problem.

'When you wake up in the night and your mind starts churning and you can't get back to sleep, what are you thinking about?'

He looked startled, as if there was only one thing that could possibly be keeping him awake.

'Oscar,' he said. 'My son.'

I let him talk.

'It hasn't been easy for him,' he went on. 'Oscar's finding it hard – his parents splitting up. Juno – his mum – my wife – leaving. Just walking out the door for her *new life*.' He couldn't keep any of it out of his voice – the bewilderment, the hurt, the anger. 'I know divorce is not easy for any child. But Oscar's a sensitive boy, a gentle boy, and he has taken it all to heart. I think he is struggling with emotions and a situation that he doesn't really understand.'

I thought of Oscar on the village green, brandishing a knife in the face of his tormentor, and for a moment I was going to tell Ben what I had seen. And I didn't doubt that it was true – Oscar was a sensitive boy who was in turmoil because his mother had walked out of the family home and was apparently shacked up somewhere with another man. In my experience, it was never the tough kids who carried a knife. It was the ones who were petrified, and weak, and deeply troubled.

But I said nothing about the boy and his knife, and I hoped Oscar had had the sense to drop it down a drain.

Ben Cave had enough problems already. He was a single father with blood pressure so high that it was either going to come down or kill him.

'It looks so perfect, doesn't it?' he said, getting up to leave. 'The Gardens, I mean. Like a little green corner of paradise. You would never think there's a boy who misses his mother, a boy who feels broken because his parents split up. What do they say? Something about what's inside every dream home ...'

'In every dream home a heartache,' I said.

He laughed and shook my hand.

'Story of my life,' Ben Cave smiled.

18

When I arrived home, Mrs Mendoza – Virginia, the middle one of the Gardens' three Filipino helpers – was standing in the hallway, a lightweight Dyson in her hand and a terrified expression on her face.

'Mrs Mendoza? What's wrong?'

She gestured upstairs with the spout of her Dyson.

'It's Ma'am ...'

I went up the stairs two at a time and found Lana on the floor of her studio, peering under the small sofa bed that we had not yet got around to throwing out.

'Lana?'

'It's got to be here somewhere.'

'What?'

She twisted her face up to look at me.

'The CCTV hard drive,' she said.

'Why would it be under the sofa bed?'

'Then where is it? We have to find it for the police.'

Mrs Mendoza was hovering just outside the doorway. She cleared her throat.

Lana and I both looked at her.

'You're looking for that video recording, right? For the film – for the film of the boy who was in the accident. But maybe the police took it away?'

'But we would *know* if the police took it, Mrs Mendoza,' Lana said, failing to keep the irritation out of her voice.

'No, I meant maybe they took it *before*,' Mrs Mendoza said. 'Maybe they took it from the other time – from the *Clutter* family time.' Her face clouded with the memory of the tragedy. 'Maybe the police took it away then.'

Lana slowly got to her feet. The possibility had not occurred to her, or me, that the CCTV hard drive could conceivably have been taken long before we ever moved in, when the police were investigating another incident.

I nodded at Lana and smiled with what I hoped was reassurance.

It made perfect sense – didn't it? – that the police should have bagged the hard drive of the CCTV recorder after Captain Clutter wiped out his family.

'Thank you, Mrs Mendoza,' Lana said stiffly, brushing dust from the knees of her jeans, her black bell of hair falling over her face.

Mrs Mendoza went off to get on with her work, and a few moments later I heard the Dyson start up in the hallway.

I took a breath, held it, and slowly let it out, relief flooding through me as I saw Lana visibly calming down, glad we had got that awkward moment sorted out.

I pushed the sofa bed back against the wall and that was when I saw the writing.

It was carved into the skirting board where two walls met, like initials cut into the schoolboy's desk in the last century.

There was not much – almost nothing – just three letters and three numbers. But it was dug very deep, it did not look as if it was done casually or in an idle moment. Like a message in a bottle or drawing on the wall of a cave, it looked as though it meant something to whoever had made it.

I crouched down to read it.

REV 21: 1

'What is that?' Lana said.

'I don't know. Someone's initials?'

She was beside me now, tracing the trio of letters and numbers with a fingertip.

Mrs Mendoza was in the doorway, uncertain how to do her work around this strange new couple who spent their time crawling around on the floor. She looked from me to Lana.

'Should I do downstairs or upstairs?'

'Rev 21:1, Mrs Mendoza,' Lana said. 'Who was that? Was that the people who used to live here?'

Mrs Mendoza, who wore a tiny gold cross around her neck, touched it briefly and replied without hesitation. 'It's from the Bible, ma'am.'

'What?'

'Rev 21: 1. That's from the Bible, ma'am. May I?'

She came into the studio and bent down with some difficulty – lower back pain of some sort – and traced the carving with a careful fingertip.

'Yes.' She carefully stood up again. 'Book – chapter – verse. See?'

'The Bible?' I said, as if I had seen the film but never got around to reading the book.

Mrs Mendoza nodded. 'The Revelation of St John the Divine – Rev 21: 1 – chapter twenty-one, verse one,' she said. She closed her eyes and recited from memory. '"*And I saw a new heaven and a new earth: for the first heaven and the first earth were passed away; and there was no more sea.*"'

She opened her eyes, smiled pleasantly, and shifted awkwardly. The Mendoza women were all hard workers and I could see that we were keeping the middle Mrs Mendoza from her labours.

'The end of days,' I said.

'And the world to come,' Mrs Mendoza said.

Lana and I stared at her. Did she still really believe this stuff?

'People forget that part,' Mrs Mendoza said. 'Revelations is the final book of the Christian Bible, so it's very important to us. Believers like me, I mean. Those with faith. An ending, yes – but also a new beginning.'

'All of that Four-Horsemen-of-the-Apocalypse stuff,' Lana said.

Mrs Mendoza again touched the gold crucifix she wore around her neck, and I was afraid we had offended her. 'The text is actually full of hope,' she said, the mildest of rebukes. Once more she recited from memory, this time with her brown eyes wide open. '"*He will wipe away every tear from their eyes. There will be no more death or mourning or crying of pain, for the old order of things has passed away.*" One world ends but a better world begins.' She laughed apologetically. 'Although that's all a little bit later in the book.'

Then she smiled sweetly, as if she wished that we had a cheerier Biblical verse carved into the skirting board of our home.

'So shall I clean in here next, ma'am?'

'Did you work here for the old family, Mrs Mendoza?' Lana said.

'No, the Clutters had their own lady. From their life before, when they were living in Hong Kong. When the Captain was flying out of Hong Kong for Cathay Pacific. They had their lady over there and that lady – also Filipino – came back with them. I used to see them all in the Gardens. They were a normal, nice family. They looked . . .'

'What?' Lana said.

Mrs Mendoza shrugged. 'I always thought they looked *happy*.'

'And was the lady that worked for them here on the night they died?' Lana said.

Mrs Mendoza shook her head. 'Marta? She wasn't live-in.' She nodded towards the window. 'She lived on Rosa Parks. The council estate.'

'What happened to Marta?' Lana asked. 'Is she still in the village?'

'Oh, Marta's long gone, ma'am. Back to Manila, I think. Or maybe back to her province.' She sighed sadly. 'They're all long gone now, ma'am.' A beat. 'Upstairs or downstairs?'

Lana was staring thoughtfully at the skirting board.

'Downstairs, please, Mrs Mendoza,' I said.

When she had gone, I helped Lana to her feet and I held her in my arms, loving the feel of her small, strong body, desperately wanting her to see sense.

'I want you to stop tying yourself in knots,' I said. 'I want you to be happy here.'

'I'm happy if I'm with you,' she said. 'That's all I need. The rest is just bricks and mortar. Don't you know that by now?'

I pulled her close, and she rested there in my arms, and I felt her warm, familiar body pressed against mine, and some ache deep inside me seemed to ease at last.

She spoke against my chest. 'What's going to happen to the boy? The boy who was hit by Goran's van. John Carter.'

'I'm not one of his doctors. I have absolutely no idea—'

She looked up at me and something in her face stopped me.

I took a breath. 'He's got an epidural haematoma. That's bleeding and swelling inside the brain. That's why they've put him in a medically induced coma. To reduce brain activity. Even if he survives, everything will be a struggle. Speaking. Walking.' A pause. 'He's never going to have children.'

I could feel her body trembling with shock. The enormity of what had happened was kicking in hard. Lana had a far kinder, better heart than me, and it was another reason to love her.

'But Sailor's crazy about him,' she said.

I searched for something pretty to say and came up blank.

'I want to see him,' Lana said. 'At the hospital. It's right that we should go to see him, isn't it?'

'I'd like to see him too,' I said. 'Yes – it's the right thing to do.'

And some ice that had been between us began to crack. Lana took a step away from me and laughed. 'Look at the state of me!' she said, looking down at hands and jeans that were smeared with dirt from her forensic search.

We both laughed as I wiped a streak of grime from her forehead.

'Take a shower,' I said. 'Change your clothes. Then we'll go to the village and have dinner at the Italian. I'll join you for a bottle of rosé. Sound OK?'

'Sounds great.'

'OK.' I stretched my arms above my head and groaned. 'I can really tell I've been sitting down all day. I'll take a stroll while you have your shower.'

She kissed my mouth, grabbing a fistful of my hair and smiling at me as if I was still her boy.

'Come back soon. I'll be quick. And when will we go to see John?'

John? I felt a normal amount of human empathy for the ruined young man. But he would never be *John* to me.

'Tomorrow,' I said. 'After work. We'll see him together. I promise.'

I could hear the shower running as I went downstairs and grabbed my bag where I had dropped it in the hallway. Mrs Mendoza looked up at me from the kitchen and I gave her a thumbs up by way of apology and thanks, and she grinned with relief.

I walked out of the Gardens.

There was a country lane directly opposite the entrance, a former cart track, now a winding dirt road flanked by tall elm trees that led into real countryside with thick woods on one side and farmland on the other. At this time of day you might expect to see a dog walker or jogger but now there was no one and I was alone as the lane seemed to dip and the pale green light darken as it wound deeper into woodland.

There was a storm drain at the foot of a small rise and it was here that I paused and took the CCTV hard drive from my bag. It was the size of an old video tape but the weight of a brick.

I dropped it down the storm drain, hearing the soft splash of water as it fell into the darkness.

19

Friday, 11 September

John Carter was unrecognisable.

Lana gasped as we stared through the window of the Intensive Care Unit. A profusion of tubes, wires and cables seemed to snake into every part of his body. His arm, his mouth, his neck. A light blue smock was placed on top of him, but for some reason he was not actually wearing it and his shoulders were bare. There was a bandage around his skull and his two closed eyes were blackened with bruises. A thick light blue tube was taped to the side of his mouth and slid down his throat. Machines surrounded and engulfed him. I had seen hundreds – no, thousands – of patients in ICUs but it was always more of a shock when it was someone you knew.

On one side of his bed was a woman who could only be his mother. Mary Carter was not yet forty, no doubt considered attractive once, but she looked older with her long hair and no make-up and shapeless work clothes.

She held the boy's hands in her own hands in a gesture that looked exactly like a prayer.

And on the other side of the bed was Sailor.

Her school things were scattered behind the plastic chair she had pulled to the bedside. Her SAS-sized rucksack stuffed with books. Her sports bag with a hockey stick protruding. And the hard cherry-red case that contained her cello.

'Who are you then?'

We turned to look at four women cradling what looked like the entire contents of a vending machine.

One of them was around the age of the woman keeping watch at John Carter's bedside, perhaps Mary Carter's sister, and another was much older, an ancient crone whose advanced age was only emphasised by the modish tattoos on her beefy forearms. The other two were young, late teens or early twenties, clingy tops and miniskirts and heels, dressed more for a night on the town rather than a visit to a hospital's ICU.

All four of them looked at us with real venom in their eyes, as if they could smell where we came from.

And then they flew at us.

The two young women slapped at my head with wild inexpert swings, but the older women were much more adept, the forty-something catching my chin with a neat left hook while the old crone punched me full in the mouth. I reeled backwards, tasting the silver of her multiple rings, catching sight of the two younger women slapping at Lana.

And then Sailor was there.

'Stop it, stop it! He's the *doctor*! He's Doctor Wade, the one who *saved* Johnny!'

Lana rushed to my arms and I held her, feeling the metallic taste of blood in my mouth where Granny had slugged me. The women considered us with sullen calm.

'Should have told us, shouldn't they?' Granny said defensively, inspecting her knuckles where my front teeth had grazed her skin.

When they had come touting for work in the Gardens, John Carter's family had seemed like a tribe ruled by men. But it was not the same at the hospital. At the hospital it was the men who killed time in the cavernous lobby and smoked their endless cigarettes in the area immediately outside the great glass doors.

I had recognised some of them from when they came to the Gardens with their special offers for this week only, but of course they stared straight through me, just another middle-class local walking quickly by, trying to avoid making eye contact with their kind as the reception desk gave us directions to the Critical Care Unit. No, at the hospital the men of the family kicked their heels on the periphery while the women kept watch over John Carter.

More women joined us, all apparently returning from a mammoth vending machine run. There were women and girls everywhere for John Carter. Older women, who looked like aunts, some of them red-eyed with crying, and younger women, teenagers who wore scant clothes even in the autumnal chill. They looked at us, and it was as if they understood exactly where we had come from but were giving us a pass, because of what I had done, and they said nothing, and they parted to let us look through the glass.

The vicious old dear who had punched me in the mouth indicated the bunch of flowers I had forgotten was still in my hand.

'You can go in if you want,' she said.

Inside, the air was thick with electronic sounds. Little red lights everywhere monitoring heart rate, blood pressure and other bodily functions. But the confusion of wires and cables made more sense to me in here and I could recognise exactly what they were doing to the patient to keep him clinging to life. A feeding tube up his nose. IV lines in his arm. That thick blue pump in his mouth was keeping him breathing. A thin catheter wound into his bladder, draining urine. But John Carter was still more dead than alive.

Sailor and the woman were staring at me.

I saw that Sailor held the Newsboy flat cap that the boy had worn, and her thumb and index fingers moved around its brim as if it was rosary beads.

'My neighbours,' Sailor said, looking at the woman, as if confirming that our presence was permitted. 'Lana and Roman. The doctor who saved John.'

The woman rose. I saw the strength in her and felt a flash of concern, but she reached out and took our flowers.

'Thank you,' she said. She touched Lana's arm. 'Both of you. I'm Mary Carter. John's mother.'

Then she resumed her bedside vigil.

Lana was staring at Sailor, as if dumbfounded by her presence.

'John doesn't understand what's happening,' Sailor said, by way of explanation. 'Before they put him in a coma, he stared at us as if he couldn't understand why all his relatives were standing around the bed. He might have to have surgery to reduce the pressure on his brain.'

I nodded. That seemed like the inevitable last shot. I understood the thinking of his doctors, but I did not know what to say to offer comfort or hope or explanation.

'Do you need a lift, Sailor?' I said, my voice sounding strange to myself. 'We can give you a lift if you need one. When you go home.'

Lana and I had both wanted to come to see John Carter but now I found I wanted to escape as soon as I could. In the end, there is no point in being at a hospital if you are neither one of the sick or one of the healers. All you can do is make meaningless trips to the vending machine or make small talk. And that's what we were doing.

'Don't you have a cello lesson later, Sailor?' Lana said.

Mary Carter did not look up.

'Cello's cancelled today,' she said.

20

Sunday, 13 September

I tossed and turned in my bed that night as the foxes screamed at each other, their cries unearthly echoes at the bottom of the empty swimming pool. I must have slept at some point because suddenly it was light, and the foxes were gone, and I was waking up to the sound of the guns.

You heard them every day now, the strange staccato rhythm of massed shotguns suddenly erupting all at once, always followed by the stuttering sound of a solitary one or two popping close behind, as if they were trying to catch up with the rest. Most of the guns were miles away, but the explosive, weirdly drawn-out sound they made always seemed much too close, even when they were in the next county.

I tried to remember what Ben had told me. Grouse were from August to December. Partridge from September to February. Pheasant from October to February.

So from now on the early-morning wake-up calls from the guns would intensify as we approached the peak of the shooting season. I lay there listening to the dead silence that always followed the sound of the guns, Lana moaning in her uneasy sleep beside me, and I became aware of the sound of running water.

As Lana slept on, I slipped out of bed and went to her private alcove at the back of the house. Ben's boy Oscar was in the back garden, staring into the swimming pool as it began to fill with water. A green hosepipe snaked into the pool and it twitched with life as water began to cover the cracked tiles at the bottom.

Oscar was sitting by the poolside when I came into the garden, the hosepipe held loosely in one hand as he read the crumpled postcard he held in the other.

The water in the pool had just about covered the cracked tiles.

'How's it going, Oscar?'

He brushed his long hair from his eyes and his thin undernourished face squinted up at me.

'Vince asked me to watch the water. It takes twenty-four hours to fill her up and if the water stops then it leaves a mark on the plaster. And that's no good, so you have to do the filling all at once.'

'Makes sense,' I said, sitting down beside him, our legs swinging far above the water at the bottom of the pool. 'You're a big help to Vince.'

Oscar tapped his chin with a bent corner of his postcard. 'I might come and help him tomorrow. If he needs me.'

'No school tomorrow?'

He grimaced. 'I've been having a bit of a stomach-ache.'

He was a terrible liar.

'How's school going?'

'Fine.'

'Anyone bullying you?'

His pale face flushed with anger and embarrassment. 'Nobody bullies me,' he said furiously. Then he was suddenly calm. 'You don't have to pay me or anything for helping Vince, if that is what you're worried about.'

I smiled. 'That's not what I'm worried about.'

We watched the water for a while and then I nodded at the postcard he was clutching by his side.

'Did you hear from your mum?'

He nodded, hesitated for a moment and then shyly showed it to me – a glossy image of fireworks exploding around the London Eye on New Year's Eve, the postcard already bent and dog-eared from being carried around.

'You can read it if you want,' he said, all studied nonchalance.

'Thank you.'

The message from his mother was short and businesslike, a brief homily to be a good boy and work hard, printed in block letters, as if the writer was unused to writing without a keyboard, signed off with the stilted admonition *love your mother* which seemed part greeting and part command.

'Do you think man can live on Mars?' he said.

'I never really thought about it.'

He grinned slyly. 'Some people think that Mars is our back-up planet. They think that when it all hits the fan on Earth, we can just take off to Mars! But it's a fantasy! You know why?'

I shook my head.

'*Because children can't grow up on Mars!*' he said, his grin growing wider. 'The high radiation, the lack of sunlight and subterranean existence – none of that is good news for children. It would either kill them or drive them *insane*.' He carefully adjusted the hosepipe. A light breeze blew through the garden and wildflowers skittered across the surface of the shallow water that now covered the pool. 'But that's not the worst of it. What matters most is the lack of gravity on Mars. The gravity on Mars is about a third of what it is on Earth – did you know that?

'I don't think I did.'

What a strange boy he was, always alone if he wasn't with Vince or his father. But I liked him.

'Children's bones develop in response to gravity,' he was saying. 'That wouldn't happen if they were living underground. The human race wouldn't survive the first generation born on Mars. And it's the lack of gravity that would kill us. You know what that means?'

I shook my head. 'No.'

'This planet is all we've got,' Oscar said.

Lana came into the garden cradling a coffee cup. She ruffled Oscar's hair and laughed as he recoiled, blushing hotly.

'We should fix the pool before we fill it again,' she told me.

'But I can't sleep with those foxes at it all night long. The water will keep them away. Unless they want to mate under water.'

Lana looked doubtful. I changed the subject.

'Oscar heard from his mum,' I said.

I looked at him, and he lifted his chin, giving me permission to show the postcard I was holding to Lana. She read it and smiled at him.

'I love postcards,' she said.

Vince came into the garden, and I got a strong blast of that eau de Vince, his unique combination of sweat and weed.

'Vince, we don't want the pool topped up any more,' Lana said. 'We want the leak repaired.'

'Dr Wade asked me to fill it,' he said gruffly. 'To keep out them foxes.'

Vince looked at me for arbitration, but I just grinned and shrugged.

'Vince?'

He turned to look at Lana.

'Please look at me and not my husband. I'm telling you the pool doesn't need filling. It needs *fixing*. There's something wrong with it.'

'But—'

'Drain it, Vince,' she said, frowning at the dog-eared postcard she held in her hand. 'Drain it or we'll get someone else to do it.'

On Sunday afternoon Lana and I drove to the next village.

This neighbouring village was prettier, smaller and far more popular with tourists than our own. Our village was lovely, but it was unmistakably a place where people lived and worked, whereas the village next door was achingly beautiful, the yellow stone façades of the old town totally untouched by modern times. Like our village, there was a river running through it, as clear and sparkling as a mountain stream, but there were no spotty schoolkids on the village green, no modern cafés with complicated coffee to spoil the view. This was the former wool town as ye olde theme park and here it was easier to buy a cream tea than a sliced loaf and a Lottery ticket.

The downside was that it attracted coachloads of tourists in the way our village simply did not.

From Beijing to Birmingham, they poured in and sucked on their ice creams as they glided in rowing boats down the glistening river, laughing as they ducked their heads under the five arched bridges, shaded by weeping willows that dipped their branches into the water.

It still felt like high summer here.

At the edge of the old town, far away from the main tourist drag, there was a tiny but high-end camera shop run by some old hippy who had fled here on some back-to-nature trip after taking too many drugs back in the Eighties. The shop was why we had come.

The old hippy knew his stuff and he talked Lana through mirrorless cameras, a leap forward in technology that had happened after her retirement.

'They're small,' she smiled, her hands full of the Sony A7R IV.

'They're really geared towards the professional photographer,' the old hippy said.

Lana's face froze. 'I *am* a professional photographer,' she said.

'Right on, man,' the hippy said, looking sorry for himself.

I looked away, out to the street, at the scattering of tourists who had wandered off the main drag and were strolling by the river in the afternoon sunshine.

And then I saw a familiar face.

'It's Ben,' I said.

Ben Cave came out of a newsagent on the other side of the river, and stood there for a moment, his thoughtful, elaborately scarred face frowning at the slow-moving tourists.

'Thanks,' Lana said curtly to the old hippy, handing him back the camera and heading for the door.

I called out to Ben, but he ducked his head and seemed to hurry on, giving no sign that he had heard me. I stared after him for a moment and then Lana and I crossed the bridge and went into the newsagents he had just left. I bought two Magnums while Lana wandered the shop. There was an old-fashioned postcard carousel just inside the door and she slowly turned it around. I joined her with our Magnums.

The carousel was mostly what you would expect – postcards of the photogenic Oxfordshire hamlets, the grand stately homes, the honey-stone houses and green hills and clean rivers calling you to a slower, better, more beautiful life. But there were also images from further afield, aimed at the coachloads from the People's Republic of China. The façade of Buckingham Palace; Harry and Meghan on their wedding day; the Queen on horseback in a red military uniform, saluting; William and Kate and the children. You could tell these images were slipping into history because some of the postcards were curling a little at the edges and gathering a thin film of dust from standing too long on the carousel.

'Look,' Lana said.

It was a postcard of the London Eye on New Year's Eve, lit up with a sky ablaze in a riot of fireworks. And I knew that I had seen exactly this shot of the London Eye before.

Because it was the same postcard that Oscar had received from his runaway mother.

'It's the same shot, isn't it?' Lana said.

'I think so.'

She laughed with disbelief. 'It's *exactly* the same shot, Roman.'

'So what?'

She shook her head with disbelief. 'Didn't you see what was wrong with Oscar's postcard?'

'Wrong with it? What was wrong with it?'

'Are you really telling me that you couldn't see it?'

'The language was a bit stilted, I guess.'

She gasped with exasperation. I was still holding our two Magnums.

'I'm not talking about semantics, Roman.'

She walked out of the shop and I followed her. I held out her Magnum and she didn't notice.

'The picture on the front was of London,' she said, her eyes gleaming with a triumph that unnerved me. 'But the *postmark* was local. The *postmark* was from here.'

'Sorry, but I don't understand what you think you've discovered.'

'What I *think* I've discovered?'

She shook her head, her black bob swishing, as if she could not believe me.

'You think I imagine these things, don't you? You think they're all in my head.'

'Lana,' I said. 'Please – just calm down and have an ice cream.'

'Don't tell me to calm down! Don't tell me to relax and don't tell me to get a grip. I'm not your *patient*, OK,

Roman? I'm your wife. And I don't feel like a bloody ice cream.'

We glared at each other as the tourists ambled by, taking their selfies in front of the golden architecture and sucking on their Cornettos, glancing at us with curiosity, the man and wife who could not count their blessings and enjoy an ice cream even on a sunny Sunday afternoon in a place that looked a lot like paradise.

'Juno Cave,' she said. 'Oscar's mother. She's meant to be in London shacked up with some Brazilian stud, isn't she? And it's a lie. She's *here*. She's nearby. And – I don't know – maybe she's scared to come home. Do you know what they're like, Roman? Our respectable neighbours? Do you have any idea of the way that Guy treats Willow?'

'What are you saying?'

'Wherever that boy's mother is, she's not far away,' Lana said, wild-eyed and finally reaching for her Magnum. 'Someone's telling lies.'

21

Monday, 14 September

It is the start of the working week, and I am about to have a panic attack in the supermarket.

I am at the back of the queue and I can feel it coming.

It happens when I feel trapped – stuck on a tube train paused for too long between stations, or inside a lift that grinds to a halt between floors and – yes! – stranded at the back of a queue that does not appear to be moving, with the exit door and fresh air and freedom so far away.

That's when they begin.

And this is the way they always, always feel.

I lick my lips and look at the back of the heads in front of me.

And here it comes now. A distant dread that builds slowly and then very, very quickly, the symptoms numbingly familiar– the dry-as-sand mouth, the beating drumbeat of my heart, the sudden inability to breathe, and the palpable terror that has no discernible cause or cure. And then it is on me, and I feel like my heart wants to explode out of my chest, I feel certain that I will die here today at the back of the supermarket queue with a bottle of still water and a banana and plastic-wrapped New York deli sandwich in my sweaty hands. And I feel like weeping with frustration because I had thought – believed, prayed, hoped – that this feeling was behind me now.

This is the first attack I have had out here in our new life, and I see how pathetically naïve I was to believe it was something I had left behind me in the city.

And there's that feeling of – what to do?

Here are the practicalities of a panic attack, the terrible logistics, the ugly choices that must be made – *right now*. Do I stay where I am and risk passing out? Not a good look for the new doctor in town, flaked out on the floor of the supermarket still gripping his banana. Or just run – drop everything, or better still toss the water and sandwich and fruit on an unoccupied till and make a break for the door, and sunlight, and open spaces, and freedom.

But that's not a good look either.

So I do what I have done in the past. What I always do. I do nothing. I endure the unendurable. And the terror manifests itself in sweat that makes my shirt stick to my body, and a sick bile that rises in my throat, and my breath coming in short gasps so comically dog-like and desperate that the young woman standing in front of me half turns to see if she is standing in front of some sort of weirdo.

Then I see him.

Standing on the street, the village green gloriously empty behind him, staring through the glass straight at me and also perhaps straight through me.

Professor Alan Hall.

He is not in the pristine sports gear that I usually see him wearing when he is out and about. He is dressed surprisingly formally, in the tweed jacket, corduroy trousers and shirt and tie combo that he probably taught in.

And he holds my gaze and somehow I find that it helps, because the queue is slowly but suddenly moving, and I know I can do this thing – I can pay for my lunch without dying or disgracing myself or fainting. And the queue is moving forward a bit faster now, and we never break eye contact, not once, and then I am standing in front of him on the street and I realise how small he is, how he is a part of that mid-twentieth-century generation who were physically smaller than we are today, but who were somehow so impressive that you never noticed.

'Magda,' he said. 'My wife. She's missing.'

There was already a search party out looking for Magda.

Goran was cruising the main streets of the village in his van. All three Mendoza women were out and about, roaming the backstreets on foot. Ben Cave and Oscar were in their car, scouting the country lanes.

'Your help would be invaluable,' Professor Hall said.

'Of course,' I said.

He checked his phone for alerts from his search party, and he looked at me with the desperation that I had seen in other spouses in his situation.

It is hard to watch someone you love losing themselves.

'Magda talks increasingly about seeing her two older sisters,' he said, trying to keep the tone light.

We stared at each other for a moment and then lifted our heads at the sound of a train in the distance.

'Do they live nearby?'

'They died in 1945.'

We found her at the railway station, a tiny woman dressed in what my grandmother would have called her Sunday best, a smart coat and handbag like the Queen, staring thoughtfully at the bulletin board for a train that was never going to pull into the station.

I was overwhelmed by the tenderness Professor Hall showed her.

'My dear, where on earth are you off to? Come now. Let's go home, shall we?'

Magda responded with meek acceptance, and he led her away, his thumbs flying on his phone.

By the time we reached the village green, the entire search party had gathered to greet us. Ben and Oscar.

Goran in his van. Three generations of Mendoza women. And as they all stared with real concern at the old lady clutching her husband's arm, it was impossible to tell apart the hired help and the neighbours.

'You silly old thing,' the oldest Mrs Mendoza gently scolded Magda. 'We were all worried about you. Why do you go off wandering around like that?'

'I don't remember,' said Magda.

There was a moment of silence.

And then, taking our cue from her husband, we all had a good old laugh about that.

Ben drove us back to the big house.

As Mrs Mendoza was helping Magda inside, Professor Hall gave me a quietly pleading look.

'Would you mind coming inside?'

'Not at all.'

We watched Magda and Mrs Mendoza carefully ascending the stairs, and then I followed Professor Hall to the rear of the house where the two-storey-high glass wall looked out over the garden and the miles of countryside behind. The Sunshine Room.

He silently poured us two glasses of sherry. I took it for granted that he wanted to talk about his wife, about where she was now and what was likely to happen next. I already felt close enough to him to not need any explanation.

'Isn't it around a year since Dr Cox's diagnosis of Alzheimer's?' I asked.

He sipped his sherry. 'Less. Feels like longer.'

'As you know, and as I am sure Dr Cox told you, Alzheimer's is like a road with a slow downward slope. And the first thing to go is memory. But sometimes the road rises a little bit, and sometimes it turns back on itself. It's never a straight road. You must know that Dr Hall will have good days and bad days.'

He shook his head.

'They are all bad days now,' he said. 'But I wasn't talking about my wife. As much as any layman can, I understand what is happening to Magda. I have made myself an expert on cognitive decline. I understand that it is a slowly progressing disease, and death usually happens four to ten years after initial diagnosis, but patients can live for twenty years.'

He filled up my glass. I found I had bolted it down in one gulp.

'I meant *you*,' he said.

'Me?'

'Yes – what was wrong with you? I was watching you for a long time in that supermarket – far longer than you were aware. What's wrong, Roman?'

I stared at him, dumbfounded. I raised my glass but did not drink from it.

And then I told him.

I told him about the night it happened.

The night they came into our home.

The feelings it left behind. The damage – mental and physical.

The way a crime – that kind of crime, the kind of crime that strikes at everything that should be safe and untouchable – is never truly over.

The act echoes through lives, leaves scars you can't see, and wounds that still ache even when they heal.

I told him the panic attacks had started after that night.

I hoped they would end when we moved out to our new life.

I was wrong.

They made you feel that you were going to die but that wasn't the worst of it. 'The worse thing is that they are embarrassing,' I said, trying to make light of them, laughing it off, grinning with tears in my eyes, trying not to spill my sherry.

He did not smile back.

'That's why Lana and I are out here,' I said. 'We are starting over. New life. Leaving the past behind. Safe and sound and home and dry at last. When I put it like that, it sounds insane.'

He shook his head, although I could not tell if it was in sympathy or disagreement.

I stared at the spectacular view. The distant hills glittered with autumnal gold in the soft morning sunshine, and I knew I would remember the way they looked now on the day that I died.

I could hear Mrs Mendoza murmuring gently to Magda in the room above.

'Protecting those you love,' Professor Hall said. 'Being ready to do anything to stop them ever being hurt. These are the most natural instincts in the world, Roman.' He watched me as I stared at the miles of Oxfordshire fields beyond that wall made of glass. 'Grief is so personal, and yet we all have our tragedies, our traumas. *How small and selfish is sorrow. But it bangs one about until one is senseless.* Do you know that quote?'

And I tore my eyes from the view and met his gaze.

He was looking at me in a way that no one had looked at me for a long time.

Not the police who came on that night, and not the doctors and nurses who treated us for our injuries. Even Lana never looked at me the way that smartly dressed, slightly built old man looked at me.

He looked at me as if he understood.

22

Tuesday, 15 September

In the small hours I was jolted from sleep by the foxes howling at the bottom of our drained swimming pool. I was almost used to it by now.

I lay there listening to their cries, that strange sound that seems to carry both every torment of the flesh and the best feeling in the world, amplified and twisted by the tiled sides of the pool.

'You hear them?' I asked Lana, rolling over.

But Lana's side of the bed was empty.

I listened to the screams in the back garden and waited for the tell-tale sounds of my wife moving through the house in the middle of the night, anticipating the sound of a tap running in the upstairs bathroom, or a fridge door being opened down in the kitchen, and a cork being pulled out of the inevitable bottle of rosé, and finally the clink of a glass, like a punchline.

But tonight there was nothing, only the shrieks of the foxes in the back garden.

Lana was not in the house.

I jumped up and slipped out of bed and walked quickly to her private little alcove at the back of the house, overlooking the back garden. It was empty. Then I saw her out in the garden. She was standing by the drained pool in just her T-shirt and pants, barefoot, a heartbreakingly slight figure staring down at the foxes, her head tilted down, the lush black hair falling forward across her face, her thin limbs washed by moonlight.

I felt a burst of panic, afraid of what these wild animals might do to her if they felt threatened. Did foxes attack if they were cornered? Surely any frightened animal would. But Lana stood there as if she had no fear. And I remembered the night I saw her for the first time at a soup kitchen at a homeless hostel in the middle of the night. She was not afraid then, I recalled.

And she should have been.

It was easy for me and my fellow medical students to move among the homeless, wearing our shiny new blue scrubs like a badge of honour, doing what we could to ease the burden of men and women who had nothing. The homeless were glad to see us in our blue scrubs, always, all of them, even though they covered the gamut of humanity – from those whose lives had been wrecked by addiction to those whose lives had been wrecked by bad luck, from young kids who had fled abusive families to the old men and women who should have been in a home with supervised care, if we still lived in a world where such places existed. We were idealistic baby doctors, and we genuinely wanted to do some good among the desperate, but there was no denying that it tickled our egos to be treated like heroes in that blighted place. It wasn't like that for Lana with her camera in her hands.

She seemed so young, her Japanese-like hair much longer in those days, in tight white jeans and a beat-up old leather jacket, heels that were gloriously impractical in that place, but that she wore to make her taller. The junior doctors all noted her presence but nobody else wanted to have a photographer wandering that refuge for the homeless, and nobody treated her like a hero. Some – the drunk, the mad, the instinctively violent – were outwardly hostile. Nobody wanted their photograph taken. She charmed the ones she could, she moved away from the ones who swore at her.

But she never backed down. She was brave and that was when I think I fell in love with her. She got her shot. And she got me too.

She had me before we even had our first shy conversation at three in the morning over scalding black coffee. She had me for life when I saw her bravery. And it was more than raw courage. There was a wildness in her, and it is the kind of wildness that you only ever see in the lucky souls who come from loving, stable, unbroken homes, the reckless ones who can dance on any tightrope because they believe there is always a safety net.

I loved the wildness in Lana, then and now and forever. I loved her brave, reckless heart. I admired, envied and needed it. And it terrified me.

I tapped on the window. She didn't hear me. I tapped harder.

Suddenly the foxes pulled violently away from each other.

They were watching Lana as she climbed down the ladder into the empty pool, her bare legs white in the moonlight.

I went back to the bedroom and pulled on a pair of jeans. The clock by my bedside said just after 4 a.m.; I cursed Lana and this madness, and I wondered if there was an almost-empty bottle of Léoube sitting on the kitchen island.

By the time I came out of the French doors, the foxes were disappearing into the bushes at the back of the garden.

And Lana was on her hands and knees in the middle of the empty swimming pool.

'Lana?'

No response.

She was staring at the bottom of the pool. The tiles all looked some years past their best but those in the centre were very badly cracked. I stared at an almost imperceptible dip in the middle of the pool, as though it had partially collapsed.

No wonder the water kept leaking.

And then Lana began tearing at the tiles in the middle of the pool, clawing at them with her fingers.

'What the hell are you doing, Lana?'

'Sandy was right,' she said, not turning around. 'Those foxes – they're not fighting and they're not mating.' Finally she turned to look at me. 'They're *digging*, Roman.'

She began to pull up the damaged tiles with her hands. Fragments came away easily at first but then most of them stayed stubbornly in place.

She slapped them in frustration.

'Please come back to bed, Lana.'

She was not listening to me. I climbed down the ladder into the empty pool and she stood up, still staring down at the shattered tiles in the damaged centre.

'Please, Lana,' I said, touching her arm, her skin so cold.

She looked at me and smiled.

'I know what I need,' she said.

She climbed out of the pool and I could hear but not see her rifling around in the old garden hutch, searching among the gardening tools and the ancient paint tins and the insect killer until she found what she was looking for.

She came back and as she climbed down the ladder I looked up at the house of our neighbours, their windows dark and silent, peacefully oblivious to this insanity.

And even now there was still a part of me that believed she would allow me to take her back to our warm bed, where we could hold each other and make slow love and reassure each other that everything was going to be all right.

Then I saw she was holding a claw hammer, its silver steel head dappled with rust.

'This should do the trick,' she said.

She went to the centre of the pool and got on her knees.

Then she brought the claw hammer down on the cracked tiles.

They shattered like a smashed mirror, suddenly split by a spider's web of damage. It was loud, very loud in that still dark hour before dawn, and I looked back at the sleeping house next door, certain that a bedroom light would suddenly come on, feeling sure that Willow and Guy must have heard.

But nobody stirred.

We were all alone at the end of the night as I watched my wife destroying swimming pool tiles with a rusty claw hammer.

'Lana!'

She was scaring me now, as though she had reached a place that she would never come back from, and I tried to pull her to her feet, but she shoved me away with an animal snarl, and with a strength that I did not know she possessed.

'What exactly are you looking for, Lana?

'I'm looking for *Juno*. I'm looking for Oscar's mother.'

'This is crazy! Oscar's mum is in London!'

'Those foxes are not mating or fighting – they're *digging*. And Juno Cave is not in London with some Brazilian stud – she's *here*.'

She hit the tiles again as hard as she could, and then again, and on and on until her arm was aching and I could see the sweat shining on her face and clinging to her T-shirt, and the tiles were smashed to pieces, ruined so completely that you could see the dark soil beneath them. Then she turned the hammer around and began to dig with the claw, the chunks of wet dirt coming up easily at first, and then hitting a harder, deeper layer as she went down a few inches.

But she kept going, tearing with the claw, until she seemed to break through to another level again, where the earth fell away.

She threw the claw hammer to one side, the tool skittering across the scattered fragments of tiles, and then she reached down, all the way to her shoulder.

'I found it,' she said, more to herself than me. 'I knew it was here. I *knew* it.'

'You didn't find that hole, Lana. You dug it.'

'It's not a hole, Roman.' A moment's silence. 'It's a grave.'

And then, with something hard and sick rising inside me, I watched as she slowly began to pull them out, the thin shards of bone, more yellow than white in the light of the harvest moon.

She placed them carefully by her side.

And there were more, there were always more, and the pile of bones by her side was growing as Lana smiled to herself with grim satisfaction.

'Lana,' I said.

It sounded like a word of warning, soft as a prayer.

Then we both looked up at the house next door as a bedroom light came on.

PART THREE
LANA

23

We faced each other across the kitchen island.

And Roman smiled at me.

But for once in my life, his smile did not work on me, and it did not make me melt, and it did not make me weaken.

The clock on the wall was clicking down to dawn, although there was still that bright moonlight outside.

Roman scratched inside his pyjamas top and yawned, as if we had all the time in the world, as if this was all just a bad dream, as if my bare feet and filthy, bloody hands were not covered with mud and muck from the bottom of the empty swimming pool.

As if there was not a long thin shard of bone resting on the kitchen island between us.

'I'm going to the police, Roman. And don't try to stop me.'

'May I ask you a question, Lana?'

His voice totally calm. That professional the-doctor-will-see-you-now tone. The voice they use to calm the hysterical, to give sweet balm to the newly bereaved, to tell you that the tumour has grown and you have had your time, sorry.

'Go ahead,' I said, trying to sound as cool as him, though I was not even close.

He raised his chin, indicating the fragment of bone. 'What exactly do you think you've found?'

'Isn't it bloody obvious?'

'Not to me.'

We both stared at the bone I had carried into the house.

It was perhaps ten inches long, more yellow than white under the kitchen lights, and it looked small, almost insubstantial lying there, just a random piece of garbage, like something you saw on the street when the foxes had been feasting on the recycling bins. The bone had definitely been more impressive under the glare of the harvest moon. But there was still something terrible about it, there was still something about it that twisted your guts, and I knew with total certainty that this was something that was never meant to be found.

'Somebody was buried under that pool, Roman.'

There was something wrong with my breathing. I touched my chest. My heart felt all wrong.

Roman looked unconvinced. He came around the kitchen island, sat down beside me, took my hand, flashed his baby blues from under his thick black eyelashes.

I could feel it working on me. That old Roman magic.

Come back to bed, angel.

But I knew what I had found. 'And I think ...'

He was politely waiting. I licked my lips.

The thought was too horrible to say aloud.

I took a breath and exhaled the words that were stuck in my throat, stuck in my heart. 'And I think it is Oscar's mother. I think it's Juno Cave.'

Roman nodded, as if his interest had finally been piqued, as if this was intriguing dinner table chit-chat. His face was impassive. Not disinterested but a long way from shocked. Mildly curious, at best.

'But – forgive me – isn't Juno Cave in London?'

His bedside manner was at its most exquisite. His voice was so calm, so soothing and so reasonable that I wanted to scream in his face.

'Why does she never visit?' I said. 'Whatever she thinks of Ben, whatever problems they may have had, why doesn't she ever see her son? Why doesn't she see Oscar? All parents love their children, don't they?'

He laughed out loud. A nasty edge to it. He was pulling rank on me, playing the doctor who had seen things that my empty, arty, quasi-bohemian head could never imagine.

'Do you have any idea of how naïve you sound? I understood that this woman – Juno Cave – fell in love with her – what? – personal trainer?' he said. 'Some sex-bomb yoga teacher or Pilates stud? As I had it explained to me by more than one of our neighbours, the reason young Oscar does not see his mother is because she's too busy with her new life. It's very sad, but – believe me, Lana – it happens all the time. It's a cliché – the absent parent too preoccupied with their exciting new partner to do any dull parenting chores in the life he – or indeed she – left behind. And as for your question about all parents loving their children – if only!'

I sucked in air to calm my pounding heart. It didn't work. 'Or maybe Oscar doesn't see his mother because she's buried in our back garden.'

Roman raised a wry eyebrow.

'And Oscar *does* hear from her,' I continued. 'That's the thing. The boy gets a postcard once a month from London. But I don't think his mother sends them. I think *Ben* sends them.'

'You never even met the woman!'

'I have proof.'

'Proof?'

'Look.'

My jacket was on the back of a chair he was sitting on and he edged forward politely as I rifled inside the pocket and took out the postcard of the London Eye I had purchased in the neighbouring village.

I placed it before him and he stared at the image of the London Eye garlanded in fireworks and then looked at the back, his mouth twisting with distaste when he saw that it was totally blank.

'This your evidence of foul play? Really, Lana? A blank postcard?' He shook his handsome head. Then he was suddenly disgusted. 'Just look at you.'

It was true that I was in a bit of a state. My knees and hands were smeared and sticky with oily dirt. There was something wrong with one of my fingernails where a corner had been torn off by my digging and now it would not stop bleeding. But the state of me seemed beside the point.

'This is the same postcard as the one Oscar received from his mother. *Exactly* the same shot! Listen to me, Roman! Oscar gets regular postcards, all right, allegedly from his mother in London.'

He snorted. 'Allegedly. I love the allegedly!'

I ploughed on. 'But the postmark – or at least the postmark of the postcard I saw, the one he showed me – the one he showed *us* – wasn't from London. It was from the next village. How do you explain that? Her son is here! She's apparently just down the road! Almost next door! So why do we never see her?'

'Maybe she's not the mothering kind, Lana. Maybe she's in the neighbourhood but she's afraid of Ben.'

'But why should she be afraid of Ben?'

Roman placed his fingertips on his lips, stifling a yawn. 'Because she cheated on him? Because she left him for some gym bunny?' He raised his hands in mock surrender. 'I would not speculate. But you know what Tucker told me? Juno's in Notting Hill living in a studio flat with a Brazilian guy in his twenties who is giving her the best sex of her life – and making her feel *wanted* again. Sorry, but that sounds entirely plausible to me. And where do *you* think she is?'

My eyes drifted to the back garden. 'I think she's buried under our swimming pool.'

'I prefer Tucker's theory. Your theory just sounds a little ...'

'Insane? Don't fucking patronise me!'

'I was going to say *thin*. It all sounds a little *thin*, Lana. Can you hear yourself? Look, we've both been under a lot of stress. After what happened to us ...'

'I'm not crazy, Roman.'

'I'm not saying you're crazy. I'm just saying you're stressed. We both are, God knows. And I'm saying you're mistaken. You're upset. Oh, Lana.'

He got up and tried to take me in his arms, but I shook him off.

'No.'

I pulled further away from him.

He jabbed an authoritative finger at the bone.

'This – I can tell you right now – this is an animal bone.'

'They're not animal bones! Why would animal bones be buried that deep? We have to go to the police!'

But there it was in some secret chamber of my mind – the first moment of doubt. I stared at the bone on the kitchen island and wondered if the police would be as instantly dismissive as Roman. And what then?

My husband filled me in.

'If you go to the police about this then you are going to embarrass yourself, and me, and you will cause an enormous amount of genuine distress among our neighbours. You're going to make it very difficult for us to carry on living here.' He threw up his arms. 'But maybe that's exactly what you want. Maybe that's your secret plan. Is that your secret plan, darling?'

'Don't say *darling* to me like that.'

He laughed. 'Like what?'

'As if you don't mean it. As if *darling* is an insult. And I don't have a plan. But people *died* in this house, didn't they?'

'Yes, they did. But you know what, Lana? People have died in most houses.'

'Died like the Clutters?'

'Perhaps not. I grant you that. But in any house of any age in this country, a large number of people have fallen off their perch.'

'And who killed them, Roman? Who killed the Clutters?'

He stifled another yawn, covered his mouth with his hand and looked at the clock. His voice sounded very tired. 'Excuse me. You know who killed them.'

I shook my head. 'No,' I said. 'I don't know, Roman. Not really. But I know that Bill Clutter – that father, that husband, that man – he didn't do it.'

'And you know this – how?'

'Because he was a happy man. A *decent* man. A *good* man. A loving father, a loyal husband. Everybody says.'

'Jesus, Lana – I've seen the poor guy's medical records, OK? He was depressive, stressed, and good old Dr Cox had him on the kind of happy pills that make you lose your mind. I don't doubt Bill Clutter's essential decency, but he was under enormous emotional – and financial – pressure. And in the end – he cracked. As many men do. Do you know the suicide rate in this country among middle-aged men? It's off the scale!'

'Don't play the doctor's card. The all-seeing, all-wise, I've-seen-things-you-little-people-wouldn't-believe bullshit. Don't do that, Roman. Stop pretending you're God for five minutes of your life, will you?'

'And stop pretending that this is about anything apart from you wanting to leave this house. Oh, Lana – exactly what do you think is going on here? Explain it to me – who killed the Clutters if it wasn't the mad, over-medicated old dad? What has happened to Juno Cave if she's not being fucked blind by some Brazilian stud muffin in Notting Hill?'

'I don't know. How could I know? All I know is that there are bones in our garden.'

'Animal bones.'

'Look at what they did to that boy.'

'To John Carter? That burglar? Is that who you mean?'

'Yes – they ran him down like he was less than nothing.'

'*They* didn't do it. *They* didn't do anything. Our security guard did it when he was responding to an emergency call. It was an *accident*. You make Mr Carter sound like some kind of innocent soul who was taking his evening stroll. But if you break into someone's house, I'm afraid you take your chances.' A moment of bitter silence, while we both remembered our own home invasion. 'And it was an *accident*, Lana. I know what you think you saw but, let's face it, you *were* a few sheets to the wind.'

'Liar,' I said.

He sighed, rolled his eyes, threw up his hands in resignation.

'Don't sigh. Don't roll your eyes. Don't you fucking dare.'

His handsome face contorted with frustration.

'Lana, you were *drunk!*'

This last word screamed, and finally, beyond the bedside politesse, I saw the real fury in him.

And I knew that I was going to the police.

And he knew it too.

'You're talking about our *neighbours*,' he said. 'You're talking about the people next door. You're talking about our friends.'

'There's something wrong with them. They're like some kind of batshit-crazy cult or something. Tucker and Ben and the old folks in the big house. Even Krissy. Don't you feel it? There's something *wrong* here. They're like the Manson Family in Barbour jackets and muddy green boots.'

His superior smile. A slight chuckle.

I wanted to slap him.

Silence.

'I think someone's getting away with murder, Roman.'

We stared at each other, and it was as if we were both deciding something about the other at long last.

And I tried one last time.

'I think they – someone, I don't know if they're all involved, I don't think Willow would hurt a fly – or Sally or Oscar, come to that – and I know Ben seems like a sweet guy, and a great dad to Oscar – it's all mixed up in my mind – but I think *somebody* killed Juno Cave and got rid of her body. And I think there's something off about what happened with the Clutters. And there was a housekeeper – Marta – whatever happened to her?'

'Sorry? Who? I feel like I should be taking notes.'

'The Clutters' housekeeper. Marta. She disappeared.'

He barked with disgust. 'Is Marta perhaps under the swimming pool too? Who's next for the unmarked grave, eh? Someone's got quite a little murder factory going on here!'

I took my jacket from the back of the chair. I was going to have to put on some shoes. We had talked enough. I went to the sink, ran the cold tap, rubbed most of the dirt and blood from my hands.

'I'm going now.'

'Do what you want. I'm going back to bed.' The first milky white light of dawn seeped into our kitchen. He looked at the clock and dragged his finger through his tight golden curls. 'I can't believe I've got to be at work in a few hours.'

'Sorry to disturb your sleep.'

He suddenly seemed on the verge of tears. He was always the weak one in our relationship.

I'm sorry, but it's true. I was the one who whined, moaned and complained. But Roman was the one who broke.

I pulled on some jeans and trainers and threw on my jacket and picked up the car keys and headed for the door.

And then suddenly he was blocking my way.

'You're scared,' I said. 'You're scared I might be right, aren't you?'

'I'm scared you might be having a nervous breakdown. I'm scared you are going to destroy our chance of a new start. I'm scared you are going to make it impossible for us to live here.'

He was still blocking the door.

'Look – maybe Ben sent a few postcards to protect his son from the fact that his mother has moved on and has absolutely no interest him,' he said. 'Did that ever cross your mind? That it might be an act of kindness? Lana – I love you, darling, but you need help.'

Perhaps he did love me, I thought. But *darling* was always our unsafe word, *darling* was our trigger word, *darling* always told me that I had deeply pissed my husband off.

'Please get out of my way, Roman, please.' Saying please twice.

'You're not going to the police.'

His chiselled features were white and tense with fury and fear. He did not look quite so handsome now.

'Who's going to stop me – you?'

Then his hands were on me, grabbing me by the shoulders, and I was shoving him away, slapping at his face with my open palms.

We briefly scuffled in the doorway, a pair of nerds attempting to fight and not really knowing how, me trying to get past him and Roman stopping me from leaving.

And then it was suddenly over.

'Go on then,' he said, abruptly standing aside. 'Fine! Tell everyone your conspiracy theory! Embarrass yourself! And me!'

'I will.'

'Are you really going to do this?'

'Just watch me,' I said, pulling open the front door.

And as the door slammed shut behind me, I could already hear him talking on the phone.

24

Outside the police station the sun was coming up and revealing our village in all its golden autumnal glory. Swans on the river, leaves of yellow and rust blowing across the green, nobody about apart from the first of the dog walkers and the early runners.

'I need to speak to DCI Jim Baxter,' I announced.

The sergeant on the front desk was not a young man, and not a fit man, and he looked as though he was at the rough end of a long night shift.

'My name is—'

'The boss doesn't get in until ten.'

Waking up a bit, he gave me the professional once-over. I dragged my fingers through my hair, thinking I should have washed my hands a bit more. And then he seemed to sense the panic in me and something frozen inside him began to melt. He was not a bad man, I could tell.

'You're welcome to talk to someone else. Can I be of any help to you, miss?'

I considered blurting it all out to the desk sergeant and I did not know where to start.

'I would really prefer to speak to DCI Baxter.'

Baxter was the only one I trusted. He was the only one who would not look at me as if I was a crazy woman. There was something about his calm, courteous manner that told me he was the one I should talk to.

The desk sergeant sighed, shrugged, and closed up inside again.

'Then you'll have to wait.'

And so I did.

I took a seat in the waiting room by a sad little play area for children, a melancholy pen of random Lego and stuffed animals who were long past their best-by date, and I read the posters on the wall.

Sexting – so what? Don't regret your decision later. A little stick insect posing in a bikini.

UNLOCK YOUR POTENTIAL. UNLOCK YOUR POTENTIAL. Smiling young cops in recruitment posters who looked nothing at all like the sleepy desk sergeant, who observed me out of the corner of his beady eye, as if I may suddenly run amok in his reception area.

But most of all, the wall was full of advertisements for the lost.

MISSING.

MISSING.

MISSING.

There was an entire section dedicated to the missing. An entire wall of the missing.

A thin-faced teenage boy with an elaborate haircut, his poster curling at the corners with age.

An old man with a vacant look in his eyes.

A boy, not even school age.

These were the missing. The adolescent, the very old, the very young. Especially the young: *4 feet 10 inches, blond hair, freckles. 4 feet 8 inches, red hair, freckles.*

Uniformed cops started to come and go in pairs, the end of the night shift and the start of the day shift.

I half expected Roman to come and claim me, or at least to call me, but he did not come, and he did not call, and the sun was starting to blaze through the grimy glass doors of the police station when DI Hunter, DCI Baxter's surly helper, strolled through the door carrying her reusable coffee cup.

The desk sergeant raised his eyebrows. 'This lady's waiting for DCI Baxter.'

DI Hunter turned her large pale head towards me, gave scant sign she even recognised me, then nodded.

'Follow,' she said, unsmiling.

She took me up two floors – we used the stairs, me struggling to keep up with her long strides as she took the stairs three at a time – and walked through a semi-busy open-plan office to some kind of interview room. Everything looked worn out, exhausted, frayed at the edges.

She closed the door behind us.

I cleared my throat. 'I was hoping to talk to DCI Baxter.'

She scratched her close-cropped hair and gave me a sour smile. 'I'm afraid you are going to have to make do with me.'

'This will sound crazy,' I said.

We sat facing each other. DI Hunter's reusable coffee cup sat untouched on the Formica tabletop. Outside carefree voices drifted by the frosted glass. Laughing, not-a-care-in-the-world office banter. The day was starting.

'Bones,' I said.

'Bones?'

'I found bones under our swimming pool,' I said. 'That's why the water level kept going down.' *Don't babble, Lana.* 'Because there are bones buried under the tiles and the tiles are all cracked.'

'Sorry – bones? What kind of bones are we talking about, Mrs Wade?'

I cleared my throat.

Just say it.

'Human remains,' I said.

We stared at each other as I controlled my breathing.

Oddly enough, I felt better now.

'Human bones,' I said, gaining confidence. 'And I think they belong to the ex-wife of one of my neighbours. Her name . . .' Once it was said in this place there would be no going back. I licked my lips. 'Her name was Juno Cave. Or is Juno Cave.' *But the present tense would mean that she is still alive, wouldn't it, Lana?* 'And our house – a family died in our house,' I added, although the gory digression seemed to remove some force from what I was saying. Because I wasn't telling this large sceptical police officer something she wasn't aware of already.

'The Clutters. I know. Very sad.'

'I don't believe he did it!' I blurted. 'Captain Clutter. William Clutter. I don't care how stressed he was about money and work and all of that. I don't care what kind of medication he was on. I don't care how depressed he was – *he wouldn't do such a thing.* And John Carter – the boy in a coma – the one who was run down on our street.' I shook my head. 'There are too many bad things happening on that street.'

She held up the palms of her hands.

'Wait a second,' Hunter said, narrowing her eyes as if to see me better. 'John Carter getting run down was an accident.' We stared at each other for a long moment. 'Wasn't it?'

I shook my head. It was hard to admit. It was hard to say it out loud.

'There was nothing accidental about it,' I said.

She stared at me, mulling it over, finally seeming to take me seriously.

'There's something *wrong* about that street,' I went on. 'I don't know what it is – but if you upset them, if you get in their way, they just snuff you out.' I paused, tried to steady my breathing, to slow my pounding heart. 'And the housekeeper – what happened to her?'

'Whooh,' she said. 'Back up. What housekeeper is this?'

'The Clutters' housekeeper. A Filipino lady. Marta. She just disappeared. Nobody seems to know where she went. I know it all sounds mad.'

'It doesn't sound mad,' Hunter said, and I wanted to hug her.

Tears of relief were suddenly streaming down my face. 'Thank you,' I said.

She stood up and stretched to her full length, her fingers scraping the ceiling.

'It's just a lot to take in.'

'Of course.'

'These are very serious allegations.'

'I know!'

'Are you in danger, Mrs Wade? Has anyone been violent to you or made threats against you?'

I shook my head.

'Is your husband violent towards you?'

I shook my head, flashing on the clumsy tussle we had had as I was leaving the house.

'My husband – Roman – would never hurt me.'

'Are you sure?'

'He's a decent man. A kind man.'

But Roman could not see what was so horribly obvious to me. He would see it all clearly when DI Hunter did her job.

'And are you suggesting to me that one of your neighbours is responsible for these crimes?'

'Yes. I think so. What other explanation is there?'

'What do you want me to do, Mrs Wade? Shall I send a couple of officers to your house to take a look at these bones? Shall we do that first? You can stay here at the station while we make this initial investigation. Someone can take a statement from you while my officers check it out.'

I felt the panic fly in me again. I could feel something slipping away.

'You,' I gasped. 'It has to be you that goes to that pool. It must be you.'

I was standing up now, my voice getting louder in the tiny interview room.

I sensed heads turning beyond the frosted glass.

DI Hunter held out her hands, palm down, asking for calm, and I sank back into the seat.

All at once I felt very tired yet totally awake.

'Let me make a quick phone call,' DI Hunter said.

She was back in the room in less than five minutes.

'Thank you again,' I said, aware that I was babbling now, repeating myself, but I was overwhelmed with the relief of being believed.

The fat sergeant was no longer on the desk when we were leaving the station.

'Don't we need other people?' I said. 'To search and dig and investigate and all that stuff?'

DI Hunter touched my arm with infinite kindness and my eyes suddenly burned with more grateful tears.

'Everyone is on their way,' she promised.

25

The sun was up now, the glare blindingly white on the tiles of the empty swimming pool, and I shielded my eyes as I led DI Hunter out the French doors and into the back garden.

There was no sign of Roman. The car not on the drive. No message on my phone. I hesitated, gripped by a sudden dread that unspeakable things had happened in our home, and then I felt DI Hunter's hand lightly touch my shoulder, as if offering gentle encouragement.

I wheeled around, wiping my eyes with the back of my hand. 'Thank you for believing me,' I said, my fear replaced by relief in the reassuring presence of the big detective.

'Let's take a look at what you found,' she said.

I was aware that we were alone in the garden.

'And everyone else is on their way?'

'They will be here soon. Come on, Mrs Wade.'

I went to the ladder and climbed down into the pool.

At the bottom I looked up at DI Hunter, who was pulling on gloves and staring back at the house.

She started down the ladder as I went to the smashed tiles in the centre of the pool and sank to my knees.

But there was something wrong.

The hole that I had dug out under the smashed tiles had a lot more bones than I remembered seeing in the night, as if they had risen up from some unmarked grave in my absence. And these bones were different.

More like an animal's bones.

And – although I knew it was impossible – there was what looked like a skull, a small skull that had not come from anything human, with a long narrow snout that had fierce-looking canines at the top of its extended jaw.

I could feel DI Hunter's breath beside me. 'May I see?'

'This isn't what I found,' I blurted.

'Excuse me,' she said, politely ignoring me, and her gloved hands reached into the hole.

She lifted out the skull and held it up between us.

'Is this what we're looking for, Mrs Wade?' she said, a thin veneer of courtesy over what felt like her ice-cold contempt.

Before I could answer, I heard voices in the garden, and I understood that it was not more police officers who were on their way.

It was my neighbours.

I looked up as their faces appeared at the top of the empty pool and they stared down at us. Krissy and Tucker. Willow and Guy. Sally Berry. Ben Cave and, inexplicably, the youngest Mrs Mendoza, the doe-eyed Angel, shyly holding hands with him. And young Oscar, peering between them, his lank fringe falling over his eyes.

The clothes my neighbours wore were an odd jumble of pyjamas and bathrobes and day clothes that had been hastily pulled on.

Guy was dressed for a shoot, all Barbour and green boots. Willow's lovely face was covered in a pale cream mask, as if she had been interrupted in the middle of her elaborate skincare regime, giving her a spectral look.

The youngest Mrs Mendoza – Angel – was wearing some skimpy baby doll nightdress under a white towelling robe. But what was she doing here? What were they all doing here?

Oscar drifted to one side, a parka thrown over his old-fashioned flannel pyjamas, his mouth slack with shock. And then there was suddenly Roman, waiting by the top of the ladder, holding out his hand.

'Please come out of there now, Lana,' he instructed softly.

I turned to DI Hunter.

'But I found bones,' I said, aware of the shake in my voice.

She nodded soothingly. 'Yes, of course, and now I've seen them, haven't I? And now we can all have a good think about where the bones may have come from. How does that sound, Mrs Wade?'

'*Different* bones, I mean.'

I stared at the pool, and the leering animal skull seemed to mock me. 'These are not the bones I found. Someone must have swapped the bones.'

DI Hunter looked up at Roman, and I saw her eyes were asking him for assistance.

'Do you need help getting out, Lana?' Roman asked, his infuriating voice smooth with that hushed bedside manner, as if he was talking to a raving basket case.

I went back to the broken tiles and I threw off my coat and sank to my knees and I began scrambling in the dirt with my fingers, angrily pushing the animal bones aside, ripping at the soil, feeling the sharp little bones biting into my hands, my fingers, knowing that what I had found must still be here somewhere.

I heard Guy stifle a snort of laughter.

'Don't,' Willow told him.

'Mrs Wade?' DI Hunter said. Her hand gripped my shoulder.

But I kept digging, frantically clawing at the dirt, gasping with sudden pain as something very sharp – a fragment of broken tile, a shard of animal bone – stuck in the fleshy ball of my thumb, drawing blood that splattered on the white tiles. And still I kept digging.

Then arms were gently but firmly pulling me to my feet, Roman on one side and DI Hunter on the other.

I stared at them. 'I don't understand,' I said.

'Then let me explain it to you,' Roman said. 'May I?'

I nodded mutely, my gaze drifting from his face to the smashed tiles, the pile of bones, the grinning skull of the dead animal.

'When we are under a lot of stress we sometimes create stories so that the world around us makes more sense,' Roman was saying. 'There's a condition called fantastic confabulation—'

I pulled away from him. 'I'm not fucking crazy.'

DI Hunter patted my arm. 'Nobody's accusing you of anything, Mrs Wade,' she said.

Apart from being wrong, I thought. Apart from being delusional. Apart from making a screaming fuss about nothing. Apart from auditioning for the role of village idiot. I could see the contempt in her eyes, and I could feel Roman's repressed anger.

'Let me help you out,' he said. 'Darling.'

I pushed him away. 'I know what I found!' I said.

I looked one last time at the long, low skull of the animal, which DI Hunter had placed next to the broken tiles, as if it was some kind of conclusive evidence. Then I furiously turned away and climbed the ladder out of the pool.

My neighbours were all waiting for me.

Willow and Krissy immediately came to my side.

'Are you OK, sweetheart?' Krissy said. 'Oh, you poor thing, look at the state of you!' She began brushing dirt from my hair.

'There were *bones*, Krissy,' I said. 'I saw the bones, I felt them.' I glanced back at the pool. 'They were not animal bones. These ones – they're the wrong bones.'

'The wrong bones!' Guy laughed.

Roman had climbed out of the pool now but DI Hunter was still down there, taking photographs with her phone. To be filed under crazy lady, I thought.

'There were more bones than that – and *different* bones.'

'Roman told us everything,' Willow said, her fabulous face frowning behind her kabuki mask of night cream.

'Everything?' I asked, shocked that my husband had shared our secrets with the world.

'Everything.'

No, I thought. Not everything. Never everything. Roman would never tell them everything.

'We know you lost your baby,' Willow said. 'The night you were burgled in the old place.'

Then Guy stepped forward, as if to make some kind of formal announcement. He was smiling. There was something slung over his shoulder. He tossed it at my feet, and it immediately seemed to cleave apart. Because it was two things, not one.

A brace of dead fox, and as I looked down at them I saw that one had a shotgun wound near its hind leg and the other was missing half of its head.

And I knew with total certainty how they had died.

The fox with the wound in its hind leg had been unable to run away after Guy had shot it and the other one had been reluctant to leave its side. So one had died slowly, bleeding out with its leg wound, while the other had died quickly, executed at close range, the barrel carefully placed against its head. I could imagine Guy strolling into his back garden in his bathrobe, whistling tunelessly, the shotgun over his shoulder, loving every moment.

'*That's* what was in your pool and that's also what was under your pool,' he said. 'One of their dearly departed.' He grinned. 'The mortal remains of Basil Brush.'

I stared at him with loathing.

'Boom boom,' he said.

I looked at Ben Cave. 'You,' I said. '*You* send those postcards to Oscar, don't you?'

He looked pained. 'Please,' he said. 'Do we *really* have to do this in front of my son?'

Oscar stared slowly from his father to me and back again.

'Don't deny it!' I said. 'I know those postcards are not from Oscar's mother. They're not from Juno. *You* send them.'

I expected him to treat me with outraged contempt. I expected him to deny everything. I expected him to call me crazy.

But instead I saw Ben's eyes well up with tears. He nodded, as if his head was unbearably heavy, and the youngest Mendoza woman, the lovely Angel, reached out to rub his back, her robe slipping open to reveal a long creamy expanse of thigh.

'Yes,' Ben said. 'I send Oscar a postcard every month and I pretend it's from his mother.' He looked at his son, smiled through his tears and touched the boy's long, lank hair. 'You know why? Because it would break his heart to know that his mother has broken off all contact with us.' His mouth twisted with hurt and disbelief. 'She doesn't even send him a birthday card.' Father and son hugged each other. 'Sorry, buddy,' Ben croaked.

'No, Dad, please,' Oscar said, both of them in tears.

I looked wildly at Krissy and Willow.

'But what about the old housekeeper?' I said. 'The one who took care of the Clutters. What happened to her?' The name had slipped my mind. This was bad. It suddenly came back to me. 'Marta! What happened to Marta?'

'Tell her,' Ben Cave said to Angel, and I finally understood that they had slept in the same bed last night. His voice was hard now. 'Go on,' he said. 'Tell her.'

And Angel came towards me with her phone, a latest model iPhone, her face very young, her huge brown eyes watching me warily, as she scrolled through the photos on her phone.

She held it out to me to reveal images of a stout and smiling lady somewhere in her late sixties, the same lady surrounded by grinning relatives and animals – a scrawny dog, some stray chickens, an anorexic cat – and the same lady at the church and especially at dinner time – there were lots of family meals in the photographs. And in the background of every photo, the lush green vegetation of the Philippines, heavy with the tropical heat and rain, crowded in behind every image.

'Marta went home,' Angel said.

I stared at her in disbelief.

She shrugged, and Ben squeezed her bare shoulder in encouragement. She tugged at her silky robe and modestly covered her skin.

DI Hunter had got out of the pool and was talking to Roman. Then they shook hands, two pillars of the community.

I watched their lips move.

'Thank you for your call,' he said.

'Happy to help,' she said, and they both turned to look at me.

'So do you feel better about everything?' Krissy said. 'The bones were from a fox, OK? The housekeeper – Marta, who worked for the Clutters – is back in the old country. And Ben ...' We both looked at him, one arm slipped around the slim waist of the young Miss Mendoza, the other round his boy. 'Dear old Ben sends those postcards to Oscar *as an act of kindness*,' Krissy said, a note of firmness in her voice now, telling me to start seeing the world as it really was, and not as it was in my head.

Oscar looked up at his dad, wide-eyed. Ben hugged him fiercely and the boy gulped back a sob.

Willow stroked my arm, her ghost face too close. 'So are you all right now, Lana?'

I did not reply and she stepped back as Roman approached me.

He put his arms around me and pulled me close and at first, I thought he was holding me with some of the old tenderness.

So soft they felt, his deft fingertips on the skin of my dirt-streaked bare arm, his skin on my skin, so gentle and so loving, and I found myself filling up with a love for him that I thought had been lost. I was almost ready to apologise for whatever they wanted me to apologise for. Let's just turn back the clock, can we?

But then I saw the needle in my husband's other hand, his little black doctor's bag open on the scrubby grass by the side of the empty swimming pool.

Roman was not stroking me.

Roman was not comforting me.

He was looking for a vein.

'This will calm you down, darling,' he said, and then I felt the bee-sting of the needle as it slid smoothly into my flesh.

26

Sunday, 4 October

It no longer felt like summer.

In the two weeks since we had all stood by the empty swimming pool at the end of the night, the days had grown colder and shorter and darker. The clothes that Roman and I had unpacked together when we first moved in were no longer warm enough. I slept late every day now, the pills that I was taking to calm my mind making me slow and listless, everything a little blurred around the edges, but when Roman had been at work for hours I rose from my bed and, down in the basement and in the guest room, I tore open cardboard boxes, looking for clothes to match the season. But it was a slow process.

Roman had prescribed white pills to help me sleep and yellow pills for my anxiety. But the white pills left my brain foggy in the daytime, and the yellow pills left me feeling tired, so tired, even after I had slept for twelve hours.

But the routine of unpacking the boxes that were still piled up all over the house was soothing. When I had a stack of the flattened cardboard boxes from the basement and a collection of boots that would be good for walking the fields if – *when*, I mean – I left the house again, I carted the boxes out to the recycling bins and Sally Berry waved from the doorway of her cottage, a sweet old hippy lady in double denim surrounded by pink flowers, giving me a big grin and a jaunty thumbs up.

Everyone had been so kind. Everyone had been so understanding.

Everyone had been so nice about my problem.

I waved to Sally and went back inside and up to the spare room. I was looking for more winter clothes, for the coats and fleeces and sweaters and beanies Roman and I would need very soon. But I was unearthing other things too in all the neglected boxes. DVDs. CDs. Wine glasses. Books.

I unpacked it all, because it had all been put off for too long, as if – I could admit it now – I had secretly harboured the delusion that we might not really be staying here forever. Then I carried our winter clothes to the walk-in closet in the master bedroom, and stacked up the DVDs, CDs and books to be transported to the empty white shelves in the living room.

Because it is time, I admitted it to myself. *This is our home now.*

I was emptying a cardboard box full of books when I saw it. *After Eden* by Professor A.V.R. Hall. A stolid-looking hardback sitting among all the well-worn paperbacks.

Was that really him?

Was this book really written by our neighbour in the big house?

Yes – because there was an author's photo – Professor Hall as a younger man, much younger than I had ever known him, almost rakish in his corduroy jacket and floppy bow tie, back in the day when he was the hotshot academic in his prime who enthralled his students and BBC TV producers alike.

You can tell in a moment when a book has been read, I thought as I flicked through it. You can tell when a book has been loved. And this book had been read, and this book had been loved, for there were entire passages underlined in yellow marker. I was too weary to read full paragraphs right now but I registered the chapter headlines.

The End of Jobs. The Collapse of Capital. The Death of Politics. The Last of the Oil. And yellow-marked phrases floated up to me. *The final reckoning for Wall Street. The privatisation of clean air and water.* It seemed to be a book about endings. I looked at the photographs. Armed militia in the United States. Two shuttered banks, one hundred years apart, one in 1928 and one in 2008. A monkey in a laboratory with death in its terrified eyes.

There was an inscription at the front of the book.

To Roman
Sine timore.
Alan Hall

And I didn't understand.

Because there was a date scrawled above the inscription and it was before we moved here.

In fact, the date scrawled on the title page was a couple of months after that night, the terrible night they came. *The home invasion*, I thought. *The burglary*. But that didn't quite cover it, did it? Those descriptions would never quite cover it.

I stared at the date, the signature, the Latin pep talk. So this meant – what did it mean? It meant that Roman had met Professor Hall – where? At a book event? Some time and place before we moved here.

Sine timore. No fear.

And that made no sense at all to me because – checking that date again – those were the days immediately after that terrible night, when Roman and I huddled together, afraid of the world, and there was nothing in our hearts but fear.

'Lana?'

The afternoon nap had become the highlight of my day. It broke things up nicely. Sleep until noon, potter around doing a little light unpacking and then back to bed for a few hours before getting up just before Roman got home and we ordered dinner online.

But today he was early.

Roman stood in the doorway of the bedroom, and he was dressed for the guns.

I sat up in bed and blinked my eyes. He wore a sleeveless tweed shooting vest with huge pockets. A checked button-down shirt with a prissy little knitted tie. And the funny thing was, Roman never wore a tie to the surgery. There would have been a time when Roman wearing grouse moor drag would have been a source of amusement between us.

I would have laughed out loud. But not today.

'You're back from work early?'

He smiled patiently. He was being very patient. 'It's a Sunday. No work today. The surgery's closed.'

'Oh, of course. Sunday.'

'There's someone to see you, Lana.'

'To see me?'

'She's waiting downstairs.'

'To see *me?*'

He nodded, grinned, held out his hand. 'Please don't worry. Please don't worry about anything any more.'

I followed Roman downstairs and heard a mumble of soft voices in the kitchen.

Ben Cave and Oscar turned to look at me.

And there was a woman with them who I had never seen before. A black-haired, milky-faced beauty, maybe forty, although her tight white jeans and heels and elaborately distressed leather jacket made her look years younger.

She smiled at me as if we knew each other. And then she stepped towards me and gave me a fierce hug, as if she couldn't help herself.

'Lana? So nice to meet you. I understand you've been concerned about my welfare.' She was still smiling. Everyone was smiling at me.

My voice caught in my throat. There was something magical about this woman's presence in my home.

When I finally spoke, my voice seemed to come from somewhere far away.

'You're Oscar's mother,' I said. 'You're Juno Cave.'

We sat in my alcove on the first floor.

Roman brought us tea.

Everyone was very kind. Especially her. Especially Juno.

She scrolled through her phone, showing me her pictures of Oscar, all the way from blurry, curled-up foetus on a black-and-white twelve-week scan to newborn baby to stumbling toddler to gap-toothed kid to the long-haired shy boy in the outer suburb of his childhood, and scrolling through her gallery was like watching Oscar grow up before my eyes.

'It hasn't been easy for any of us,' Juno said. 'Not for Ben. Not for me. And especially not for Oscar.' Her eyes were hot with tears. 'Adults move on. We find a new partner. We find a new life. But children don't have that luxury. You don't divorce your parents, do you?'

'I feel like an idiot,' I said. 'I thought you – I don't even know what I thought.'

But that's not true, is it, Lana?

You know exactly what you thought had happened to Oscar's runaway mum. You thought Juno was buried under your swimming pool when there were only some dead foxes in there.

'It will get better,' Juno said, nodding at the hundreds of photographs, spooling out like her own private movie of motherhood. 'I'll send for him soon. He can spend more time with me. After the wedding.'

The wedding? I imagined she was talking about herself, that she was formalising her relationship with her well-oiled Brazilian stud muffin. Who wouldn't?

But I had the wrong end of the marital stick.

'Not me!' she laughed. 'God, no! That's all been over for months! Manolo ran back to his wife and three kids in Rio! He wasn't quite so keen on me when I was part of the furnishings. It is amazing how fast the sex wears off. No, I mean Ben and Angel – didn't your husband tell you they were getting married? I thought he would have told you.'

Did he? Sometimes Roman told me that we had already had conversations that I couldn't recall, for the life of me. I blame the pills, I really do.

I licked my lips and sipped my tea. I didn't know what to say to this woman.

'I'm not proud of any of it,' Juno went on. 'And I know that I carry my share of the blame. I thought that someone I hardly knew – Manolo – my friend, a real friend – was the love of my life. But he was just the catalyst to get me out of a bad marriage. Manolo was my exit door and, to be honest, I had been looking for one for years.' She stared at the back garden. 'I had what you could call a rather disrupted childhood.'

I remembered what Krissy and Willow had told me. The mother who was a drug addict, the beloved brother Juno was separated from when they both disappeared into care, the bad luck that some people are born with and then have to live with.

'Our mother was a mess,' she said. 'She did her best, but drink and drugs and men – one rotten choice after another – meant it would only end one way. Her children in care. My brother and I didn't just lose our mother, our home, our childhood – we lost each other. I sound like I'm making excuses, don't I? And there are no excuses – not for the way that Ben and I treated each other towards the end, and not for the way that I have neglected our son. There are no excuses. But there are *reasons*. You think you're starting a new life but it's a lie. There's only the one life. And you can't start it over again.'

'Did you ever find him? Your brother?'

She shook her head. 'I heard he got into drugs. He turned out to be just like dear old mum. He's probably dead by now. I think my marriage to Ben – and the thing with my friend, Manolo – was just me really wanting a family. And maybe wanting it too much.'

My theories were dust. And I saw that they were already dust long before Juno Cave came to tea. There was no grand conspiracy, no bodies buried under the swimming pool, no trail of blood. Just a bored and unhappy wife with a deeply damaged childhood, distracted by the welcome resurrection of her sex life, then neglecting her maternal duties and finally feeling the burden of a terrible guilt.

It all seemed so ordinary, it all seemed so commonplace.

Juno Cave fled maternal duties for freedom, better coffee and regular sex. And so – surely? – it followed that Captain William Clutter really did crack up and take it out on his family, the poor man.

And that the family's housekeeper – Marta – truly had turned in her duster and her bucket and gone back to the old country, where she seemed to be very happy surrounded by her chickens and grandchildren.

There was a simple explanation for all of it.

There was even an explanation for me and my madness.

Because it was painfully clear now that I had been feeling the strain of recent events. And now there were cracks in me too.

'I'm sorry, Juno,' I said. 'I've caused so much trouble. For you. For Ben. For Oscar.'

She reached out and squeezed my wrist. 'No,' she said. 'No, Lana.'

'I've been unwell. Things have been – they've been very stressful. I won't bore you with the gory details. But I'm going to get better. I *am* getting better.'

'I know you will. I know you are.'

'Oscar,' I said. 'He thinks it's all his fault – you and his dad breaking up, I mean. He thinks he's to blame somehow. I guess all the children of divorce have a little of that in them. That's what you have to fix, Juno. But he's a lovely boy. He really is. You can be so proud of him.'

She smiled with a mother's pride, the tears streaming down both our faces now, and there was no need for any more words.

Juno left me in the alcove, and I could hear her and Ben and Oscar saying their goodbyes to Roman downstairs.

When the front door closed behind them, I went to the front of the house and watched them together talking in the middle of the Gardens.

The Caves lingered, as if reluctant to say goodbye. Ben and Juno with Oscar between them.

They had the strained formality of old lovers, striving to be polite as they conversed across all those burned bridges.

Juno reached out and rubbed Oscar on the back of his neck and he turned his face to look at his mother.

After all the drama, I couldn't help feeling that this family gathering – the broken family gathering – was strangely sedate. Whatever hurt and anger there had been in the dying days of their marriage, Juno seemed relaxed in the presence of her ex-husband.

Ben was civil and soft-spoken.

Oscar was dry-eyed and calm, considering his mother with a mild curiosity as she reached out to stroke his smooth cheek.

I couldn't help feeling that they seemed far happier than most families who stay together.

I turned away.

If I wasn't so heavily sedated, I would have definitely felt embarrassed.

27

Monday, 5 October

If I had not become unwell, and if I had not been resting at home, I would never have known about Willow and Vince's affair. But then you never really know your neighbours until you spend all day spying on them.

I was padding back from an early-morning walk to the bathroom when, glancing from the bedroom window, I saw Guy going off in Ben's Range Rover to the guns – that's what they called themselves, *the guns*, as if those pulling the trigger were inseparable from their weapons – and Vince's battered old van pulled up next to Guy's Aston Martin only moments later.

After quickly casing the street – which, quite frankly, was when my suspicions were aroused, all that surreptitious checking when the Gardens was conspicuously deserted, for it was still too early even for Goran to be sitting in his van – Vince slipped inside the house next door without troubling the bell.

Because he had his own key.

Which was how I knew for certain.

And as it was still so early, Willow and her sun-baked handyman had the entire day ahead of them for all those hard jobs about the house where you have to get your knees dirty when you are fiddling with the stop cock.

I wondered how long it had been going on.

Quite a while, I guessed, to develop a schedule this slick. And from far away across the neat endless fields, there came the sound of the guns.

There was a small green outhouse at the side of our garden.

Something less than a shed, but a bit more than a hutch, and it contained the remnants of all the previous occupants. Chlorine tablets for the swimming pool, garden tools speckled with rust, a stainless-steel barbecue grill, a deflated basketball, an air pump and a jumble of burned orange vinyl that, on closer inspection, turned out to be some kind of an inflatable lilo.

When I took it out and wiped it down, I liked it even more.

It was a Water Hammock Pool Lounger – that's what it said on the side, the tops of the letter 'o's all starting to peel away from the surface – and it was basically three inflatable supports for the arms and head, joined together by a flat backrest and seat. I glanced at the pool, now fully repaired and brimming with sun-spangled water, and it looked inviting.

The day was unseasonably warm, possibly the last day in double digits for many months, so I went up to the bedroom and put on my bathing costume. Then I came back to the garden, hosed down the Water Hammock Pool Lounger, pumped it up and dragged it to the pool.

I stayed in there, semi-submerged and drowsy, until I heard laughter on the other side of the high garden wall. I listened for a while and then I climbed out, as quietly as I could, and went back inside and upstairs to my secret alcove to watch.

Willow and Vince were sitting with their feet dangling in the pool. Laughing, sated, a happy couple with all the time in the world. Vince in jeans rolled up to his knees, his T-shirt around his neck, Willow in just a white bath towel. Nothing underneath. Then it all came off so easily and quickly and they threw themselves laughing into the pool, and into each other, frolicking like a pair of mating seals.

I realised that I had never seen either of them look anywhere near that happy before. They looked lovely together.

And that's when I heard the car pull up outside. I went to the front of the house. The sound of the guns had intensified as the day went on and I could not help feeling that there was a fury and a desperation about them now. So it seemed premature for Ben Cave's Range Rover to be back in the Gardens so soon with Guy sitting in the passenger seat, his shotgun between his legs.

Christ.

Ben and Guy conferred for a moment, and then Guy slipped out of the car, Ben drove off and Guy began crossing the street, adjusting the gun slip on his shoulder. My phone was already in my hand, calling Willow, as I went upstairs to my alcove at the back of the house. I stared down at them. Willow and Vince were in the middle of the pool, his arms around her neck, her legs around his waist, both of them naked. I could see her slab-sized phone vibrating on a lounger by the pool. I shook my head as it flicked to voicemail, her message breezy and light, telling me to leave a message and she might possibly get back to me. Heart pounding, I dashed to the front of the house and watched Guy steady the shotgun on his shoulder as he took out his key.

And then he stopped.

Professor Hall, in a pastel-coloured polo shirt and shorts that came down to his knees, was making his stately progress towards the big house. Guy paused, turned back down the drive and approached him. Professor Hall made some point with the tennis racket he was carrying – he seemed to be indicating the sound of the guns – and Guy nodded in agreement, polite, deferential, respectful.

I rushed to the back of the house.

Willow and Vince were out of the water and lying by the side of the pool, the same white bath towel draped over both of them, Vince on his stomach, Willow on her side, one hand lazily exploring the crack in his beefy butt.

I smacked my fists again the window once, hard, and their startled faces looked up at me.

Then I went back to the front of the house. Professor Hall was heading for home.

And Guy was nowhere to be seen. I returned to my alcove, my mouth dry, fearing the worst.

But Willow was reclining demurely on a lounger at the far end of the pool, her eyes hidden behind big black shades, wrapped prim and tight in her giant white bath towel. Vince was socially distanced at the other end of the garden, on his hands and knees by the French doors, barefoot but miraculously back in his T-shirt and jeans, tampering with one of the garden lights.

Guy strolled into the garden, glanced at Willow and then began talking to Vince. Then Willow got up and, watched by both men, began to walk towards the house, taking her time, her white bathrobe tied up secure and chaste. She stopped to place a lingering welcome home kiss on Guy's mouth. Guy watched Willow every step of the way as she walked back into their home as if she was coming down a Paris catwalk. Vince concentrated on the garden lights. Then he got to his feet, wiping his hands on his jeans, murmuring a question, and Guy seemed to snap out of his reverie.

Vince was asking about the gun.

Guy unzipped the leather slipcase and pulled out the shotgun – a thing of exceptional beauty and superb craftsmanship, even a snotty city girl like me could appreciate that, all deep dark wood and ornate silver decoration gleaming in the sun – and the two men stood there admiring it.

And I shivered, drenched in sweat.

As if someone had stepped on my grave.

The day was dying now.

I swam, then slept on the Water Hammock Pool Lounger, drifting across the pool in a mild autumn breeze, enjoying the mild warmth of the sun on my face and the sharp cool of the water on my legs and feet. How many more days like these? Perhaps none, not until next summer.

And at last, I could imagine us being here next summer.

The garden next door was silent now. No laughter and love-making this deep into the day. The guns were silent.

I don't know how long I dozed on the water hammock, but I came awake to the sound of voices by the side of the pool. My brain still foggy with sleep, and with the low sun shining in my eyes, they were all indistinct black shapes, huddled close and holding their drinks, and they looked as though they might have been there for a while, their voices soft and low, as if they were trying not to wake me. My neighbours. Who had let them into our garden?

Tucker, Krissy's husband, was braying in his Boston accent. 'One solar storm and it's over, man. One eruption on the sun and we're burnt toast. An EMP – electromagnetic pulse – would unplug the world in a moment. Everything would end. The Internet. The electronic grid. Telecommunications. Food chain, water supply, finance industry. Puff! All gone, man! You think this couldn't happen? *It already did.* The Carrington Event in 1859. Google it, dude. But we weren't addicted to technology in the nineteenth century. And we are now.'

Voices of friendly dissent.

Then Ben was talking. 'Before that ever happens someone will eat a bat or a cat or a rat in the soup-of-the-day in some Chinese city you never heard of and the next thing you know there's a hundred million people dying across the planet because this time big pharma can't come up with a vaccine.'

And then a woman was talking – Krissy – telling them that they were both wrong.

'You don't have to wait for the sun to explode or the next plague,' she said. 'Because long before that happens, one day you will go to an ATM and find that the banks are shut, your money is worthless, and your savings are all gone.'

'Roman thinks we're crazy,' somebody said.

'I hope I *am* crazy,' Sally Berry said. What was she doing here? 'But, oh, we have taken so much out of this planet ... we have taken *everything* ...'

They were all black shadows against the last of the sun. But I could identify their voices now.

'No, Roman doesn't think we're crazy,' Professor Hall said, and they all fell silent. 'Because I think he's seen it. Roman has seen how your world can fall apart in a moment. Am I right, Roman?'

'Yes,' Roman said.

I slid off the Water Hammock Pool Lounger and into the water and gasped out loud at the shock of the cold. It was freezing. I wanted to get out of the water immediately. But there was something wrong. The sides of the pool had risen, I realised, with a surge of panic. No – the water level had dropped, it had dropped dramatically while I was sleeping, and no one could see me, no one knew I was there.

My hands reached for the edge of the pool, but it was far too high for me to pull myself up, and from somewhere far away I seemed to hear rushing water as it leaked away beneath me. The pool hadn't been fixed properly. The leak was still there. Or was it just the white pills and the yellow pills that were making me so weak?

I raised my hands, fingertips clawing at the edge of the pool, and as if in response a flock of birds erupted from somewhere without warning against the sky and then were gone. The water was very cold now, and the sides of the pool were impossibly high, and the modest warmth of the autumn day had gone. The black silhouettes above me were still talking in their soft voices, impossibly distant, and I called out, longing for Roman to notice me, and to reach out and offer me his hand.

'This is not some rivers-of-blood fantasy, man,' Tucker said. 'This *will* happen.'

'Who's going to protect your family?' Professor Hall asked.

'Nobody,' Roman said, and there was something in his voice that I had never heard before.

I screamed his name again and as one of the faces turned towards me – those blank, featureless faces rubbed out by the low sun – I felt like an intruder at a party that I had not been invited to and where I was not wanted, and my eyes blurred with the sting of chlorine and tears.

28

Tuesday, 6 October

'You look awful.'

These were Sandy's first words to me when he got off the train from London. He stood staring at me on the empty platform as my face grew warm with embarrassment.

And then I felt that special flicker of resentment that we reserve for old friends.

Doesn't he get it?

'I haven't been well, Sandy.'

He continued to frown at me, genuinely shocked by my appearance. We were still standing on the platform as the train pulled out, and I caught a glimpse of my face in the passing windows. The flesh hollowed out. The circles under my eyes as black as bruises. The old bomber jacket hanging on my frame in a way that it never had before.

'I'm worried about you,' he said, his voice softer.

'It's all been difficult for me.'

I remembered Juno Cave's painfully sympathetic smile, and I remembered sitting so close to her in my upstairs alcove that I could feel the warmth of her body. *How could I have been so wrong?* Last night I had jolted awake from my rest, the medicated fog lifting for a moment, and before the deep and dreamless sleep had sucked me down again, I wondered if I was going insane.

The things that I had believed to be true had all been in my head. And now, my total certainty that I was right terrified me.

'I've just let things get on top of me,' I said, attempting a smile. 'But I'm getting better now.'

'I don't mean to be rude,' he gruffly apologised. 'And I know things haven't been easy for you. But – my God, Lana. *What has Roman got you on?*'

'Vitamins, mostly.'

He exhaled with disbelief. 'They must be very powerful vitamins to make you look like this.'

I hesitated, because I knew that Roman would not like me discussing my health care with anyone, not even my oldest friend. Especially not my oldest friend.

'And just some other stuff to calm me down.'

He nodded, waiting.

'Benzos,' I said.

Sandy shook his head. 'You're going to have to help me here. I have no idea what *benzos* might be.'

'Benzodiazepines.'

'They sound very modern.'

'They work.'

'And what are Benzodiazepines for exactly?'

'Insomnia. Panic disorder. Generalised anxiety disorder.'

'Ah. Magic pills.'

I wanted to tell him about Juno Cave. I wanted to tell him about my madness. I knew that then he would understand. But all he cared about were the pills that calmed me down, and helped me sleep, and got me through the day without feeling that my heart was going to burst out of my chest.

I felt a stronger surge of resentment. I didn't like Sandy looking at me as if I was sick. I wanted him to look at me in the old way, as if I was special, as if I was going to conquer the world.

'And what are the side effects of these – what are they? – benzos?'

'The side effects,' I say, repeating the line that I had learned from Roman, 'are that they make me well, Sandy.'

'And they're working, are they?'

I tried to force a laugh. 'Sandy, don't worry – I'm married to a doctor.'

'Doctors kill people all the time, don't they?' he said.

Sandy and I were already settled in the Italian restaurant overlooking the green when Roman arrived.

I watched Sandy take in the new Roman. For we had both changed in our new home, we had both been transformed. As the flesh had fallen off me, Roman had been piling on some new muscle.

After his daily weight training, grunting his way through the reps with weights at the end of the bed before breakfast, Roman's slender frame had pumped up in a way that it never had before. You could see it across his shoulders, around his neck, the way his biceps strained against the jacket of his dark Paul Smith suit. As I had lost strength, Roman had seemed to gain it.

He shook hands with Sandy and then brushed his mouth lightly across my sunken cheek, not really a kiss, not really catching my eye. The token physical contact of a marriage that has seen sunnier days.

I smoothed my hands on the soft linen tablecloth.

Roman looked at me slightly differently these days, as if he was looking beyond me, to another version of me, somewhere in the past or perhaps the future, as if hoping to see a different Lana.

'Lana and I went for a walk around the village,' Sandy said, and I had a sinking feeling.

Roman smiled brightly. 'It's beautiful at this time of year, isn't it, Sandy? Some people think the county is at its best during the colder months. Something to do with the light.' He grinned in his disarmingly boyish way. 'You two photographers would know more about that than me.'

Sandy glanced out of the restaurant windows, the soft afternoon haze casting long shadows across the village green and glinting like burnished old gold on the river. Then he looked back at Roman.

'What I really noticed was that Lana was struggling to keep up with me,' Sandy said. 'And I'm an old geezer with a touch of rheumatoid arthritis and a dodgy hip.' He looked over at me. 'But Lana was the one who needed to sit down and catch her breath.'

Roman touched my hand. 'Lana's not been herself lately, but she's doing a lot better.'

I felt like telling the pair of them to stop talking about me as if I wasn't there. I felt like telling them to shut the fuck up and choose some pasta. But I was so tired, I wanted to curl up and sleep the afternoon away. I stifled a yawn as my husband and my friend glowered at each other over the breadsticks.

Roman's smile was uncertain now. He paused as the waitress brought him a menu, her eyes lingering on his face for slightly longer than was strictly necessary, her features registering a kind of quiet delight.

This is the way women look at my husband, I thought.

And men too sometimes.

Don't forget the men.

'I'm worried about our girl,' Sandy said.

It was the wrong thing to say.

Roman didn't lift his eyebrows but he looked as though he just might. I saw him wince. *Our girl.*

He didn't care for Sandy's proprietorial air. And he never had.

'As I say, Lana hasn't been well,' Roman quietly repeated, the doctor who is growing tired of the dumb questions.

'I mean – look at her,' Sandy continued, ignoring him as if reports of me being a bit under the weather didn't quite cover it. 'So thin. So tired. She's like a bad photocopy of the old Lana.'

I snapped a breadstick in half. 'Gee, thanks, Sandy.'

'Yes – thanks for your concern, Sandy,' Roman said, with no detectable sarcasm, the good doctor placating a sick patient's difficult relative. 'We both appreciate it, we truly do.' He patted my hand, his eyes on a point somewhere beyond my shoulder. 'But Lana's fine.'

Sandy stared at me, his mouth twisted into a disbelieving smile. My heart went out to him. I knew he cared about me. They both did. But it felt like this argument had been coming for years.

Because Sandy wouldn't let it go. 'This medication,' he said. 'Benzodiazepines. Am I saying it right? When Lana was having a rest – catching her breath – I looked them up online.'

Roman sighed as he carefully laid down the menu. 'Always a wonderful idea, Sandy! You know the worst thing that you can do for someone's health? *Google their symptoms.* Self-diagnosis is – forgive me – plain stupid. Really, Sandy. It's stupid. Truly, you should know better.'

The waitress was back to take our orders.

Sandy waved her away and I gasped with relief. I was dreading the food. I was dreading the moment I had to decide how much I could force down without throwing up and how much I could leave on the side of the plate without causing a fuss.

'And I read that you're not meant to take these *benzos* for more than a few weeks,' Sandy continued. 'Because there can be other side effects. You know – apart from the side effect of making her well.'

And suddenly Roman was furious.

I watched him struggling to contain his rage, his new muscles flexing inside a shirt that was suddenly a size too small for him. When he spoke, his voice was so quiet it was almost inaudible. 'Sandy,' he said. 'Just to be clear – are you asking me to justify myself as a doctor or as a husband?'

'Neither.' Sandy raised his hands, helpless, retreating. 'I just care about Lana, that's all.'

Roman smiled tightly and picked up the menu. He was anxious to order. He wanted to be away. He would be skipping the starter and the dessert today, I reckoned.

'Lana's getting better,' Roman smiled tightly, signalling for the waitress.

And I knew that he would make sure he never saw Sandy again.

*

Sally Berry emerged from her cottage as Sandy and I arrived back at the Gardens, almost as if she had been waiting for us. She had a beatific smile and a wicker basket loaded with fruit and vegetables. She crossed the street and held out the basket to Sandy. An unmarked jar of honey sat in the middle of the gnarly-looking fruit and veg.

'From my garden,' Sally Berry said. 'September is harvest time.'

Sandy seemed genuinely touched, and lost for words, and admired the basket as if it was a newborn babe.

'Apples. Onions. Tomatoes. Courgettes,' Sally said. 'Autumn-fruiting raspberries. And a jar of my honey.'

Sandy cleared his throat. 'Lana tells me you have your own hives.'

'The human race could learn a lot from bees,' Sally said. 'Their work ethic. Their selflessness. Their unconditional love. Their respect for timeless values. Work. Family. Sacrifice. Duty. And love. They live their brief lives in the service of a greater good.'

'Magnificent creatures,' Sandy agreed.

'Bees are the essence of resilience,' Sally said.

Sandy and I went into the house and I smiled at him as I made us tea and he inspected his harvest basket.

'You wouldn't get that from your next-door neighbour in the city,' I said.

'No, they'll mug you for your autumn-fruiting raspberries soon as look at you,' Sandy laughed.

'What are you going to do with all that stuff, Sandy? You never cooked in your life.'

'Maybe I know someone who will cook for me. Did that ever occur to you? That I might not be sitting at home alone every night tapping away at the Deliveroo app for my lonely dinner for one?'

I smiled. After the death of his wife, Sandy's love life had always been a bit of a mystery. There had been women since his beloved Angie died, I suspected, but I had assumed they were all kept at a safe distance of a few thousand miles.

'You've got a new girlfriend?'

He flinched.

'At our decrepit age, I am not sure that's the term either of us would use. But I have *a friend*, yes. Why don't you come to the city and meet her? You can spare an old man one day out of your exciting new life, can't you?'

I smiled at him. 'Always.'

He took a seat at the kitchen island. 'It never works out very well for any of us when I come out here to the sticks. Not you. Not me. Not Roman.'

'True,' I sighed.

'So next time, you can come to me. We can take a walk in St James's Park. Visit the National Portrait Gallery. Have lunch at Wiltons. Look at the second-hand books on Charing Cross Road and the tenth-hand guitars on Denmark Street. We'll have afternoon tea at Fortnum and Mason, and you can meet my new friend. Her name is Melanie. She was born in Hong Kong but grew up here. And it will be fun.'

Something lifted within me. 'It sounds like fun. And I'm glad you've met someone. I look forward to meeting Melanie.'

He fumbled in the pocket of his jacket and placed something between us on the kitchen island.

It was a key. Or rather two keys, a front door key and a deadlock, both freshly cut and golden.

'The key to my apartment. For you.'

I stared at him, my throat choking with emotion.

'Because you're not stuck out here, Lana. OK?'

'OK.'

'Come any time. And if we're not home – if by chance we are eating dim sum in Hong Kong – then let yourself in.'

I picked up the keys and clutched them in my hand.

'I don't know what to say, Sandy.'

'You don't have to say anything. But know this – you're not crazy, Lana.'

I smiled at him, deeply touched by his act of kindness, the key to his home held tight in my fist. 'That's the nicest thing anyone's said to me for ages!'

'I mean it. And it happens to be true. But will you do me one favour?'

I looked at him. 'Anything.'

He wasn't smiling any more. 'Stop taking those bloody pills.'

We sipped our tea in the upstairs alcove and looked out at the back gardens.

'So I take it you're not working?' Sandy said.

I shook my head. My photography felt like it belonged to some other lifetime. I was often so tired that I felt like weeping. I could just about make it out of bed. And even if I did, I knew now I wasn't going to be the next Dorothea Lange.

So, what was the point?

Sandy said nothing but I knew he was disappointed in me for giving up something that he had devoted his life to. And I couldn't stand to see him disappointed in me.

'But I was good at it, wasn't I? Photography, I mean. Not a world beater, not touched with genius. But I had the eye, didn't I? And I had the technique, and I was willing to put in the hours. I was all right, wasn't I?'

He grimaced. 'Christ, you talk as if your life's all over. But yes – you were good at it, and you still are, if you give it a chance. You are not too old to do anything, Lana. Just – get well.'

'I'm trying, Sandy. I really am.'

There was a stir in the garden next door as Willow and Vince came out of the house. They kicked off their shoes, rolled up their jeans and sat on the edge of the pool, holding hands as they dipped their bare legs in the water.

It was getting too cold for splashing around in an outdoors pool now, and their appalled laughter drifted up to us.

Sandy watched them for a while and then suddenly he leaned forward.

'That's not her husband, is it?'

'Is it so obvious?'

He screwed up his eyes. 'Who *is* that guy?'

'That's Vince. Our handy man. And special friend to the fabulous Willow, who you've met.'

'Yes, and I've met him too,' Sandy said. 'But he didn't call himself Vince.' He shook his head with disbelief. 'It's him. It's really him. My God.'

He got up and left the room.

'Sandy?'

I followed him to my studio. Dorothea Lange's *Migrant Mother* stared down at Sandy as he put on his reading glasses. And then he peered at his own photograph, *The Crack Shack*, and at all those lost souls in that drug den staring out of the twilight.

'Look,' he said, tapping it. 'There's your Vince, years before he was Vince.'

I stared at Sandy's photograph. Towards the rear of that unlit room there was a man in his late twenties, his face in profile and his body bent over as if he had some business on the filthy ground. Or as if he was trying to avoid being photographed. There must have been twenty men and women in that filthy, cavernous space. And he was the only one not looking at the photographer.

'That's him, isn't it?' Sandy said. 'That's the man in the garden next door with Willow.'

'I don't know.'

But I did know. I just couldn't believe it.

Vince was in Sandy's award-winning photograph of a crack den. There was Vince, many years younger, a lifetime younger, right at the back of the room, his long rat-tailed hair falling across his swarthy face as he turned away from the camera, as if half of him did not want to be in Sandy's photograph, and the other half of him actually didn't give a damn.

But that handsome, midnight dark face was unmistakeable. And I recalled the smell that always followed Vince around, the insistent sickly sweetness of his weed.

'Was he a drug addict?'

Sandy stared at his photograph with wonder, still not quite believing it.

'When I knew him, he was into everything. One of those non-discriminating drug users. Constitution of a rhino. Was he a drug addict? If he was, then he was a high-functioning junkie. But Vince – although he was called something else back then which slips my mind – was the reason that most of the people in this photograph got busted and went to jail.'

'Vince was an informer?'

Sandy shook his head.

'Your Vince was a cop.'

29

Wednesday, 7 October

I thought I heard Roman whisper my name, but I was not quite sure until the moment his hand gently smoothed my hair. I buried my face into the pillow, so sleepy I could hardly open my eyes.

'How's my favourite patient?'

'Tired.'

'Can you sit up for me?'

I knew why he wanted me to sit up.

'Later,' I said, muffled by the pillow. 'Leave them by the bed. I'll take them later.'

A beat.

'If you take them now then you can go back to sleep.'

That gently cajoling daddy-knows-best doctor's voice.

He was not going to go to work until I took my pills. I wearily hauled myself up, rubbed my eyes and stared at what he was carrying. A tray with an egg cup containing a cocktail of pills. A blue pill and a white pill and a yellow pill. And a glass of water to wash them all down. Yum yum.

Diazepam? Xanax? Temazepam? And were they all benzos?

The drug diet was constantly evolving. He did explain it to me. I should have taken notes.

'How long do I have to take them for?' I asked, aware that I sounded like that most difficult of patients, she who dares to doubt her all seeing, all knowing doctor.

'You know how it works, Lana,' he said, with just a trace of professional irritation. 'We give you the lowest possible dose for the shortest possible time. Like any medication.'

'They just make me so *knackered*, Roman.'

'But they also make you feel *better*, don't they? Less anxious. Less ...'

He decided not to go there. Deluded? Was that what he was about to say then thought better of it?

The crazy lady obediently picked up her pills and Roman nodded encouragement as I popped them in my mouth.

I brought the glass to my lips to take a modest sip and as I was replacing it on the tray, I knocked it over. Suddenly there was water all over the sheets, the empty glass clattering to the floor, bouncing once but not breaking as it skittered away.

'Shit,' Roman said, getting down on his knees to clear up my mess.

'Sorry, sorry.'

'No, it's OK, don't worry, it's only water.'

I got out of bed and watched Roman fussing over the wet duvet. The water was mostly on his side of the bed so when he was finished mopping up as best he could, I slid back onto my half.

'Roman?'

He turned in the doorway, his hands full of soggy tissues, the tray tucked under his arm, empty egg cup in his hands.

'I just want us to be happy,' I said.

He nodded and gave me the saddest smile. 'Of course,' he said. 'And I want you to be well.' He thought about it for a moment. 'And I want us to be safe.'

I lay in bed, breathing, resting, letting my fingertips trace the edge of the wet sheets, listening to the sounds of Roman leaving the house. I could hear the unbroken whine of a leaf machine passing by outside.

When the front door finally shut behind Roman, I retrieved the three pills that I had stuffed inside the pillow, balled them up into a tissue, and held them tightly in my fist.

I was tired of feeling tired.

I went to the window and watched the street.

Krissy was taking Sailor to school. It must be netball practice before class and then a music lesson later, because Sailor was dressed in sports kit and lugging her cello in its cherry-red hard case.

Vince was blowing leaves outside Sally's cottage, wearing safety glasses, earmuffs and bright yellow gloves as Goran watched him from his white van.

Ben Cave and Professor Hall were coming back from their exercise, heading for the big house as Guy came down his drive and quickly crossed the street to Vince, who turned off his leaf machine and removed his earmuffs. Guy was jabbing his finger at Vince, who watched him with an impassive face.

No protests of innocence, no defensiveness. He could have been listening to a list of urgent chores for the garden.

But it was not that. Guy looked exactly like a man who has just discovered some digital dirty laundry on his wife's device.

Vince was thick bodied with all the hard-earned muscle of manual labour and Guy, though taller and bigger, was soft and flabby from living the good life for so long. But at that moment, my money would have been on Guy to clean Vince's clock. Because what they were discussing seemed to matter much more to Guy than it ever could to Vince.

I saw Guy's mouth move. You didn't need to be a lip reader.

'*Stay away from my wife*,' he said.

Then he marched back into his house.

I went into my studio and looked at *The Crack Shack* by Sandy McKay.

In the end, I reflected, there is no such thing as a secret life.

No matter how deep they are buried, all your dirty little secrets are dragged kicking and screaming into the light.

It was definitely him.

It was Vince in the photograph, in that crack den, in that other life.

When I returned to the window and watched the street my neighbours were all gone and Vince was alone, moving through the Gardens methodically, getting on with the job, blowing the leaves in one direction, always moving towards the manor house, a thoughtful frown on his dark face, as if he was giving Guy's words serious consideration, or perhaps just thinking about the falling leaves and reflecting on the turning of the seasons and the transience of all things.

Beyond the treeline, the ancient fields were empty for as far as the eye could see. It was a beautiful day. No guns today. My fist clenched around my balled-up morning pills.

I felt better already.

Vince was smoking weed when I found him.

One of those little soggy roll-ups that he favoured, the Vince equivalent of a tea break, his recreational drug elevenses, as he stood among the curiously neat piles of leaves. His expression when he saw me coming was neither friendly or unfriendly, but he made no special effort to greet me and I realised that he was the only one around here who did not treat me as if I was about to break, the only one who didn't act as if I was a fragile child, or off my rocker.

'Girl trouble?' I said.

He laughed shortly.

'Husband trouble, more like.' He smiled at me, weighing it up, wondering how I knew. But not for long. 'Willow doesn't delete, you see,' he said. 'That's the problem. You've got to delete, I always think, if you're going to play the game. Then delete again – delete from the trash. Then erase your browsing history. Better yet, get a second phone. But Willow is surprisingly innocent for someone who was modelling in Paris when she was fifteen years old. But there we go. It's all right. Just deny everything. That's my policy.'

'Do you love her?'

He laughed again. 'A romantic, are you?' He thought about it with a rueful smile. 'I want to be with her all the time. I want her to have a happy life. I can't get enough of her body. Is that love?'

'Close enough.'

He sucked the last of his soggy joint and flicked it away. The morning air was full of mists, mellow fruitfulness and the sweet, cloying stink of the handyman's weed.

'Is that why the police kicked you out?'

He wasn't laughing now.

'What?'

'The wacky baccy. Did they kick you out of the police force because you got too much of a taste for the wacky baccy?'

Some emotion I could not read flitted across his lean, lined face.

And then he smiled at me with what seemed like genuine amusement, and I wondered if I had got it wrong, if Sandy was mistaken, if this was one more thing to add to the list of lies that I had believed to be true.

And he saw my doubt. 'Hubby got you on the happy pills, has he, Mrs Wade?'

But I remembered his face in profile in that filthy room and my mind felt totally clear for the first time in a long time.

'You were an undercover cop,' I said. 'I saw you in a photograph that I have in my studio. You were working among druggies and dealers and junkies. And then you went native, didn't you? You got into drugs. And I was wondering – was that why the police kicked you out?'

He licked his lips. Glanced up and down the Gardens. Not so cocky now.

'I really don't know what you are on about, Mrs Wade.'

I smiled. I enjoyed seeing him off balance.

'Ah, but I think you do, Vince. Is that your real name? You worked with druggies and your job was busting the druggies and then you became a druggie yourself. Is that how it happened? It probably all got a bit too much. The pretending. And so they kicked you out.'

He was still smiling at me, but it was taking a lot of effort.

'What exactly has your husband got you on, Mrs Wade? And can I have some?'

But now I could clearly read what was on his face. And it was fear.

Goran slowly approached us in his van, restlessly doing his rounds, killing the long hours of watching all our honey-stoned houses, and Vince turned on his leaf machine and with one fierce blast, blew some stray leaves towards one of his neat piles.

Goran passed, raising his hand to both of us, unsmiling.

We waved back and watched as he drove slowly back to the other end of the Gardens.

Vince hefted his leaf machine onto his shoulder.

'Do you want to get us both killed?' he said quietly, not looking at me. 'Because you will get us killed if you keep opening your mouth.'

'I just want you to admit—'

'Please stop talking, will you?'

And then I understood.

They did not kick him out.

They had never kicked him out.

Vince – or whatever his real name was – had never left the police force.

He was exactly what he had always been. An undercover cop.

I stared wildly up and down the street.

'Why are you here?'

He had regained some of his composure.

'I really don't know what you're talking about,' he said. 'I think you have me mixed up with someone else. But perhaps – for both our sakes – you should watch what you say around your neighbours.'

'I don't understand.'

'I think you do. You just find it hard to admit it.'

I shook my head. But I heard the sudden sound of the guns rolling across the fields and, as a black cloud of birds burst from the trees, something stirred deep inside. Because I thought of my husband's new shotgun. And I thought of Krissy coming out of Lehman Brothers with her degree from Harvard and her career in a cardboard box along with the rest of her belongings and her plans for the future.

And I thought of Sally Berry's honey, and food that lasts forever, and I thought of Ben Cave with half his face sliced off.

And I thought of Magda Hall, the old lady in the big house, and the tiny girl she had been when in April 1945 in Berlin with her pretty older sisters fussing with their hair when the Russians came.

Goran got out of his van at the far end of the Gardens, and I thought of him moving in his mother's womb as Yugoslavia disintegrated.

All of them. They all had their private stories of collapse and chaos and endings.

They had all been burned.

And despite living in this blessed place, they all expected to burn again.

I thought of Guy having to get out of the changed South Africa. I thought of Willow in Paris, when she was what she called 'messed up' and with nowhere to turn.

And – yes – I thought of Roman and me, on the night our world fell apart.

Somehow all the broken parts of all these broken lives fit together here.

Guy – or Krissy or Tucker or one of them – it could even have been my husband, I suppose, or it may have been Professor Hall over sherry and civilised conversation – it could have been any of them – had said that you could feel it everywhere now, this sense that everything was finally falling apart.

'What's happening here?' I said.

'You already know what's happening here,' Vince said.

I turned towards the sound of the guns.

'They're waiting for the end of the world,' I said.

30

Thursday, 8 October

Vince lived in a field with a sizeable settlement of yurts, about a dozen of them, all looking surprisingly solid and clean and permanent and respectable, as if it was full of well-heeled grown-ups who were nostalgic for Glastonbury back in the Nineties. Around these parts, even the tents were middle class.

He had been expecting me. And I had been expecting male squalor but there was a fussy neatness about Vince's home, a slightly off-kilter domesticity. Small but neatly stacked shelves of old vinyl and paperbacks, his fresh work clothes drying on a hanger, clean boots and a toolbox by the zippy flap that acted as front door. No photographs.

He put the kettle on and pottered around the kitchen the size of a phone booth.

'Milk? Sugar?'

'Have you got camomile?'

'Do I look like I've got camomile?'

'Anything then.'

'I can put honey in it.' He nodded at the harvest basket on the work surface of his tiny kitchen. It was exactly like the one that Sally had given Sandy. Bruised-looking fruit and vegetables with a jar of home-made honey sitting at the centre.

A jar of Sally's honey. 'Or are you sweet enough already?'

'Anything,' I said again, unsmiling.

He made builder's tea for two and began to roll himself a joint. It was not like the small, wet joints he discreetly chain-smoked at work in the Gardens. This was a home-alone joint. This was an off-duty spliff. This was the size of a Cornetto.

I sat at one end of the only sofa in his yurt, and he knelt before the scarred old coffee table. He licked three Rizlas and stuck them together in a T-shape, broke open a cigarette, scattered the tobacco on top and finally produced a bag of dark brown hashish. After heating it with a disposable lighter, he crumbled some on top of the tobacco.

'Ready for some dirty secrets?' he said.

I nodded, feeling a surge of nausea, afraid of what I was about to hear.

'Just over eighteen months ago Bill Clutter and an unidentified white male attempted to buy destructive devices from a man in a pub in Brixton,' he said, rolling the giant spliff with expert fingers.

'What? Wait. Bill Clutter? You mean William Clutter? The pilot?'

He nodded. 'That's the one. Mad Bill. Cap'n Clutter. The one who killed his family and then himself. Allegedly. Clutter came to the attention of the authorities when he attempted to purchase two destructive devices from a man in a pub.'

'Destructive devices?'

He sparked up his joint. The tip flamed and then flared red as he sucked on it. Billows of smoke shrouded his dark head and filled the yurt.

'Hand grenades,' he said. 'These hand grenades were made in Croatia. Cetinka – that's the name of the manufacturer. Quite distinctive-looking. Black, lattice-faced spheres with a gold-coloured handle and a ring pull that looks just like a key ring. They should have been destroyed twenty years ago at the end of the Balkan wars. But – like decommissioned ordnance throughout history – these had been stolen, stashed away and sold on the black market.'

'How do you know all this?'

'Because the man who Mad Bill tried to buy his hand grenades from was not an arms dealer. He was from the Metropolitan Police. A former colleague of mine. The hand grenades didn't exist. But the law likes to know when someone is in the market. My bosses thought they were destined for extremists of one ilk or another. Some eye-swivelling, ideologically certain cabal of nutjobs ready to spill blood for their noble cause.' He grinned, took a hit of his joint, held it, released the smoke with a sigh. 'They could have been anything. Marxists, Nazis, anarchists. Animal rights or eco-warriors. Pro-life or anti-capitalism. Racial supremacists. Or just some little country lines drug dealer who wasn't content to scare his rivals with a shooter. But as it turned out, it was none of the above. This was for the Gardens – where you have a higher class of nutjob. It turns out that they – your neighbours – are getting ready.'

I took a shallow breath. 'For what?'

He shrugged. 'They're getting ready for when the shelves are empty and the lights go out and the Internet is dead, and the policemen are throwing away their uniforms. They all think they've seen the future, but they've all got their own private extinction event in their heads. Some of them – the American couple, Tucker and Krissy, and Willow's hubby, my mate Guy, and the old geezer in the big house, Professor Hall – are waiting for total global economic collapse. Capitalism falling on its fanny one more time and this time not getting back up.'

He nodded at the jar of honey.

'Sally, the spirit of Woodstock, believes that the human race are disrespecting Mother Earth and in the end the planet is not going to stand for it.' He sucked on his joint. 'And maybe she's right. Maybe they're all right. The ex-copper – Ben Cave – was in some of the same riots as me. That's where he lost half of his face, whatever he may tell you now. He knows the rage that is out there, waiting for an excuse to erupt. He would have seen it every day of his working life.'

The tea was scalding hot. I carefully placed it down, my tongue burning.

'And you have to admit, there have never been so many ways for the world to go badly wrong,' Vince said. 'The ice caps melting. A terrorist attack that unplugs everything. Some new plague. A nuclear cock-up. Or a cosmic blip that we can do bugger all about – a solar flare on the sun that turns off our technology. And although it sounds like the batshit-crazy club – *it's all happened before*. Everything they're scared of, everything that haunts their dreams. Plague, starvation, radiation, riots, the asteroid that did for the dinosaurs. Nothing they have in their heads hasn't happened before and couldn't happen again. And probably will.'

He took a suck of his giant joint and offered it to me.

I shook my head.

'And it's not illegal to be scared about tomorrow,' he said. 'It's only illegal when you start stocking up on hand grenades. It's only illegal when you start acting like your neighbours.'

'My neighbours? Sally? Krissy? *Willow*?' I felt like laughing in his face. 'Willow's not getting ready for the end of the world. She has trouble getting ready for dinner.'

He smiled fondly. 'True. An extinction event for Willow would be having a security block put on her black Am Ex card. Then let's say – some of your neighbours.'

'But what exactly are you talking about? Do you mean they're the kind of people who have a thousand cans of chicken soup in the basement?'

'Their plans are a bit more advanced than that. This lot have even got their own private doctor.'

It took me a moment to realise he was talking about Roman. The idea was absurd.

'Whatever they are – whatever William Clutter was – Roman is not one of them. He's not a ... a Prepper.'

'You sure about that, Lana? May I call you Lana? I notice he's bulked up with some muscle recently. He spends hours chatting to Professor Hall. More than you know, perhaps. Didn't he buy a gun? I don't know what your hubby's frightened of, lady. Bad people standing at the end of your bed at three in the morning? Is that what happened? You tell me. What *did* happen to you two?'

My face was burning. 'You're crazy.' I coughed, waving away his smoke.

Vince's smile faded. I had hurt his professional pride.

'And Bill Clutter is dead,' I said.

'Maybe Captain Bill developed cold feet. Or perhaps his lovely wife – April – or his son – Josh – wanted out. Who knows? Maybe he really did have a breakdown and top his family and himself. Maybe it's all true. And maybe not.'

The tent was too small. The air was thick with smoke. I could not breathe.

'You think someone killed the Clutters?'

'I have no idea what happened to that family.'

'People don't get away with murder.'

He laughed out loud. 'You really are a mad housewife, aren't you? *People get away with murder every day of the year.* And you know the biggest reason they get away with it? *Because they look normal.* They look like your neighbours. Yes, there are other reasons why people get away with murder. A lack of evidence, a lack of witnesses, police incompetence, a narrative that sounds credible even when it is totally invented, a story that rings true even when it is a pack of lies. But the *main* reason that people get away with murder is because they look like they are incapable of murder. Impression management, we call it in the game. Rich people in nice houses tend to be very good at impression management.'

'How did you get here?'

'Ah, that was the easy bit. Struck up a conversation with Goran in the Rat and Trumpet in the Village. Got my round in, and then another one. Then I had one interview with Ben Cave where I wasn't even invited to sit down.' He indicated Sally's harvest basket. 'And the next thing you know, I was the new handyman in the

Gardens, doing household chores for the minimum wage. It's amazing how gullible the totally paranoid can be.'

He stared thoughtfully at his smouldering spliff. 'People are attracted to apocalyptic thinking,' he said. 'People like your neighbours. It's a kind of narcissistic self-pity. You lose your job. You stub your toe. The Red Army marches in. And you see the world in ruins.'

'Or you get messed up on drugs.'

He laughed shortly.

'I'm not messed up on drugs! I've been smoking this stuff every day for the last thirty years – and I can give it up any time I like!'

I did not smile.

'I'm not a junkie,' he said, more firmly. 'I never touched the hard stuff. You know why? Because I grew up around it. My mum was a heroin addict. And it ruined everything.'

He took another suck on his joint, his eyes rolling back onto his head. He was very stoned now. He blinked, refocused, scratched under his arm. He didn't look as though he was capable of smashing drug rings or secret cults.

He looked like he would struggle to catch a cold.

He held the jumbo-sized spliff out to me again with a small, stifled cough.

I shook my head with disgust.

'Are you're here to keep them under surveillance?' I asked.

'No,' he said, the fog in his eyes lifting. 'See, I don't care what your neighbours are preparing for. And I don't care what they believe. I don't care what they're afraid of when they wake up in the middle of the night, or what weapons they have stashed under the floorboards. I don't give a damn, lady.'

'Then why are you here?'

He had closed his eyes. I thought he had nodded off. I got up to leave.

'Thanks for the tea, Vince. Or whoever you are.'

Then his eyes opened, and they blazed with a light I had never seen in them before. 'Because my sister lived on your street,' he said.

He let that settle between us.

'And then one day she went missing. Not a word. Not a peep. Gone, baby, gone. Meant to be shacked up in London. Well, maybe. But if that was true, then she would have been in touch with me, sooner or later. Even if she was in trouble, *especially* if she was in trouble. Because we were separated when we were kids, you see, and we swore that if we ever found each other, then we would never let it happen again. And I found her, all grown up. It's not difficult to find someone if they're still breathing and still using their real name. She wasn't happy – her marriage hadn't worked out. She wanted to change her life. But here's the thing – we had only just found each other, and she wouldn't leave me alone again. So I want to know what happened to my sister. I want to know what scared her. I want to know what happened to the only family I have left. And that's why I'm here. For her. Only her.'

And finally I understood.

'You're Juno Cave's brother,' I said.

PART FOUR
ROMAN

31

Saturday, 10 October

I came out of the treeline and the open field lay stretched out before me. The shotgun I carried pulled down hard on the muscles in my arms. The grass was still the lush green of late summer but the distant trees were now full of the brown and gold and rust shades of autumn.

I looked across at the others. Ben and Guy and Tucker, all dressed in the strange rustic formality of the shoot – check shirts and silk ties under wax jackets, wellington boots and flat caps pulled low down over our eyes. We cradled our shotguns with an almost parental tenderness.

Ben smiled across at me. 'Tenpin bowling for posh people,' he said, then lifted his scarred face to the far side of the open field, towards a dense thicket of trees and bushes.

Even as I watched it seemed to shiver with a rustling noise and suddenly erupt as an unbroken black cloud rose from it, nothing but that full blackness for an instant, and then the dark cloud shattered into countless tiny pieces as the birds took off into open sky and made their bid for life, flying straight towards our guns. A ragged-looking spaniel and an old black Labrador burst out of the thicket, tongues lolling, panting with excitement, racing towards us.

'Over!' Ben called, meaning the birds were coming our way.

It was a rough shoot, a walked-up shoot, meaning that there were no beaters and no gamekeeper, no glasses of champagne or corporate hospitality, no townies and no tourists. Just the landowner's two dogs to flush out the partridge, grouse and pheasant from their hiding places to where our guns were waiting.

I filled my lungs with the cold air. Then I lifted my gun, nestled the stock hard against my shoulder, and I squinted at the sky, grey slate smeared with rain clouds, alive and teeming with terrified life, looking for a target as I felt my finger on the trigger.

My telephone vibrated somewhere deep inside my jacket.

I heard the guns beside me, one after the other – *boof* – *boof* – *boof* – *boof* – the sound of 12-bore shotguns fired close by and in the open air, the sound seeming to extend and carry its own echo with it, and I focused on the sky as my phone continued to vibrate on my hip. I lowered my shotgun. The spaniel was already haring across the field towards a fallen bird, the old black lab lumbering close behind him. My phone was still vibrating, and the birds were already high above and far away, already back in formation and flying as one as my companions reloaded their guns.

Then I took the phone from my jacket and read the text message from Lana that told me she was leaving me.

I'm sorry but I just can't stay.
I will call in a day or so.
I love you all ways.

I read Lana's message again, the panic rising, and something fell away inside me, and it was the stuff that we built our marriage on, it was the foundation we constructed with all those countless small, shared moments over the years, the essence of all the memories we made our lives upon, dissolved by a single text message. It was everything, or at least the best part of my life, and I could feel it falling apart.

And then I read Lana's message again, looking for some deeper meaning, looking for a reason to hope. *I love you all ways.* Did that mean that there was still a chance for us? Was that a mistake? *All ways?* Did she mean *always*? Would Lana love me always or was loving me always already finished?

I felt my jaw seize up and my teeth clench, the sudden tears burning and blurring my vision, smearing the words on the phone that I read again and again and again. *All ways* sounded like a consolation prize, it sounded like a kind-hearted brush-off, as if she was dumping me as gently as she could, it sounded like – *I hope we can still be friends*. I stared at her text message, looking for that buried meaning, or even any meaning beyond the terrible message that she had left, and that she had reached some breaking point, and all the sadness and fear and unhappiness in her had not abated. I saw the face I loved, the serious beauty of Lana's wide-eyed Fornasetti face, and I imagined her writing these words that said she was leaving. And I saw how totally I had failed her. I had not given her the help she needed, the support she craved, the love she deserved. I saw with horrible clarity how all my pathetic efforts to make our lives good – moving out here, stealing her away from the city, our new home, my new job, the soothing medication I had carefully prescribed like some drug-dealing deity – had not made her happy and had not calmed her or made her feel safe, and if I had lost Lana then it was because I deserved to lose her. I was not worthy of her love. I was a husband who had let down his wife at every turn. Lana was my best friend as well as my lover, but I had not done enough to stop this day from coming, when my best friend packed her bags and left.

And the tears I choked down under the grey sky of the rough shoot were for myself, but they were for her too, because I knew she would never have gone unless she was right at the very end of what could be endured.

'Lana,' I said, the two syllables caught in my throat, and my heart, because our life together had stepped off the edge of the cliff, and I had done nothing to stop it.

When I looked up, my neighbours were surrounding me, and I could feel their concern, and that they knew something was very wrong. Guy's hand rested on the head of the spaniel. A dead bird was hanging from its mouth, as big as a bouquet of flowers, a red and green head on a golden-brown body, at once beautiful and grotesque. A pheasant, I guessed. The sight of it sickened me.

I stared at Lana's text message and felt the panic churning in me. Unusual for me to feel this way, this soaring dread, this roiling panic, in the great outdoors. In the past, my panic attacks happened when I felt confined, trapped, buried inside a situation that I could not escape from. But here it was in the wild open spaces, that familiar feeling of suffocation, my heart pounding, the sudden awareness of blood pumping in my veins. I clawed open my waxed jacket and I pulled at the too-tight collar of my dinky little checked shooting shirt and neat silk tie, and I felt the sudden sweat sliding down my back.

'My wife,' I said. 'Lana. I think she's left me.'

Guy cursed softly, glancing at Ben. 'Another bolter,' he muttered, and then to Tucker, his words little more than a whisper now. 'I knew it the first time I saw her.'

Ben was staring at me, a man who knew how it felt to be left by your wife. 'Any idea where she might be?' he said, matter-of-fact, and the way he said it made me understand that it wasn't over, that I still had a chance, that I could get Lana to come back.

'I might know where she's gone,' I said.

There was something wrong in the Gardens.

Oscar was sitting on the pavement outside Sally's cottage, not moving, his fingertips pressed against his forehead, his long lank hair hanging in his eyes, his face chicken-breast white. Sally was by his side, in floods of tears. Krissy was on her hands and knees, bending over something. As Ben's Range Rover pulled up, I saw it was the lifeless body of Oscar's dog, Buster.

A scattering of pink flowers from the oleander bush drifted across the pavement and clung to Buster's rich red fur. I was out of the car and on my knees next to the dog, touching his heart, pulling back his eyelids, but the old boy was long gone.

The apricot smell of the oleander bushes filled the air.

Sally was raving. 'I told you – I begged you! – *keep Buster away from the bushes!* I told you again and again! Didn't I tell you, Oscar?'

Ben was on the pavement with Oscar in his arms, and it was only now, with his father wrapping his arms around him, that the boy came undone.

'Dad.'

'I know, I know, I know,' Ben said, not letting him go. 'But this is the price we pay, the way you feel now, this is how much it costs for loving someone the way that you loved your Buster.'

I stared at Sally's fairy-tale cottage, and the pink tangle of flowers that covered the front of her gingerbread home. *Nerium oleander*, I thought, getting to my feet.

Toxic for pets.

Toxic for anyone.

You would never dream something so pretty could do so much harm.

Krissy was doing her best to comfort Sally, who was unmoored somewhere between anger and guilt.

'I *told* him to keep the dog away from the bushes!'

Ben took Oscar into their house. Krissy led away Sally. The smell of apricots was everywhere as Guy and Tucker looked at each other and then at me. Guy raised his eyebrows with a sigh and Tucker turned away, as if remembering a previous appointment.

'I'll take care of Buster,' I said.

I gathered the dog in my arms and carried him down the side of my house, gently laying him in a quiet corner of the back garden. I found an old tartan blanket and wrapped him in it, thinking that would do until we had a chance to bury him. Then I went looking for my wife.

32

Any other woman would have had friends her own age to run to when she was bailing out of her marriage. Ageing girls-about-town, young mothers, friends from work or university.

But Lana had Sandy.

Sandy lived in one of those big mansion blocks across the street from Harrods. More like a hotel than a home, I always thought, because of the doorman, the lift, the anonymous corridors, and because of the ever-changing cast of residents from every well-heeled corner of the planet. It exuded a kind of impersonal luxury, discreet urban privilege coated in a thin film of travel dust.

Sandy had lived his life here, using it as a bolthole when he was jetting off to war zones, then in his brief marriage to Angie, and beyond to widowhood. I had only been here once before – some press awards ceremony that Lana had dragged me along to in our courting days, when a crowd of us went back to Sandy's place in Knightsbridge to pay homage to the great man, and the inevitable prize the craggy old genius had just picked up.

I remember that Lana and I had a row on the way home. That was my memory of this flat, as the doorman announced my arrival, and I felt the ache of the long drive in my back and my bones.

I had always told myself that Sandy got under my skin because the world worshipped him for taking pictures of human suffering while a poor sap like me did twelve hour night shifts actually trying to relieve human suffering. That made my dislike sound very noble. But it was not quite the full story, or even the real story. Between you and me, I didn't resent Sandy McKay because the world loved him.

I resented Sandy because my wife loved him.

Sandy's girlfriend let me in.

I say girlfriend – Melanie was an attractive Cantonese woman in her middle years, one of those glossy, good-looking older women you see in Hong Kong who appear to have always been around money.

She gave me a smile of genuine warmth. 'You're Roman. And you're so welcome.'

Lana and Sandy were in the living room.

Lana had a book on her lap. I was expecting some learned, self-improving tome on Alfred Eisenstaedt or Weegee or Don McCullin or Diane Arbus or Brassaï, someone Sandy could drone on about for hours. But it was a hardback copy of *After Eden* by Professor A.V.R. Hall.

They looked up at me. 'I'm not coming back,' Lana said, and I stared at her, speechless, because I saw her clearly now, I saw her outside of the context of us, outside the universe of Lana and me – our home, our marriage, our life together – and with a jolt of shame I saw how unwell she had become, how pale and frail, and how all my efforts to make her healthy and happy had failed.

I stood there like a fool, lost for words, for there were no words to say how sorry I was to have lost her, and to have let her down. Yet I struggled to comprehend that there was a life now when we were no longer together. You think – or rather you grow to believe – that you will be together forever. Then you see it's just a delusion, that everything has its ending. Lana's serious face framed by that black bell of hair – I was so accustomed to seeing that face across the table from me in the morning and at the end of the day, so used to seeing that Japanese hair on the pillow beside me, that it was a shock to the system to be in a room with Lana and know that I could not reach out and touch her, that I could not take her in my arms, that she would be happier if I had never come.

How many nights together? They were in the thousands now. And already it felt like another time. We felt light years away from us. Together.

I felt the defective muscle by my eye start to pulse, and I stared around the room because I found that I could only look at Lana in short bursts. She did not need her marriage to me, I saw. She could have a different life, a better life, within walking distance of the food hall at Harrods.

How pathetic my dreams of redemption in the countryside seemed in the cold luxury of Sandy's apartment.

It was different from what I remembered. Smaller – a neat if outrageously expensive one-bedroom apartment in Knightsbridge with a generous living area, the walls covered with framed photographs by the great man, but now there was evidence of Sandy's new life. Framed photographs above the fireplace of Melanie with her late husband, Hong Kong harbour shimmering in the heat behind them, and laughing with their baby girl in a park, and the proud parents with their grown-up daughter graduating. Then later pictures of the daughter and Melanie grinning over blazing cocktails in some resort that might have been Bali, and the husband apparently dead by now. And there was one photograph of Melanie and Sandy, the pair of them dressed like explorers, off on some adventure on the wilder shores of the tourist trail. Angkor Wat, by the look of those temples. And there were invitations above the fireplace, to dinners and a reception and two weddings. A popular couple, a special couple, still living a full and active life.

'I mean it, Roman,' Lana said. 'You shouldn't have come. I would have called.'

Melanie was offering me tea, trying to act the gracious host, not quite sure how to play it, but her natural courtesy winning out. Sandy stared at me with blank-faced belligerence, as if there was still some of the Glasgow hard man in him if I wanted to take my chances.

'No,' I said to Melanie. 'Thank you.'

'Vince is Juno Cave's brother,' Lana blurted, as though we were in the middle of a conversation I had missed. 'Vince was a policeman. He *is* a policeman. Undercover. He's in Sandy's photograph – *The Crack Shack*.'

She looked at Sandy, who nodded his self-important affirmation.

I shook my head. 'What?'

'Juno and Vince were separated when they were children,' Lana said. 'Then Juno married Ben. And now Juno's gone, and Vince says that it doesn't make sense that she hasn't stayed in contact with him.'

I was struggling to keep up. 'Wait. Vince the handyman?'

'Why doesn't she get in touch with him? Why did she break off contact?'

I thought about it. 'Probably she's afraid Vince will ask her for money to buy drugs. Doesn't that seem like a reasonable expectation? Lana, you *met* Juno Cave.'

She swallowed. 'I know.'

'Did she seem afraid to you? Maybe she's not the greatest mother in the world, or the happiest wife, or the most generous sister. I don't know. But falling apart is what families do. I don't know why she blanks her brother. I don't really care, to be honest.'

There was a small suitcase in the corner, open, and I could see a few items of clothing that I recognised as Lana's favourites, and the sight of them pulled at my heart. A leather biker jacket that she'd been wearing the night we met. A beloved Prada sweater with so many holes it was falling apart. A few pairs of high-heeled shoes that she wore because she had never been happy with her height, she never thought she was tall enough. And the camera that she had not picked up for so long.

'Oh, Lana,' I said.

'She looks awful,' Sandy said, his accent more Scottish now he was at home in Knightsbridge. 'I don't know what you've got her on, but they're killing her.'

I felt a stab of fury. 'No,' I said. 'They're to stop that happening.'

'Look at her,' Sandy told me – he *told* me. 'Skin and bones, black circles under her eyes. She looks like death warmed up, Doctor.'

It was true she looked awful. But I remembered Lana on her hands and knees, digging up animal bones as our neighbours watched, and I remembered her full of fear, and her head reeling with nightmares that she had conjured out of nothing, and I remembered all the nights I woke to hear her wandering the kitchen, getting a bottle of rosé from the fridge, unable to sleep yet again. The pills I had prescribed were never to make her unwell. They were to calm her nerves, to help her sleep, to keep her sane. And I found I had zero inclination to explain any of this to Sandy.

'It's not you, Roman,' Lana said. 'And it's not us. It's that place. There's something in the air that is pure poison.'

Poison, I thought, and I felt the weight of poor Buster in my arms as I carried the dog to our garden, looking like he was sleeping, a few stray pink petals from Sally's toxic oleander bush still clinging to his red fur.

Lana smoothed her hands on the book on her lap. It was an older edition than my copy, but it looked as if it had never been read. It had the same quote they were still using on the cover.

'The Nostradamus of your worst nightmares' – The Times.

'Your Professor Hall is a hero to some,' Sandy sneered. 'With his predictions of collapse and chaos and the coming apocalypse. They love him – the survivalists, the preppers, the catastrophists, the doomsday cults of every kind.' Sandy stood, drawing himself up to his full pompous height. 'But he's not a hero to me.'

I laughed at him.

'I just want my wife back, Sandy. I just want Lana to come home. I don't care if there's an elderly academic living at the end of our street who has seen the end of the world. That's nothing to do with me, or Lana, or the family we were planning to have.'

I let that hang there.

Then I took the book from Lana's lap. A first edition of *After Eden* by Professor A.V.R. Hall. I turned to the title page, where it was signed.

To Mr McKay
Thank you for making being shot so painless!
Sine timore.
Alan Hall

I flicked through it, shaking my head. 'It's about how societies end. How everything is going to hell in a handcart. Capitalism, the environment – you name it and it's buggered, basically. He gave this to you when you photographed him, Sandy?' I closed the book. 'It looks like it's never been read.'

Sandy had lost the ability to blush fifty years ago, but he looked slightly uncomfortable. I smiled at Melanie and she smiled back, still hoping the evening could end without a nasty scene.

'What did you do, Sandy?' I asked. 'Look at the pictures?'

'But *you've* read it, haven't you, Roman?' Lana said. 'And you've got your signed copy. What does it say again? *To Roman – carpe diem.* That means – what? – fish of the day, right? Beautiful.'

'My Latin is a bit rusty,' I said, 'but I think the dedication is the same as in Sandy's copy. Professor Hall's catchphrase – *sine timore.* Without fear.'

'But why didn't you ever *tell* me that you met him before we moved in?' she asked.

I shrugged. 'Because it wasn't a big deal. And I hadn't really *met* him. I stood in line at the Waterstone's on

Islington Green, bought his book, told him my name and he signed my copy. There was quite a queue.'

Lana shook her head, her eyes suddenly brimming with tears.

'Why do you lie and lie and lie, Roman?' she said.

'I don't lie!'

'Do you believe in all his batshit-crazy theories?' she demanded. 'That the economy is going to crash and burn? That some new plague is going to come sweeping out of the back of beyond and wipe us all out? That someone – or something – is going to pull the plug on civilisation?'

I smiled sadly. 'No, Lana, I think everything will work out fine. Capitalism will survive. The poor and the sick and the ignorant and the hungry and the diseased will all gambol unto the sunny uplands of tomorrow. Planet Earth will be lucky with the weather. I think peace, prosperity and good health will cover the planet for ever and ever, amen.'

'Oh, fuck off, Roman.'

I gave Lana back the signed book. 'Lana has not been well,' I said, telling all of them the bitter truth. 'I did my best. As a husband, as a doctor. I guess I'm not very good at any of it.'

'She's frightened,' Sandy said, not giving me an inch.

'She's frightened because she's not been well,' I said, flashing again on the night we watched her digging up animal bones in our empty swimming pool.

'The Gardens is toxic,' Sandy said. 'Lana is staying here.'

I finally lost my temper with the old fraud. 'No, Sandy – *you're* the one who's toxic. You really need to keep your groupies close by, don't you? It's the only thing to help you forget that your heyday was thirty years ago.'

'My goodness!' Melanie exploded politely. 'What is *wrong* with the pair of you?'

Sandy smiled slyly. 'Roman and I both want what's best for Lana,' he said. 'It's really as banal as that.'

I turned to Melanie. 'I'm sorry, I really am.'

She looked sympathetic, and it made me weaken.

I didn't want to fight. All I wanted was the woman I loved to come back to me. But I understood that was not going to happen, no matter how much I wanted it. I hung my head, heavy with surrender.

'Go home, Roman,' Sandy said, not unkindly. 'You can see that Lana doesn't want you here, can't you? You're an intelligent man. You see that she doesn't want your suburban dreams and your clinging devotion and your fucking magic pills. Just go home and let Lana get on with the life she's meant to be living.'

I nodded. Lana was no longer looking at me. She hung her head too, as if in some last act of solidarity, and the black bell of her hair covered her face.

'I'll go but it's not home if you're not in it, Lana – it's just bricks and mortar and some numbers on some fucking estate agent's screen. It will never be home if you're not there.'

And I smiled at her. I smiled at her because I wanted her and she knocked me out and all that boy-girl stuff, but I also smiled because some people just make you happy that they are alive and living their life in this world, even if in the end they are not for you. Lana looked up at me and I smiled at her the way I had smiled at her on the night we met.

I wiped my eyes and held up my hands.

'Don't worry, folks!' I told them. 'He's not going to cry!'

The room was silent as they watched me leave.

Lana's voice stopped me at the door.

'Wait,' she said. 'Just wait, will you?'

And we stood there in silence in that home like a hotel room, while Lana stared straight at me, and straight through me, and my wife calculated exactly what it would take to give us one last chance.

33

Sunday, 11 October

It was just after midnight when I lifted Lana from the passenger seat and she awoke in my arms, her eyes scrunched up, for the night was too bright.

There were swirling blue lights all over the Gardens, two squad cars parked at the entrance, their blue emergency lights pulsing.

A woman was screaming.

Her long hair flying, she was just about being restrained by two uniformed policemen, one holding on to each arm, as she howled, maddened with grief.

John Carter's mother, Mary.

Her family were with her. A man of about forty, two boys in their late teens, and a woman in her early twenties. But the men hung back, as if uncertain how to act, while the young woman wrapped her arms around her mother and attempted to comfort her.

It was very late now, past all our bedtimes, but our neighbours were all coming out to look. Sally Berry was already on her doorstep, framed by the pink oleander. Krissy and Tucker appeared, and Sailor padded out behind them in her pyjamas, barefoot, her face streaming with tears.

Krissy ordered her to go inside. Sailor did not move. Mother and daughter stood shouting in each other's faces.

'Mary wants us to share her pain,' Sailor cried.

'No,' Krissy said. 'Mary wants to rub our noses in it.'

I blinked my eyes, exhausted from the drive, not understanding what I was looking at, still not understanding what had changed.

Ben Cave came out of his house with his arm around Oscar. They looked at the scene for a moment and then went back inside. Willow and Guy emerged from their house as I carried Lana up the driveway.

'Is Lana OK?' Willow said.

I looked at Willow's beautiful face, hidden behind a coat of milky cream. 'She's going to be fine. Thanks.'

I nodded at the disturbance at the entrance to the Gardens. The police were trying very hard to not arrest Mary Carter. 'What's happening here?'

The wailing woman broke free from the cops who were restraining her. She sank to her knees and began to beat her fists against the ground.

'My beautiful baby!' she moaned.

Guy chuckled.

I closed my eyes, understanding all at once, and imaging the well-rehearsed ritual at the hospital when the bed is stripped and the equipment wheeled away and the sad personal belongings of the newly deceased are bagged up for collection by the next of kin.

'Her son,' Guy told me. 'That little thief. They unplugged the worthless bastard.'

Sunday morning in the Gardens.

I was standing at our bedroom window, watching the street as our neighbours busied themselves with the rituals of self-improvement and pleasure.

Guy was sauntering down to his car, booted and suited for the guns, his shotgun in its slipcase slung over one Barbour-clad shoulder. You can't shoot game on a Sunday in England, so either Guy was off to blast clay pigeons from the sky or else he truly did not give a damn about their rules. Ben Cave was leading Professor Hall in a slo-mo jog back to the big house.

Krissy was loading Sailor into the Range Rover – Sailor dressed for what looked like hockey practice, but dragging her cherry-red cello case, so there was an afternoon music lesson after the morning's sport.

Sally hacked ferociously at the pink tangle of dying oleander shrubs.

Downstairs in our kitchen, I could hear Lana talking to herself.

And then she was suddenly emerging from our front door, dressed in the T-shirt and pants she had slept in, screaming at Guy.

'I *know* what you do!' Lana shouted, on the edge of furious tears. 'I *know* how you treat Willow! You bastard! You fucking *bastard*!'

Guy had his driver's door open, a frozen grin on his face.

He placed his shotgun on the back seat.

'Lana,' he said. 'I must ask – have you ever considered switching to decaf?'

Willow came out of her house, wrapped in a kimono, a kabuki-like cream covering her face. 'Lana,' she said, not quite touching her. 'Please. It's OK.'

'It's *not* OK, Willow!' Lana said, advancing on Guy. 'He touches you again and he'll regret it!'

I was out of the house and attempting to put my arms around Lana, but she shook me off.

Guy had lost his frozen grin. 'Go inside and take your happy pills,' he ordered Lana. He looked at me and raised his chin, as if to ask – *Are you going to deal with this or not?*

'Lana,' I said, afraid that she was going to launch herself at him.

Everyone was watching now.

Krissy and Sailor.

Professor Hall and Ben.

Sally, the garden shears still in her hands, the chopped pink petals fluttering around her faded denim jeans.

Professor Hall was the first to turn away, embarrassed on everyone's behalf.

He broke into his careful run and Ben followed him.

'You dare touch her and I'm calling the police!' Lana screamed at Guy.

'Again?' Guy said, wide-eyed with wonder. 'You're going to call the police *again*, Lana? Because calling the police worked out so well for you last time, didn't it? You crazy bitch.'

'Hey!' I said, Lana in my arms as Guy took half a step towards us, then stopped.

He turned on me furiously. 'Control your wife!' he shouted.

Which was a stupid thing to say.

Because nobody could control my wife.

I expected the argument to start the second we got back inside the house.

But Lana was silent and thoughtful as she climbed the stairs. I heard her settle into her alcove at the back of the house. That was where she was sitting, gazing down on next door's empty garden, when I joined her.

'Guy hits her, you know,' she said calmly, not looking at me. 'Willow hits him too. Sometimes she hits him first, I know. But there's no excuse, is there? There's no excuse for a man to raise his hand to a woman, is there?'

'No,' I agreed. 'There's no excuse.'

Lana continued to stare down at the back gardens.

'Do you want to take these?' I said, as casually as possible, and she turned to look at me standing there with a wine glass that was empty apart from the three pills at the bottom.

I held my offering out to her as if it was a bouquet of red roses and she laughed.

'To stop me making scenes?' she said. 'To keep me quiet?'

'No,' I said. 'Never that, Lana. To make you better. To just make it easier to deal with things.'

'I hate them. I hate my pills.'

'I know you haven't been taking them,' I said, my face reddening. 'Did you honestly think I wouldn't notice if you're not taking your medication?'

'How could you tell, Roman? Because I'm capable of stringing two thoughts together?

'No, because you're *angry*. I can tell, because you're *upset*, because you are *anxious* and because you want to beat up Guy.'

We smiled at each other. Then my smile faded.

'And because I can see that you've been working yourself into a state,' I said. She wasn't looking at me. 'They calm you down, Lana. That's what they're *for*.'

'That's right, Roman. They make me so calm I'm practically in a coma. They make me so calm that my brain curls up and dies.' She shook her head. 'But now I'm looking for other ways to calm myself down. Ways that don't put me in a coma. Alternative remedies.'

I felt a wave of despair. 'Don't waste your time with digital quacks. Just take the medication you need to get through this difficult patch. And you should be resting.'

'I just slept for ten hours!'

I was struggling to stay calm. 'So you don't want to take your pills?'

'No, Doctor. I'm done with the pills.'

'Then that's fine. Don't take them. But you have to see this can't go on, Lana. All the obsessing about the past. And all the accusations.'

'Guy *hits* her!'

'I don't doubt it. You know what I mean. The night the police were here. The obsession with Juno Cave, who seems perfectly happy to me. Constantly worrying about the Clutter family, who are beyond anyone's help. It can't go on like this, can it? Because it's not going to end well.'

'You're afraid I'm going to embarrass you again!'

'No,' I said. 'I think we're way beyond being worried about feeling socially awkward.' I gestured to the world beyond our window. 'Our neighbours – all the people who live next door. They're starting to think you're ... unbalanced.'

'You mean *unhinged*. And is that what you think?'

I sat next to her in her alcove. 'I think it's been hard for both of us since that night at our old flat. I think the stress has been unbearable. I think we are both struggling in our own ways. I have panic attacks in supermarkets. And you – you get these crazy stories in your head that have no basis in reality. And it scares me.' She was silent. 'Because how long before our neighbours call the police about *you*, Lana?'

She laughed shortly. 'To do what? Lock me up?'

We stared at each other. And she finally saw I was serious.

She drew herself away from me as if she had been scalded.

'What are you going on about? Do you think they're going to come and lock me up? Are you talking about them putting me in a nut house? My God, Roman – you're talking about having me sectioned!'

I tried to touch her arm. She pulled away. Her thin bare arms were wrapped around herself for protection, and when she drew her legs up I could see her feet were filthy from confronting Guy on the driveway.

'You just can't keep raving and ranting and think that there are no consequences,' I said. 'Because there will be, Lana. Here – and anywhere else we might live.'

'Sectioned. Locking me up in a nuthouse. They can't do that to me!'

I took her hands in mine.

'But they can. Under the Mental Health Act, anyone can be admitted to hospital without their consent if it's for their own well-being. And that's where all these scenes – digging up bones, screaming at the neighbours – are leading.'

'You wouldn't let them do it!'

'I wouldn't be able to stop them. And that's why I'm scared.'

'You've been scared for a long time, Roman.'

I left her and went to our bedroom at the front of the house.

I sat on our unmade bed and after a few minutes I could feel her standing in the doorway, staring at me. Then her hands were resting on my shoulders.

'We can't go on like this,' I said, not turning around. 'I want you to be well – I want that more than I ever wanted anything in my life. But look what happened with Juno. Look how wrong you were about all of that. Remember how bad that made you feel – how upset we all were because of your … delusions.'

Lana bent over me and put her head close to mine. She knew how much I loved her hair, she knew how much I loved it swishing in my face.

'You would never let them come for me,' she said quietly. 'You would never let them take me away. You love me, Roman. I know you do.'

I almost laughed. 'A lot of good that will do you,' I said. 'The world narrows down, Lana. When I was young, I thought I was going to save the world. Now I know the truth. It turns out that I can't even protect my wife.'

She came and sat by my side. 'I'm sorry,' she said. 'I'm sorry I left you. I'm sorry you had to come and get me.'

I placed my hand on her leg and smiled. 'You had to get away. You told me. I get it.'

'No,' she said. 'That's not what I mean.'

The room was very still.

'That night in the old place,' she said. 'I'm sorry I left you that night. I'm sorry I ran away. I'm sorry I left you there alone. And I'm sorry, Roman – I'm sorry about what those men did to you.'

I shook my head, denying it all, wanting her to stop, to please just stop talking.

When I could work up the nerve, I looked at her.

She touched my cheek. 'My beautiful man,' she said.

We held each other, and we did not talk, and we sat like that for a long time.

And out on the street, we could hear the low murmur of discreet voices.

Our neighbours were talking.

34

Monday, 12 October

The rains came.

Torrential, driving rain that woke me at first light as it hammered on our roof. Lana slept on as I quietly slipped out of bed, and padded to the window where I saw that the weather was repainting the world. The rain turned the stone of our houses to a deep old gold and transformed the distant fields and countryside to darker shades of green, brown and yellow.

A fast-flowing stream was running from the manor house to the entrance of the Gardens. Oscar and Ben came out of their home in their running gear and splashed through it, lifting their bare legs, laughing with appalled delight, then father and son jogged from the Gardens towards the country lane on the far side of the main road. I watched them disappear under the tall elm trees.

Sally Berry came out of her pink-garlanded cottage and stared up at the furious skies. She hesitated for a moment, as if contemplating going back inside, then stepped out to the middle of the Gardens, her faded double denim outfit turning from sky blue to indigo as it became more sodden. But Sally just stood there, looking up, as if all her worst fears about what mankind had done to our planet were being confirmed.

And it was true – this felt like some new kind of weather that was nothing like you remembered.

Sally went back inside her cottage, and I got back into bed with Lana, spooning against her bed-warm body, feeling the sleepy heat of her back and butt and legs. I said her name and she murmured my name, somewhere between sleep and waking. It was nearly time to get up for work.

Just a little longer, I thought, holding my wife as the rains beat down.

It rained all morning and well into the afternoon.

From the window of my surgery, I watched council workers sandbagging the river. The streets of the village were deserted. Rachel, my receptionist, frowned at her phone, reading about cancellations on the trains. I told Rachel that she should leave early, so when my last appointment of the day arrived, Krissy and Sailor, there was only me to greet them. They came in, dripping on the carpet, Krissy with a face like thunder and Sailor avoiding eye contact.

I took them through to my surgery.

'How can I help?'

'Show him,' Krissy said.

Sailor didn't move.

Krissy seized her daughter's right arm and roughly pulled up the sleeve of her white school shirt, and I saw the cuts on the pale flesh of Sailor's forearm. I came round the desk and examined the wounds. Two cuts, very recent. One short horizontal line, just below the crook in her arm, the dried blood livid red, and then another cut shaped like a fishhook, the dried blood black on this wound, longer and deeper, as if she had gained confidence with her cutting.

'Please,' I said, and Sailor followed me to a corner of the surgery where there was a sink. I examined her arm again, looking at the depths of the wounds, looking for signs of infection, and then took her wrist and held her arm under cold running water. Krissy sat watching us, ready to explode.

I silently soaked a gauze pad in saline solution, cleaned the cuts and dressed the wounds in a sterile adhesive bandage.

'What did you use, Sailor?' I said.

Krissy exploded. 'Who cares what she used? Christ, Roman! I want to know *why* did she do it? It's insane! You don't seem surprised. Jesus! Is this normal now, a world where our children butcher their bodies?'

I went back to my desk. Sailor sat down beside her mother.

'There are multiple reasons for self-harm,' I said. 'Anxiety. Depression. Low self-esteem.'

'My God – look at her! Low self-esteem? What does this one have to feel low self-esteem about? She's the girl with everything! You should have seen the mess I was at her age! And I wasn't cutting chunks out of my body!'

'It's a cry for help, Krissy,' I said.

'Oh *please*. You're in private practice now. No clichés, please. Not at these prices.'

'Or a cry of something else. Despair. Sadness. Anxiety.' I looked at Sailor and then at Krissy. 'And it can happen to anyone.'

Krissy stared at Sailor pulling down the shirtsleeve, covering the bandage, doing up her button. Her long blonde hair fell over her miserable face.

'Do you know why you cut yourself, Sailor?' I said.

'It presses the mute button in my head,' she said.

'I'll press your mute button for you!' Krissy said.

'Self-harm is a way of expressing complex, distressing emotions, a way of working through a difficult time,' I said. 'Our next step is finding other ways for Sailor to express herself, possibly finding a sympathetic professional for her to talk to, if that's what she wants. And developing coping mechanisms, such as breathing exercises for stress.'

Krissy snorted with disbelief. 'Take a deep breath?' Krissy said. 'You're really suggesting she takes a deep breath?'

I told them what I knew about self-harm, and the options that were open to us now.

But what I did not tell Krissy was that Sailor's wound looked like the letter *J* to me, and I did not tell Krissy that sometimes the cut in a teenager's flesh was the first initial of somebody's name.

Lana called as I was locking up the surgery.

'They found it, Roman.'

'What?'

'The police found the hard disk from our CCTV. The one that went missing. They found it down a storm drain, Roman.'

I stared out of the window, speechless.

The council workers had finished laying the border of sandbags along the edge of the river. The rain was not stopping. The river's level seemed far higher than I had ever seen it.

'A storm drain?' I said stupidly, as if I had never heard of such a thing. 'I don't understand.'

'Remember when the police came to our house the day after John Carter was run down? They wanted to see our CCTV. But the hard disk wasn't there. Remember that?'

I remembered walking down the cart track under the tall elm trees, the sound of the summer fields all around, and I remembered that the CCTV hard drive felt as heavy as a brick in my hand. And I remembered the sound the water made when I dropped it into the blackness.

'Yes.'

'The police found it down a storm drain.'

I was silent, a sick dread rising in me now.

'It's a drain to run off the water from the fields, to stop them flooding,' Lana was saying, as if I needed some further explanation. 'There's one in that lane opposite the Gardens where the joggers and dog walkers go. And it overflowed, Roman. Ben and Oscar saw it when they were running, and they called the police because it was full of things that should not have been there, things that had been dumped, things that had no good reason to be there. Women's clothes, apparently.'

'Women's clothes?'

'And other things that should not have been there. And one of them was a CCTV hard disk.'

'How can they know it's the one from our house?'

'You're right, Roman. Maybe it's somebody else's CCTV hard drive. There must be loads of them down there. But that's not what the police think. Our old pal DI Hunter was down there, nosing around, and she told Ben and Ben told Tucker and Tucker told Krissy and Krissy told me. And now I'm telling you.'

The silence hummed between us.

'Hello?' she said.

'I'm still here,' I said.

'They found it, Roman.'

A young policeman was laughing under the tall elm trees as he watched an even younger policeman pulling objects from the storm drain.

DI Hunter watched the officer on his hands and knees without expression as he fished out what looked like a clump of leopard-print silk, covered with the black grime of the storm drain.

The source of the laughing cop's amusement was strewn all around the storm drain.

It was all lingerie. Wardrobes of it.

Thongs and bras and fishnet bodysuits. Pink and black and leopard print. High-heeled shoes that were not made for walking. Swimwear that wasn't designed to get wet. Stockings and knickers and what were now unidentifiable pieces of silky rag. It all lay strewn in the mud.

And there were other things. Books – perhaps they had once been school exercise books – and unopened jars of home-made honey. But mostly it was all that lingerie, that was what had caused the storm drain to overflow. The CCTV hard drive that I thought was gone forever now lay on a silky slip of black gauze that had once been a nightdress.

DI Hunter was taking photographs.

But none of it, I realised, was bagged up as evidence. There was no sense of urgency, it did not feel like a crime scene. DI Hunter glanced at me as I stood gawping.

'There's a Victoria's Secret store down there,' Hunter said.

'Who did it belong to?'

The detective shrugged. 'Your guess is as good as mine. But we found a CCTV hard drive which I am assuming belonged to the system in your house.'

She squinted at me in the rain. But she did not look suspicious, and I wondered if this was some professional façade.

I made an effort to not speak, to not ask the obvious question.

But she answered it for me.

'The footage is probably ruined,' she said, not sounding too concerned. 'But we will get our lab boys and girls to have a look.' And she smiled at me, a mirthless grin. 'Because you never know your luck, do you?'

I stared at the ruined, muddy pile of women's lingerie.

It looked like it had been thrown away by a cuckolded husband or an abandoned mistress.

Someone who must have been burning with fury.

I was soaked to the skin when I got home.

'I know you put it down there,' Lana said, sitting at the kitchen island with an untouched glass of rosé in front of her.

I did not bother to lie. I was sick of lying to my wife.

'I was trying to be a good neighbour.'

She shook her head. 'You do things behind my back.'

I stared down at the puddle on the kitchen floor I was standing in.

'I threw it away because I didn't want to get our security guard arrested for an accident.'

'An accident?' She picked up her wine glass but did not drink. 'Keep telling yourself that and one day you might actually believe it.'

'I didn't want our neighbours to hate us. It would have done nothing to make things better for John Carter or anyone else. Certainly not for you and me.'

'You took it. You threw it away. And you did it all in secret.'

She lifted her wine glass and put it down again.

'I want this place to work for us, Lana! I believe it's our last chance for happiness. I did it for the reason I do everything. *Because I love you.*'

Lana shook her head, but I saw something in her soften, and she left the room and came back with a big white bathroom towel.

'Get out of those wet things,' she said, pulling off my jacket, undoing the buttons of my shirt, helping me out of my clothes until they were crumpled and wet on the floor and I stood there stock-still and naked in our kitchen, Lana drying me off with a kind of brisk tenderness as the world grew dark outside.

'You're going to catch your death,' she told me, and my fingertips touched her face.

PART FIVE
LANA

35

Tuesday, 13 October

They buried John Carter and they made us watch.

I got out of bed at the sound of the horses and looked from the bedroom window as the procession paused before the entrance to the Gardens. Four black horses pulled a glass carriage, the horses wearing blinkers and feathery black plumes as extravagant as a showgirl's headdress, guided by a hatchet-faced undertaker in a top hat who looked like he was auditioning for a production of Oliver Twist. The Victorian solemnity was undercut by the wanton modern-world bling of the gold coffin in the back of the hearse, shiny as a box of Ferrero Rocher chocolates on Christmas Day, the coffin almost covered by an extravagant wreath of carnations that spelled out JOHN. The glass carriage was followed by a convoy of black Rolls-Royces, their orange warning lights pulsing with the steady rhythm of heartbeats.

They had stopped at the entrance to the Gardens, as if to allow us to pay our respects, or to taunt us. Or, yes, simply to make us watch, to make us see. And we did.

I saw Roman come out of our house just as Guy appeared on the driveway next door, dressed in a tweed four-piece shooting suit. Willow padded behind him in a white bathrobe, barefoot, sleepy, shivering in the cool of the early morning.

We all looked at the stalled procession.

Then Guy snorted with bleak amusement and his sneering voice drifted up to me.

'My big fat gypsy funeral,' he said.

There were two police cars parked at the entrance to the Gardens, and DI Hunter stood by the open driver's door of one of them, talking to Goran, apparently suggesting with a lift of her chin that he might like to put some distance between himself and the mourners. Goran stuffed his hands into the pockets of his black bomber jacket and wandered slowly into the Gardens, as if it was all his choice.

Now more of our neighbours were coming out of their houses to look at the funeral cortège.

Ben Cave and Oscar, the boy breaking away from his father to trot to the entrance of the Gardens, to get a better look. Then Sally Berry. And Krissy and Tucker, followed by Sailor in her school uniform, lugging her cello, her already pale face now chalk-white with shock.

Sailor hung back, her arms wrapped around the cello, embracing it, but the rest of them drifted to the middle of the road and stood in a loose group with Goran on one flank, the hired help slightly apart from the families.

There was no sign of Vince. And I suddenly wondered if he would ever be coming back now his secret was out.

DI Hunter walked over to the little group. Guy made an impatient gesture, indicating the road was being blocked by the procession and DI Hunter raised her hands, palms facing the ground, as if asking for patience until the cortège has passed. The neighbours muttered among themselves. There was no need for the cortège to stop at the entrance to the Gardens, and we all knew it.

DI Hunter went back to the police cars. Oscar stood next to them, and some of the faces in the black convoy of mourners turned to look at the boy.

DI Hunter spoke to Oscar, and he stared up at her as Ben jogged over, put his arm around his son's shoulder, and gently led him back to the grown-ups.

The cortège suddenly lurched into movement, the orange warning lights of the cars flashing so bright in the autumnal mist it felt like the first day of winter. Then I saw the middle-aged woman's face at the window of the leading Rolls-Royce, staring at my neighbours as they watched her bury her son.

Mary Carter's face was no longer lost in a rage. She looked helpless. Heartbroken. But she was also shockingly calm now. And before the car had passed, she took one final look at the Gardens, as if she finally understood something about these big houses with their money and their security and their privilege and protection, as if she was doing some final accounting, some final reckoning, and measuring the difference between us and everyone she loved.

In the early afternoon there was a soft knock on the door, and I rushed to answer it, thinking it was Roman, come home early to claim me, and tell me that we were still strong together, and nothing would ever change.

But it was my neighbours. Willow and Krissy and Sally Berry.

Willow threw her arms around me.

'You're back with us now,' Sally said. 'Back where you belong!'

I laughed with embarrassment.

'Anything that we can do to make you happy here,' Krissy said, close to tears, her voice cracking with emotion. 'Just ask.'

I stared at her.

Willow and Sally were happy to see me but Krissy seemed ready to fall apart. And she wasn't simply upset about me running off to London and then coming home to scream at my next-door neighbour. There was more.

'Sailor,' Krissy said, answering my unspoken question. 'Sailor's missing.' She looked around wildly. 'Well, not *missing* exactly. It's just – nobody knows where she is. I dropped her off at school, but they phoned and said she wasn't there for registration. Her cello was in the playground. What was her cello doing in the playground?'

Across the street, Tucker leaned on his car horn, anxious to get moving.

'I've got to go,' Krissy said, her tears spilling. 'We've tried her friends. Nobody's seen her. She's just run off.'

'Silly young thing,' Sally said. 'Moping about that horrible boy.'

'He *was* kind of cute,' Willow said.

'Oh, he was a feral little prick, Willow!' Krissy said viciously.

'Hashtag – just saying,' Willow said.

Then I was comforting Krissy, or perhaps we were comforting each other, holding each other awkwardly, patting each other on the back, and I knew that Krissy and I had not grown close, not the way that I had grown close to Willow, but perhaps we could, perhaps we would.

'Look at us!' Krissy laughed, wiping her eyes. 'What a mess!'

I laughed with her. 'Sailor will be back,' I said. 'I know she will. You do so much with her. You do everything with her. You're such a great mother, Krissy.'

I meant it.

Tucker leaned on the horn of his car again, breaking the spell, and Krissy and I came apart, smiling bashfully at each other, as if something had been revealed.

My neighbours cared about me, and I cared about them, and sometimes in life we put down roots without even noticing that they are growing.

'Thanks so much for coming,' I said to the three of them.

'That's what neighbours are for,' said Sally.

Night was falling and they still hadn't found Sailor.

Roman came back from work, spoke to Ben on his driveway and immediately went out again.

The police had been called. Sailor's disappearance was serious now.

Most of the street was out looking for the missing girl and the ones who were not – Sally, Oscar, me – hovered in our doorways, or watched from the window, or wandered down the driveway, waiting for news, waiting for Sailor to come back home, just waiting.

Then Sally went back into her cottage and Oscar stood on his driveway alone, looking bereft, and as I watched him from my kitchen window, I suddenly realised that this poor awkward kid was helplessly, hopelessly in love with gorgeous, high-flying Sailor. And then Oscar went inside his home too and finally the Gardens were silent and empty.

I stood at the window of our kitchen and stared at our street for a long time. The days were growing noticeably shorter now and as the night grew dark the only splash of colour left in the Gardens were the pink flowers of the oleander bushes growing in mad profusion around Sally's cottage.

Sally had chopped it back after the death of Buster the dog, but the pink flowers still clung to the house as if they were a part of it.

When it was too dark to see the pink flowers, I went to my laptop at the kitchen island and typed 'oleander' into the search engine and I sat there for the longest time, scrolling through the infinite images of the flower in bloom, usually pink but also white and red, a hardy evergreen and perennial favourite, it said, and I let myself get lost among the flowers, and I felt comforted by them.

Then, among all that glorious colour, there was a solitary black-and-white image from what I could only think of as the olden days. A group of stern, rail-thin men with moustaches and top hats and shirts with high collars, standing around in a field that was inexplicably covered in dead horses.

It could have been a war zone.

But the men did not wear uniforms. They wore the clothes of the ordinary world. So how to explain all the dead horses?

'Plants cannot move to escape their predators so they must find other means of protecting themselves,' I read.

Then there was a sudden spasm of pain in my neck, an excruciating jolt in some stress-stiffened muscle, and I half-turned my head towards the window and the night outside, as the sweet scent of apricots drifted in from the darkness and the cottage across the road where the oleanders grew.

36

Roman was still out helping them to look for Sailor and so when the night was silent and the street was empty and I was sure that no cars were coming, I put the door on the latch and quickly crossed the street to Sally's cottage.

I had tried calling Vince, but his phone went straight to voicemail.

So I was going to have to do this part alone.

I stood staring at the pink flowers that still ran riot over the front of her house, even after Sally's brutal chopping, feeling giddy with the sweet heady apricot scent of the oleander.

I shivered in the cold night air. *Should have worn a coat, Lana.* Or perhaps it was not the night that was making my flesh crawl.

I took out my phone, paused for a moment, listening to the sounds coming from inside Sally's house. Stevie Nicks was singing, giving some departing lover her bitter-sweet hippy-chick best wishes – and Sally was warbling along at the top of her surprisingly strong voice. I began taking photographs of all those pink six-petal flowers surrounded by their strangely sharp-looking leaves, getting as close as I could without touching them, uncertain exactly what I was doing, but very aware that I could look but not touch.

Because I knew now that these pretty flowers could kill you.

Then headlights suddenly blazed behind me.

I turned, shielding my eyes, as the lights began creeping towards me. My heart hammered in my chest as the thought crossed my mind that those lights were not going to stop, that I would be run down where I stood.

Just like that boy. Just like John Carter.

And then the vehicle slowed and came to a stop with the headlights and the front bumper inches from my legs.

The driver's door opened, and the bulky black figure of a man emerged, unhurriedly closing the door behind him as he started towards me, the engine still running, the headlights still on, still blinding me.

I averted my face from the glare, one hand pressed to my forehead.

'You OK, Mrs Wade?' Goran said quietly.

I was aware of the white van in the darkness, the engine rumbling, Goran coming towards me, so close now I could smell his sweat and scent mixed with the fruit smell of the oleander.

I felt my legs going. 'Please,' I said.

'Sorry, Mrs Wade?'

'Please don't hurt me.'

He laughed with aw-shucks embarrassment.

'I'm not going to hurt you!' He ran a hand over his shaven head. 'Nobody is going to hurt you, Mrs Wade! My job is to make sure that you're safe. That we're all safe here in the Gardens.'

He waited, and in the blaze of the headlights his breath was steam in the cold night air.

I gestured feebly towards Sally's front door.

'I just wondered if there was any news about Sailor. But then I …'

The big security guard stood there, letting me babble, watching my face grow hot from my lies. 'I was watching you for a while,' he said casually, deciding that I had finished, that I had run out of feeble excuses for doing what I was doing, namely taking photographs of my neighbour's house. He half-turned his head and gestured towards the entrance of the Gardens. 'You were just standing there, so I wondered if you were feeling all right.' He paused. 'I know you haven't been very well.' A pause. 'That's true, isn't it?'

I nodded.

'I didn't notice your phone,' he said. 'I didn't really see what you were doing. Until now.'

He took a step towards me and only stopped when he saw me freeze with terror.

'Don't,' I said. 'No closer.'

He raised his hands, placating me, as Sally's front door opened, and Fleetwood Mac blared louder from inside the cottage.

'Lana?' Sally said.

They both stared at me and the scent of the oleander, that ripe fruit smell, was suddenly sickening.

I felt beads of sweat break out on my back and slide down my spine, and I suddenly thought I was about to vomit.

Then the pair of them were holding me, Goran on one side and Sally on the other. I stumbled away from them into the road, breaking their grip and I ran across the street to Willow's house, banging on the door as Goran and Sally watched me without expression. Willow answered the door with her perfect features covered in a coating of ghost-white face cream and wearing some kind of floaty gossamer-thin kimono. She looked like a recently exhumed geisha.

'I need Vince,' I said.

Willow laughed shortly. I realised I may have woken her. She seemed to be on something that slowed her down.

'We all need a Vince in our life, Lana.'

'Is he at home? He's not answering his phone.'

Beneath the mask, her lovely face looked peeved. 'Well, he's not here, is he?'

'He didn't come to work today,' I said in a rush. 'Did you speak to him? I need to see him urgently.'

Willow sighed, and tiny fissures appeared in the white paste around her mouth.

'I'm the wrong person to ask, Lana. Believe me, this is the last place he is going to be, and I'm the last person he is going to see.'

She sounded somewhere beyond sad. She sounded all chewed up inside, yet not remotely surprised.

She raised a hand in greeting to Goran and Sally across the street and the sleeve of her kimono slipped up her arm, revealing one of her lucky tattoos. Then she folded her arms across her chest, a defensive gesture.

'Look, Guy's still going stark raving crazy because of what he found on my phone, OK? He's talking about throwing me on the street, so I have to be careful. I can't go back to Paris. I can't go back to modelling. I'm too old, I'm too fat and I'm too ugly.'

She was by some distance the most beautiful woman I had ever seen in my life.

'What was on your phone, Willow?'

'A photograph. Something that I had sent to Vince. A shot of one of my tattoos.' A beat. We both looked at the number 7 on her arm, half-covered by her billowing silky sleeves. A significant number in all major religions, I recalled. 'Not that one,' Willow said, pulling down her sleeve. 'I sent him my number 8,' she said. A rueful, lopsided grin. 'Men always love my number 8.'

I remembered Willow pulling down the waistband of her skirt to show me the number 8 just above the crack in her world-class ass. The luckiest number of all because 8 in Mandarin – *bā* – sounds the same as 'to prosper'.

Unlucky for some, I thought. Unlucky for Vince.

'I need to see him now, Willow.'

She smoothed the white paste around her lips and the tiny flaws were gone.

'Vince doesn't work here any more,' she said.

I turned away, stumbling to the middle of the road, and they were all still standing there, just watching me. Then I ran.

37

The blue lights of the emergency vehicles swirled around the yurts.

The scene looked almost festive, like disco night on a Native American reservation. Between the two lit-up squad cars and an ambulance there was another vehicle – an unmarked, anonymous-looking van with blacked-out windows, backed up against the entrance to Vince's yurt, its back doors open and waiting.

Curious faces gawped in the flaps of the other yurts. Uniformed officers conferred as they unspooled yellow-and-black tape around Vince's home while another group pulled on sterile white suits and blue gloves and booties. Digital radios chattered in the night like birds. It looked like they were just getting started.

So nobody challenged me as I stepped over a streamer of the yellow tape and approached Vince's front door.

Two young, uniformed officers were standing right outside, smiling at a phone, as if one of them had just taken an amusing selfie that was sure to get a lot of likes on social media. They should have stopped me, and they could have stopped me, but they didn't. I went inside and the first thing I saw was Vince sitting on the small sofa where I had sat, the right sleeve of his denim work shirt rolled up around his bicep, kept in place by what looked like a rubber tube tied around his bicep.

Drug paraphernalia covered the rickety table in front of him, mingling uneasily with the remains of his tea. A half-drunk mug of char, an almost-gone pack of chocolate digestives and a box of Tetley teabags. And an unsmoked joint, a bag of weed, and a much smaller bag of white powder and a syringe, the needle shining silver in the candlelight.

A strange mix of the domestic and the debauched.

The scene was so mundane that it took me a long moment to realise that Vince was staring at me with lifeless eyes.

It was crowded with police in here, plodding white ghosts in their bulky sterile suits going about their business. Events were more advanced than they were outside. Somebody was taking photographs of Vince and his tea and his drugs. Somebody else appeared to be sketching the position of his body in relation to the rest of the yurt. There were numbered yellow markers all over the floor.

One of the white ghosts was down on all fours, his or her knees resting on little see-through stepping stones, picking up something with infinite delicacy. A few seconds went by without any of them registering my presence in the doorway. Then an index finger was furiously jabbing at me from inside a blue latex glove and all their faces were turning towards me and an angry northern accent was shouting.

'Get her out of my crime scene *now*!'

The voice belonged to DCI Baxter, but it was DI Hunter who unceremoniously escorted me outside. She was wearing one of the baggy white suits and a blue face mask, but I would know the freakish bulk of her anywhere.

'Is Vince dead?' I said.

'No,' she said. 'He's taking a power nap.' She sighed, sick of me. 'Yes, he's dead.'

'But it doesn't make any sense! Vince would never touch hard drugs! Because of their mother.'

DI Hunter did not respond but as I was dragged away, I caught a glimpse of what was still sitting in Vince's tiny man-alone kitchen.

The harvest basket.

Then we were outside the yurt, but we kept walking, or rather DI Hunter kept walking and the way she held me – my elbow gripped tightly and elevated in one of her big bony fists – ensured that I was dragged along in her wake, as I struggled to keep up with her brisk, long-legged pace.

When we were beyond the police tape, she began ripping off her protective suit and I pulled away and faced her.

'I want to know how Vince died,' I said.

DI Hunter glanced back at the yurt. The lights from the cars swung on and off her face. 'Heroin overdose.'

'How do you know?'

'Because I've seen a dead junkie before. The needle and the white powder and the corpse are always a dead giveaway.'

'Listen to me. *Please*. Vince didn't kill himself with drugs. I know he didn't. He's been poisoned. That stuff – the syringe, the powder – it must have been planted.'

'Planted?'

'Someone wanted him dead. Because of where he was sticking his nose. And because of what he knew.'

DI Hunter was suddenly furious. She seized me by the shoulders and shook me and for a moment I thought she would slap my face.

'Will you stop talking? He's got half a gram of heroin on his coffee table and the other half in his bloodstream!'

'No,' I said.

'Just go home!' She shot a look at the door. 'Please, Mrs Wade. Do yourself a huge favour. Just go away before you get arrested or hurt.'

'Who's going to hurt me?' I said.

'I'm warning you,' she said. 'I called your husband once to bail you out. I'm not going to do it again, OK?'

DCI Baxter had come outside now, pulling off his blue shoe coverings and gloves, looking up when he saw me, shaking his head with a resigned smile, annoyed yet forgiving. I believe he pitied me.

DI Hunter took a step away from me, as if something had passed between us that she did not want her boss to see.

I shouted at DCI Baxter. 'I need to talk to you.'

'Christ on a stick,' DI Hunter muttered, stepping further away from me.

DCI Baxter slipped under the police tape and approached me. He was sweating from being inside the white suit. He began to pull it off, more slowly than DI Hunter. But his face was sympathetic.

'You have to check,' I told him. 'Vince didn't die from an overdose.'

He looked at the yurt and back at me. But he didn't tell me I was mad. He didn't tell me that Vince's hippy tent was full of heroin.

'I think he was poisoned,' I said. 'Because of what he knew about my neighbours.'

DCI Baxter nodded, as if this was a perfectly reasonable assumption. I clutched at his sleeves and he patted my arm, like some kindly mind-how-you-go policeman from an old movie.

'They'll do an autopsy,' he said. 'When someone dies suddenly, they always do. So if there's any foul play—'

'But it doesn't show up!' I said, and I saw him glance at DI Hunter.

She shook her enormous head with cold contempt.

'The stuff they use!' I said, the panic threatening to overwhelm me now. 'It's brilliant, can't you see? Even if you check him for poison, it will not show up in the autopsy *because it's oleander.* And oleander doesn't show up in any autopsy.'

They stared at me, waiting for more.

'I read it online,' I said, and it sounded pathetic, even to me.

DCI Baxter and DI Hunter exchanged looks. She raised her eyebrows and shook her head again. She did not tap her temple with her finger, and describe little circles, but she may as well have.

Crazy lady.

But DCI Baxter was different. Even when I was grabbing at his sleeve and feeling myself on the verge of hysteria, he looked at me with almost paternal concern. 'Who exactly are we talking about, Mrs Wade?'

'My neighbours. I'm not sure which ones. But Vince was on to them. He didn't care – that's the sad bit.' I shot a tearful look at the yurt and saw a body bag on a stretcher was being loaded into the blacked-out van. 'He knew about them, but he was only here to find out what had happened to his sister. Ben's wife. Juno Cave. She was his sister.'

'Mrs Cave – Juno – was an only child,' Baxter said gently.

I shook my head, more confident now. 'That's not true. Juno grew up in care. She grew up being bounced between foster homes and care homes. But she had a brother who she was separated from when they were children. And that was Vince. And they found each other as adults. Then she went missing.'

They did not look convinced.

'Vince knew what my neighbours are,' I said.

DI Hunter smiled with mocking amusement.

'And what are they, Mrs Wade?'

'"Elite preppers", Vince called them. Survivalists. They're people who think everything is about to fall apart.'

DI Hunter snorted, and I hated her. 'What – like some sort of doomsday cult?' she said. 'On *that* street? In *those* houses?'

I saw that even kindly DCI Baxter was struggling to believe me. 'I think we need to get you some help,' he said. 'A doctor. Not necessarily your husband.'

'I know what he is,' I blurted. 'Vince, I mean. What he was, I mean. He was a policeman. An undercover cop.'

And now both of them were chuckling at me.

'Vince claimed he was still a policeman?' DCI Baxter said. 'Is that what he told you? The sad truth is that Vince *was* a policeman – once upon a time.'

'In a galaxy far, far away,' DI Hunter said.

'What?'

'Vince was a fantasist,' DCI Baxter said. 'Vince had not been a serving police officer for many, many years. Whatever he may have told you. It's true that back in the day he was an undercover surveillance officer – and a very good one, by all accounts – but then he went native. He became an enthusiastic participant in the very thing he was meant to be investigating.'

'Your hero Vince was a junkie,' DI Hunter said brutally.

'Tragically, it happens all the time,' DCI Baxter said. 'The undercover cop who becomes the crime he is meant to be busting.'

'So, they kicked him out,' DI Hunter said bluntly. 'Because Vince was a smackhead. Because he had a sweet tooth for the Class A drugs he was meant to be cleaning up. Not just the wacky baccy that you could always smell all over him. The hard stuff. The white powders. The kind of drugs that killed him tonight. That's the only poison anyone is going to find in him.'

I was speechless.

'Vince was discharged years ago,' DCI Baxter continued. 'They tried to do it gently for old time's sake. They usually do. Nobody on the force wanted to see Vince in jail. Former cops do not thrive in prison.' He looked at DI Hunter. 'But you could smell it on him, couldn't you? I don't mean the drugs, I mean the desperation to still matter, to still belong.' He looked back at me. 'You lose a job and it can be hard to let go. You hear about these commuters who get made redundant but still get their morning train for the next ten years. Because the new reality hurts so much. Vince, as I say, was a fantasist – that's why he worked so well undercover for so many years. *Because he believed in the lies*. So – whatever fanciful yarn he may have spun you, Mrs Wade – Vince was a recovering drug addict trying to make a living as best he could.'

'Doing odd jobs for the gentry,' DI Hunter said. 'That's the only reason he was here.'

'And tonight, he fell off the wagon,' DCI Baxter said. 'Vince wasn't a policeman, Mrs Wade. He was a *former* policeman. A disgraced cop. And a drug addict. I don't think he ever met Juno Cave.'

I shook my head, trying to control my ragged breathing.

'Vince wasn't a heroin addict,' I said. 'I know he liked his weed, but I never saw him on anything stronger. You must check the basket. That harvest basket with the vegetables and the fruit and the honey that's in his kitchen. Especially the honey – they have to do checks on the honey, OK? You have to tell them about the honey.' I took DCI Baxter's hands in mine and I felt him recoil and then relax, letting me hold them. 'You're a good man,' I said. 'I can tell. You have to believe me.'

'She's off with the fairies, boss,' DI Hunter muttered.

A white-suited figure appeared in the door of the yurt and gestured to DCI Baxter. He was needed inside.

DI Hunter sighed with exasperation. 'I'll take you home, Mrs Wade,' she said, taking my arm.

I pulled away. 'Not *you*! You already stitched me up once! You phoned my husband that night I found the bones.'

'I phoned your husband because you were very upset, Mrs Wade,' DI Hunter said, professionally polite in the presence of her boss. 'Your husband was worried about you. Everyone was very worried about you. And as I understand it, they still are.'

She reached for my arm again.

I shoved her away. She stared at me with disbelief.

'And that's assaulting a police officer right there,' she said, a mean glint in her eye. 'Please may I book her, boss?'

'I think I should hear this,' DCI Baxter said, and suddenly the night grew still. The three of us stood there, waiting for him to decide what happened next.

'One of my officers is going to take you to the station,' he told me. 'When DI Hunter and I have finished here, and that may be a while yet, I'm afraid, we'll tape a formal interview and get all of this on the record and get it sorted once and for all, OK?'

I swallowed hard. 'Thank you.'

'And when we're done, we will *both* take you home.' He smiled kindly. 'All right?'

I nodded, speechless with relief.

DCI Baxter hailed one of the uniformed officers and told her to drive me to the police station.

'You'll be safe there,' DCI Baxter told me.

And DI Hunter watched me, her large face impassive, her coarse features illuminated and then hidden and then revealed again, caught between the blue lights and the darkness.

38

HAVE YOU SEEN JIM?

Jim was an old man who was suffering from dementia. The A4-sized poster on the wall of the waiting room at the police station said that Jim had gone missing from his care home ten days ago. Now Jim's face – a ruddy face, smiling shyly under a purple paper hat at what looked like some heartbreaking care home Christmas party, the face of a man who had had a good life that was now winding down – was at the centre of the wall of the missing.

No, I thought, I haven't seen poor Jim, and I wondered where he was tonight. And what unearned familiarity, I thought. How disgraceful. Who are we to call Jim by his first name? Who are we to not address him with more respect?

I glanced at my phone as it beeped yet again.

Missed Call – Roman.

I turned the thing off.

I sat alone in the waiting room of the police station as the clock crawled closer to midnight. There was a fat sergeant who looked oddly familiar on the front desk, although they seemed to have an endless supply of them, these lard-arsed desk jockeys in blue who couldn't catch a cold. This one yawned extravagantly, making no attempt to cover his great gaping mouth.

I turned my head away, disgusted, and tired beyond belief.

DCI Baxter would make it all right, I believed. I knew he was not yet convinced by me, not by a long way. But DCI Baxter was a good man, a decent man, and he would listen to my suspicions about the dead and the missing without automatically thinking I was a madwoman, and he would listen to me without phoning my husband behind my back like that duplicitous cow, DI Hunter.

And that was all I wanted, I swear. Even if I was wrong about some of it. Even if I was wrong about all of it. Even if Vince was just the congenital, drug-addicted fantasist they claimed. Even if Juno was happily bonking her brains out in the city. Even if it had really been an accident when Goran ran down John Carter. Even if the Clutters had died exactly as everyone said, a husband and father cracking up in the modern world and just wanting it all to please stop, please.

Even if my mind was inventing things because I wanted to get away, to find my old life. Even if I was making it all up because there was some sickness inside me. Even if I was as crazy as they all thought me to be.

That's all I wanted now.

Someone kind to listen to me.

My eyes kept drifting back to the wall of the missing.

The missing all looked so uniformly happy in their photographs, and those smiling faces clawed at my heart. You would think that it would be all digital these days, that you would have to scroll through these faces online, but there was a real wall with its paper wanted posters, all those lost souls of every age, from toddlers to the elderly.

And the young. Especially the young.

4 feet 10 inches, blond hair, freckles. 4 feet 8 inches, red hair, freckles.

All those families, I thought, always waiting, never knowing, as the hours and the days and the months and the years and the lifetimes drifted by. Suspecting – *almost* knowing – but never *really* knowing, not quite. There was always someone new being put on the wall. I half expected to see Sailor's shyly gorgeous face going up there. How long would Krissy and Tucker have to wait before they put Sailor's smile on that wall?

HAVE YOU SEEN SAILOR?
5 feet 5 inches, blonde hair, freckles, cello.
Dead boyfriend.

The wall had changed since the last time I sat here, staring at the other jolly policeman behind the desk. I knew the system now. They never took anyone off the wall, they couldn't be bothered, and of course they couldn't be certain about what had happened to the missing, so they only tacked and pinned the new faces on top. The missing were really piling up. The wall contained layer upon layer of the missing, like geological strata of rock reaching back into history. There had been a young woman in the very centre that last time but now it was this lost old man – poor Jim. And already Jim's picture was curling away from the wall in one corner, as if nobody cared enough to put it up there properly, where it would stay and people could study it and think – you know what, I think I may have information that will be helpful to your inquiries – they didn't give a damn about any of that, it was as if they were just going through the motions, as if nobody really expected that any of the missing would ever be found again.

It was not good enough. So I stood up and crossed the room and pressed down the corner of Jim's picture.

It immediately curled back up.

I glanced at the fat sergeant and saw he was smirking at my pathetic effort to give some tiny shred of dignity to the missing. That infuriated me.

So I licked the tip of my index finger, delicately wet the back of Jim's poster and pressed it down. It curled back up again, worse than before, so that part of the face underneath was suddenly visible. I heard the fat cop chuckle. A woman's beautiful blue eye stared at me. It rang a distant bell, that eye, and I was seized with a longing to see the rest of the face. I pulled off Jim's picture, careful not to tear it, and I saw I was wrong. It was not a woman beneath – the eye belonged to an adolescent boy, a pretty teenage boy, he had a little of Roman's dreamy male beauty about him.

HAVE YOU SEEN LEO?

Suddenly I found I could not breathe. All those smiling faces, all those missing children and grandparents and spouses seemed to crowd in on me. To fight off what felt like a panic attack, I tore off the picture of the boy, not quite as careful as I had been with Jim.

'Oy!'

It was the fat sergeant.

He was staring at me as if he did not quite believe what he was seeing. Below Leo there was a slightly older teenage girl – Sailor's age – but nothing like Sailor. A plain girl in glasses with a bit of weight problem.

HAVE YOU SEEN MARY?

The fat sergeant was coming out from behind the desk when I tore Mary's poster from the wall.

'Oy, you can't do that!'

But he was dead wrong. For now I could not stop myself.

Something drove me on. Both hands flying, I began ripping down all those A4 posters from the wall of the missing. The runaway girls, the bolting wives, the wandering old folk who strolled out of their care home and went in search of a partner who was fifty years in the grave. The toddler who climbed into a stranger's car outside the playground, the tipsy twenty-something in her best dress who never made it home after getting a lift from the club, the depressed father who was being buried alive in debt, the teenager who could not stand one more day of the mockery of her spiteful peers.

HAVE YOU SEEN, HAVE YOU SEEN, HAVE YOU SEEN?

Two uniformed officers, both women, came into the station and nearly collided with the fat sergeant as he waddled angrily towards me.

'Are you mental?' he asked me.

'You can't say that any more,' I told him.

I was tearing at the wall in a frenzy now. Ripping with both hands, pulling the posters down, needing to know who was buried at the very bottom of the wall of the missing.

Because somehow, I already knew who I would find there.

The sergeant's podgy hand was on my arm as I ripped off the penultimate poster with a flourish.

The posters were scattered all around me, smiling up from the floor, some of them still intact, the more recent ones torn to pieces.

And there she was waiting for me – not quite the very bottom of the wall after all, but buried deep – smiling in all her youthful beauty, as if life was sweet, never guessing what was waiting for her down the line. But then who does?

HAVE YOU SEEN JUNO?

And I had seen Juno, hadn't I?

Because Juno had come to see me, and we had sat drinking herbal tea in my little alcove that overlooked the lush back gardens, and Juno had smiled with a touching gratitude that I had been concerned for her welfare. And she had carefully – kindly – explained to me that wives become unhappy, and marriages come to an end, and sometimes children have to be left behind with dear old dad, but love remained, and love endured, and everything came out all right in the end. All that I-got-to-be-me bullshit.

And I did not understand what I was looking at because the face that smiled back at me from the wall of the missing was not that woman.

This was some other Juno Cave.

HAVE YOU SEEN JUNO?

This was a different face.

A different woman.

A different Juno.

I turned away, heading for the door.

'You're not going anywhere!'

The fat policeman had his hands on me. His fingers – surprisingly strong for such a spectacularly unfit man – dug so deep into my arms that I could feel them pressing against bone.

I cried out with the pain.

And then I bent my head and sank my teeth into his hand until he let go with a scream.

And as I left the station, I shook my head with disbelief.

Because I had no idea who had come to see me with Ben Cave, Oscar and my husband.

But I knew that she was not Juno Cave.

39

Wednesday, 14 October

A distant church bell struck midnight in the village.

I stayed off the road on the way home, keeping to a footpath that ran beside a line of sparse trees and a low drystone wall. It was bitterly cold now, but the path was made hard by both the summer that was gone and the winter that was coming.

A smell hung heavy in the air that I had never noticed during the daytime, and it was the smell of the country-side – of horse and hay, ancient ponds and dense spinney. The fields looked very different in the dark.

My heart hammered in my chest.

What had they done to the real Juno Cave?

Halfway to home, there was a car parked by the side of the road, its orange emergency lights flashing. Figures moved around it. I heard voices and saw torchlights piercing the night, aimed into the black fields on either side of the road. I half-crouched and edged away from the footpath, deeper into the darkness.

A man was calling a name.

Tucker's voice, I thought I heard. There were other figures with them. A woman who had to be Krissy. And Ben, definitely Ben, still in the driver's seat, illuminated by the interior light, his scarred face drawn tight with tension.

And a slimmer man – Roman? At first, I could not be sure.

Then the slight figure moved, and it was something about the way he lifted his head – a certain quick raising of his chin, a gesture that always struck me as hopeful and curious and brave – and I would have known him anywhere, and I wanted him to call my name.

Even then, especially then, I wanted Roman to call my name.

And I know I would have gone to him. I would have stepped out of the dark fields and into the light. But they were all calling for Sailor. That's who they were looking for.

'We're not angry!' Krissy cried, in a sing-song voice that seemed to seethe and burn with furious rage. 'We're not mad at you, baby girl!'

I walked further into the fields, much deeper into the darkness, and then I stopped and stood there, waiting, shivering in the cold midnight air, watching their torchlights sweeping across the black, afraid to breathe.

Then they all got back into the car and drove away, very fast, towards the village, and I pressed on, slowly at first, and then increasing my speed when the Gardens became visible through the branches of the trees, sporadic lights showing in all of the houses. The footpath ended and I made my way across the last of the field, hauling myself over a stile, tired now and fighting for breath, but then getting a second wind when I knew I was almost there.

And then I was running towards the lights of home.

Which, when I think back on it, seems insane.

Because sometimes home is the place you should run away from.

I waited for what felt like a long time among the last of the trees, watching the entrance, and when I was sure there was no sign of Goran and his white van, I quickly ran across the road and into the Gardens.

Oscar was standing in the middle of the street.

As I got closer I saw the tears streaming down his face.

'They still haven't found her,' he sobbed, brushing a lank veil of hair from his thin face. 'Sailor. She's gone. Where do you think she is? Where is she *sleeping* tonight? I'll probably never see her again.' His hand covered his eyes, ashamed of his tears. 'She loved him, didn't she? She loved that dead boy. That fucking ... *thief*.'

'Who was she?'

He started, then wiped his nose with the back of his hand. 'What?'

There was a car in the distance.

I glanced back at the entrance to the Gardens, waiting for it to turn into the street.

But the car kept moving.

I looked back at Oscar. I put my hands on his shoulders and shook him.

'The woman who came to my house,' I said. 'The woman with you and your father and my husband.' We stared at each other. 'That wasn't your mother, was it? *Was it?*'

He looked up at his house, all lights blazing but nobody home, and I saw the dread in him. And I felt a sudden surge of sympathy for this poor, broken boy. He seemed undernourished, in need of everything. I put my hands on his shoulders again but gently now, trying to soothe him, and to shake some sense into him.

'You can tell me the truth, Oscar. You don't have to be afraid of anyone.'

'I'm not scared,' he said tearfully. '*You're* the one who's always so scared.'

A child's jibe. But it was true enough.

I put my arm around him.

'I'm not going to let anyone hurt you, Oscar. We're friends, aren't we?'

He looked at me steadily, as if weighing something up.

Then he nodded. Friends, then.

I placed my hands on the back of his neck. I drew him to me, our foreheads almost touching.

'But I want *the truth*. She wasn't your mum, was she? I *know* it wasn't her. So tell me – that woman who sat with me, and drank tea with me, and thanked me for worrying about her. And pretended to be Juno. That wasn't your mother, was it?'

He slowly shook his head. 'She was just some woman.'

'Why would you all *lie* to me like that?'

'I think they just – I don't know – I think they all wanted to put your mind at ease or something. Everybody was worried about you. Cracking up, causing trouble. They were worried about all the stuff you were coming out with. Calling the police round and all that. They wanted to – I don't know – calm you down. Cheer you up.'

'Cheer me up?'

'Yeah.'

'Who?'

'Everybody. The neighbours. My dad.'

'And who was that woman?'

Oscar sniffed.

'Just someone my dad hired. An actress. An actress and a waitress. It's the same thing most of the time, my dad said. A resting actress. I think she was in some soap opera once. Playing a dead person. I don't really watch television.' He smiled slyly. 'She was good though, wasn't she? Convincing.'

He saw my eyes flare with anger.

'They didn't mean anything bad,' he said quickly. 'They were just trying to – reassure you. My dad said you were having a nervous breakdown.'

He looked up at his empty house again. And I saw he was terrified of his father.

'Does your dad hit you?'

'No. Sometimes. Hardly ever.'

'Where's your mum, Oscar? Where is she really?'

I watched the great sadness settle upon him.

'It's just like they always told you. She's with that new guy. Busy with her new life. Too busy for us. Too busy for *me*. She moved on. Isn't that what adults call it? Moving on?'

'And is that the truth? Or is it another lie?'

Sally came out of her house, bustling across the street to us, her face frowning with concern. I looked at the garlands of pink flowers that surrounded her door, cut back so brutally after the death of Buster, and I remembered how beautiful they had looked on that summer day we moved in, and I also remembered how the lifeless eyes of Vince had stared right through me, and the open jar of home-made honey on the shelf of his yurt's tiny kitchen, and how the pretty flowers could kill you.

And I felt a stab of pure terror in the presence of this kindly old hippy.

'Vince is dead,' I said.

'Drugs,' Sally said. 'I heard. Very sad.' She blinked at me with her watery blue eyes and then turned to the boy. 'Just say *no* to drugs.'

'I do,' Oscar said, scowling. 'I *do* say no to drugs.'

'And what on earth are you crying about?' she asked him. 'You're not wasting your tears on a girl, are you? She's not worth your tears. Not even a girl as lovely as our Sailor.'

'This child is terrified,' I said.

'Old Oscar?' she chuckled. 'My Oscar? What's he got to be terrified about?'

She ruffled his lank locks.

'Stop it,' he said.

'Stop it!' Sally mimicked, laughing now, mussing his hair even harder. 'Stop it, stop it, stop it!'

'Don't touch him,' I said quietly.

Sally stared at me with those blank blue eyes.

I put a protective arm around Oscar's shoulders, hugging him close, feeling the frailty of him.

'Don't you ever touch him,' I said. 'Come on, Oscar.'

I started for my house, Oscar trailing after me, leaving Sally standing in the centre of the road, still staring at me without expression. Oscar followed me into the house. There was nobody home.

I quickly searched for what I needed. Car keys. Money. I would need money. Credit cards. What else? A few clothes. That would be enough. Our car was on the drive. It had been a stupid mistake to come back and to kid myself that it was ever going to work. I was leaving tonight. I was leaving right now.

'What are you doing?' Oscar said, trailing behind me as I grabbed what I would need.

'Leaving,' I said.

I went upstairs and Oscar trotted after me, whimpering softly, like a puppy with separation issues.

I went into the bedroom, pulled out a suitcase.

'But where are you going?' Oscar said. 'Everybody's leaving!'

'Anywhere,' I said. 'I can't stay here.' I turned and looked at him. 'If you want, you can come with me. We can find your mother. I can leave you with her until you work out what you want to do.'

He stiffened. 'They don't want me there,' he said, his face darkening. 'But it doesn't matter. Because I have to stay here and wait for Sailor. And I *know* she'll be coming home. You watch.'

'Fine.'

I threw a few clothes into a suitcase.

Oscar was at my shoulder, watching me with interest. As if taking notes about how to leave home. He was a bit too close because I could smell sugar and sweat. I turned and stared at him, and he took half a step backwards.

'But why are you so *scared* all the time?' Oscar asked me.

His voice was almost conversational.

I thought of the Clutters, and I thought of Vince, and I thought of the bones in the swimming pool. Was Juno Cave really in the city having the best sex of her life? Perhaps it was true. Tears sprang to my eyes.

Either the danger was real or it was all in my head. There was either something evil in this place or it was all a crazy lady's imagination.

And either way, it broke my heart.

I turned back to my packing.

I had to get out of here now. I had to get away, and I had to get well. For good, this time.

'Did you hear me?' Oscar said, his voice a plaintive whine. 'What exactly are you scared of, Lana?'

I don't think he ever called me *Lana* before.

I turned to look at him.

'I'm scared because I think they're going to send someone to kill me,' I said quietly. 'They're going to get shot of me. The way they do with anyone who gets in their way. Vince died tonight and I know it wasn't the drugs that killed him. I *know* it.'

'But who's *they?*' Oscar said, laughing with disbelief.

I turned back to my suitcase, snapped it shut.

'I don't know. But I think that if I don't get out tonight, something very bad will happen to me.'

Behind me, I heard Oscar's giggle slide into a higher key.

'Do you really think so, you crazy bitch?' he said.

As if I had been struck, I turned to look at him.

And then I saw the knife.

40

Oscar was pointing his knife at my chest.

The same knife that I had once seen him brandish in a bully's face on the village green, the knife I had urged him to drop down a drain before it got him into trouble.

I slapped his ear.

It happened almost too fast to register. I took a step towards the boy and – my sense of distance miraculously perfect – I brought the open palm of my right hand down hard on his left ear. There was something profoundly shocking about the precision, the violence, and the effect it immediately had on Oscar. One smack to the ear and he was undone, the knife hanging down by his side.

Then I slapped his other ear.

The knife fell to the bedroom floor.

He reeled backwards, the tears filling his eyes.

'Are you going to start blubbing, Oscar?' his father said.

Ben Cave was standing in the doorway of my bedroom. He frowned with disapproval at his son.

I did not understand how he could be here. 'How the hell—'

He jangled a set of keys, so many that they filled his fist, the keys of a medieval gaoler.

'You should always have a set of your neighbour's keys,' he told me. 'You never know when the people next door might need a hand.' Then he focused on Oscar. 'I asked you a question, young man. Are you going to cry like some pussy boy just because this nice lady gave you a little tap?'

'No,' Oscar said, the word choking in his throat.

Ben raised his eyebrows.

'No? Because you really look like you're about to have a good old blubberoo to me.' He glanced at me. 'Does Oscar look like he's going to have a bit of a blub to you?'

'You're out of your mind,' I said. 'You're insane.'

'I think you'll find that *you're* the one about to be carted off to the loony bin,' he said, stepping into the bedroom, slipping the keys into the pocket of his leather jacket. 'Oh, sorry – we can't say loony bin any more, can we? Mental health issues. That's what you've got, isn't it, Lana?' He turned to Oscar, the mark on the side of his oddly smooth face twisting with amusement.

'Sweet on her, are you? Not another one of your pathetic crushes, is she? Thinking about Lana behind that locked bathroom door, are you, you dirty bird? Hoping to get in a few lessons with her, are you, son?' Ben picked up the knife and his jaw clenched with barely suppressed rage. 'What did I tell you? Don't point this at someone unless you are prepared to use it. Wave it about again for no good reason and I'll shove it up your spotty little arse! Got it?'

Oscar whimpered an affirmation. 'Yes, Dad.'

Ben waved the knife like a conductor's baton. 'And are you going to *cry* when the ice caps melt, and the planet is boiling, and banks are shut, and the supermarkets have all been picked clean? Is that what you're going to do, Oscar? Burst into tears?'

'No!'

'Be a man!'

'I'm trying!'

'Try harder,' Ben said.

'You killed Vince,' I said. 'I know Sally poisoned him.'

Ben looked genuinely surprised.

'Poisoned Vince?'

'The oleander. Sally put it in the honey. In the harvest basket. Oleander's poisonous, and it doesn't show up in an autopsy.'

Ben laughed. 'You don't need to poison a recovering heroin addict! You just give them heroin! You just slip half a gram of street smack through the letterbox of their yurt and wait for them to poison themself. Sally wouldn't hurt a fly.'

Oscar's eyes were bright. 'Did you find Sailor?'

'No,' Ben said flatly, not looking at his son. He gestured towards me. 'This one's been prattling to the police again,' he said.

'I know,' Oscar said. 'A little bird told me.'

Ben shook his head. Then he smiled.

'Alone at last,' he said. 'Just the three of us.'

He came towards me with the blade held out, dancing with the big ugly knife, teasing me, Oscar snorting with amusement behind him, watching me over his father's shoulder, both of them enjoying my terror as I backed away, away from the suitcase on the bed, stepping back into my studio, the old safe room and – I realised as the bile rose in my throat – away from any possibility of escape.

'Your face!' Ben chuckled. 'I do enjoy it when you're falling apart. That's when you're at your most attractive, Lana. You always struck me as a bit plain. From that day I met you. A bit of a plain Jane when stood next to your gorgeous husband. But when you are all wild-eyed with terror – then you look almost pretty!'

He followed me into the safe room. I banged hard against the wall where the migrant woman looked down. Ben lifted the point of the blade to my face, very slowly, his grin spreading and growing across his features like a malignant disease.

'You touch me, and Roman will kill you.'

He laughed shortly. 'That seems unlikely.'

He lightly pressed the tip of the blade against my upper lip, pushing it up, away from my teeth, and I felt the metal press against soft flesh and the fight drain out of me, to be replaced with terror.

'Please,' I begged. 'Please don't hurt me, Ben.'

The knife slowly came away from my face, hovered around my waist. He slowly lifted the hem of my T-shirt. I felt cold air on the naked skin of my stomach.

'Go on, Lana,' he said, his eyes half-closed. '*Ask me*. You know you're dying to.'

I swallowed hard.

'Where is she?' I said. 'Where's Juno?'

'Ask the lad,' he said.

Oscar lounged in the doorway of the safe room, his face blank as he stared up at *Migrant Mother*. He looked at me.

'Mum's out back,' he said calmly. 'Mum's in your garden.'

'That's right,' Ben said. 'She's in the pool. Or rather – she's *under* the pool. Or at least she was until some mad housewife called the cops.' He sighed elaborately. 'Talk about stupid! Who do you think you are, Lana? The Neighbourhood Watch?'

'But the bones,' I said. 'The bones I found. Roman must have known they were human bones …'

'I think Roman didn't *want* to know,' Ben said. 'That's my theory, Lana, for what it's worth. The clever doctor couldn't face the truth because he couldn't handle the truth. And by the time the law showed up – thanks to you! – we had Basil Brush buried out there.'

I shook my head, the sickness and dread rising.

'What happened to her?' I said, and it came out soft as a prayer.

Ben frowned, leaned towards me, pointing the tip of the blade towards my ear.

'Louder,' he said.

'What happened to Juno?' I said.

'Mum got sad,' Oscar said.

Ben looked at his boy and smiled. He touched his shoulder and turned back to me. There was no air in the tiny space now. I could feel the walls squeezing the life out of me. Ben shook his head, as if trying to lose some troubling thought, and indicated the world beyond these walls, the green fields, and the rolling countryside. 'Juno was never happy here. Like a lot of you townies – maybe all of you townies! – she *thought* she would be – and then she just wasn't. She became depressed. She was diagnosed with clinical depression, in fact.' His features creased with frustration. 'Nobody can be just *unhappy* any more. They have to be *depressed*. They can't just be miserable. They have to have *mental health issues*.

Everybody's got mental health issues these days, haven't they? It's all the rage.'

'What did you do to her, you bastard?'

'Juno didn't like the way I was bringing up our son,' Ben said. 'Didn't like it one bit. The emphasis on clean body, clean mind, physical fitness, discipline and decency. That all contributed to her depression. And she was grotesquely over-medicated. Doctors, eh? Bunch of drug dealers, the lot of them. Big pharma, right? It's all about the bottom line. But you would know all about that, wouldn't you?'

'Juno wouldn't leave,' I said. 'Juno wouldn't leave her son.'

'Wrong!' Ben said. 'That's exactly what the bitch was planning to do. Breaking up our happy home.'

'You remind me of my mum in lots of ways,' Oscar reflected. 'Never happy. Always complaining. Always with something new to whine about.' His eyes narrowed. 'Always causing trouble in our street.'

'Juno started coming to this house,' Ben said. 'She started spending more and more time here. Making new friends in this very bedroom.'

And I suddenly believed I saw it all.

'Juno had an affair,' I said. 'Juno fell in love with Bill Clutter, and you found out, and then you killed her.'

Ben and Oscar smiled at each other.

'Mum wasn't fucking the pilot,' Oscar said. 'Mum was fucking the flight attendant.'

'Juno was taking her clothes off for *April Clutter*,' Ben said. 'Not Bill Clutter! Juno was hot to trot for *Bill Clutter's wife*. Miss Saigon, 1999. That's who she was in love with – or claimed love is what it was!'

'They came to see you, didn't they, Dad?' Oscar said.

Ben nodded grimly. 'Bold as brass! Claimed they were going to take the boy and shack up together in the village.' He shook his head again, still finding it all so difficult to believe. 'Then April went home and told her husband the same thing,' he said. 'And that was the night Captain Clutter cracked. That was the night that Bill reached for his shotgun and killed his wife, their son and himself.'

'Then it was true,' I said. 'It was all true about the Clutters.'

Ben nodded. 'The Clutter family massacre was exactly as advertised,' he said. 'But being a redundant airline pilot didn't have anything to do with it. It was because Bill was suddenly redundant as a husband, a father, a breadwinner. It was because Bill Clutter was suddenly redundant as a man.'

'But Juno,' I said. 'What happened to Juno?'

'I'll show you,' he said, almost conversational, and started leading me back into the bedroom, giving his instructions to Oscar. 'Shut the door and stay here until I say you can come out.'

I hit him in his ruined face.

It was a wild, clumsy, instinctive blow with a half-closed fist, a lashing out more than anything resembling a punch, but it caught him somewhere between his nose and an eye and sent him stumbling backwards, back into the studio, crashing into the little desk where the CCTV monitor stood, losing his balance and almost tumbling to the floor. Then I was past him and into the bedroom and heading for the stairs when he slammed the sole of his boot down on the back of my leg just behind the knee.

I collapsed. He picked me up and threw me on the bed.

'Dad—'

'Shut the door, son. Give your old man some privacy.'

Oscar quietly closed my studio door.

Ben Cave lay on top of me and pressed a pillow over my face and immediately I could not breathe, and I struggled against him, I sank my nails into his neck and felt them dig into skin and flesh, and I clawed and writhed and fought like some dying animal, I fought with my last remaining strength and then the exhaustion washed over me. I was done. I felt his erection pressing against the top of my leg. He removed the pillow.

'Get it now?' he said. 'Penny dropped, has it?'

'That's what you did to Juno,' I gasped. 'Oh God – that's what you did to her, and then you buried her out there because you could not risk an autopsy because she fought you and scratched you and she had your skin under her fingernails and then you came up with that bullshit story about running off with some guy to London.'

'Smart, aren't you?' he said. 'For a crazy woman.'

'Crazy? You're insane. All of you.'

He stood up and unbuckled his belt.

'Really? That's your opinion, for what it's worth. Which is nothing. I think you'll find out pretty soon that we're the last sane people alive in these parts. I think that in the end you'll see that it's the rest of the world that's insane.'

'No, you're a bunch of rich crazies, hurting innocent people while you stew in your sick fantasies and play with guns and knives and wait around for the end of the world. I don't blame Juno for wanting to leave you. I don't blame April Clutter. I don't blame them for falling in love. Who would want to live with you evil bastards?'

He looked at me calmly, wanting me to understand, as he sat on the bed and began pulling off his trousers.

'Look – when everything falls apart, it's only the end of the world for people who don't see it coming, Lana. It's not the end of the world for those who have *trained* for it, *anticipated* it, *expected* it. Preparation is key.'

He folded his trousers and placed them neatly at the end of the bed. He felt himself, as if to make sure his erect cock was still there.

'Well?' he said, his scarred face frowning with irritation. 'Are you going to take your kit off or do I have to rip it off you?'

Oscar's voice came from the safe room. The door had been opened a crack.

'Dad?'

Ben reeled around in fury. 'I told you to shut the door!'

'You better see this, Dad.'

Ben got to his feet, reached down and hauled me up by the scruff of my neck as if I weighed nothing. Holding me up with one hand and his folded trousers with the other, we returned to the safe room where Oscar was staring at the CCTV monitors.

On the middle screen in the top row, I could see DCI Baxter and DI Hunter standing on the front step of my house.

The doorbell rang.

We did not move.

We stood there, transfixed by the two figures on the tiny screen, just down the stairs and on the other side of my front door.

So close, so close.

DI Hunter was at the door, her head half-turned as if listening for signs of life inside, and DCI Baxter stood behind her, hands in his pockets, surveying the street.

I opened my mouth to scream, and Ben's hand clamped down hard, covering most of my face, pinching my nose between his thumb and index finger, expertly stopping my breath.

This is what he did to control you. This is what he did to stop women complaining. He stopped you breathing.

Oh Juno, I thought, and bitter tears burned in my eyes.

'Don't,' he said, his breath hot in my ear.

I nodded, briefly, fully compliant, and he released my nose but not my mouth.

The doorbell rang again.

And then – as if ringing a doorbell wasn't quite enough – knuckles rapped hard against the front door. DI Hunter bent over to shout through the letterbox.

'Lana?'

She called my name and there was so much concern and kindness in her voice that I saw I had been wrong, so wrong about DI Beth Hunter all along. Then she was straightening up to her full height.

And DCI Baxter and DI Hunter were conferring.

They were deciding if they were going to kick down the door.

On the monitor we watched them step back into the street, look up at the house, consider the solitary light in the bedroom.

DCI Baxter was thinking.

Then he shrugged, shook his head, looked at his watch.

They were not kicking down a door for a crazy lady.

We stood still as they walked to their car, got inside and drove away.

Ben took his hand from my mouth.

'We can't stay here,' he said.

41

The oldest Mrs Mendoza opened the front door of the big house.

She was wrapped up in a livid purple bathrobe, so synthetic it looked like a fire hazard. A thin skim of night cream concealed her kindly face.

She looked as if she had just been roused from a deep sleep and yet somehow was not even remotely surprised to see us.

She blinked at us from behind her spectacles. 'They're out the back, sir,' she told Ben. 'For drinks on the terrace.'

She stepped aside as we entered, and at the top of the stairs I saw Dr Magda Hall, the old lady stick-thin and wraith-like in a long nightgown that time had turned off-white, like curdled cream. She clutched the banister for support, as if she might be blown away in a strong wind, and she and I stared desperately at each other, both dumbfounded and lost for words. I saw her attempt a smile but then Ben glanced back at me, frowning with impatience, and Oscar gave me the smallest of shoves from behind.

'Back to bed with you now,' Mrs Mendoza told Magda, clapping her hands, padding back up the stairs. 'It's so late!'

There were lights shining on the terrace where we had drunk champagne on the day that the rains came and John Carter was run down. Roman was with Professor Hall at the far end of the terrace, taking the old man's blood pressure. Guy and Tucker were arguing, both of them drunk and reeling. They were holding small glasses of something red. No champagne tonight. And no sign of Willow or Sally or Angel, the new Mrs Cave. Krissy sat bent double, staring intently at her phone, wild-eyed with worry.

'Did Sailor come home?' Oscar asked her.

Krissy glanced up at him, then shook her head before turning back to her phone.

'The police have got a CRA out,' she said. A beat. 'Child Rescue Alert.' She snorted with derision. 'What does *that* mean? Her picture is going to be on some milk carton? Don't make me laugh.'

I was staring at Roman, waiting for him to notice me, wanting him to just come to my side, needing him to hold me, to tell me that we were leaving, to wake me from the nightmare.

He was unfurling the rubber band around his patient's arm, taking the reading. 'One hundred and forty over ninety,' he said as we approached them.

Professor Hall beamed with delight, rolling down the sleeve of his strangely hairless arm. He shared a gentle fist-bump with Ben Cave. Then he smiled warmly at us, as ever the perfect host.

'Please,' he said, indicating the tray of drinks by his side.

'Roman,' I said, and he finally looked at me, nothing in his eyes but pain.

'Are you all right?' he said, and I shook my head.

Ben sighed. 'I'm sad to say Lana went to the police *again*. And she's going to *keep* going to them until they come back with their search teams and their diggers and root around like good piggies until they find the tiny speck of DNA that puts us all away.' He drained his glass. 'You know she can't be trusted, Alan. I know you love the good doctor here.' A nod at Roman. 'But his missus truly can't be trusted.'

Professor Hall's smile slipped, and he looked at me as if he was my disappointed favourite uncle and I was a problem that needed to be urgently fixed.

'Lana,' he said. 'All we ever wanted was for you and Roman to be a valued part of our community. All we ever wanted was for you to be safe, secure and happy in our little neck of the woods.'

'Roman,' I said. 'Ben killed Juno.'

I watched his face change, and I saw the horror settle upon it.

'Ben killed her and everyone here helped him to cover it up. Because Juno was unhappy here. Because she was an unhappy wife and she wanted to leave and start a new life with April, with Mrs Clutter.'

'That's a filthy lie!' Oscar roared, furious tears in his eyes. 'My mum wasn't like that! She wasn't that sort!'

His father wrapped him in his arms.

'Bill Clutter didn't kill his family because he lost his job again,' I said. 'He killed his family because his wife was in love with another woman. With Juno Cave. Bill Clutter must have stuffed all April's lingerie down that storm drain in a jealous rage and then gone home and killed her and their son and then himself.'

Oscar sobbed in his father's arms, our friendship over.

'They murder difficult women here, Roman,' I said. 'That's what they do.'

'Please!' Professor Hall said, as if all this could be resolved, as if it was just some heated disagreement over the dinner table. He beamed at me. 'Lana! Do have a drink.'

I picked up a glass and bolted it down, recoiling from a jolt of something sweeter than honey. Not red wine then – cream sherry. They were drinking sherry as they discussed the end of the universe.

I stared at the empty glass, and I felt my grip tighten around it, and I knew what I had to do.

'Is it true?' Professor Hall said gently. 'Did you go to the police again, Lana?'

'Vince was on to them,' I told Roman, ignoring him. 'Vince knew all about them. And they didn't like it because he was getting too close to the truth about Juno – his *sister*.'

'My wife did not have a brother,' Ben sneered.

'Vince is dead,' I said. 'He died tonight, Roman.'

'Drugs,' Professor Hall sighed. 'Very sad.'

'I thought – I thought there was oleander in the honey,' I said, 'I thought they poisoned him with the honey.'

A chorus of mocking laughter.

'The police say he took an overdose,' I said. 'And maybe he did. But it was because our neighbours got to him. They dropped heroin through his letterbox. And Vince was a recovering addict. They knew he wouldn't be able to resist. They knew it would kill him.'

'So, as you see, we have a problem,' Ben told Professor Hall, his stitched-together face hideous under the night lights of the terrace.

Roman was staring at me, paralysed, dumbfounded. I wanted him to do something. But he did nothing.

'A *problem*?' I said, a great choking sob rising up in my throat. 'Ben killed his wife! He suffocated Juno with a pillow. He buried her in the back garden of our home because an autopsy would have revealed the truth. *Our home*, Roman. They have keys, Roman! They have the keys to our home! That's the problem they have, Roman!

That's who they are, Roman. They're not going to protect you. They're not going to save us.'

The others had gathered round for the breaking news.

'The police have been knocking on their door,' Ben said. 'Tonight. Again. Just now.'

'Jesus Christ,' Krissy said. 'Is this really true, Lana? Why do you do these things? Why do you try to hurt us when all we've ever shown you is kindness?' She shook her head, turned away, done with me, staring at her phone.

'Bury her under your patio, Tucker,' Guy suggested with a lopsided leer, and I saw how reeling drunk he was.

'Bury her under *your* fucking swimming pool, man!' Tucker told him.

'Roman?' I said.

But he hung his head, and he could not look at me.

'We know what happened to you,' Professor Hall quietly told me.

He placed his hand on Roman's arm.

He would not look at me, he still could not look at me.

'To both of you,' Professor Hall said gently. 'We know what those men did to Roman when they broke into your house, and we know what they did to your lives.'

'Made him their bitch!' laughed Oscar, pointing at Roman with huge amusement. He thrust his skinny hips and grinned obscenely. 'Gave him a little of that old jailhouse rock!'

Guy turned on the boy. 'Will you shut your moronic mouth? I'm sick of hearing your puerile jabber.'

Ben Cave bristled. 'You don't get to talk to my son like that!'

'Oh, back off, Scarface,' Guy said.

Professor Hall was still staring at me with deepest sympathy.

'All we want to do – all any of us have ever wanted to do – is protect those we love. Isn't that the most natural thing in the world?'

I stared at him. 'Protect them from *what*?'

Krissy looked up from her phone. 'From when the world goes to shit. Simple as that, Lana.'

'After the money's gone,' Professor Hall said. 'When the politicians can't give all those morally corrupt banks one last kiss of life. When the vaccines don't work for the next pandemic. Who knows what the next time will look like? When the planet bites back. When the angry mob kicks down your front door.'

I stared around wildly. 'You're all crazy,' I said.

Guy beamed at me. 'I hope so!' he said.

I flew at him, wanting to kill him, but Ben Cave held me back.

'You evil bastards,' I said.

Guy's smooth, well-fed face creased with amusement.

'No, really – I hope we're crazy! But let's face it, summers are *not* the same as when we were children.' He pointed at Oscar. 'Summers are not even the same as when this unfortunate specimen was born.' Guy's pampered face was a mask of blank conviction. 'Our planet is *burning*, Lana. You *know* it's burning. But I hope you're right. I hope we are all totally mad.' He was not smiling now. 'But it doesn't feel like it, does it?'

'We're getting ready for anything that Mother Nature throws at us,' Professor Hall said calmly. 'Or anything that the human race throws at itself. It's not complicated. Some kind of end is coming.'

'Lady, you don't learn to dance the day before the disco,' Tucker said, turning to Krissy. 'Anything on Sailor?'

Krissy shook her head, gnawing at her lower lip. 'She'll be in London by now,' she said, staring at her phone.

Oscar whimpered with love-sick grief.

I felt my fist tighten around the empty glass in my right hand.

Some light deep inside the sherry glass shimmered.

And I thought – *without the old man, they would not be here. Without the old man, they would not be getting away with murder. So it's the old man you have to kill. If you stick this glass in just one of them, it has to be the old man. Even before the wife-killer, you must get the old man. He is the reason they are all here.*

'Things are not normal any more,' Ben said. 'You can taste it in the air.'

He put his arm around Oscar's shoulder as his son sobbed for Sailor.

'When there's no more fake money left to print,' Guy slurred, draining his sherry glass, reaching for another.

'When the supermarket shelves are empty and the mob goes looking for what it can grab,' Ben said, thoughtfully stroking his scar, which seemed to pucker up tight and cause him some irritation when he was agitated.

'It's going to get pretty bad, pretty quick,' Tucker agreed.

'We're a canary in the coal mine of western civilisation,' Ben said.

Krissy was suddenly shaking her phone, her eyes wide with excitement.

'Sailor's not in London,' she told Tucker. 'The *Find My Brat* app has tracked her down.' She looked up at her husband. 'She's *here*! She's in the village! She's coming home, Tucker!'

But Tucker was drunk and distracted.

'The plan is just – be ready,' he told me, swaying unsteadily. 'You're not going to get a two-minute warning when the shit hits the fan. Plague, starvation, radiation – bring it on. Global economic collapse. Man-made diseases. A massive solar flare. A dirty bomb that makes every other terror attack look like a fender bender. A nuclear weapons screw-up by the Russians or the Iranians or the Pakistanis or the Indians.'

'Or the Americans,' Guy said.

'Polar shift,' Tucker continued, ignoring him. 'Peak oil. All entirely possible! Even probable. We'll be ready when the rest of the world are killing their children as an act of mercy. *We dig in here*. We have food, water, weapons. *We bug in*. Then – if we must – we bug out, right? We can bug in for months and we can bug out in minutes.'

Murmurs of assent. But Krissy was wandering away, her head inclined towards her phone as if in prayer, waiting for her daughter to come home.

She did not care about the end of the world right now.

She just wanted her daughter to come home.

'There's an old tin mine in Cornwall all stocked,' Ben told me. 'Ham radio that exists independently to the power grid. N95 masks. Dehydrated, freeze-dried food. Lots of it. And if we have to get out of the country, then there's a pilot who lost his job when all the airlines died. In fact, there's *ten thousand unemployed pilots* who would be happy with the gig.'

Guy knocked back his sherry, reached for another. 'Stage one – stay put. Stage two – leave for deep countryside. Stage three – leave the country.'

'Yes, I can't imagine Willow climbing into your bunker,' I said.

'Willow will do what I tell her to do,' Guy snapped. 'Or Willow will be back in the same gutter where I found her.'

They were fanatics, I realised. We had been living next to people who had all the murderous cruelty of fanatics.

'And are you taking Goran with you?' I said. 'Does the help get to survive?

'Not everyone will make the final cut,' Ben admitted. 'But Goran will be taken care of.'

Guy guffawed. 'We'll chuck him so much dehydrated, freeze-dried food he'll be the richest man in Swindon.'

My hand was so tight around the stem of the sherry glass that I thought it would break.

'You're right,' I said. 'I see that now. It's coming. Something bad. Everything will change soon. And we have to be ready. Damn right we do.'

Roman glanced up shyly at me, and I saw his pain, and his love for me, and I recognised the depth of it for the first time, and for a moment it was just him and me, and I knew that you only need one person to love you.

'Let's go home, Roman,' I said quietly. 'Can we?'

But Professor Hall was smiling sadly, and I saw it was impossible.

It had gone too far. I had talked too much.

Going to the police again – that sealed it for me.

Knowing the truth about Juno did for me.

It was like they said – not everyone would make the final cut.

I was already dead.

Professor Hall settled it with a small lift of his head and as bodies moved towards me, I lurched forward and in one motion I smashed the sherry glass on the side table and then suddenly I was holding just the thin sharp stem in my bloody hand.

And with all my force I tried to bury it deep in Professor Alan Hall's chicken-skinned neck.

42

Roman stopped me.

Of course he did.

He threw himself between the old man and me, wrapping his arms around me tight, holding me as if it was for the last time, both of us crying now, and with our helpless tears, the fight seemed to drain from me.

What remained of the broken glass slipped from my fingers, smashing against the flagstones of the terrace. I could feel something warm and wet in my palm where I had sliced my hand open when breaking the glass, but the pain had not yet begun.

'Lana,' Roman whispered. 'Please.'

Professor Hall touched the loose folds of skin on his neck. He was really disappointed in me now.

'Lana,' he said, stiff with disapproval, as if I was a dinner guest who had disgraced herself after hitting the aperitifs a bit too hard. 'I really think it's best if you go home now.'

For one mad fleeting moment I felt my spirits soar, because I thought that even now, I would be allowed to walk away. But no – Professor Hall was looking beyond the husband who still held me in his tight embrace. Ben and Guy and Tucker and Oscar were all watching me, and as one they took a step towards me, until Roman's voice stopped them.

'No,' he said. 'Don't you touch her. Don't you ever touch her.'

He let me go then, and gently steered me to one side, and placed himself between them and me, and I had never loved him more than I loved him at that moment.

'But she went to the *police*,' Guy said, exasperated. 'And she will go to them again. Come on, Roman – you know she will.'

Tucker and Ben and Oscar held back, but Guy brushed past Roman, a soft shoulder charge that turned him sideways. Guy took my hand, not roughly, but without apology, as if it could not be any other way, and he was standing close enough that I could smell the sickly-sweet sherry on his breath. Krissy called out excitedly for Tucker with breaking news on Sailor and the pair of them retreated to a quiet corner of the terrace, consulting Krissy's phone, making plans for the return of their only child.

Guy stood there, holding my hand, almost formal, like a neanderthal on prom night.

'We would never let you suffer,' Ben told me, patting my arm. 'You know that, don't you?'

'You'll be taken back to your house and given something to help you sleep,' Professor Hall said quietly. 'In your own home, Lana. In your own bed. Just to calm you down. That's all. And – there'll be no pain.'

'No,' Roman said, and they all turned to stare at him. 'I'm telling you for the last time – no.' He looked desperately at Professor Hall. 'We can work this out.'

Then it was just Roman and me, looking at each other, and I smiled because he was holding back the world for me. My boy – still my boy, always my boy – putting himself between me and all the bad that was out there. Because he loved me, and that is what you do if you love someone, you get between them and the bad, even if you know in your heart you can't stop it, you will never stop it. That's what we should have done before, I saw now, that's what we should have done on that other night.

I should have stayed. I should never have run away.

We should have fought.

But we were fighting now.

'Lana is leaving with me,' Roman said, his voice shaking. 'And we're leaving now. Please don't try to stop us.'

Professor Hall shook his head. 'No,' he said.

'Lana,' Roman said, wanting me to finally understand. 'I swear, all I ever wanted for us—'

Professor Hall nodded and Ben touched Oscar's shoulder twice and the boy stepped forward and punched Roman in the stomach three times, a trilogy of pathetic little punches, pussy punches, the tentative blows of a coward who is afraid of being hit back, the punches of the bully's craven sidekick.

And it was only when the boy stepped away and back into the arms of his father that I saw the knife in his right hand, and I saw that the blood was already everywhere on Roman's stomach, and his eyes were on me even as they fogged over, his eyes were always on me.

I screamed as Roman slumped sideways, knocking the table with the drinks flying, and collapsed to his knees and then fell onto his side, as if he was folding himself up, as if he was suddenly just too tired for this world, and the blood was on his hands and his stomach and his chest and all over the flagstones of the terrace.

Guy tightened his grip on me. 'Jesus Christ,' he muttered. 'Was that necessary?'

'I promise you're not going to feel a thing,' Ben told me soothingly, taking my other hand.

Oscar laughed with excitement. 'You might feel a small prick. Can I watch, Dad?'

Guy whirled on him, grabbing the boy by the scruff of his T-shirt with his free hand and then Ben had his hands on Guy and Oscar was slapping at him and the two men and the boy were locked in a fitful scuffle, Ben somehow still gripping me, while Tucker watched, grinning with drunken amusement, until everything stopped at the sound of the voice that came faintly from the French doors.

'*Was geht?*'

Magda Hall stood at the entrance to the terrace, ghost-like in her long white nightdress. Under the terrace night lights she looked like an apparition.

Mrs Mendoza scuttled out after her, angrily ordering her to come back to bed immediately, but Magda just stared at her without even a glimmer of understanding and I realised with a start that her second language had gone completely now.

There was only the German left.

Magda looked at Guy holding my hand.

She stared at Roman on the floor, his hands on his stab wounds, pressing down hard, desperately trying to stem the blood.

Then Magda looked at me.

'Please help us,' I said, my voice steady and clear.

Professor Hall went to her side.

'*Die Russen kommen?*' Magda asked him.

Professor Hall smiled.

He touched his wife's arm and I saw the endless love that was still there, and I felt a surge of what could only be envy.

'Don't upset yourself, my darling. All is well.' An indulgent smile. 'I assure you the Russians are *not* coming!'

Suave as ever, he turned to the assembled guests, inviting them to smile along, turning a moment of confusion and madness and abject horror into witty supper-time banter.

Then he turned back to his demented, beloved wife.

'Mrs Mendoza, if you would be so kind?'

'Sir,' nodded Mrs Mendoza, and she gently steered the old lady away with one brief horrified look at Roman bleeding on the floor, not wanting to see.

I broke away from Guy and I had Roman in my arms, the blood everywhere, my hands, his stomach, the flagstones.

I said his name and I kept saying his name as his eyes fluttered closed, almost as if he was sleepy, and I felt multiple hands take me by my upper arms and pull me away, as if I might wake him.

Then I heard Krissy cry out with alarm and we all turned to see that Dr Magda Hall had returned.

But now she was holding a 12-bore shotgun.

Mrs Mendoza was crawling on the floor behind her, going in the wrong direction, trying to get away, her hands over her ears and a silent scream trapped in her gaping mouth.

Magda hunched forward, the curdled cream night-gown slipping off her bony shoulders, concentrating, as if the weight of the shotgun she held might bend her until her bones snapped.

But then she seemed to locate some long misplaced inner strength and she slowly straightened, the 12-bore double-barrelled shotgun glistening under the night lights of the terrace, black as an oil slick.

We all froze.

And then Ben was approaching her.

Very slowly, with a kindly smile slowly spreading across his scarred and weathered face, one hand outstretched, his professional decency dialled up to ten.

'Everybody relax,' he said. 'Let's all just calm down now, shall we?'

Magda looked beyond him at Guy, who was paralysed with terror but somehow still holding onto me.

And then she looked at me with the glint of recognition.

And it was as if she saw it all for the first time.

In one surprisingly smooth movement she lifted the shotgun and pointed it at Ben. He stopped dead.

Guy let slip my hand. 'Is that thing loaded?'

'*Lauf, Mutter!*' Magda said.

She steadied the shotgun, taking careful aim at the smiling man walking very slowly towards her.

'Relax,' Ben told Magda, and she shot him in the face.

The noise seemed to go on and on and on, it seemed to last forever, and they were both blown sideways by that never-ending moment, Magda by the unexpected shock of the recoil and Ben with half of his head gone to a ruined mush of blood and bone and pulp and then Oscar was kneeling over his dead father on the floor, the boy's mouth wide open but the ringing in my ears too loud to hear his screams.

Then Magda was staggering forward, raising the gun, more confident with it now, and almost casually she fired the second barrel at Guy and suddenly he was shuffling backwards, his eyes popping so wide he looked as though he had been plugged into something, and his right arm was gone below the elbow, just gone, nothing there now, and the blood would not stop and his fingers clawed desperately at nothing.

'*Lauf, Mutter!*' Magda shouted.

And I realised that she was talking to me.

'*Lauf, Mutter!*'

Run, Mother.

I hauled Roman to his feet and with all my strength, I propelled him towards the door of the big house, and he staggered forward on drunken legs, too weak to walk without my help but still on his feet, both hands pressed expertly against his wounds, the blood dripping on the floor, a boy screaming for his father behind us.

And we ran.

43

Roman staggered like a drunk beside me, almost dragging me off my feet as he leaned on me for support. We came out of the black iron gates of the big house, and although his hands were covered in his blood, he seemed to have stemmed the flow, for his eyes were open, staring, measuring the distance we had to travel to home.

We were almost there when I saw them.

At the entrance to the Gardens, Sailor lounged by the Goran's white security van, a secret smile on her face, still in her school uniform but with her stripy tie hanging low, her grey skirt hiked high, and a tobacco-coloured Newsboy cap perched on the back of her head.

Goran stood before her with a different kind of smile on his face.

A witless, grateful grin, as if he could not believe his good fortune.

Sailor leaned forward, murmuring something close to his face and he looked at her with disbelief. One of her long, cello-playing fingers languidly stroked his black bomber jacket and he lurched forward, but she pulled away with a laugh and gave him instructions on how it was going to be, and how it had to be, take it or leave it.

He broke away from her and quickly opened the passenger door to his van.

Sailor slipped inside, tugging at the hem of her skirt with no discernible effect. Goran slammed the door and went quickly round to the driver's side. He could not move fast enough.

Oh, Sailor, I thought.

That's not the way. That's not how you get even with them. That's not the way to hurt your mother.

I half-carried, half-dragged Roman up the drive of Willow's house and hammered on the front door. Nothing. I leaned on the doorbell until she finally appeared in some diaphanous robe, her hair an explosion of dark curls, scratching at the tattoo of the number 7 in the crook of her skinny arm.

'If you want to live,' I said, 'then you have to come with us.'

Roman sank to one knee and Willow's gaze drifted from him, towards the big house, and back to Roman.

'Shouldn't we call . . .'

'I'm taking him myself,' I said. 'It's faster. And safer. I mean it, Willow.'

I eased Roman to the ground, his back against the wall, as I fumbled for my door key. His hands were pressed hard against the wounds, but I could see him weakening.

'When he can't keep his hands there, you have to do it for him,' I said.

'OK.'

'Watch Roman for me. We're leaving. And if you're coming with us, it has to be now.'

She was still standing there, staring towards the big house.

I steadied Roman against the jamb of her front door and I went inside my home. I found the car keys where I had left them on the kitchen island and snatched up the green first aid kit from under the sink. Halfway to the front door I stopped, staring out the kitchen window at the white van and the two figures close together in the front seat, Sailor's blonde hair shining with some inner light, Goran's stubbled face further away, hidden in shadows but turned towards her. I saw her push the hair from her face as her head ducked down out of sight below the dashboard.

Goran leaned back with a sigh, his neck white in the night.

I did not see the face of the person in the back of the van, the one who had been waiting for him. But I saw their hands emerge from the darkness and I saw them slip the wire over Goran's head and around his throat and I saw what happened when they pulled tight. For then there was only fury in the front of the van, Goran clawing at the wire around his neck, his nails raking at the strong hands that held it in place, fighting with the desperation of the dying, his eyes bulging with terror and pain, lashing out at Sailor as she leaned against him, trying to hold him down.

Her Newsboy cap went flying.

Then one foot shattered the windscreen and the other suddenly burst through it in an explosion of broken glass, his boots flailing in the streetlights as he fought for his life.

When he was finally still, Sailor rummaged around on the floor. She was looking for her Newsboy cap, and I realised it was the one worn by John Carter on the day he first came to the Gardens.

As I came out of our front door she was adjusting the hat on her head and getting out of the passenger seat, carefully straightening her skirt. She went to the back of the van as the doors opened from inside. She took two cans from the van and started up the driveway of her home.

I came to the end of our drive.

'Sailor!'

The girl looked at me for a moment and then went into her family home.

Mary Carter climbed out the back of the van.

She reached inside, collected two more cans of petrol and followed Sailor.

Willow was carefully easing Roman to his feet. The blood seemed to have stopped but his eyes were getting sleepy again.

'Let's go,' she said.

She must have left Roman for a few minutes because she was in T-shirt and jeans now, trainers worn with no socks, one of her husband's dark green shooting jackets thrown over the top. No bags. There was no time for bags tonight. I should have felt angry with her for leaving Roman alone but her hands were already covered with blood as she pressed down his hands, encouraging him to keep the pressure on his wounds.

We got into the car, Willow and Roman in the back seat.

As I turned on the ignition, I could see Mary Carter dousing petrol all over the hallway of Sailor's home. Then she was working her way deeper into the house, emptying the contents of one can and then starting on the other with the stoic patience of a woman who was accustomed to hard physical labour.

Sailor briefly appeared upstairs in the window of what I knew to be the master bedroom, only one can of petrol in her hands now, sloshing the contents over the bed, the curtains, the windows.

Then she was gone from my sight.

The front door of the house across the street was still wide open as I put the car in drive.

And from somewhere deep inside, there was a sudden burst of flames.

The fields flashed by dark and silent on either side but ahead I could see the lights of the motorway, and their promise of safety and help.

Then there were suddenly other lights coming towards me and I touched my brakes at the sight of them, this fast-moving convoy of blue lights going in the opposite direction.

The emergency vehicles heading for the Gardens.

They flew past us, their sirens wailing, their lights pulsing in the bright midnight, and I watched them go in my rear-view mirror and then pushed my foot down on the accelerator. The fields were once again dark and unchanging on both sides of the road.

The motorway was very close now.

Roman moaned with pain and Willow's voice softly soothed him, and as I pulled the car onto the slip road the world was suddenly exploding with light in my rear-view mirror. It held my gaze, demanding that I watch, as it raged with sparks and plumes of fire that had no place being there, whining and flashing and lighting up with stars that lived and died and were replaced by new stars, brighter stars that were born and faded away but still kept shining. I gasped with shock, mesmerised by the dazzling light of long-dead stars, caught between a memory and a dream.

'Just look at the road, will you?' Willow snapped, and Roman smiled at me in the mirror.

He closed his eyes as I turned my eyes ahead and pressed my foot down, impatient for the place where he would sleep in my arms forever.

And behind us the sky was full of fire, like those fleeting moments just after midnight on New Year's Eve, or perhaps the end of the world.